THE FIRST CUT

The blow surprised her. It was dull, as if she had been pounded by something blunt and heavy, and she wondered if he had, unaccountably, used the wrong side of the cleaver. But when she opened her eyes she saw the severed finger lying on the board. It looked unreal, like one of those gruesomely unfunny objects one might buy in a novelty store . . .

Nella

JOHN GODEY

SPHERE BOOKS LIMITED
30-32 Gray's Inn Road, London WC1X 8JL

First published in Great Britain by Sphere Books Ltd 1982
Copyright © John Godey 1981

Set in Lasercomp Plantin

Printed and bound in Great Britain by
Collins, Glasgow

CONTENTS

Part I

THE PACKAGE

Chapter 1

The package sat squarely in the centre of his desk when Roehmer returned to the squad room from an early lunch. Passatino was standing beside the desk, looking down at it. Murphy was catching squeals, chatting into the phone in that high humorous voice of his that sought consciously to make light of, or even belittle, aggrievement.

Passatino said, 'You got an early-mailed Christmas present.'

The package was a four-inch square covered with brown wrapping paper which, from its criss-cross of wrinkles, suggested that it had been used before. Roehmer read from the odd lettering:

> Det. Wm. Roehmer
> 18th Police Precinct
> New York, N.Y. 10021

Passatino was smiling. Roehmer gave him a suspicious look. 'How did this get here?'

'US mail. A dollar and thirty cents worth of stamps. They must have money to burn.'

Roehmer shook his head. 'You don't go up to a post office window and have a package like this one weighed; you put a lot of stamps on it so it won't be stopped for insufficient postage, and then drop it into a box.' He bent over the desk to attempt to decipher the smudged post office cancellation. 'We'll check out the station, but . . .' But it would be a different post office station from the other notes.

'The magazine letters,' Passatino said. 'It's the exact same thing as the other ones, right?'

'It looks the same, but anybody could imitate it if he wanted to take the trouble.'

'It must be a lot of work, cutting out those little letters,'

3

Passatino said. 'Still, what else has he got to do all day long?'

'You know what he does all day long?'

'Sure,' Passatino said. 'Sit around playing cards and drinking booze, and every once in a while get up and peek out the window, and then sit down again and drink booze and play cards. You know how I know?'

'No.'

The syllable was abrupt, even challenging, and Passatino paused for a moment in surprise before going on. 'Because I see it in the movies all the time. Booze and cards and peek out the window. Cutting out and pasting up the little letters too.' Passatino smiled. 'You know why perpetrators all do the same thing? They see it in the movies.'

Roehmer picked up the package. It hardly weighed anything. A couple of ounces. An innocent lightness. He studied the letters of the address – the familiar, distinctive type font of *Playboy* – painstakingly cut out and pasted up.

Passatino, watching him as he turned the package in his hand, said, 'Careful, there might be prints.'

'Oh, there's prints, all right. Of about six or seven post office employees.'

'You gonna open it?'

The package was neatly sealed on its underside with Scotch tape. He shifted it in his palm so that it balanced at the end of his fingertips. Suddenly it started to topple, and he had to bring his other hand up quickly to save it from falling. He held it cupped between his palms for a moment, hidden, contained. He was reluctant to open it: premonition – which was a fancy word for cop smartness. He began to bounce it up and down on his right palm. Passatino was breathing on his neck.

'Watch out, Rome!' Murphy said, his hands raised in front of him defensively. 'There may be an explosive device in there.'

Roehmer snorted, but stopped bouncing the package.

Passatino said, 'Come on, Murphy, quit kidding. Who would want to send Rome a bomb?'

'His wife, for one.' Murphy said. 'Or some PR kid he slapped around for laughs.' Murphy covered his head with his hands. 'If you're gonna open that thing, I want a couple minutes' start out of the squad room.'

'You're a scream,' Roehmer said.

'What I would do,' Murphy said, 'I wouldn't be no posthumous hero. I would call in the Bomb Squad to handle it.'

But there was a certain wariness about Murphy's smile. And some of the other detectives in the room were looking a little nervous too. Roehmer said, 'That's all I need – the Bomb Squad driving up in that big iron wagon.' His fingers curled around the edges of the box to hold it more securely. 'That's all I need.'

Passatino said seriously, 'Maybe he's right, Rome. In today's atmosphere?'

'Murphy, the squad room comedian,' Roehmer said. 'Don't you know Murphy yet?'

Murphy slid off his chair and cowered behind his desk. 'Okay, open it up. But when you end up jelly, don't say I didn't warn you. Better hide, Pass.' He peered around the corner of the desk. 'I got another idea, Rome. Give it to Mr Special Agent Fairborn. Let it blow *his* ass off.'

The phone rang. Murphy got up and answered it, grinning, his head ducked protectively in the crook of his arm.

'Right,' Passatino said. 'Let Special Agent Fairborn open it. Then if there's a bomb – '

'Bullshit,' Roehmer said. 'The package is addressed to me. Since when do I give my personal mail to the FBI to open?'

'Maybe not a bomb,' Passatino said, 'but a deadly spider, a whaddayoucallit, tarantella.'

Roehmer rummaged in a drawer for scissors. Murphy was grinning and winking. Roehmer slit the wrapping paper carefully. Passatino inched backwards as Roehmer examined the wrapping paper briefly before placing it to one side of his desk. The box was made of white cardboard and there were no identifying marks immediately visible. The lid was held in place by two small pieces of Scotch tape. Roehmer cut the tape and removed the cover.

'Boom!' Murphy crashed his palm down on his desk. '*Kah-rumph!*'

A wad of crumpled newspaper eased upwards with the release of the lid's pressure. Roehmer noted absently that it was the *Daily News*.

'Well, no bomb,' Passatino said.

'A deadly South American poison,' Murphy said. 'If you feel a little pinprick, Rome, it's too late even for a priest. It acts instantaneous.'

In the instant before he removed the clump of paper from the box, Roehmer arranged his features in a blank professional set, although he could not have said later whether he did so for the benefit of Murphy and Passatino, or because he had already guessed what the box contained, or a combination of both. He lowered the box so that Murphy and Passatino could see into it.

Murphy gagged in mock horror. A few of the other detectives came over for a look.

Roehmer lined everything up on the lieutenant's desk: box, wrapping paper, crumpled newspaper. The lieutenant leaned forward in his chair and looked into the box. He made a face.

'This is not a nice case,' the lieutenant said. 'Kinky. And by the way, where does this leave your hot theory?'

Roehmer didn't say anything.

'This puts a whole different complexion on the case – you know that?'

After a pause Roehmer said, 'Yes, sir.'

The lieutenant gave him a stare. 'You better believe it, Detective Roehmer.'

'There's also a ring in there,' Roehmer said. 'And a note.'

'Don't tell me,' the lieutenant said. 'The note says there are nine more of these to go. Right?'

'I didn't read it yet,' Roehmer said. 'I just wanted to show you the whole set-up first.'

'Let's see the note.'

Roehmer picked up the box and tilted it. The finger rolled on to the desk, stiff, etiolated, the flesh slightly retracted at the severed end, with a joint of grey-white bone protruding. The ring skittered towards the edge of the desk. Roehmer put out his hand and stopped it from falling off. It was a small gold ring with a chip of red stone set in a simple mounting. A girlish ring.

'The note,' the lieutenant said.

Roehmer picked out a folded sheet of unlined paper, tinged by a pale watery bloodstain. He unfolded the paper and glanced at it before handing it across the desk.

The lieutenant read the cut-out letters aloud. ' "This is Nella Massey's finger. Only nine left." Did I tell you? "We are not fooling around. Pay up or else." '

'Could be a joker, of course,' Roehmer said.

'A cut off finger is a joke?'

'I mean a hoax,' Roehmer said. 'What do I do with it?'

'Turn it over to the G-man.'

'The question is, is it the girl's finger or not? Can't I find that out as good as the G-man?'

'The trouble is you want to be a star. Ain't you tired yet seeing your name in the papers and answering dumb questions on the TV news every night?'

'I'm a detective,' Roehmer said, colouring. 'I know the routine as good as Fairborn does.'

'Maybe better, but you ain't co-operating. You want to make the Department of Justice mad at you?'

'It's mine,' Roehmer said. 'The letter. Technically, I mean, it's addressed to me.'

'*Technically* is the right word. They expect you to pay the ransom? At that, why *you*? If they were gonna send it to *any*body here . . . Not that it would make any difference if they did send it to me. Or the captain.'

Roehmer started to say something about hating criminals who went over the boss's head, but decided the lieutenant's funnybone couldn't stand it.

'But I'm glad it wasn't sent to the girl's uncle. Can you imagine opening the mail if you were the old guy, and finding your own flesh and blood's finger in a box?' The lieutenant shook his head. 'It must have hurt like hell, chopping that thing off.'

I don't want to think about that, Roehmer thought. He said, 'I'd like to run with it, check out if it's really her finger. After all, technically, it's my case.'

'Technically again,' the lieutenant said. 'You sure have got a hard-on for this case.'

The lieutenant was not a sensitive or discerning man, Roehmer thought, but he had a cop's nose on him for sniffing out suspicious behaviour. Well, what do I think – that I'm invisible?

'I can move real fast on it, Lieutenant. Run it down to the lab for classification, and then round-robin all sources for a match-up.'

The lieutenant scowled. 'What about the ring? Do we know that it's the girl's ring?'

'Even if it was, it would be like her clothes that they mailed. It wouldn't mean all that much.'

'But if it *ain't* her ring, *that* means something, don't it? Check out the ring with whatsisname, her ex-husband.'

'Laurence Adams,' Roehmer said. 'The guy's a bit of a jerk.'

'Even a jerk can identify a ring, can't he?'

'Yessir.'

'I shouldn't have to tell you something like that,' the lieutenant said with a scowl. 'The ring is probably hers, or they wouldn't have bothered sending it, but that don't mean the finger is hers. Check out the nail polish. That wouldn't be proof either, but it would give an indication. The only thing that would be proof would be a print match-up. But I wouldn't count on that too strong. The kind of family she comes from, there's usually no fingerprints on file anywhere.'

Roehmer nodded. 'If the check shows up negative, I can go up to the place on Park Avenue and toss her room for prints.'

'I understood she didn't live there steady with the uncle.'

'In and out, but she stayed there recently. There's bound to be prints.'

'Unless they gave her room a real good cleaning. Anyway, they got to be nearly two weeks old.'

Roehmer knew that someone of the girl's age – the mid-twenties – secreted more oils than an older person, and that her prints would be viable after two weeks or even longer. He was tactful enough not to mention it to the lieutenant.

'Even if the room was cleaned, they might not get everything. It's certainly worth a try, Lieutenant. In my opinion.'

'In your opinion. You going to tell the old man about the finger? You want to give that a try too?'

'First thing, I have to find out if it's hers or not.' He risked a smile. 'If it is, I'll tell Special Agent Fairborn, and *he* can tell the old guy. That way, I'll be co-operating.'

'Occur to you,' the Lieutenant said, 'that even if it is her finger, she could still be dead? What's to prevent them cutting it off after they killed her?'

'I'll check it out with Forensic. See if it's fresh.'

'What does it prove? She could be fresh-killed, too, couldn't she?'

What the lieutenant was saying was true but irrelevant. Identifying the finger came first; anything else would have to follow from there. Besides, he knew she wasn't dead. But he couldn't tell the lieutenant *how* he knew: whatchamacallit, empathy, wasn't acceptable police procedure.

The lieutenant frowned. 'You going to call that husband about the ring?'

'*Ex*-husband.'

'Whatever. Just make sure you call him.'

'Yessir.'

'Okay. Take that thing out of here, and get back to me as soon as you can.'

Roehmer held the box just below the edge of the table and, with the eraser of a pencil, nudged the finger along the desk until it fell into the box. It stood up at an odd angle. He jiggled the box gently back and forth until the finger became dislodged and fell flat. Then he put the pencil point through the circle of the ring and carried it to the box, where he placed it to one side of the finger.

'You afraid to touch the finger?' the lieutenant said. 'You think it might be contagious?'

Roehmer said, 'I don't want to smudge it, in case the perpetrator slipped up and left some prints on it.'

'Certainly,' the lieutenant said.

'I'm not leery of it, chrissake. I've seen things a hundred times worse. Hell, one time – '

'Tell me your fascinating police stories some other time,' the lieutenant said.

Reddening, Roehmer put the lid on the box, picked up the wrapping paper and the balled-up newspaper, and left the lieutenant's office.

The open-topped partition of Laurence Adams's office admitted a hubbub from the hallway outside, where a number of students were waiting to see their instructors. A political argument was going on, and a booming voice, rising over a counterpoint of mocking interpolations, was advocating what seemed to Adams to be some kind of technocratic utopia. A science major, without a doubt. Across the desk, Metcalfe was frowning, his lips still formed exaggeratedly to the shape of the last word he had spoken before falling silent.

When the clamour subsided, Metcalfe said, 'Where was I?'

I'm not supposed to keep your place, am I? Adams didn't say it, knowing that his restraint was wholly due to the colour of Metcalfe's skin. What greater love, he thought – or payment on account of conscience – than to curb our hieratical privilege of professorial sarcasm? He said, 'Well, you were defending your position.'

'Hey, come on, I wasn't *defending* it, I was, ah, *expositing* it.'

'Expounding.'

Metcalfe said, 'You expound, I exposit, okay?'

Not okay, but okay. The din in the corridor started up again, and Metcalfe stared at him accusingly. Leaning back in his chair, Adams pushed his door open a few inches and said, 'Keep it down there, please, I'm trying to hold a conference.'

He shut the door again. There was a moment of silence, and then an outraged voice said, 'Well, fuck *you*, Professor.'

Voices rose outside, a hubbub of laughter and *shhh* sounds. To his relief, after what he took to be a critical moment of indecision, feet scuffled as the group moved off down the hallway.

He settled in his chair and said, 'Go on, please, Metcalfe.'

Metcalfe was smiling slyly. 'You gonna take that shit, Professor?'

'What would you like me to do – go out there and beat hell out of them?'

Metcalfe shook his head in hopelessness, then turned businesslike. 'My position,' he said briskly. 'As you call it. But it isn't *my* position, I was simply expounding – I mean expositing – the concerns of the black experience.'

Adams glanced at Metcalfe's paper and its – literally – inflammatory title: 'Burn: The Crimes of Shakespeare, Twain, Poe, and Other Literary Racists.' Its thesis was that works offensive to blacks should be burned, and not metaphorically, either. It covered a wide range of writing – good marks for research – but concentrated its fire on Nigger Jim in *Huckleberry Finn* and on Othello, who was characterised as an establishment buck nigger who sold out his glorious African heritage for a piece of white pussy. Adams felt disappointed. He had expected something more original from Metcalfe, who was a bright, superior student.

He said, 'Do you think your view represents a pressing concern of black people? That, other priorities notwithstanding, they're clamouring for a bonfire stoked by *Othello* and *Huckleberry Finn*? How many do you think have even *read* them?'

'I don't want *any* of them to read racist shit, especially the young kids coming up.'

'I don't suppose you'd care to look at it in perspective – in the light of the prevailing outlook of people towards blacks when these works were written?'

'No, Professor, I definitely wouldn't care to look at it in your perspective.'

Metcalfe was slender and handsome, and, excepting his elaborate Afro, not particularly Negroid. In fact, Adams thought, his lips and nose are thinner than mine, and his skin isn't all that much darker, either. He realised that Metcalfe was amused at his success in sucking his teacher into an argument, which wasn't at all the purpose of a conference. For all he knew, Metcalfe's whole paper was a put-on, a red rag to wave in the professor's face. Okay, he's had his fun, Adams thought, let's get on with it.

He said, 'You write well and interestingly, your animadversion to Shakespeare notwithstanding.'

'Shakespeare? If God himself had written *Othello*, I would have his ass.'

'Yes, well . . .' Adams picked up the paper. 'You have a tendency to write too many one- and two-sentence paragraphs. Admittedly a minor point, but it chops up the rhythm of your thought . . .' He paused. Metcalfe was regarding him with scorn. 'As I say, it's a minor point – '

The telephone rang. Welcoming its intervention, he snatched up the receiver.

'This is Detective Roehmer, Professor. The Eighteenth Precinct?'

The tough, demotic voice, almost a parody of a street voice, took him by surprise, and he heard an impatient tapping through the phone before he collected himself and answered. 'Oh, yes. Hello, Detective Roehmer.'

'A development has turned up in the case, Professor, that you can help us out with. It's a question of identification.'

'Identification? It's not Nella? I mean, you haven't found . . .'

'No, we haven't found her. It's an object we'd like to have you try to identify. We would appreciate your coming down here to the station house – '

'An object? I don't get what you mean. Detective.' Across the desk, Metcalfe was looking elaborately bored.

'We're in possession of an object which purports to be a personal possession of Nella Massey.'

'What do you mean by a "personal possession"? I mean, why not tell me what it is?'

'It's a ring which purports to be Miss Massey's.'

'What do you mean by "purports"?' Adams saw Metcalfe draw his brows together in simulated pain.

'The ring in question is a gold band with a setting of, I believe, a ruby.'

'Nella had such a ring. But it couldn't be hers, because hers didn't come off.'

'Will you explain what you mean by that, Professor?'

'Yes, I suppose I was not clear. I mean unable, unable to be taken off. She's been wearing it since she was twelve or thereabouts, and actually her finger, where she wore the ring, was thinner than her other fingers. The knuckle, however, grew normally, so the ring couldn't pass by it and come off. It would have to be cut through to be taken off. Is the ring cut through?'

'No.'

'Then it can't be Nella's.'

'Well, we would like you to come down here and look at it anyway. Can you do that, Professor?'

'Yes. I'm having my last conference of the day. I should be finished in about ten minutes. I'll come directly thereafter.'

Roehmer thanked him and hung up. Adams looked across the desk at Metcalfe, who shrugged and said, 'Go ahead, Professor, I'll waive the ten minutes.'

'Will you? That's good of you, Metcalfe. Thanks.'

Metcalfe shook his head pityingly, and left.

Roehmer returned to the precinct house at four o'clock. He felt winded, as if he had been running, which in a figurative sense was the case. He had taken a taxi, at his own expense, down to the police lab on East Twentieth Street, where a technician, responding to his urgency, had run a print of the severed finger through the computer. With the classification report in his pocket, he had taken another cab to the medical examiner's office at Bellevue.

13

There he had been told that he would have to leave the finger for examination by a pathologist. He took a third cab back to the precinct house, completing destruction of ten hard-earned dollars, and had the classification of the severed finger put on the wire to all fingerprint banks (including the Army's in St Louis, although he knew that was a waste of time; but Detective First Grade Roehmer was thorough, right?).

In the squad room Murphy told him that Laurence Adams had come in and made a positive identification of the ring. It was Nella Massey's.

'It's a common kind of ring,' Roehmer said. 'What makes him so sure?'

'She had this nervous habit of biting the ring. He showed me indentations on it, like tooth marks. The only thing that bothered him was how the ring came off her finger. He said it was probably ten years since she last had the ring off.'

'He didn't make any wild guesses about it?'

'Not him. He don't look like the wild guesser type.' Murphy grinned. 'I told him there were ways of getting rings off that the public didn't know about.'

'He bought it?'

'He ain't exactly what I would call worldly. Nervous? Jesus. I think he's still got a bad case on the girl.'

'Maybe. But it's a one-way street.'

Murphy looked at him sharply. 'How can you tell?'

'That's the way I heard it.' Christ, Roehmer! 'Thanks for handling it, Murph.'

Fending off questions from several of the other detectives in the squad room, he went back to his desk and busied himself with paperwork until his phone rang and the wire man told him that the responses to his queries about the prints on the severed finger were in. Negative all around. He dialled Julian Massey's number.

'Good afternoon, sir. Detective William Roehmer. Eighteenth Precinct?'

'What do you want?'

'I'm very sorry to trouble you, sir. It's just a slight

procedural detail. If I could drop by at your apartment for a few minutes – '

'Do you people have to bother me all the time?' Massey's metallic old-man's voice was querulous.

'This is just, you might say, a purely technical thing. We need a set of Nella's fingerprints, that's all it is.'

'What for?'

Julian Massey's tone was brusque and commanding. Taxpayer to the servant its considerable levies supported. Superior to subordinate. Upper stratum to lower stratum. In this precinct, with its well-to-do residents on Park Avenue and the elegant side streets, the tone was a familiar one; so Roehmer didn't allow himself to become upset or impatient.

'It's departmental routine, sir, required by new regulations in cases of missing persons for computer classification purposes.' Gibberish, but maybe the old man wouldn't examine it for meaning. Cops could be con men, too, when they had to be.

'Then why didn't you do it ten days ago, for Godssake?'

A note of triumph in Julian Massey's voice: I may be old, and I may forget something now and then, but that doesn't mean I can't put two and two together. He thinks he's scored off me, Roehmer thought. Good. Let him think so. The con.

'You're right, Mr Massey, I got to admit that we slipped up. It's my fault. I just forgot all about it.'

'Well, tough luck if you don't know your job.'

Kiss my ass, you old fart. 'Ah, gee, sir, I wish you wouldn't say that. I'm in a real bind. When my lieutenant discovered that I had neglected to secure prints, he almost busted a gut.'

'I'm sorry to hear that.' Massey snickered.

'I asked him if he could make an exception in this case so I wouldn't have to bother you, but he's one of those rules-and-regulations jockeys. He said he was accountable for the performance of the men in his squad, and as long as he was accountable . . .' Murphy was looking over at him, his head thrown back, laughing silently, shovelling bullshit in pantomime. Roehmer lowered his voice as he went on: 'I must throw myself on your mercy, Mr Massey. I've been threatened with disciplinary action; I may even be suspended for several days with loss of salary. So I wish you would allow me – '

'Nobody asked you to become a cop in the first place.' Julian Massey's voice was openly gleeful. 'But you did, so you have to abide by the stupid rules.'

'I can't afford a suspension, Mr Massey. Especially at this time, when my wife is expecting.' Overdoing the soapsuds? We'll see. 'If you just let me attend to this little matter, I'd surely be grateful. I promise you it won't take more than fifteen minutes. All we'd do is take a few photographs . . .'

'Of what? Nella isn't here, you know. She's been kidnapped.' Julian Massey cackled; he was breaking himself up with his own wit.

'Her room, sir. It would contain prints, and we would simply try to pick them up. I give you my solemn word, sir, you'll hardly know we're there, and we'll be in and out in fifteen minutes. I would appreciate it deeply.'

In the long pause that followed, Roehmer held his breath, trying to sense the current of the old man's thinking in the humming silence.

'All right. I'll allow it this one time. But only fifteen minutes. After fifteen minutes, ready or not, I'll kick your rear end out of here.'

Roehmer let out his breath and said heartily, 'It's a deal. In and out in fifteen minutes or you'll kick my butt.' He pondered adding a chuckly 'and I'll bet you're the man to do it,' but the old man couldn't be that vain. Or could. In either case, it was a bad idea.

Forensic technicians, as fingerprint experts were officially designated, normally worked in pairs, but Detective Vassos showed up alone in the lobby of Massey's building: his partner had gone home with a stomach ache. Roehmer told him about his arrangement with Massey.

'Fifteen minutes ain't enough,' Vassos said, 'but I'll try to live with it. I know how these rich sonofabitches can be, I sympathise. But I'm just one man.'

'I know,' Roehmer said. 'You want me to, I can work the one-on-one camera.'

Vassos grunted.

The doorman announced them over the intercom, and the stony-faced elevator operator, wearing a maroon uniform with white piping and a wing collar and white gloves, took them up to fifteen. As they passed the eighth floor, Roehmer's eyes flickered, but he didn't feel much. I've transferred my affections, he thought bitterly.

Julian Massey opened the door for them and they followed him into the drawing-room. Vassos was goggling. Except for the clutter, its size and munificence was like a movie set, everyman's idea of how rich folks lived. Massey waved them towards the corridor leading back to the bedroom, but didn't accompany them. As they started off, he reminded Roehmer that he had fifteen minutes, not a tick more.

Nella Massey's room was as Roehmer had remembered it from the first time he had been here, when he had caught the squeal almost two weeks ago. It was not a large room and it was furnished with simplicity, even girlishly, with a flounced pink and white bedspread and curtains, an ancient doll or two in places of honour, a dressing table strewn with a clutter of perfume bottles, toilet water, lipsticks standing in a rack like a platoon of soldiers. The photographs on a white side table were a synopsis of her life, toddler to young woman. The first time he had looked at the pictures it was from a purely professional point of view, as a means of identification, but now he studied them with a depth of interest that was almost proprietary. Centred – favoured, he guessed – were three pictures that showed her in a white ballet costume, one leg raised, arms outstretched or curled gracefully above her head, her expression rapt, innocent, and touching. Barring one picture, taken when she might have been fifteen or so, and in which she was almost comically puffed up with fat, the pictures were remarkably similar from early childhood on; the face sombre, intense, vibrant. Only the eyes had changed though the years, narrowing and elongating from rounded innocence, as if, Roehmer thought, she had learned to look out at the world with suspicion, or, at least, guardedly against the piling up of hurt, betrayal, disillusionment.

Vassos went to work speedily, dusting everything in sight, every conceivable surface that might have held a print: mirror, chair arms, dressing-table, bed posts, glass-top desk, doorknobs, closet and dresser pulls, telephone, bathroom drinking glass, medicine cabinet and mirror, back of silvered hairbrush, faucet handles, even the wooden john seat.

Under Vassos's watchful eye, Roehmer worked the one-on-one camera on the flat surfaces, up-ending it, centring the lens housing over a print, and snapping a picture. Vassos, meanwhile, was picking up prints in the traditional way (the camera, made by Polaroid, was a recent development in police work). He would cut an inch-and-a-half strip of cellulose tape from a roll, place it over a print, and then lift it away; the print would transfer to the gummy tape, which Vassos would then protect by placing it against a strip of photographic paper. He admitted grudgingly to Roehmer that, thanks to nobody having been over the room with malicious intent (by which he simply meant cleaning it), he had taken a few good solid prints as well as a number of promising latents.

Julian Massey was waiting for them in the drawing-room. He tapped his finger against the crystal of his watch. 'Fourteen and a half minutes, by God. I guess I don't get to kick your rear end.'

Roehmer smiled. 'I try to keep my word, sir. It builds credit for the department.' Vassos was staring at him. 'Well, thank you again, Mr Massey. Appreciate it.'

As he was unbolting the door to let them out, Julian Massey said, with a sudden note of anxiety, 'Nothing new? I mean . . .' The timbre of authority, the rich man's certitude, had drained out of him suddenly; he was a rheumy-eyed stick of an old man with a quavering voice, sick with anxiety. 'No new development, or anything to tell me?'

'Nothing at all, sir,' Roehmer said firmly. 'If there was,

we would inform you at once and immediately.' Which, he thought, uses up exactly all my credit with him when we have to tell him about the finger.

He went back downtown with Vassos and waited anxiously for the new prints to be classified and coded and compared with the print of the severed finger.

'Perfect,' Vassos said. 'You can see for yourself – an exact match-up.'

Behind the closed door, the lieutenant and the captain, the precinct commander, were in conference. Roehmer smoked and fidgeted for almost fifteen minutes before the door opened and the captain came out. As usual, his uniform jacket was unbuttoned, with his gun stuck down inside his pants, the hammer resting against the edge of his belt, the butt pressed into the swell of his gut. He always wore it that way. One day, Roehmer thought, and maliciously hoped, the gun would go off accidentally and shoot his dumb cock off. Then he wouldn't get any more freebies from the hookers they routinely rounded up from time to time before routinely turning them back on to the street again. The captain brushed by him without greeting or interest, and Roehmer went into the lieutenant's office.

'So?' the lieutenant said.

'Nothing on record any place, so I went up to the apartment with Vassos from Prints and we took prints in the girl's room. Here's the report.'

The lieutenant took the paper but didn't look at it. 'Well?'

'Hers.'

The lieutenant glanced at the report and then put it down on the desk. 'Where's the finger?'

'I left it with the pathologist to check on when it was cut off, and so forth.'

'You tell Massey about it?'

'No.'

'Get on the blower to the special agent. Tell him what you've got. Tell him to tell the old man.'

'I'll have to make up a story – you know, why I went off

on my own with the finger and didn't call him.'

'So make up a story.'

'Okay. But tell him to tell Massey? – that's giving him an instruction. You want me giving him instructions?'

'Christ, I have to be a goddamn mother around here.' The lieutenant sighed. 'Never mind. I'll take care of it. About the finger – who knows about it besides you and me?'

'Forensic, the guy at the medical examiner's, Vassos, Passatino – '

'They all know they have to keep it quiet?'

'That's what I told them,' Roehmer said. The lieutenant didn't seem quite satisfied. 'I made it real strong.'

'You better be right. I don't want any of the medias to have this until after the old man himself knows about it. It would be a terrible blow if the poor guy had to read about it in the papers. So I don't want no leaks. Understand?'

'Yes, sir.'

When Roehmer left, the lieutenant got up and shut his door. He found a phone number written on his desk blotter, picked up the phone, and dialled. After a couple of rings a voice came on, speaking over a flurry of clacking typewriters.

'Severinsen.'

'Lieutenant Boyd. Hold this for about one hour, and then you can go with it. A severed finger came into this precinct through the mail. We checked it out. It's hers, the Massey girl's.'

'By checked it out, you mean what?'

His voice was speedy and staccato, just like the sound of the typewriters, the lieutenant thought. 'The print on the finger matches the girl's print.'

'Give me the details, Lieutenant.'

'Look, this is not attributable.'

'Okay. Not attributable.'

'But payable,' the lieutenant said.

'Okay. Payable. Let's go.'

Part II

NELLA IN THE HOUSE OF APOLLO

Chapter 2

As Nella fled, the prolonged resonance of her screams ricocheted in her head, and the scene played itself back: Julian hugging the picture protectively against his thin chest, flopping backwards in a glitter of splintered glass, his right hand, glossed with blood, splayed out on the deep blue pile of the carpet to cushion his fall.

She raced across the cluttered expanse of the sitting-room towards the entry hall, plunging like a fullback in a straight-ahead line, leaving a fair sampling of Julian's quirky possessions quivering in the wake of her path: a Bengali terra-cotta horse, eight feet tall; a ponderous chair, late Viking (or early Hollywood, more likely), covered in the pelt of some unidentifiable cervine animal, surmounted by two great branching antlers; a clutch of African violets implanted in the chamber pot Nell Gwynne was thought to have piddled in; a pigmy blowpipe; a brace of duelling pistols gathering dust on a scarred surgical table said to have been used for illegal dissections at the University of Padua in Galileo's time; on a marble pedestal, a bald feminine head from Schiaparelli's atelier in Paris, rakishly adorned by the hat supposedly worn by Errol Flynn in *Robin Hood* . . .

She wrenched the outer door open and was halfway through it when she remembered her coat. She opened the guest closet and yanked the shearling off its hanger. Trailing it behind her, she ran out, slamming the door. The vestibule was decorated with odd pieces that Julian deemed inappropriate for the apartment itself, although Nella had never been able to determine what criteria he employed for such judgements, since in her own estimation one item was just as much junk as another. She rushed towards the elevator, skimming over remnants of threadbare Persian rugs scattered on the tile floor, and pressed the call button. Above the elevator door Julian had hung a replica of a pair of Etruscan horses joined together at the withers like Siamese twins. As a child she had named them – not without calculation – Damon and Runyon.

Fred, the night operator, opened the elevator door, and she barged inside without a greeting. He slid the grille shut with a tiny shrug of his shoulders. When the elevator started downwards, she backed against the teak panelling of the rear wall, eyes straight ahead to avoid meeting her reflection in the bevelled mirrors framed at the sides of the car. She put her hand to her throat. It felt constricted, the muscles taut and aching, and it hurt when she swallowed. She could not remember having screamed like that ever, not even in a childish tantrum, and it struck her now as being a class of violence more abandoned than knocking Julian down or wilfully smashing the picture, his idiot treasure.

The image of Julian collapsing to the floor recurred, and she began to tremble. His hand, with its slick of blood. She steadied herself by pressing her back against the panelling and stiffening her legs. She held that posture, barely breathing, until the elevator reached the lobby floor. Fred opened the grille, then the outer door, with ceremonial slowness. She paused for a moment, as if to test the stability of her legs, before stepping out. She put the shearling on as she turned the corner of the lobby.

Karl, the doorman, was sitting on the high-backed rococo bench, opening a carton of milk. At the sound of her footsteps he hid the carton behind his back, but then, when he looked up and saw her, brought it out again.

She walked towards him slowly, with icy deliberation, to within a foot of the bench, and looked down at him. 'How dare you turn this lobby into a cafeteria.'

His broad, age-pleated face concealed itself behind that profound absence of expression it had mastered in forty years of absorbing insult and disdain. But for all that, she knew that his servant soul detested her: she was a transient here, she dressed improperly for anyone who lived in his house, and, of course – never mind that Julian did – she never tipped him.

She glared at him, then turned away and walked to the door. She planted herself squarely in front of it, waiting. Nella, you're being ridiculous. Suppose he doesn't come. Will you stand here all night? Yes, all night! But presently she heard a stirring, and she knew he had risen, was straightening the heavy skirt of the maroon coat, perhaps was touching the visor of his cap to settle it. She heard him shuffling across the lobby, but she didn't move until he said, ''Scuse me, ma'am.'

She stepped to one side so that he could reach the knob. The door opened, and she went out. She did not look back at him as the door closed behind her. In the street, traffic was flowing by on both sides of the centre divider; the kerb as usual was lined with cars parked bumper to bumper. She stood for a moment facing to the north, and the stiff night wind whipped against her face, drying the sweat of her anger, and the tears she had not been aware of shedding until now.

She put her back to the wind and walked aimlessly south. At the corner she paused, and the image of Julian's bloody hand flashed before her. *Hand that once held mine* . . . She turned abruptly westwards, as though the sudden movement might dislodge the red hand and send it skimming off into the night. She walked on, head down, and found herself at Fifth Avenue without any conscious memory of having crossed Madison. She headed south on Fifth, past one monolithic apartment building after another, each with its glimpse of a doorman inside. Across the street, in the park, the dried stiff limbs of the trees creaked in the wind.

The sound of a bus bearing down on the yellow-lined kerb across the street triggered an impulse. She turned sharply and ran into the street, setting off squealing brakes and horns and invective. The cars might have killed her – and perhaps would have if their drivers had had time to think about it instead of instinctively stamping on their brakes – but they screeched to a stop. She threaded her way across the street between front and rear bumpers, signalling to the bus driver, who gazed at her blankly through the window as he waited for a passenger to leave through the centre door. She knew that he wasn't going to wait, and so, enraged by his rejection of her (it didn't matter now, all rejections were equal: Julian's, the bus driver's, the doorman's), she ran in front of the bus as it pulled away from the kerb. The driver jerked to a stop. She stood on watery legs with the huge bulk of the bus rocking on its springs six inches away from her.

The driver was on his feet, screaming at her through the windshield. 'You trying to get killed, you crazy . . .' He was a black man with a round face that might ordinarily have been pleasant and, even now, succeeded only marginally in being ferocious.

Behind her, traffic was in full spate again, rushing on to its next crisis, its next aggravation. The driver was waving at her furiously with a pink-faced palm, as if to waft her out of his way, on to the sidewalk, or even further, into the park, dark and whispering beyond its stone retaining wall.

She shouted at the black face behind the window. 'I want to get on this bus. Open your door.'

'Out of the way. Step out of the way, lady.'

'I'm not going to budge until you open the door.'

The mild face contorted. 'Get the hell out of the way, damn you!'

A passenger appeared in the window, glanced down briefly, and then, his meagre curiosity appeased, disappeared.

'You are gonna get run down, lady!'

She folded her arms across her chest, and the gesture seemed to infuriate the driver. He sat down. In the next moment the gears of the bus began to grind. Nella's body jerked in terror, but her feet didn't move, and neither did the bus. The driver half rose in his seat to glare down at her, then sank back again. The front door clattered open.

It occurred to her as she moved towards the kerb, trembling, that the driver might close the door and shoot off once she was clear of the bus, but she didn't hurry, and

26

the door remained open. She climbed in. The driver folded the door shut at once and swung out into the stream of traffic. She saw that there were a half-dozen people in the bus, and that they were glancing at her covertly, torn between curiosity and the unacceptable risk of involvement.

Bracing her hip against the coin box, she rummaged through the pockets of the shearling and dug two quarters and a dime out of a deep pocket crammed with packets of matches and crumpled bills and Kleenex and, from its feel, half a candy bar. The driver watched the coin box with exaggerated attention as she dropped the coins in the slot.

In a cold voice she recognised as identical to the one she had used with the doorman, she said, 'Aren't you supposed to wait when somebody flags you down? Isn't that what you're paid to do?'

'I stop when I *see* somebody, lady.'

'You saw me. You turned your head and looked at me.'

He said indignantly, 'You trying to tell me what I see or don't see? Whose eyes is it?'

First Julian, then Karl, now a bus driver. What are you trying to do, Nella – become the witch of the whole wide world?

She walked to the rear of the bus, challenging the averted eyes of the other passengers, and took a seat. The bus lumbered down Fifth Avenue, and she watched the streets go by, peering out through her own indistinct reflection in the window. To the right, the park ended; the tall staid apartment houses were replaced by office buildings and the great stores. Forty-second Street and the huge pile of the library, then Lord & Taylor . . .

The bus stopped at Thirty-fourth Street, across from the Empire State Building. When it moved on again, she pulled the signal cord. The bus driver edged into the kerb obediently enough at the next stop. She left properly through the centre door, and the driver waited patiently for her to step down before shutting the door. Confrontations that pass in the night. Incident closed. An errant wind swirled dust and small bits of debris around her ankles as she waited for the bus to move on, excreting a cloud of blue exhaust smoke, before she crossed to the east side of the avenue.

The stores of lower Fifth Avenue – wanly lit by the meagre glow of night lights – had a distinct flavour of their own, a blend of shabbiness and the exotic: oriental rugs, vases, lace, chinoiserie, Asiatic objets d'art, set out in display windows marked WHOLESALE ONLY. She barely glanced at them before turning off the avenue. The side street was dark and deserted and the old buildings harboured shadows. She felt a stab of misgiving, but moved onwards, walking close to the kerb (Manhattan lore: if someone came at you, he was likely to do so from a doorway, so you left yourself space to manoeuvre), nervously alert, scanning every building or store entrance that might shelter her eventual mugger. Except for an occasional figure on the avenues, she saw no one until she was approaching Lexington, and then, fifty paces ahead of her, a man loomed up, walking lurchingly towards her, speaking aloud in an argumentative voice. She weighed crossing the street, but decided against it, and went straight on towards him, quickening her pace. More Manhattan lore: if you walk briskly, you're less likely to be accosted than otherwise; a slow pace is considered an invitation. The man stopped when he saw her and fell silent. He stared at her as she swept by, but didn't move. She didn't look back.

As she turned into Third Avenue, two men came around the corner. They paused for a moment, then changed their direction and angled purposively across the pavement towards her. Her hand rose from her side, fingers outstretched, groping blindly for something that was not there.

If she had not been mulling over the movie, formulating the way she would tell him the story, another thought might have sprung more quickly into Agnes Massey's mind when she came in and saw Julian stretched out on the carpet amid a scattering of glass. He was lying on his back, his eyes shut, his cheeks hollow, his mouth partially open, his arms crossed on his chest. The fingers of one hand were bloodstained.

As she paused in surprise, an odd notion struck her: of all the dozens of people she had seen die, none had ever passed on like this, on the floor, unattended, with their boots on. Well, not actually boots, Julian was wearing the chamois slippers she had bought for him at Saks . . . And then it occurred to her that all the money, the apartment, the house in Sag Harbor, the car, the junk he had picked up all over the world, that it all belonged to her now, without effort, without having to lift a finger. But after the first thrill of excitement, what she felt most of all was disappointment and regret. So that, when he stirred and calmly opened his eyes, she was relieved: nothing would have to change now.

'Where have you been, for Godssakes, when I needed you?'

First words out of his mouth, Agnes thought, and he didn't leave any doubts that he was alive and kicking. She said, 'The movies, you know damn well. I invited you and all, didn't I?'

He gave her a scheming smile. 'Did you think I was dead?'

'You're too mean to die. What all happened, for Petesake? How long have you been lying there?'

'Half hour, about. In need of professional assistance. A whole half hour, waiting for you to come back.'

She noticed the picture, its glass splintered, lying on the carpet beside him. 'How the devil did you do that? Did you fall?'

'I didn't do it. *She* did.' To Agnes's surprise he spoke mildly, without vehemence.

'*She* broke it? On purpose?'

'A face is scratched,' Julian said.

'A face? Scotty's? Gawd!'

'Don't call him Scotty,' he said irritably. 'We didn't call him that. I've told you a hundred times.'

'I'm sure glad it isn't *his* face that's scratched. That would be awful. Or yours. Is it yours?'

He shook his head impatiently. 'While you're standing

there yapping I could be bleeding to death. Aren't you going to help me?'

She stooped and picked up his hand. 'A couple of little cuts, Petesake, and it's all coagulated.'

He pushed her hand away. 'The uniform. Put the uniform on, nurse.'

'Okay.' She stood up. 'But aren't you going to get up meanwhile?'

He shook his head, grinning. She started to unbutton her blouse as she left the room.

The two men separated to flank Nella on either side. Her heartbeat raced but she didn't falter. Keeping her eyes to the front, she walked on without changing her pace. The only other pedestrian in sight was a full block ahead and walking swiftly away from them. There was a steady flow of cars, but there was no comfort in them; if she were to scream, they would simply accelerate.

'Hello, baby. How you doing?'

Conversation. Okay. All right, Nella, you can relax a little. They probably haven't got robbery in mind, or murder, maybe not even rape. In fact, it might be just a simple old-fashioned pick-up. Although she was still tense, she no longer felt intimidated. As she crossed a street, she flicked her eyes to the left, to the man who had spoken, and then to the right, at the second man, and instantly characterised and named them. Apollo to the left, Richard Widmark to the right.

Whether he was baffled by her failure to respond to him or had merely exhausted his repertoire of opening gambits, Apollo lapsed into silence. But a half block further on he stepped forward a few paces and then turned around to face her. She felt a resurgence of tension, thinking that he meant to block her path, but that wasn't his intention; he kept walking backwards, still facing her. Her first impression of him was confirmed. He was ravishing: a steep classical forehead, straight dark brows, clear, high-coloured skin, thick brown wavy hair, a Hollywood chin. His face might have been a trifle too broad to be movie-star handsome, but it was a very near miss. She realised that he was deliberately putting himself on display. Okay, Apollo, I'm dazzled. But she hadn't seen the half of it. He skipped backwards a few paces, extending her angle of vision so that she could drink in the rest of him: terrifically broad shoulders under a creamy leather sports coat, tapered waist, columnar thighs in skin-tight Levi's jeans . . .

But his backward movement had suddenly reminded her of a time in Rome when she had been tailed – *front*-tailed – for more than an hour. Her admirer had first appeared at the top of the Spanish Steps, beside the Trinità dei Monti, and he had followed her down the steps themselves, backwards, at the risk of breaking his neck, and then along the Via del Corso all the way to the Monumento a Vittorio Emanuele. She had been tailed before, but always conventionally, from behind, and usually ending with a ritualistic pat or pinch on the ass, and so she had wondered where a front-tailer would wrap matters up. She had laughed out loud at the absurdity of her notion. The Italian, perhaps thinking he was being mocked, had stalked off in a huff.

Now, remembering the episode, she smiled. An instant too late she knew that Apollo would misinterpret her smile and take encouragement from it. He stopped, then ranged himself alongside her again.

'Buy you a drink, baby?'

He wasn't smiling himself, either because he was trying to project sincerity or because such a blatant appeal constituted overkill for someone with his assets. Himself unadorned, himself was adornment enough. She continued at her steady pace, head to the front. She could see Apollo from the tail of her eye, but not Richard Widmark, who was trailing a step behind her. Nevertheless, she sensed his presence, a wraith with an expressionless face caged tightly in its own bone.

'You're a real nice-looking chick. You know?'

You're not the Dr Johnson of pick-up artists, Apollo, but maybe you don't have to be. Maybe all you've ever had to do was put your radiance on display, and everything else would follow.

31

'And you got a great bod too. I mean it.'

He drew the syllable out lovingly, so that it became *bahd*. Where had she heard that self-conscious pronunciation before? Where?

'You don't want to frown, baby, it puts lines in the pretty face.'

Oh, God, yes, a porno film she had once seen – to what pointless and desperate end? – in which the male protagonist, pumping away furiously upon his companion, had (it was easy to deduce from his freezing in mid-thrust and nodding his head in agreement) been instructed by the off-scene cameraman to say something (*we got sound, chrissake, we want more than a few grunts, don't you ever say nothing to the broad you're fucking*) and, with effort, awkwardly and even shyly, had said to the tense face beneath him, 'I like your *bah-dy*.' But there was certainly no further resemblance between Apollo and the protagonist of the film, a scrawny young man with the deprived face of a jockey and a surrealistically long penis.

'Why the hell don't you say something?'

Apollo's irritation took her by surprise, until she realised that he wasn't addressing her but Richard Widmark, still trailing a pace or two behind. For a moment there was silence, followed by a deep, uninflected voice.

'Hello, baby.'

'Jesus.' Apollo bent towards her, as if asking her to endorse his disgust with his friend. Well, you've got my sympathy, Apollo, he isn't scintillating. But neither are you. Apollo's annoyance broadened to include her, as well. 'What a pair. You both don't know how to speak?'

A blinking neon sign ahead read PLEASANT TIMES BAR AND GRILL, and she was surprised that it still existed, that it had survived all the years since her childhood. As they drew abreast of it, she could have sworn that the dusty half-curtains and flickering neon beer signs in the window had never been changed. The interior looked as dark as ever, too, relieved only by a dim light far inside. That darkness now, as it had been when she was a child, gave it an air of secrecy, of mysterious, illicit goings-on.

Apollo's hand closed around her waist, not roughly but firmly enough to be a restraint. She was startled; she had not expected, after all this time, that he would touch her.

'Come on, baby, come on.' His tone was complaining. 'Why don't you just let yourself relax and be friends.'

She wrenched her arm out of his grasp and, looking at him squarely, said, 'Why don't you just fuck off?'

He was taken aback, and before he could recover, she walked swiftly on. She risked a rearward glance over her shoulder. They were entering the Pleasant Times Bar and Grill: Apollo first, Richard Widmark slouching behind.

The changes of the street reflected the shifting and often contradictory flux of the restless tides of the city. A half dozen of the houses on the block were handsomer than they had been in her childhood, bought up by ambitious people of means, and by costly renovation turned into 'town houses'. At the corner, Schmidt's grocery, predictably, had become a bodega. The ageless tenement still stood, little different in appearance except for the graffiti that festooned its old brick at street level. Where once a doctor's shingle had been screwed into the wall at the entrance, there was a sign reading: DOLORES GONZALES, ELECTROLYSIS. Many of the Irish and Armenian surnames on the letterboxes would surely have been replaced by Hispanic names.

She was making a pilgrimage to her childhood. Yes, a pilgrimage. She hadn't been on the bus for two minutes before the impulse that had sent her skittering across Fifth Avenue had translated itself from mindlessness to underlying purpose: a visit to the faraway country of her childhood to celebrate – or consecrate, or mourn, or expiate, or all of these – the irredeemable burning of bridges. This time there could be no coming back, no return to Julian's nest.

She walked along the street slowly, reaching out to the past through a consciousness burdened with the overlay of fifteen years. *Hand that once held mine*. She remembered her hand rising unbidden, groping, when Apollo and Richard Widmark had first borne down on

33

her. It had been seeking Julian's hand, as it had done so often, so trustingly, when he walked her to school. Julian's hand, embodiment of wisdom and strength and sanctuary.

The house. She noticed at once that the giant stone tubs Julian had brought back from South America (when she was a child, the snakes that coiled around their plump girth had amused and frightened her at the same time) had been removed and the tiny garden space was planted with evergreen shrubs and white frost-bitten chrysanthemums. The sandstone façade had been cleaned recently, and the trim touched up with blue paint, so that the house looked as fresh as when she had lived in it. The parlour-floor windows were covered by pale blue venetian blinds where in the old days there had been lacy curtains and brocaded wine-coloured drapes running from the high ceilings to the floor. The ground-floor window was open at the bottom, leaking music, a bass thump that might have underscored anything from a symphony to rock and roll, or even the insipid cocktail music that her mother had listened to for hours on end, feeding her silly romantic soul with memories of old proms.

She could not people the house. Her father, Poor Philip, was dead, her mother a ghost, Julian an old man with a bloody hand lying on a blue carpet. She felt a stab of guilt. Had she not loved her father, that irresponsible weakling, and even felt his torments? Had she not pitied her mother and tolerated her foolishness? Had she not adored Julian? But too much had happened; she couldn't bring the past and the present together in the same place.

She crossed the street so that she could look up at the third-floor room she had once inhabited. The blinds were rolled up there, but all that was visible was a portion of blank white ceiling. She could not bring to life the room with hobbyhorse, dolls, four-poster bed, closets full of clothing, chests full of toys, all bought for her by an indulgent uncle; and she could not visualise Nella, pretty and spoiled and fair-haired. Nothing to be seen. It was just a house with memories that had gone cold. Once you left a house it was empty, no matter who else moved into it.

She turned away and began to walk back towards Third Avenue. Pilgrimage finished. She turned the corner. Ahead, the neon sign of the Pleasant Times Bar and Grill flickered blue and white and yellow.

Chapter 3

In her early years Julian had co-opted the role of father, mother, maid, and walked her to school each day. Their route took them by the Pleasant Times Bar and Grill. Once, when she expressed curiosity about it, he had told her that it was a wicked place, that working men, poor people, went there to get drunk. Working men equals poor equals bad. But this sociological assessment had eluded her. She took the point, but modified it drastically: the Pleasant Times found a place in her fantasies as a forbidding castle occupied by a treacherous knight or a scheming grand vizier. The darkness of its interior was the darkness of a castle dungeon.

The 'poor' or 'bad' men who frequented the Pleasant Times were often unshaven and dressed in seedy clothing, or they reeked of beer fumes. ('They're dirty,' Julian said.) Occasionally one of them, hanging around outside for a breath of air, would give her a smile and say something like 'Hello, sister,' or 'Aren't you a pretty thing.' She would pretend to be frightened and tighten her grip on Julian's hand or duck her head and hide. Julian would hurry her by, warning her that she was never to respond because these men were 'tough', and often beat their own children mercilessly. Later on, in early adolescence, the secret darkness of the Pleasant Times struck her as being erotic, and she would experience an excitement of another kind when one of the men took notice of her. As she had done in her younger years, she hurried by. But she would throw her shoulders back to accent her budding breasts, and feel a strange weakness in her legs.

Now, pushing the door inwards, crossing the threshold, she felt a momentary thrill of excitement: the sinister castle, the grand vizier lurking. She felt her way to a red-backed stool near the door, where the bar curved inwards at a right angle before it made a long straight sweep to its end in a matching inwards turn. It was so dark that her hands, clasped in front of her, were grey blurs. Only the centre of the bar, where a clot of men was congregated, was even moderately lit. To the rear of the bar, pin-up lamps with opaque shades, spaced at regular intervals on the wall, suggested a row of booths. To her right, half-way down the length of the room, a jukebox stood against the wall, its colours muted and swirling dispiritedly.

The bartender had marked her entrance with a sharp, alert turn of his head, but continued to make drinks, whirling between his work area and the back bar with that special almost-showy efficiency of his trade. The cluster of men at the bar were talking animatedly and with broad gestures. Now and then one of them would seem to appeal a point to the bartender, who never said a word, only shrugged. After a moment the general conversation would resume.

She spotted Apollo at the centre of the group. He was seated on a barstool, and next to him, almost hidden by his bulk (or simply dimmed by his glitter), was Richard Widmark. Apollo was facing in her direction, squinting his eyes to penetrate the gloom. You'll need the eyes of a lynx to see me, Apollo. She stared back at him, and presently he gave a little start and nudged Richard Widmark with his elbow. Lynx-eyes! Richard Widmark barely glanced up before returning to his drink.

The bartender came towards her, bouncing on the creaking duckboards.

'Help you?'

She judged him to be in his early forties, with elongated eyes that might have been round in his Irish boyhood but had narrowed with age. He seemed to be looking her over, checking out her credentials; Lexington Avenue, a block away, was teeming with hookers. But what could he see, coming from light into darkness? If her own eyes, which were becoming accustomed to it, could barely make out his features, then her face would be little more than a dusky smudge to him.

'What'll it be, ma'am?'

He knows a lady when he sees one – right? She guessed that the determining factor was the shearling coat and, beneath it, the cashmere sweater. Hookers dressed more provocatively.

She said, 'Scotch and water,' and named a deluxe brand of premium whisky. 'That is, if you have it.'

She could tell by his slight stiffening that he had taken offence. He turned without saying anything and went back to the centre of the bar. Chalk up another score for the witch of the whole wide world.

From the midst of the group at the bar, Apollo was staring at her. In the grey, faceless crowd he stood out as if spotlighted, a peacock in a nest of mudlarks. She watched the bartender pour her drink. She recognised the bottle, even though his hand covered the label. Or, rather, she recognised it negatively; it was not the distinctive bottle of the Scotch she had ordered.

He carried the drink to her and put it down on a tiny napkin. She picked the glass up and sipped from it.

'This tastes like bar Scotch.' The witch of the whole wide world never relented. She thought she could detect the skin tightening over his cheekbones.

'Would you like to see the bottle?' He paused a beat and added, 'Ma'am?'

'Never mind.'

He said, 'Dollar and seventy-five cents,' adding, as she began to rummage in the pocket of the shearling, 'bar or other brands is only a dollar fifty.'

Whatever the whisky was, she thought, his brand of logic was certainly worth an extra quarter. She separated a crumpled five-dollar bill from the junk in her pocket and gave it to the bartender. He smoothed it out fastidiously before going back to his cash register. He was returning with her change when she heard the door open. The bartender cast a sharp, wary look past her shoulder.

'Oh, Martinez,' he said. His tension eased.

A yell rose from the group at the centre of the bar as Martinez came into view. He was a slim, dark man in a black suit, with a large bandage wound around his head

38

like a turban. When he joined the crowd, everyone started talking to him at the same time. He put his hands over his ears, shaking his head, and presently the hubbub died down. But Martinez still waited, like a stern conductor at a concert demanding absolute silence before giving the downbeat.

Apollo broke the spell. 'Just because you got a hit on the head don't mean you know what happened,' he said. 'You were sleeping it off on the floor.'

A babble of voices rose again, shouting Apollo down. Martinez looked pained. When the noise died away, he said, 'Ju want to hear the story or ju do not?'

Apollo mimicked his solemnity, but said nothing, and after a moment, appeased, Martinez began his recitation. He spoke emotionally, with sweeping gestures, occasionally glancing at the bartender as if for confirmation. His voice carried clearly down the length of the bar, and Nella had no trouble piecing the story together. Last night, four men had entered the bar with drawn guns, lined up the customers, and robbed the till. It was a typical enough city episode, occurring almost exclusively in lower-middle-class neighbourhood bars, as if, Nella thought, the robbers were inhibited by a sense of fitness that limited their crimes to their own social stratum.

'Even with the masks,' Martinez said, his expressive fingers covering his face, 'even with the masks I could tell they were Puerto Ricans.'

Apollo's hand rose, palm out, like a policeman halting a flow of traffic. 'You got X-ray eyes, Martinez?'

Before Martinez could reply, one of the men at the bar said, 'Even if they were for sure Puerto Ricans, that don't mean they were the *same* Puerto Ricans that knocked off the bar the last time.'

'They were the same,' Martinez said excitedly. 'I will swear they were the same.'

'McGarry?' the man said to the bartender.

The bartender shrugged. 'Could be. But I haven't got no eye for them kind of people. Especially if they're wearing masks.'

'If they were the same ones,' Apollo said, 'that ain't robbery, that's persecution.'

He repeated himself, but now he was looking past Martinez in her direction, inviting her to share in his self-appreciation. She stared back at him expressionlessly over the rim of her glass.

'The same,' Martinez said. 'I swear it by God.'

'McGarry don't swear it,' the man said.

Martinez turned to McGarry with appeal. The bartender shrugged again, and Martinez's shoulders drooped. Nella thought: Martinez has just run up against a difference in temperament; if McGarry was a Latin he wouldn't have hesitated. But McGarry was Irish, the cautious, cool side of the Irish character. Commitments could turn out to be costly.

'So,' Apollo said, pointing his finger at Martinez, 'so you couldn't see their faces. Then how could you tell they were the same ones as last time? In fact, how could you tell they were Puerto Ricans? The defence rests.'

He didn't take his eyes off her. He was strutting his stuff for a gallery of one.

'How I know,' Martinez said, 'they were talking *puertoriqueño* Spanish and also they were very short people.'

'I suppose you measured them?'

Not quite equal to the brilliance of your opening speech, Apollo, but we can't always measure up to our best work. I'm listening, Apollo.

'I did not say they were the same size,' Martinez said.

'Let him tell the story, chrissake,' one of the men at the bar said.

'Ju let me tell it, I tell it,' Martinez said indignantly. 'Okay. I was standing right here. And I say to them, "Brothers, please do not hurt any of us." This was after they threaten.'

'How do you say that in Spanish?' Apollo said.

'*Hermanos, por favor, no nos hiera* . . . What is the difference?'

'I want to hear it in Spanish, that's the difference.'

'We all want to hear it,' the man who had spoken before

said. 'So why don't you leave him tell it?'

Richard Widmark turned to him. 'What's your business if he feels like talking?'

Apollo held up his hand, as if in restraint of his friend, and nodded graciously to Martinez. 'I pray you to proceed. What happened next?'

'Next, the leader of them, he say, "Shut up your fawking mouth".'

Everyone laughed. Apollo, eyeing Nella down the length of the bar, winked. Martinez waited impatiently for the laughter to subside.

'So then I say to the leader, in Spanish, you understand, "*Hermanos, yo tambien soy puertoriqueño.*" Brothers, I am also Puerto Rican.' He paused reflectively.

'So then what?'

'Then he slug me. The leader, he lift up his gun and *boom*! he slug me with his gun.' Martinez pantomimed a blow to the head. 'I start to bleed and I fall down.' He staggered dramatically, and mimicked falling. Then he smiled. 'But I din' have to fall down. I could have hold on to the bar. But I think they like it better if I fall down, so I fall down.'

Apollo winked at her again. 'Terrific, Martinez. You tell him you're his Puerto Rican brother, so he brotherly slams you on the head with his gun. If that's brotherhood, Martinez, I'll take sisterhood.'

'Don' laugh,' Martinez said. 'If I don' say I am his Puerto Rican brother perhaps he is not so nice as to hit me with the gun, perhaps he shoot me with it.'

'Terrific,' Apollo said, 'you Puerto Ricans sure have a funny idea of nice.'

'Ah,' Martinez said, 'there is the joke. I am Cuban. You see? If he know I am Cuban he would not be so nice to me.'

Winking a third time, Apollo said, 'A real Cuban? Just like Castro?'

'*Fawk* Castro,' Martinez said passionately.

A stocky middle-aged man materialised from the rear, shrugging on his coat, accompanied by a worn, dowdy woman with an elaborate hairdo fresh from the beauty parlour. The man listened for a moment to the discussion while his wife peered at herself in the mirror behind the bar, patting her hair, then joined in. He was sure that the Puerto Ricans were the same ones as before.

Apollo said, 'Look, Doyle, don't try to be an expert. You were just a Pinkerton, not a real cop.'

'It's a uniformed force,' Doyle said. 'Some of the things we knew and did the cops *wished* they knew and did. Ask McGarry. Even McGarry will admit it.'

Apollo said, 'The Boy Scouts are a uniformed force too.'

Richard Widmark guffawed. Doyle gave him a look and said, 'It's a known fact among cops that cheap rip-off artists like these ones haven't got much brains or imagination, and if they make a score in a place they usually come back and hit the same place again. You read in the papers about a grocery or drugstore that gets hit a half a dozen or so times a year, odds are that the perpetrators are the exact same bums. Am I right, McGarry?'

McGarry said nothing.

Apollo said, 'You getting the message, McGarry? They'll be back again.'

'Wouldn't surprise me a bit,' Doyle said. 'It's the *modus operandi*.'

'Hey, Martinez – hear that? Doyle is talking Spanish.'

'Not Spanish,' Martinez said, shaking his head. 'Or it is a dialect I do not know.'

Nella expected Apollo to preen himself in the laughter that followed, but he was whispering to Richard Widmark, who glanced in her direction and nodded. She watched Apollo disengage himself from the group and start towards her. He faded out momentarily in the no-man's-land of darkness beyond the light at the centre of the bar, then took on shape again as he came closer, broad-shouldered, wasp-waisted, swaggering. He turned the corner of the bar, pulled out the stool beside hers and sat down. When he leaned in towards her, the movement released a fragrance of tart cologne and reminded her suddenly of Roland Duffield and Eau Boy (when had she

42

seen him last? – it seemed ages ago), and then of Julian, folding towards the carpet with an old man's stiff angularity, anticipating his fall with a look of terror.

Her lips parted in an involuntary grimace of dismay. Apollo, perhaps seeing her teeth, the flash of whiteness, took it for a smile.

He said, 'So we meet again.'

He gave her a smile of his own, a parsimonious lifting of the right side of his mouth. Well, maybe a half-smile was enough if you were Apollo; a full-mouthed one might be so dazzling it would reduce people to cinders.

When she found herself making all sorts of excuses to herself for the dreary predictability of his conversation, Nella acknowledged her intention of sleeping with him. Bore or not, his handsomeness excited her. He had hitched his chair closer, and his leg, resting on the foot rail, was very close to hers. Another little while and he would start playing footsie . . . Her leg quivered with expectation.

'So look . . .' He tapped the rim of her glass with a glistening, manicured fingernail, and she curled her own fingers into her palm to conceal the bitten nails. 'How about a refill?'

She nodded. He summoned the bartender with a showy wave of the hand.

'Two more of the same, McGarry. And loosen up the old wrist when you pour?' When the bartender left, he said, 'You from around here? I mean the neighbourhood?'

She shook her head. 'Not any more.'

He pondered her response briefly but didn't pursue it. 'I live right around the corner. It's an okay neighbourhood. There are a lot worse. I mean, practically no blacks, unless you count the Indians. Ever been in one of their stores on Lexington?'

'Do *you* count the Indians?'

He looked at her blankly, then shook off his puzzlement and gave her an up-from-under look. 'You know, you're a pretty chick?'

A question mark, just the barest tinge of one, and most

likely it was a speech pattern, but she decided to take it literally. 'Yes, I know.'

Her answer took him aback, not least of all, she thought, because he could be thinking: Sure, but not all *that* pretty, baby. Well, come on, Nella, don't be a smartass. Next time he compliments you, just smile and thank him.

'You a college girl?'

My turn to be taken aback. Trying to flatter me by shaving a few years off my age? No. He didn't mean *at present*, he was simply trying to triangulate her social position. Okay, an opportunity to make amends.

She said, with conscious coquetry, 'Do you like college girls?'

'I like *all* girls, baby, period.'

His smirk was visible through the darkness. On the bar railing, the edge of his shoe touched hers. Her foot tingled. Even a little of Apollo turned her on. She glanced down the length of the bar. The discussion about the hold-up appeared to be still going on, but less intensely than when Apollo had been orchestrating it. Richard Widmark, nursing his drink, was listening silently and without expression.

'Actually,' Apollo said, 'actually, it's not important. I mean, a college girl is more educated, and that's the whole extent of it. What counts is the person, the person's character. Example: I'm a college man myself, but my best friend never even finished high school. But his character is excellent, and that's what matters.'

She guessed that he wanted her to ask what college he had gone to, but she knew his answer – one of the Ivy League schools – and she was damned if she would play straight man (person?), so she merely nodded, as if in agreement with his statement of egalitarian principle. The bartender brought their fresh drinks. He set them down and waited, his eyes focused precisely midway between them. After a moment, frowning, Apollo took his wallet out of his pocket and paid for the drinks. Slow on the draw, Nella thought, he was used to girls paying for *him*. The bartender was aware of it.

'So anyway, what's your name, baby?'

He leaned towards her, making the question an intimacy, and shifted his leg so that it was touching hers from the knee down. Well, paying for the drink entitled him to a small liberty, didn't it?

'Nella.'

'Nellie?'

'Nella. With an *a*.' She spelled it for him.

'Kind of unusual name. But nice. Mine's Wally.' He put out his hand and they shook hands formally. 'My full legal name is Wallace Cornwall. But my friends call me Wally. What do your friends call you – Nellie, Nell?'

'I haven't got any friends.' But his perplexity, close to a scowl, told her she had made a mistake. Wrong to inject a sour note into the music of the mating dance. 'No, I'm joking. It's just that nobody ever calls me Nellie or Nell, only Nella.' The marble brow smoothed out.

'Nella. It grows on you. Nella. You know, I like it lots. I also like *you*. I mean, I like what I see.'

His eyes dropped for open inspection, taking inventory from breasts to crotch. She sat still for it, thinking, Now if I were a proper feminist I would return the favour, maybe even go a step further and give him a friendly goose.

She said, 'Well, I like your name, too, Wally. And I like what *I* see too. You have quite a build, you know.'

The modest duck of his head was nominal. 'I keep in shape. I take supreme care of myself. It's professional.' He paused, as if to make room for a question. When she said nothing, he went on. 'You know how a lot of athletes let themselves go to fat afterwards? Not me. I used to play a lot of football. At Yale.'

Score one, Nella. Her little self-congratulatory laugh caused her to inhale her drink and she began to cough. Apollo patted her back, and the paroxysm passed. But the strain had made her throat sore again, and reanimated the scene in Julian's sitting room, those rending screams, directed with manic force into Julian's face, mottled by its own vehemence. Apollo's hand was no longer patting her back but massaging it in slow, sensuous circles. Screw Julian, she thought, screw him and his money, and screw

45

the Creepy Housekeeper too. She turned on the stool so that, now, her leg pressed against his from foot to thigh.

'I'm gonna take off.'

It was Richard Widmark, standing next to them, although she had neither seen him rise from his place at the bar nor walk towards them.

'What's your hurry?' But Apollo – Wally – barely paused before saying, 'Well, don't wait up for me. Oh, say hello to Nella. Nella, this is Richard.'

Richard. If she had been drinking, she would have choked again. 'Hello, Richard. Richard what?'

'Richard Kowalik.'

No cigar, Nella thought. His lips were thin but well shaped, and they barely moved when he spoke, which salved her disappointment in his name a bit. Now, if he would only produce a demented laugh . . .

'Richard is my cousin,' Wally said. 'Also, we're roomies.'

And before that, roomies at Yale, and before *that*, at Lawrenceville.

As though he had read her mind, and felt obliged to set the record straight, Wally said, 'He's the one I mentioned before. My best friend. A high-school dropout, and I went to Yale. Old Eli?' She watched for some tell-tale cautionary glance at Richard, but there wasn't so much as a flicker. Okay, it was an old gambit and Richard was up on his part. 'Still, we're best friends.'

He punched Richard playfully on the arm, and as Richard brightened, she braced herself hopefully for wild laughter. But there was only the small smile, briefly relieving the intensity of the face, with its deep-socketed eyes and caved-in cheeks.

'So I'm splitting,' Richard said. He ducked his head towards Nella. 'Glad to meet you.' He left, drifting silent and preoccupied through the door.

'We're first cousins,' Wally said, 'though it's hard to believe. Being as there's no resemblance? But his father and my father were brothers. He had a rough life, Richard, a rotten life.' For an instant his expression clouded. 'But things are a whole lot better now.' He

46

turned on his one-cornered smile. 'Say, you don't do a terrific lot of talking, do you, Nella?'

'I'm the strong silent type.'

To her surprise, her simple-minded joke floored him. He threw back his head in laughter, exposing the smooth powerful column of his neck. Splendid pedestal for the splendour of the head it supported. Still chortling, his hand resting on her shoulder now, he said, 'You're a funny chick, Nella. You know, it's real rare to meet a beautiful chick with a sense of humour.'

'Thanks, Wally.' *But I don't think I'll press my luck.* 'I'm glad I met you too. And Richard.'

'You're probably wondering why Richard's name and mine are different, our fathers being brothers?'

It isn't too hard to figure out, but I don't want to come on too strong. Chick with sense of humour, okay, but brilliant deductive powers might make the mixture too rich. She looked at him questioningly.

'I had to change my name. Kowalik is a fine Ukrainian name and I'm proud of it and proud to be a Uke, but the agencies and the clients can't pronounce it. I do modelling, you know. So I decided it would be better business to call myself Cornwall.'

'What do you model?'

'Body, mostly.' *Bahdy.* 'I do some head stuff, too, but I like bahdy best. I have a physique, you know.'

'So I noticed, Wally.'

His level brows drew together earnestly. 'That must have sounded like I was fishing for a compliment. I really wasn't.'

'I know, but a fact is a fact.' *Come on, Wally, stop massaging my shoulder, nice as it feels, and let's get the show on the road.*

He found his opening when she finished her drink. 'How about a refill on that?' Then, snapping his fingers: 'I got an idea. Why not let's go to my place? I got better booze than this rotgut. Also, it's cosier. Okay?'

'Where's your place?'

'Just around the corner, off Third. Look, you don't have to worry. I mean, do I look like a rip-off artist?'

'All right, Wally, let's go there.'

Third Avenue glistened with that deceptive sheen that the city wore on cold, clear nights when the dust of the day's intensity had settled. Wally eased around to the kerbside in a display of manners she hadn't seen in years and she took his arm. She was content to walk in silence, but Wally evidently felt the need for sociability.

'Whereabouts around here did you used to live?'

'A few blocks south of here.'

'Where do you live now?'

He stopped, waiting for her reply.

'Park Avenue.'

He gave a little gasp of pleasure. A dumb thing to say, Nella, he'll be afraid to lay a hand on so much glamour.

'It figured.' His voice sounded self-congratulatory. 'It figured you would come from some place like Park Avenue.'

I don't really live there, Wally, I've just been an occasional on-and-off squatter, a young pensioner, so you can stop dreaming.

'Can't we walk, Wally? It's cold.'

He took a single step and stopped again. He was of that order of people who found it impossible to walk and talk at the same time. I'll freeze to death before we get to the corner.

He went off on another tack. 'Nella. I've been trying to figure out what kind of a name that is.'

'It's just a name . . .' And suddenly old fury boiled up in her. 'It's a stupid name. I despise it. It's Italian, it's an Italian preposition.'

'You're Italian?'

'No. Just the name. It means *in*, for Godssake.'

'It means *in*? I don't get it.'

It didn't say much for her sense of proportion that she could become just as enraged as Julian over trifling matters as important ones. She said, 'Never mind. Maybe I'll tell you about it sometime.'

They turned the corner. The house was a five-storey apartment building; its entrance was just off Third

Avenue. In her childhood it had been a place where women had congregated with their baby carriages. It appeared to have been carefully tended through the years, except for the inevitable graffiti, which, however, someone had made a determined and partially successful effort to erase. They entered a small vestibule through glass doors and went up a flight of three steps. Wally used a key on a second door to let them into a large lobby.

He stopped beside a desk placed just inside the door. 'Where is that guy?' He stood with his hands on his hips, frowning. 'He gets paid to sit here every night, ten to six. So where is he?'

There was a cardigan sweater draped over the back of a chair. A heavy nightstick hung from a hook at the side of the desk.

'We had a lot of robberies and muggings,' Wally said. 'So all the tenants got together, and we pony up fifteen dollars a month out of our own pocket.'

Let's *go*, Wally.

'You like the desk? Maybe he went to relieve himself or something. You know, aside from the protection and all, it adds some class – like a doorman?'

Ah, now I see, Wally. You want to impress the Park Avenue visitor with your building's chic, and, bad luck, the guard has to be off taking a leak. Let's *go*, Wally.

'Well, I guess you can't blame him if he has to relieve himself.' He took her elbow and steered her into a left turn that led to a staircase. 'No elevator, but I don't like an elevator. Want to see how I always get upstairs?'

He launched himself up the first flight three steps at a time, and waited for her on the landing. Then he took off again. His apartment was on the top floor. She was panting when she got there. Wally was waiting, breathing easily, displaying his one-cornered smile. She felt a slight stirring of uneasiness as he turned his key in the lock, but it didn't last; she was accustomed to taking chances.

Wally hung her shearling coat in a closet, and led her past a tiny neat kitchen with folding louvred doors through a foyer. The living room was tidy and thought-

49

fully furnished, the upholstery predominantly blue, the carpet a brightly coloured Rya rug in tones of blue, yellow, and green, the drapes drawn over the windows citron. The walls were bare except for one picture, running the length of the sofa – a long, rectangular painting of a log cast up on a beach. The log was atrociously drawn.

'Like it?'

It wasn't a rhetorical question. He was proud of the decent taste of the inexpensive pieces and the carefully keyed colour scheme, and he truly wanted her approval. She said, 'It's awfully nice, Wally.'

He gave her his half-mouthed smile. 'We got cross ventilation.' He pointed to a set of three windows facing north. 'That's the front. Over here is the back.' He led her to a single window at the opposite side of the room. 'I want to show you something.'

He drew back a corner of the curtain. There was a small yard below, and to the right a small two-storeyed building, old and weathered, with two dimly lit windows at ground level.

'You know what that is – those windows?'

He was leaning against her, not assertively but making his presence felt. She shook her head obligingly. 'What are they, Wally?'

'The first one is the Gents, and the other one is the Ladies.'

'You have outside johns?'

'Quit your kidding. That's where we just came from, the Pleasant Times. If I don't want to go out, I just let down a bucket, and McGarry fills it up with suds. Real convenient, right?'

'Do you really do that?'

'I never did, though I would like to. For laughs? But one time, I was lazy, I didn't feel like getting dressed, so I took a shortcut. I really did. There's a back door to the house that opens up into the yard. I went downstairs and out through the door, and into the saloon by climbing through the window of the john. But then you know what happened? I forgot to fix the locks on the back door, and couldn't get back in. So I had to walk home in my kimono. But let down a bucket – I was just kidding.'

Okay, you were kidding. When are you going to get serious, Wally?

He put his hands lightly, caressingly on her shoulders. 'I just thought you'd be interested.'

Oh, I am, Wally, it's the most fascinating revelation of the entire year. She tilted her head and pressed it against his hand. He smiled with the left corner of his mouth.

'Tell you what – sit down and I'll go fix us a drink. Okay?'

She sat down on the sofa. From the kitchen she heard the sound of cabinets being opened, of ice being cracked out of tenacious trays. She ran her hand over the nubby blue fabric of the sofa cushions, then looked up at the citron drapes; the colours mixed and produced green. She turned her head to the picture of the log behind her: put the yellow sand together with the blue sky and it made green. There were no plants in the room. She juxtaposed the blue of the sofa and the citron of the curtains and got green again. Anything, anything, Nella, to fill up your mind, to divert it from the image of Julian stretched out on the floor (blue carpet, yellow complexion, mixing to make green) in a scatter of broken glass. Her throat began to ache.

Hurry back, Wally, hurry. She heard ice clinking against glass. Hurry!

'Eau Boy!' Julian had shouted. 'Eau Boy, for heaven's sake! A stupid young man, that Roland of yours, but not so stupid that he isn't smarter than you, and takes my hard-earned money and throws it away on a frivolous, stupid idea, and you're stupid enough to give it to him . . . You fool – to pay ten thousand dollars for a few fucks!'

It wasn't the first time he had brought it up, or the tenth, for that matter, but the awkwardness of his locution enraged her. In the next instant she was screaming again. 'A few fucks! Ten thousand dollars! You old idiot, don't you realise you're shelling out *millions* for what you call a few fucks?'

Yet it wasn't words at all, neither hers nor his, that had

51

snapped the last thin reserve of her control. In the midst of her outburst she realised that he was gazing dreamily past her at the picture on the mantel over the fireplace. She didn't know then, or now, if his attention had been wandering, or if he was deliberately trying to infuriate her, nor had it mattered. In a headlong, heedless delirium of rage she had wheeled around and run towards the fireplace. He shouted and ran after her. He reached over her shoulder as she snatched the picture from the mantel, and they wrestled for its possession. She pushed him and sent him staggering. Holding the picture with both hands, she slammed it against the edge of the mantel, then whirled around and threw it towards him. He was still falling, a ghastly flailing of arms and legs, and the picture landed beside him, spraying glass . . .

'Hey – what's the idea of the mad face?'

Wally stood over her, holding a neatly arrayed tray with two glasses, a dish of peanuts, two small cocktail napkins. She made an effort to reorder her face by putting a smile upon it.

'That's lots better. You got a lovely smile, you know.'

She was still trembling, but she worked on her lovely smile as he set the tray down on the smoked glass top of the coffee table. He had removed his leather jacket, and in shirt sleeves his massive shoulders, tapering down to the small waist and flat belly, were almost too good to be true. He sat down beside her. He offered her one of the glasses, but when she reached for it, he withheld it coyly.

'Don't I rate a little reward?'

As close as an inch away his skin was flawless. Everybody else has *pores*, Wally. He began his kiss with pursed lips. She parted them with her tongue, thrusting deeply into his mouth. He responded enthusiastically, but broke away abruptly when the drink sloshed over its rim. Frowning, he put the glass down on the tray, took out a handkerchief, and dabbed at two wet stains on his trousers. There is a time for neatness, Wally, but not now, not now. He folded his handkerchief and put it on the coffee table, and then, without warning, threw himself on top of her, bearing her back on the sofa. His hand parted

52

her legs, and in the same motion slid upwards and probed into her crotch.

His weight drove the breath out of her. She braced her hands against his chest and pushed him off. 'Let's go into the bedroom, Wally.'

He rolled to his feet agilely. She took his outstretched hand and he lifted her off the sofa and led her towards the bedroom. The living-room gave into a small hallway, with the bathroom directly ahead, and doors to the left and right. The door to the left was closed. Richard's? She held back at the threshold to the other bedroom.

'Your friend,' she said. 'Is he . . .'

'No problem, baby.' His right hand was on her breast, his left was splayed across her buttocks. 'He won't bother us. He's asleep. Anyway, he's used to . . .'

He edged her into the room and shut the door behind them. Did Richard go to sleep with his light on? A faint spread of yellow had been visible at the bottom of his door. Never mind, Nella, Wally knows what he's talking about. Richard wouldn't bother them, he was *used to*.

'I'll give us some light,' Wally said, 'so we don't trip all over the equipment.'

He turned on a lamp beside the bed (blue sateen spread edged in yellow) and in the pause before he enveloped her again, she caught a glimpse of the equipment – a rowing machine, barbells, weights, something with handles and cables attached to the wall. A collection of photographs – pinups? He drew her against him and she arched into him, pelvis to pelvis. He slipped a hand under her sweater to her breasts, cupping, massaging, sampling them, and her nipples rose and tightened to his touch. She felt the cashmere threads of the sweater begin to give under the stress of his roving hand.

'Wally, let's take our clothes off.' He leaned back and pushed her sweater upwards. It caught beneath her chin. 'I can undress myself, it's quicker.'

She whipped the sweater over her head, baring her breasts, and worked the zipper of her jeans. She pushed them down past her hips before sitting on the edge of the bed and kicking off her shoes. She worked the jeans down

53

over her feet and slid her panties off. Quicker I promised, and quicker I delivered. Wally was in less of a hurry. In fact, she thought, he seemed to be working the room. With his shirt off he struck a pose, putting his upper torso on display. It was something to see. His shoulders were enormous, powerful, sloping off towards that enviable waist; his biceps were over-developed, but they were smooth rather than knotted; his triceps rippled, and his stomach was a grid of serried muscle.

He removed his pants with the languor of a striptease artist, and posed again. When he bent to remove his apricot jockey shorts, he made a half-turn to exhibit his back muscles, which played rhythmically under the surface of his skin. His buttocks were shapely and firm, with deep concave dimples behind the thigh bone. Okay, Wally, it's a radiant ass, now let's see the rest.

He turned about slowly, in a model's self-conscious, stylised pivot. His penis was erect and hard, pointing upwards at an acute angle, and it seemed small in the context of the overwhelming richness of the rest of his body. Be thankful, Nella, if it was in scale you couldn't cope with it.

'You like?'

'It's too wonderful for words – so far.' She fell back on the bed. 'But let's see how you use it, shall we?'

Score another for the witch of the whole wide world.

Chapter 4

Propped up on one elbow, Nella traced the strong ridge of his left clavicle with her hand, tingling to the hard line of bone under the smooth surface of his skin. Her fingers trailed downwards to the swelling mounds of his pectorals and teased his nipples. He purred. His eyes were shut, and his pleased half-smile lifted his lip to show moist white teeth. Her fingers walked down the hairless chest, stroking lightly, to the flat stomach with its rippling muscles.

Perfect post-coital harmony: my pleasure in the beauty of his body, his contentment with my adoration of it.

Her eye was caught by the pin-up photographs on the wall, and she realised that they were not pictures of four-fifths naked girls, but of a four-fifths naked man – Wally. They were professional photographs, artfully lighted, portraying Wally in bikini shorts (the contours of the bulge in front made her suspect that he was padded), a loincloth, a leotard, a leopard skin. There were back, front, and profile views, buttock shots with Wally scowling over one bulking shoulder, discus-thrower poses, chest-expanded stances, traditional strong-man attitudes with the fists clenched to bring forward the musculature of chest and arms. In some of the photographs he glistened darkly with oil, in others he was as pale as marble, in all of them he presented a supremely self-conscious gaze to the camera.

Narcissus had his own private gallery.

He had made love egocentrically, in graceful and self-absorbed slow motion, as though performing for a camera or his own pleasure. If she were to measure his performance, it would rate a passing grade, somewhere between a C-plus and a B-minus. There had been one singular moment: approaching climax, she had dug her nails into his back, and he had cried out in anguish,

'Don't, don't do that, you'll mark up the bahdy.'

But he might have had a valid point. If you made your living from being perfect, you were obliged to be a jealous custodian of your perfection, and guard it even against the stigmata of passion, however complimentary they might be.

As her hand roamed over the smooth topography of his body, she felt herself moisten. Experimentally, she touched his penis. Dormant, limp.

'Nella?'

His eyes were open, brows knit, lips moving without sound, and she guessed he was trying to start a conversation, searching for a topic. It was touching, even flattering; he wished to be sociable beyond the mere connection of their bodies.

'Nella?' His brows unravelled. 'You promised to tell me about your name.'

Had she promised? No matter. 'Forget it, Wally, it's boring.'

'But I'm really interested.' His brows were knitting again, and there was a suggestion of petulance in his voice. 'Nella, you made a promise.'

'Instead of talking, wouldn't you rather . . .' Her hand trailed down to his penis again. Nothing. Maybe he wasn't trying.

'There's lots more to a relationship than just sex,' he said earnestly.

'I never thought of it that way before.' She removed her hand. 'But the story really isn't interesting.'

'The more you keep saying that, the more you make me curious.'

There was a stubborn set to his face. If I don't tell him, he'll withhold his favours. 'Well, all right. Julian gave me the name.'

'Your father? You call him by his first name? Christ, if I ever tried calling my old man anything but Pop, he would have clouted me. I'm named after him. Wladek, Junior.'

'Julian is my uncle.'

'Even an uncle. You call your *uncle* by his first name?'

'Well, he called me by *my* first name, didn't he?'

'Yes, but there's a diff – ' He perceived that he had missed her joke; he quirked his lips in belated acknowledgement. 'But how come *he* named you instead of your father or mother?'

Bull's-eye, Wally. Because that's the system our happy household operated on. She said, 'He took the name – the word – from the inscription on a statue – and he told my father about it.' *Told* will have to do instead of *ordered*, Wally, we don't want to go too deep, do we?

'On a statue? I'll be damned.' He ran his hand down her thigh: reward and promise. 'Tell me about it.'

How did you explain to a stranger that it was Julian all over? That it was typical, predictable, that despite a lifelong love affair with Italy he had never troubled to learn more of the language than *please, thank you,* and *where's the toilet?*

'Well?' Wally lifted his hand away from her body.

'Keep on doing that,' she said, pushing his hand down to her thigh, 'and I'll tell you anything.'

'Okay. He saw the word on a statue.' He was prompting her. 'Right?'

'Right. In Treviso, a little town in northern Italy. At the museum. He was there thirty or so years ago, before I was born.'

She had made a point of visiting the museum as a sort of pilgrimage of bitterness. From Venice, where she had been spending a week, she had taken a bus at the car station in the Piazzale Roma that had dropped her on a Saturday at noontime at a terminal in the centre of town, which was jammed with students going home for the weekend. Treviso had been heavily bombed in the war, but so cleverly reconstructed that there were no visible scars. She found the museum in a neighbourhood of opulent, fenced-in villas. It was a cold wet day towards the end of October, and she was the only visitor. A *docente* had guided her past half-obliterated frescos by a Modenese artist, third- and fourth-rate northern Italian painters, shattered fragments of ancient pillars, and, at last, to the statue of a middle-aged woman by an obscure sculptor.

'There was a plaque on the wall beside the statue which read something like this: *Nella statua della matrona Romagna . . .*'

'Hey, baby. I get the Nella, all right, but what's the rest of it mean?'

'The plaque said that in his statue of a Roman matron, the sculptor had departed from the chilly idealism of the Greeks . . . Okay, the point is that *nella statua* simply means, in Italian, *in the statue. Nella*, the word *nella* in Italian combines *in* and *the* – it means *in* – but Julian, in his ignorance, thought it was the name of the woman in the statue. Nella, as a name, stuck in his mind. I guess he thought it was beautiful, and he thought the statue was beautiful, and when I was born he thought *I* was beautiful . . . Hence, Nella.'

'That's it? That's all you're mad about? I think it's a kind of a cute story.'

And so it might have been, except that it was a symptom – and a mild one, at that – of Julian's possessiveness, his exercise of power, his despotism . . . She said, 'It wasn't the name my parents had chosen for me.'

'Still and all – you hate this uncle just for that one thing?'

'Not only for that.' How had she allowed herself to blab so much to a boy she had picked up for a one-night stand? 'That and other things. It's time we made love again, Wally.'

'Other things?' He raised his head from the pillow to look at her. 'For instance?'

'For instance, he killed my father.'

He was staring at her. She rolled over, rising to her hands and knees, and began to plant quick, furious kisses down the length of his body. When she reached his penis, it was no longer limp but curved upwards to meet her lips.

'Nella?'

She stirred but was unwilling to come fully awake. They were lying under the blanket now; the heat in the radiator had lowered, and their bodies had cooled in the aftermath of passion.

'Baby?'

She looked at him drowsily. He was propped up on an elbow and his one-sided smile had a programmed fixity about it, as if it had been launched for purely technical reasons. Insincere, Wally.

'Baby, I want to ask you something.'

A warning ticked off in her. She opened her eyes fully and studied him. The smile was meant to soften her up. So that he could pursue what she had said about Julian killing her father? His eyes turned away from hers, his smile became even more strained, and with sudden insight she knew exactly what was coming.

'Baby, what I want to ask you – '

'No.'

'No, I can't ask you something?' His attempt at making a comic face was a flop.

'Quit the crap, Wally. I'm not going to sleep with your friend.'

His smile disappeared. He was silent, baffled, for a moment, and then he said, 'The way you put it, it sounds terrible. But it's not. I mean, Richard *likes* you.'

'Do *you* like me?'

'God, yes, I like you lots.'

'But you don't mind sharing me?'

'You got to understand something,' he said earnestly. 'Richard and me, we're so close, it's like being the same person. We're first cousins, but more like brothers. Twins, even. It's like we're interchangeable, like we're one person. So there's actually no difference. You see the point?'

I get it, Wally, I get your dumb little rationalisation. You must have made it dozens of times in your long history of snaring girls and passing your conquests on to your less-favoured cousin-brother-twin.

She looked him in the eye and shook her head vigorously. His mouth turned down in a sulk.

'I thought you were a swinger. I thought you liked to have a good time.'

'I thought I was *having* one.'

'All you're doing is you're twisting my words.'

'Let's get something straight, Wally. I went to bed with you because you were attractive, and that's it. I don't sleep with just anybody. I'm not a whore.' Hurrah for the virgin Nella!

'Don't I know you're not a whore, for Godssake? Don't I know a girl with real class when I see one? Besides, if you were a whore you wouldn't be here. I never paid anybody a nickel in my entire life. I don't have to.'

His vanity had side-tracked him into an irrelevancy. She continued to stare at him, and his eyes wavered.

'Well, if that's the way you feel about it . . .'

He lay back on the pillow, then shifted a few inches so that their bodies no longer touched. Petulance, even a form of extortion: if you won't be nice to Richard, I won't be nice to *you*. She turned her head and studied him. His eyes were closed, his lower lip undershot in a pout. Okay, you bastard.

'All right, Wally, I'll let Richard fuck me.' Call you and raise you.

His eyes opened wide in surprise.

'Bring him in here.'

'You sure it's okay? I mean, if you really don't want to . . .'

She said in a fading whisper, 'Go get me Richard. Hurry.'

'Nella . . .' His voice was thinned by uncertainty.

'Richard. I want Richard. Get him for me.'

He got out of bed and hesitated for a moment at the door before going out and shutting it tightly behind him. Oh, Christ, what if I'm wrong? Well, I can always get up and go home. Go home? Oh, Christ! She shut her eyes until she heard the door opening. It was Wally. He got back into bed and put his arm around her waist.

'Richard don't want to.'

'Doesn't *want* to? I thought he liked me.'

'Well, he's tired, you see, he has to get up very early in the morning . . .' He put his hand on her cheek and turned her head towards him. 'I'm going to make a confession, Nella. I didn't wake him up, I didn't even go into his room. You know why? Because I didn't want to share you.

First time I ever felt that way about a girl. What do you think of that?'

'Oh, I'm flattered, Wally, terribly flattered.'

'Does it tell you something, Nella?'

'What should it tell me, Wally? Tell me.'

'That I like you lots, really *lots*.'

I *am* flattered, God help me: Apollo cheating on his buddy for the sake of a mere mortal. 'I like you too. Lots.'

He rolled on top of her. For the first time he was smiling with both corners of his mouth.

Agnes's starched white uniform had retained its shape when she took it off. It lay on the floor beside the bed like the pelt of an animal. Some animal, Julian thought, grinning as he edged out of the bed, remembering her stepping out of the uniform stark naked, boobs swinging, pubic hair black and bushy and glistening. Venus disembarking from the half shell. He slid his feet into his slippers and shuffled out of the bedroom, not making any special effort to be quiet, knowing that nothing would wake Agnes up. She was a heavy sleeper; she called it sleeping 'the sleep of the just'. But he kidded her about it, saying it was the result of years of practice as a private night nurse in sleeping through her patients' moans and groans.

Agnes complained in her mild way – as others did, not so mildly, especially Nella, not that it was any of *her* damn business – that the sitting-room was so cluttered that it was impossible to cross it without running into something. But even in the dark he wove his way with absolute sureness past the beloved objects he had collected from all over the world, and found his way unerringly to the mantelpiece. He took the picture down carefully and carried it back to the Empire chaise-longue, which had belonged to a French countess. He sat down and turned on a lamp. The picture was bent slightly at the bottom, where he had written *Princeton Triangle Show, 1917*, but the cardboard backing had saved it from any serious damage. The broken glass had inflicted some tiny scratches on two of the faces in the photograph, but not, thank God, on either his or Scott's.

Holding the picture directly under the light, he smiled indulgently at the array of very young men got up in organdy dresses, ringleted wigs, huge false bosoms, faces rouged and lip-sticked, muscular silk-stockinged legs extended in high kicks. Tufts of chest hair stuck up from some of the necklines. Narrowing his focus, he studied the two figures at the centre of the line: himself, skinny as a rail, with a silly grin on his face, his false breasts askew, one of them on his shoulder, the other under an armpit; and Scott, handsomer than any of them, his red hair hidden under a monstrous blond fright wig, his impudent Irish face smiling, and, on the whole, good-looking enough to actually pass for a girl.

It was a marvellous show that year, not least of all because Scott himself – and his friend Wilson – had written some of the skits. It certainly hadn't surprised *him* when Scott had blossomed out as one of the great writers of the twenties. A pity he hadn't been privileged to know him very long. Shortly after that Triangle show they had both left Princeton: Scott had joined the Army, and he had transferred to Cornell to study architecture. He had been a precocious seventeen at the time, and Scott had been several years older.

Nella, always playing the cynic, maintained that the man in the photograph wasn't Scott at all. She claimed to have read somewhere that although Fitzgerald might have written for that year's Triangle show, he didn't appear in it. Well, be that as it may – after some sixty-odd years you couldn't be expected to vouch for every detail – the fact remained that Scott *had* gotten into costume, and there he was in the photograph.

It must have given Nella a great deal of pleasure to smash the picture. She had always hated it and mocked his affection for it. What difference could it possibly make to anyone if he doted on this souvenir of his youth? Whom could it possibly hurt? She resented it because it was a living part of his history, a history of considerable achievement, if he had to say so himself. And what was *her* history, despite all her opportunities? Disorder, waste, aimlessness. No vocation, nothing she *believed* in. Fashionable nihilism, though he was willing to bet that deep down – despite her professed contempt for 'doing things', for 'getting places' – she must have some kind of grudging envy of those who succeeded. It was out of this envy, he was certain, that she had vented her rage against the picture because, although he was then nine years younger than her present age, he would soon be taking steps to become – as Scott might have called it – 'a personage'.

He smiled indulgently at the photograph. He and Scott, Julian and Scott, arm in arm, good friends before their careers took separate paths. He had to admit, studying the two faces, that compared to Scott he was an ugly duckling. Though, come to think of it, at least he had decent-sized legs (Scott's legs were disproportionately short, the only flaw in his physical beauty), and he certainly was kicking at least six inches higher than Scott.

'Bad enough you're out of bed and wandering around, but without a bathrobe. You want to catch cold?'

Agnes had come into the room. She was wearing a robe herself, but it was loosely tied, so that when she put her hands on her hips it gaped open to her navel.

'It's not cold,' Julian said. 'Besides, I'm not wandering around, I'm sitting down. Also, your whatsit is showing.'

'Nearly four o'clock in the morning,' Agnes said with mock exasperation, 'and the man is talking dirty. He's a sex maniac.'

Julian grinned. 'Didn't you know that before we got married? Did I ever try to keep it from you?'

'Did you ever *not*!' She approached the chaise-longue. 'Look, why don't you get back into bed?'

He reached out suddenly and pulled the robe open wide. She jumped back, squealing.

'Sex maniac!' She closed the robe and held out her hand to him. 'Let's go back to sleep, Daddy.'

'How do you know I'll sleep?' He reached out for her robe again, and grinned when she retreated.

Agnes yawned. 'Maybe you've got the energy for more

fooling around, but me, I'm sleepy. Let's go, Julian.'

'I'm wide awake, Agnes. Go back to bed. I want to stay up for a little bit.'

She yawned again, then tilted her head to look at the photograph. 'It sure wasn't very nice of her to damage your picture.'

'Not nice!' The cords stood out on his thin neck. 'It was an evil deliberate act of vandalism that she knew would hurt me very much.'

'Don't get yourself overwrought, Julian, or you won't be able to sleep and you'll be getting up to pee every six minutes.'

'I'm over eighty, I don't need much sleep at my age.'

'Maybe not, but you need plenty of peeing.' She twisted her head to look at the picture. 'He certainly was a handsome man, your Scott F. Fitzgerald.'

'Nobody could ever equal Scott for physical beauty.' He grinned. 'Do I sound like a fairy?'

'You may sound like one, but I can stand up in court and swear that you're not.' She nodded her head towards the bedroom wing of the apartment. 'Did she come in?'

'She won't be home tonight. I know her pattern.'

'Where will she stay?'

'Who knows? Pick up some young punk or something and sleep with him. Eventually, she'll come home. I know the pattern.'

'She's a bad girl,' Agnes said.

Her simplistic judgement annoyed him, as much for its mildness as anything else. He knew that her general disposition was bovine, and that, in fact, she had no strong feelings about Nella, although she must have known that Nella disliked her.

'You know what she calls you, Agnes?' He smiled maliciously. 'The Creepy Housekeeper.'

Agnes looked blank. 'I'm not a housekeeper. Where does she get that?'

'Oh, for Godssake, Agnes. All those novels, the ones that always have a creepy housekeeper?'

'I still don't get it. What's that got to do with me? Come on, Julian, let's go to bed.'

'She's a bad girl, you say.' Julian was very fond of Agnes, but she had an irritating way of saying the first thing that popped into her mind. 'That doesn't *mean* anything. Nella is a problem, yes, a serious problem, God knows, but what does "bad girl" mean?'

'Christ, I don't know, the way she behaves and all. Bad genes, or something.'

'Genes? That girl carries *my* genes, Agnes.' Julian stared at her stonily.

'She certainly must have taken after you as a sex maniac.' Agnes smiled, but when Julian failed to react to her joke, she said, 'Well, I'm just a simple creepy housekeeper, don't try to get me involved in all this psychological stuff.'

She flopped down on the sofa beside him and put her arm around him. He pushed her away.

'Agnes, I'm trying to be serious. If you can't be serious, go to bed.'

'Well, I *tried* to be serious. Bad genes.'

'That's ridiculous and stupid. Whatever she does, however she behaves, she's my own flesh and blood, she comes from fine old stock. She has foolish ideas, she's prone to being influenced by the wrong kind of people, but basically she has a good character. When she was a child . . .'

When she was a child, she was pretty, sweet, innocent . . . and she adored him as he adored her. He had been closer to her than her father and her mother had been, and, yes, loved her more. Who had taken her to school in the morning? Not her irresponsible father, not the mother who lay abed until noon. Not that it was an imposition; loving her as he did, it was the greatest pleasure of his day. And no question but that she delighted in going with him. He could still, and would always, remember her skipping down the stairs of the old house, laughing impishly up at him as he descended more slowly, urging him, 'Hurry up, Uncle Julian, don't be such a slowpoke.' And then, when he reached the street, she would take his hand. That little hand in his, the purity of trust and love that it implied. Sometimes, when they paused at a corner, or when something along the way alarmed her, she would tighten her grasp – she had such a powerful grip for a child – and a fierce current of love and dependence would flow through her fingers to his . . .

Agnes said, 'Are you dreaming, Julian?'

'I'm not dreaming, I'm thinking. There happens to be a difference, you know. If you ever tried a little thinking yourself, you'd realise that there's nothing fundamentally wrong with Nella. Not bad genes – especially not that – a neurotic father, a lazy fool of a mother. Her father – '

'She says you killed her father.'

'She *what*?'

'You don't have to bite my head off. I'm just telling you what she told me, I'm not saying I believe her.'

Earlier in the evening, that was one of the things Nella had accused him of, screaming hysterically, but he hadn't dreamed that she would have spoken such awful thoughts to a third party. He said, 'It's a lie. My brother died in an auto smash-up. Maybe he *wanted* to die, it's possible, I don't know.'

'For Godssake, don't you think I know nobody killed him?'

'She's trying to say that I drove him to suicide. Nothing could be further from the truth. I did everything in the world I could for Philip.'

'I know that too,' Agnes said. 'Listen, Daddy, I'm dying for sleep.' She looked at him coyly. 'You come along now, and I'll tuck you in.'

He didn't answer her, but picked up the photograph and began to smooth out the damaged corner. After a moment she shrugged, rose from the sofa, and went out. He lifted the picture closer and looked at the faces, first Scott's and then his own. Who would have guessed, then, that each of them would have attained the top rung in his chosen profession?

'High-kicking golden youth,' Julian said aloud, and thought, Scott would have liked the way I put that.

Wally was shaking her shoulder gently. Still half asleep,

she rolled towards him, burrowing, warm flesh to warm flesh, instantly aroused.

'Nella?'

Ready when you are, Wally. She nudged her head beneath his chin and pressed her lips to the strong beat of his jugular.

'When you told me your uncle killed your father.' He drew his head back so that he could look at her. 'Were you putting me on?'

Oh God, Nella, what a fool you are. She thought she could feel the temperature of her body drop, as if it had suddenly lost the warmth of sleep and the warmth of desire at the same time.

'I was putting you on, Wally. My father died in an auto accident.'

He was silent for a moment, frowning, assessing the inadequacy of her response to the weight of the question that had awakened him from sleep. 'Chrissake. Then why did you say it? I mean, that's a pretty dumb thing to say to anyone.'

'I'm dumb, I guess. Julian didn't kill my father – not outright. But he drove him to suicide.' Christ, Nella, can't you ever quit when you're ahead?

'But you said he died in an auto accident.'

'It was called an accident, but it was suicide.'

He shrugged. 'Yeah, well . . .' He was sceptical, but at the same time his curiosity seemed to be allayed; murder had not been done. He lay back on the pillow and closed his eyes.

Okay, Wally, we'll let it lie there. Back to basics. 'Make love to me, Wally.'

'You're a real bunny rabbit.' He smiled without opening his eyes. 'Go back to sleep.' She ran her hand under the blanket to his genitals. His smile faded. 'Don't fool around, Nella, I have to get my sleep.'

'I know, I know.' She manipulated him furiously. 'It won't take long. I promise it won't take long, and then you can go right to sleep. Come on, Wally, come on, darling.'

He wrenched away from her and rolled over on his stomach. 'I have to have my sleep. It's one of the four fundamental factors for a healthy bahdy. The bahdy comes first.' His head flopped down to the pillow, then lifted in an afterthought. 'I'll take good care of you in the morning, okay?'

But you woke me, Wally, and stirred up a storm of old ghosts. *You* interrupted *my* sleep, and then, when I ask you a little favour, you tell me the bahdy comes first.

'What are the other three fundamental factors, Wally?'

His voice muffled by the pillow, he said, 'Proper eating and proper exercise and proper bowel movement. Sleep tight, Nella.'

Shivering, she plastered herself against his broad back and the smooth taut peaks of his buttocks. She took warmth from him, but nothing else. He was already asleep.

Chapter 5

Grunts and the warm acid tang of sweat in the gym. She swung her stick with abandonment in the ludicrous ferocity of a girl's hockey match. But when she opened her eyes, the ceiling was low, not the arching vault of the gym. Yet the grunts and the smell of sweat persisted, as if some elements of her dream had escaped across the border of waking.

'*Unh* . . . and *unh* . . . and *unh* . . .'

Wally appeared suddenly at the foot of the bed, straightening up from a knee bend, his hands clenched around a pair of barbells that he lifted overhead, pressed in to his chest, extended outwards at arm's length.

'*Unh* . . . and *unh* and *unh* . . .'

He disappeared below her sightline again. When he rose next, he was looking directly at her but his eyes were unfocused. Lift and stretch and press and grunt, his face rosy, his muscles rippling. He seemed oblivious of her scrutiny. Which for him, she thought, must be equivalent to being in a deep trance. Exactly: he was at worship in the temple of his body.

The slats of the blinds had been tilted slightly, and sunlight streaked into the room. She smelled coffee, warm and promissory. Morning in the house of Apollo. Wally rose to his feet. He was wearing Jockey shorts, and his body seemed unreal: a rendering of masculine perfection by an unimaginative artist. I have slept with a god, she thought. Wally held the barbells out at arm's length, then bent at the waist and set them down on the floor with a thump, as though to certify their weight.

He gave her his one-cornered smile. 'First thing, must take care of the bahdy.'

He turned to the pulleys on the wall, and as he tugged and grunted, the attached weights slid up and down easily. She watched the meshed play of the muscular contractions in his back, in his nearly naked buttocks.

'*Unh* and *unh* and *unh-unh-unh* . . .'

He released the weighted pulleys and turned around to face her, flushed and sweating but breathing without effort. 'Half an hour before breakfast, every morning.'

Nella threw the blanket off and crawled towards the foot of the bed. 'Good morning. Would you like to tune up a little on the bed? With *me*?'

'You do exercise?'

'You could call it that.'

She reached forward, hooked her finger into the waistband of his Jockey shorts, and peered down. Physical exertion, apparently, did not enlarge his genitals; they lay moistly unassertive in the pouch of the shorts.

He doled out his crooked smile. 'Soon as I finish the routine, baby. You skip any of it, you lose some of the good.'

Finishing the routine involved an interlude on the rowing machine, something to do with a bootlike contraption made of metal and leather that went on his feet, dozens of push-ups, chinning from a bar set in the doorway, and an assortment of calisthenics. After a while she stopped watching him, got back under the cover, and dozed off. She woke once to the sound of rain. But the sun was still pouring into the room, and she realised that she was hearing the shower in the bathroom. She dozed again.

Later, she opened her eyes. Wally was standing beside the bed, wearing a wide-sleeved terrycloth robe.

'Ready now, baby.' He took off the robe.

When she turned back the cover to admit him to the bed, she saw that he was ready in all ways: showered, shaved, after-shave-lotioned, cologned, hair combed, and penis erect.

Wally gave her a flannel robe to wear after her shower. When she came out of the bathroom, she noticed that the door to the second bedroom was open. The room was about half the size of Wally's, sparsely furnished. Wally was in the narrow kitchen, stirring eggs in a bowl. An oval table in the foyer, which served as dining-room, was neatly set with place mats, plates, cups and saucers, juice glasses, and pale green paper napkins. A coffee urn and an electric toaster stood on the table.

'You set a nice table,' Nella said. 'Anything I can do to help?'

'Just look pretty, baby, until I get the eggs whipped up. I didn't set the table. Richard did it.'

'It was nice of him.'

'It's nothing special. We don't like to be sloppy. At night we put on a tablecloth and real cloth napkins. Richard always sets the table in the morning, and makes the coffee, because he gets up earlier than me.'

The fussy punctilio of homosexuals? 'What does Richard work at?'

'Drives a cab.' He stopped stirring the eggs and looked at her defensively. 'He likes the freedom of it, no boss hanging over you all the time, and he makes good money.'

Her eye was diverted by a magazine on the table. It was called *Physique*, and on its cover was a full-colour photograph of a muscular young man who might have been Wally's twin, wearing a loincloth and sitting astride a gaudily equipped motorcycle.

'Richard's a very expert driver, I mean he's really fantastic.' Wally saw her holding the magazine and pretended to be surprised. 'Where'd you find that? Oh, I guess Richard must have been reading it and left it laying there.'

She leafed through the magazine. It consisted of a succession of beefcake pictures, with interspersed text, stories dealing with one aspect or another of body building. Several titles caught her eye: CAN BICEPS BE TOO BIG? HOW MUCH BOOZE AGES THE BODY? MUSCLES AREN'T EVERYTHING. She looked up to see Wally watching her anxiously.

'Are you in here, Wally?'

He made a show of indifference. 'Might be. Take a look if you want to.'

She found a double-truck full-colour spread featuring Wally in a series of poses similar to those that were pinned up on his bedroom wall. The headline read EFFETE

EASTERNER? NOT ON YOUR LIFE! Captions beneath the photos spoke of Wallace Cornwall, a premier New York Adonis, and contained sanctimonious recommendations from Wally as to the importance, in building a beautiful body, of diet, clean living, rightmindedness, discipline, and an intelligent regimen of exercise.

'You like?'

'They're terrific, Wally.' And then, in a frivolous attempt to make him smile with both corners of his mouth, she said, 'They're great, but they don't really do you justice.'

The left corner of his mouth lifted. The right corner quirked, but didn't quite make it. ''Case you're interested, there's more magazines over there. I mean, if you want to kill time while I finish the eggs and toast.'

'Over there' was a rack beside a lounger chair. The rack was filled with magazines. She brought several of them back to the table. Wally watched her surreptitiously as she began to leaf through one called *His Body*. It was printed on cheaper stock than *Physique*, and its pictures, she judged, were oriented to the homosexual voyeur. Male jerk-off magazines. She found Wally in a feature entitled ASPHALT COWBOY. He was dressed in the skimpiest of bikini trunks and a huge cowboy hat, and brandished a long-barrelled revolver. The gun was deployed as a movable phallus, and the picture angles were calculated to emphasise the pubic bulge. The captions were coy and suggestive. In one, Wally was holding the revolver at his hip, and the photographer had taken a profile view, so that the gun seemed to be a menacing steel cock. The caption read: *Is he made of iron? Wouldn't you like to know!* Another caption read: *Suicide? No, our handsome Asphalt Cowboy is just a little hungry* – the muzzle of the gun an inch from his open mouth.

'You don't want to look at that one.' Wally was standing over her, holding a spatula, frowning. 'Strictly for the gay trade. Sometimes you have to demean yourself to make a buck. I hate it.'

He took the magazine from her and handed her another copy of *Physique*. A strip running across the cover said,

'You'll like this one better. It's got some class.' He pointed to the stripe on the cover. 'You don't want to confuse this with the Mr America contest – that's for the iron-pumpers, you know, they're over-developed and freaky. With those knotted-up muscles and the veins sticking up and the lumps, I think they're really ugly. Mr Perfection is different, it's the *beauty* of the male bahdy.'

'Did you win the contest, Wally?'

His mouth turned down. 'Runner-up. I should have won, or at least been number two. But the fags – they control everything, they take care of their own. Still, you'll see some fine bahdies in there. Fags or not, they have very fine bahdies.'

He went back into the kitchen. She leafed through the magazine with a sense of surfeit: it contained a glut of shapely chests, thighs, biceps, shoulders. The winner, Mr Perfection himself, had two entire pages devoted to him; the second- and third-place winners a page each; the half dozen runners-up half a page each. Wally, gorgeous in a white leotard, was doing his one-cornered smile. So far as she could see, there was no way to tell the winner from the others. But then, she couldn't distinguish one good poodle from the next, either.

She thumbed quickly through the other magazines. The issue dates were all a year or more old. She returned them to the rack when Wally came out of the kitchen with two plates of eggs and a stack of toast. She tasted the eggs. He looked at her anxiously.

'Delicious, Wally.'

'I like to cook. People used to think that if a man liked to cook he was effeminate, but actually men are the best cooks, though they're famous for using a lot of pots.'

He was a compendium of clichés, Nella thought, and a man who needed reassurance. 'Well,' she said, 'if anybody questions your masculinity, I'll be happy to give you a reference.'

The compliment brought out his one-sided smile and the other side of his character: self-esteem. 'You notice how often I can do it? Around the clock.'

'I noticed, Wally. It didn't escape me.'

'Sex is related to health.' He sounded earnest. 'The amount you can do it is a matter of hygiene – clean living and a healthy bahdy.'

Penis sanus in corpore sano. 'The body is a temple,' Nella said gravely.

'You like the temple?'

'I worship it.'

His smile appeared but faded quickly. 'Seriously, I feel I have something to give to the world. My bahdy gives pleasure and inspiration to multitudes, like an object of beauty. In all modesty.'

'Don't be modest, Wally, it's a pleasure palace.'

'So it isn't only me who suffers when I don't work. It lessens the pleasure of the multitudes.'

'You haven't been doing much magazine work lately?'

'That stuff is just junk.' His lip curled. 'Modelling swim suits and Jockey shorts and bahdy shirts and T-shirts, that's the class stuff.' He looked resentfully at the magazine rack. 'That's *junk*.'

But from the dates on the magazine, he wasn't doing much junk lately, either.

'It isn't so important who you are, but who you know.' He stared moodily at his eggs, then said bitterly, 'The gays got everything sewed up. The bitches, they control the whole field. You know why I don't get work like I used to?'

She shook her head accommodatingly.

'Because I refuse to put out. I guess that sounds funny coming from a man. But it's the truth. You know, my bahdy happens to be very attractive to men as well as women.'

To Richard, for example? You could be AC-DC, Wally.

'You know how much money I made this year so far? All told? Less than five thousand dollars.'

You know how much *I* made? Less than 'less than five thousand', and all of it in handouts from Julian.

'Because I won't put out. The gays, the work goes to their own kind. If I put out, I could get all the work I could handle. But I don't go for that stuff. I strictly like women.'

'But aren't there other things you could do?'

She had meant jobs in different fields but he misunderstood her.

'The big money I had offered to me, you wouldn't believe it. By men. Mostly elderly fags, but some young too. A lot of celebrities too. You'd be surprised. I wouldn't even have to do much. You know, just let them suck me off or something. But I don't go for it. It disgusts me. And the offers to make porno flicks? Thousands of dollars. Not only for the fag trade, but straight stuff, with women. But I'm not an exhibitionist. Sex is a private matter, between two people. Porno films disgust me.'

Forget what I implied about Richard, Wally, you're straight from the word go. But – 'Have women ever offered you money?'

'It's been known to happen.' He was trying to be offhand, but a species of pride crept into his voice. 'But not the other way around, I never paid any woman for sex. Why should I, when I got as much to offer as they have – maybe more.'

Deflate him before he bursts. 'If you're making so little money, how are you getting by? Richard?'

'Yeah, Richard.' He flushed, then said defiantly, 'And when Richard isn't holding, it's me who does the supporting. It's a two-way street. We're cousins and best friends, and we share and share alike. Besides, you're getting personal.'

Sorry, Wally, I'll try to keep our relationship confined to impersonal things like fucking. 'Can I have some more coffee?'

He glared across the table at her. 'I resent you think I live off Richard. Plenty of times the shoe was on the other foot. For two whole years when he was in the slam – '

He broke off abruptly and clamped his lips shut. His eyes were clouded with regret. She watched him busy himself buttering a piece of toast. Sorry, Wally, you just made it personal; sharing a secret, even unintentionally, and especially a guilty secret, is a form of intimacy.

'I guess I made a boo-boo, right?' His attitude had shifted back to defiance. 'It's probably the first time in your life you ever met anybody who was in prison.'

'Some of my best friends have been in prison.'

He paused in surprise, then said scoffingly, 'Students or radicals, right? They lay down at an atomic plant or like that, and the cops pick them up and they spend a couple of hours in jail, waving their fists and singing songs, and then they get turned loose. A slap on the wrist.'

Right on target, Wally. She had done a half day, several years back, in precisely those circumstances, including the folksy-revolutionary singing. Still, she might surprise him yet.

'The high-class type of person doesn't go to prison, *real* prison. When they pull something serious, they hire fancy lawyers and buy their way out. There's two kinds of justice – one for the rich and one for the poor.'

'I've known two people who were in *real* prison,' Nella said, 'and both of them are what you call high-class. One of them is still serving time.'

He looked at her sceptically. 'What did they go to prison for?'

'One for pushing pot, the other for attempted murder.'

'Attempted murder? You're putting me on.'

'That was the charge. Attempted murder. But her father hired some expensive lawyers . . .' She paused for his look of triumph. 'And the charge was reduced to . . . oh, I don't know to what, but she got a year in jail and served about seven months.'

'It was a she? How did she attempt a murder?'

'She tried to run her boyfriend down in a car. She had been shooting acid.'

'Did she kill him? Who *was* this girl?'

'She hurt him quite a bit, and maybe would have killed him, but she ran into a line of parked cars and passed out. Who was she? For six months she was my room-mate at college.'

'Well, well,' Wally said, 'so maybe you're not so innocent as I thought you were.'

76

'Have I been coming on as innocent? If so, I've got some things to learn.'

'I don't mean in bed.' He smirked. 'You don't have to tell me how good high-class girls are in bed. What I meant, I didn't think you knew about the seamy side of life.'

'What did Richard go to jail for?'

'None of your business.'

'Was it for stealing?'

Wally glared at her over the rim of the cup. 'Richard don't steal.' Then his air of protectiveness turned prideful, almost boastful. 'You want to know what Richard did? He was in a fight with this guy and he damn near killed him.'

'What was the fight about?'

His face closed up. 'Never mind. You're too nosey.'

Her curiosity was piqued. 'Wally?' She looked at him innocently, winsomely, although she knew that it wasn't her style. 'Wally? Won't you please tell me?'

'Stop trying to pump me. The subject is closed.' He pushed back his chair. 'I got to go to the bathroom.' He got up, scowling, and went by her. He slammed the bathroom door behind him.

The wonderful thing about non-stop sex, like fiercely competitive tennis, was that it anaesthetised thought. Enquiring into the world of Wally and Richard pursued the same goal – keeping reality at bay. Now, with Wally gone, the suppressed ache of memory reasserted itself. Julian falling backwards, terror on his face, a fragile old man with stick-like arms and legs, the tinkling of broken glass, the vivid red of blood . . .

She stood up abruptly and began to clear the table. She piled up the dishes and stacked them in the sink, rushed back to the foyer, and brushed crumbs off the place mats. She cleaned the toaster, she put things in the refrigerator, found a place for the bread in a drawer. She washed the dishes with almost comic intensity, rubbing viciously at egg stains, tilting each plate to the light for critical examination before placing it in the dish drainer. She was scrubbing furiously at the frying pan when she became aware of Wally watching her from the doorway of the kitchen. A corner of his lip was turned upwards in a smile.

Wally, you're smiling. Good humour restored. Did you have a satisfactory bowel movement, Wally? Oh, Wally, I'm so happy to see you, you banish guilt, memory, thought.

'You oughtn't to be doing that,' he said. 'After all, you're my guest.'

Guest. A felicitous word to describe a pick-up, a one-night stand. Thank you, Wally, you're a diplomat. 'I don't mind,' she said, and bore down conscientiously on the frying pan with a piece of steel wool.

An instant before he put his arms around her waist from behind, she was apprised of his approach by a whiff of cologne. Had he given himself a fresh dose? She felt his hardness against her, and continued to scrub the pan. She had never been able to understand – except vaguely to mistrust it – why nothing seemed to incite the lust of men so irresistibly as the sight of a woman washing dishes, sewing, dusting.

'I can think of better things for a pretty girl to be doing than washing dishes.'

He flipped open the tie of her robe and began to move his hands over her body, tracing the shape of her breasts, curving down over her stomach, slipping between her thighs. She arched backwards against him.

'I mean, you like a little loving?'

Bet your sweet ass I do, Wally. She dropped the frying pan into the sink with a clatter and faced around to him.

Drowsy, relaxed, Nella said, 'I'd like to stay forever.'

'Why?'

He was braced against the headboard of the bed, combing his hair in place with doting fingers.

'Just to see if I can wear you out.'

'Never. Impossible.' His smile turned to a pout. 'I thought maybe because you liked me a little.'

'I hasten to assure you . . .' She turned her head to the side and lightly kissed the hollow below his breastbone. 'I

78

like you very much.' But why do you need reassurance once an hour, Wally?

His smile reappeared, tugging up a corner of his mouth. 'You don't see me chasing you, do you?'

She glanced at the clock on the bedside table. One thirty. 'But I really ought to be thinking of going.'

'What's the rush? You got something better to do?'

Nothing even remotely as good. She wouldn't return to Julian's apartment, not even to pick up her clothes. Last night's episode had finished everything, forever. Although Julian might forgive her for her violence, she could never forgive him for provoking it. That strangulating umbilical, woven of ancient hatreds, and the distant memory of love, was finally broken. At last, at last, true independence of Julian, not merely its false face. Yes, Nella, a familiar vow, but this time you mean it.

And where do you find shelter, Nella, until you can get your act together? Except for the few dollars in the pocket of the shearling, she had no money, no job, no place to stay. Well, she could probably phone somebody in the Old Girl network who would put her up for a few nights, although that source of refuge was no longer as dependable as it had once been. Some of her old college friends had married, others had moved out of state, and still others she was no longer on good terms with for one forgotten reason or another. Of course there was Laurence, he would take her in, but he didn't deserve to be used by her.

She couldn't stay here, either, but sufficient unto the day was the postponement thereof. 'I don't want to be in the way, Wally. You must have things to do. Don't you have to go to work or something?'

'I'm free today. No assignment. Oh, later on I might call up my agent and find out what's doing. You don't think photographers' models work every day, do you? If we did we would be rich. You know how much we get paid for a day's modelling? Hundred dollars an hour. You can figure it out for yourself.'

'It's astronomical. I can't cope with numbers like that.'

He looked at her suspiciously. 'Don't kid me. It might

be a lot of money to me, but where you come from it's bottoms.'

She licked the bulge of his biceps. 'Where do I come from?'

'Park Avenue.' His respectful attenuated drawl made magic of it. 'Even if you hadn't of told me I would've guessed. I know class when I see it, baby.'

'By class you mean money?'

'I mean class and I mean money, both.'

'About class, it's an arguable point. Money – I haven't got any.'

'Not too many people who live on Park Avenue are on welfare.'

His smile was knowing, confidential: they shared a sly secret between them. Except that we don't, Wally. Except that I *am* on welfare. I am Julian's personal welfare client. No, not *am*, no longer *am*, but was.

She said, 'It isn't my place, it's Julian's.'

He shrugged. 'But you *live* there.'

It was her permanent address, or the nearest thing she had to one. It was where she lived between relationships, after a marriage failed, in the intervals when one source of employment or another ended, when she was flat broke, when her psychological resources were exhausted. It was the lair she crawled back to to lick her wounds. Between herself and Julian, it was a fact of life neither of them ever questioned. Whatever else their relationship might be, he never refused her sanctuary and she never rejected it. It stood above her hatred for him, and outside his tyranny.

'Yes and no. I have a room there that I used to live in from time to time. Oh, Wally, it's too damn complicated.'

'How many rooms has the apartment got?'

No, it wasn't a wild irrelevancy, he was trying to pin down Julian's worth. She shrugged. 'Twelve, fourteen, I don't know, I never really counted them.'

He whistled softly. 'He must pay quite a rent in a place like that. On Park Avenue, and all.'

'He owns it. It's a co-operative.'

His eyes widened in appreciation. 'The old crock must have plenty of scratch. What's his racket?'

'He was an architect. He's retired now.'

'An architect? That's all?'

'He's a *famous* architect.' I don't want to disappoint your expectations, Wally, I really don't. 'He did the Cosgrove Building and a couple of airline terminals . . . Oh, he did a lot of things.'

'The Cosgrove Building? He built *that*?'

Muscular, sweaty Italian, Irish, and Polish labourers had built it, but that was a mere nicety. More to the point was that it had not even been designed by Julian but by three or four of the brilliant young men in his office who had since gone on to better things. The truth of the matter was that Julian was a run-of-the-mill architect who had prospered through good social connections, better luck, and a superlative staff. If he had any outstanding ability at all, it was in his shrewdness in selecting talented young architects from good schools and milking them before, as inevitably happened, they became tired of being exploited and either joined other firms or set up in business for themselves. In architectural circles his firm was known as Turnover Towers. Yet, despite all the in-jokes, he enjoyed a reputation as a great trainer of young architects, and this reputation, in turn, had attracted new generations of bright young men to his office.

She said, 'I guess you could say Julian was a master builder.'

'I never thought about architects being rich before, but I guess they do okay.' His look became deprecating. 'But not like bankers and brokers, say.'

Bankers and brokers – and corporation presidents and chairmen of the board with inside information – had often been grateful enough to Julian for his (or his young men's) designs, and he had profited therefrom, as well as from his business.

'Julian is loaded, Wally, if that's what you're getting at.'

'How much? I mean, I'm just curious. A million, two million?'

'Or three, or four.'

'You don't *know*?'

He'll start thinking you're a mental case, Nella. 'Four million,' she said firmly.

'That's a lot of money. That's one hell of a lot of scratch, Nella.'

'I guess so.'

'You guess so.' He shook his head in mock helplessness, and kissed her smackingly on the mouth. 'God, you're a kook. You *guess*.' He kissed her again.

Money begets kisses. Take a hint, Nella. 'Actually, closer to five, when you take everything into consideration.'

He lowered his head to the pillow and looked upwards at the ceiling, contented. Then he turned to her with a knowing smile. 'You're an heiress, Nella, right?'

Heiress, with its tabloid press connotation of slightly peculiar rich young women marrying obscure European nobility, divorcing, conceiving wild infatuations for their chauffeurs, endlessly litigating or litigated against; owners of yachts and country estates protected by snarling dogs, occasional committers of murder or suicide . . . Wally, your sensibility was formed by low reading habits.

'I'm not an heiress. The Creepy Housekeeper is an heiress.'

'The *who*?'

'Julian's wife. He married a woman named Agnes Morgan a few years ago.'

'A few years ago? How old is he, anyway?'

'Around eighty. And Agnes is forty. She was his private nurse when he had an operation a few years ago. They married, and that's it. She's the heiress.'

'She gets all of this Julian's money, the whole five million? You don't get anything?'

'No.'

'Not a penny?'

'When he married Agnes he changed his will and left her everything.'

'Mean old bastard!'

Give the devil his due, Nella. 'Well, he told me he would settle some money on me as an outright gift.'

'How much?'

'But he insisted on knowing what I would do with it. I told him I would give it away.'

'Give it *away*? To *who*, for Godssake?'

She shrugged. 'It didn't matter. I said the first thing that popped into my head – I told him I would donate it to the anti-nuclear plant protesters.'

'You wanted to give it to *those* freaks?' He shook his head in wonderment. 'You didn't want to just keep it?'

'No.' I don't do deals with the devil, Wally. 'Julian withdrew the offer. In high dudgeon, I might add.'

'I don't understand you, Nella. If anybody ever offered *me* all that money . . . Still and all, to cut you out of his will – that's disgusting. It's unnatural. His own flesh and blood. Doesn't it burn your ass to be screwed out of all that money?'

Much more important things than money burn my ass. 'I guess so.'

'You *guess* so. It's unfair as hell. It's criminal.' His biceps were twitching with indignation. She pressed her cheek against the surging muscle. 'He knows you all your life, and then this Agnes just comes along a few years ago. I can tell you it would burn *my* ass.'

She slid her hand under the blanket and caressed him. 'Too beautiful an ass to burn.'

'No, I'm very serious, Nella.' His brow was deeply furrowed. 'I swear, I don't understand how you can take it so calmly. If it was me, I'd want to get back at him if it took me forever. I mean, all the things he did to you, like your father, and the money going to this Agnes . . . Don't you ever want to get back at him?'

She had been trying to get back at Julian for years; that is, when she wasn't striving to earn his esteem or to avert his displeasure. She recognised that she and her father were opposite sides of the same coin. Philip had allowed himself to become indentured to Julian, and eventually won his freedom (and exacted vengeance) by running his crazy little sports car off the road and killing himself. Her own way was to resist, to defy Julian's wishes for her. By choosing to lead what he characterised as a 'bohemian existence', and refusing to 'become respectable and settle down', by which he meant marrying conventionally, profitably, and 'in her own class' (a poor college professor like Laurence had fallen well outside this rubric). But maybe, barring being alive, she hadn't had much more success than Philip.

Wally was waiting for an answer to his question. 'I smashed up his favourite picture last night.' Laugh, clown, laugh.

His brow furrowed in disbelief, but before he could speak, she turned to him full force, pressing, grinding her pelvis against him, caressing the taut peaks of his buttocks. He remained passive, unresponsive.

'Wally?'

'Don't you ever want to do anything but sex?'

Oh my God, I'm going to go hysterical – he's protesting being treated as a sex object. She raised her head and kissed him. His lips were unresponsive.

'I'm sorry, Wally. It's just that you turn me on. But I enjoy talking too.'

'Look, I'm going to tell you something, Nella.' He spoke hesitantly, almost shyly. 'We just met last night, we really hardly know each other, but I like you. I mean not just for sex, but as a person.'

Sex, yes, but what have I done to make you like me as a person?

'I'm not just saying it. I wouldn't *have* to say it if it wasn't true. I mean, you aren't going to hold out on me if I *don't* say it, so that proves it's sincere.'

The equation seemed perfectly simple and convincing to him, and he probably meant it, though God knew why. He doubtless ran the rest of his life on similarly soluble formulae. He would find it impossible to disbelieve anything he told himself.

'Do you like *me* as a person?'

Being loved for his bahdy wasn't enough for him; it was too easy, no chick could resist it. It was his psyche that needed nurturing. Gently, fangs sheathed, careful not to hurt the bahdy, she sucked on the taut skin of his arm.

'Do you, Nella? I'm very serious.'

In the deep recesses of his soul, Apollo drove no flaming chariots, but trudged among his fears and anxieties like an ordinary mortal. 'I do, Wally, I really do.' I do, Wally, so help me, I really do.

His smile appeared at the left corner of his mouth, and gradually, as if by some benign contagion, spread to the other corner. He shifted on the bed and gathered her into his arms. Quivering, panting, her voice purring non-verbal endearments, she pushed the full length of her body against him. My God, Apollo, oh Apollo, my god! She kicked the blanket free, tugging at his shoulders, and he flipped over and straddled her. She opened her legs and guided him towards her.

From the bed, Wally watched her as she entered from the bathroom. 'You have a beautiful stature, Nella.'

Thanks, Wally, I appreciate the kind words. Though to tell the truth it's about time some of the gush and flattery started flowing the other way.

'You carry yourself like a dancer. Ever do any dancing?'

Oh dear Jesus, not that! She sat down on the edge of the bed with her back to him. Don't pursue it, Wally, don't open up the most painful wound of all my many wounds. She bent and clasped each ankle – Degas, are you watching? – and remained that way for a moment, listening to the thump of her heartbeat. Then she straightened up and got back into bed. Wally swivelled his eyes towards her with curiosity.

'Don't hold out on me,' he said. 'You're a dancer, right?'

'Was. But I quit.'

'What made you quit?'

'I was too fat.' There. Simple declarative truth. Now let it lie there, Wally. Please. *Please*.

'You're kidding. Too fat? With that great slender build?'

Yes, that was the culminating irony. A year or so afterwards, when it was too late, when Julian's triumph had been sealed and she had been thrown out of the school, the fat melted away. Irony, my ass. Tragedy!

'Hey, give us a smile, baby.'

She reached to the bedside table for a cigarette. Wally didn't smoke: 'Bad for the bahdy. Bad for the lungs too.' She balanced an ashtray carefully on her stomach, then pillowed her head on his right arm and gave him a smile. He didn't seem to notice that it was forced, mechanical.

'That's much better.'

He flexed his biceps, lifting her head on the smooth swell, and then letting it subside. She took it to be a gesture of post-coital tenderness, and reciprocated by pressing her cheek against the bulge of his muscle.

'Wally, you're terrific.'

His biceps flexed, acknowledging the compliment, taking a bow.

'The exercise is very healthy too.'

'What do you mean? Intercourse?' He frowned.

'If that's what you like to call it, yes.'

'Intercourse isn't exercise . . .' He realised he was being teased. 'Intercourse is pleasure, baby, pure pleasure.'

'Isn't exercise a pleasure?'

'Well sure, but it's a different kind of pleasure.' He paused, and his brow knit in earnestness. 'There are many kinds of pleasure in the world. The pleasure of intercourse, of eating great food, of sitting in the sun, of putting on nice clothes, of the sight of a tree or a cow . . . Many different kinds of things give many different kinds of pleasure.'

That's sweet, Wally, that's really terribly sweet. She kissed his arm, lapped the velvety warmth of his skin with her tongue. And the simple pleasure, Wally, you might have added, of pleasing one's self with a pleasing body.

'Was dancing your ambition?'

It was the only genuine ambition I ever had, to go along with my only authentic talent, and after Julian murdered it, drove it to suicide, I never really had another.

'Not really, Wally. It was just a childish yearning.'

'You know what *my* ambition is?'

It was said with such studied off-handedness that she

86

knew he was about to unburden himself. 'To win the Mr Perfection contest?'

'That's just my short-term ambition. Long term, it's to own a physical culture school.'

'A health club?'

'*Not* a health club,' he said emphatically. 'A health club is just for people who want to exercise. My idea is a true, *scientific* physical culture school, dedicated to building beautiful bahdies.'

'Bodies like yours?'

'Right. To build bahdies like mine, for people who are really serious about their bahdies. It's my crusade, Nella, to dedicate myself to making beautiful bahdies.'

It's the noblest crusade since Richard the Lionhearted's, Wally.

'Can't you imagine a lot of people walking around the streets with bahdies like mine? Wouldn't that be something?'

It would be too much; a girl's virtue would be on the line twenty-four hours a day.

'That's the main, idealistic purpose of the school. But I don't want you to think it's not practical. The school, the way I would run it, it would be a real gold mine. Can you deny that thousands of people would give anything to have a physical development like mine? In all modesty?'

'I can't deny it. It's really a noble idea, Wally.'

'But there's a problem.' His mouth turned down. 'Scratch. You know what it would cost to set up a school like I have in mind, a real high-class establishment? A hundred thousand, at least.'

She pressed her cheek against his arm. His biceps jerked angrily.

'Where am I going to get a hundred thousand? Who's going to hand me a hundred big ones?'

If I had any money of my own I would give it to you, Wally, without interest, provided that I had *ius prima noctis* with the graduates.

'If I could find somebody, just one person, who was willing to put up the money, to take a chance on an investment . . .'

He was looking at her wistfully. Ah no, Wally, not me. Forget it. I bought it with Roland and Eau Boy, and that was only a lousy ten thousand dollars of Julian's money. And anyway, I'm finished with Julian. Forever. And even if I wasn't, he would laugh his head off.

Wally read the repudiation in her eyes. He turned away and stared woodenly upwards at the ceiling. But he must know, surely he must know that nobody in the world ever gave the Wallys of the world a hundred thousand dollars?

'I'm sorry, Wally.'

'You don't have the faith that I could make it work.'

She placed her hand on his chest, as if by touch to vouch for her sincerity. 'Oh, I do. I honestly do, Wally.'

'Wouldn't you like to help me?'

'I'd like nothing better, but I haven't got any money. You've got to believe me, Wally, I'm penniless.'

'Maybe so, but this rich uncle . . .'

His eyes were turned towards her now, showing an abundance of clear white sclera. She shook her head. 'It's out of the question. He wouldn't give me a cent.'

'How do you know if you don't ask him?'

'I couldn't ask him. I *wouldn't* ask him.'

'If you wanted to help me, like you said, you would at least try. You can never tell what might happen.'

'I'm never going to see him again, or speak to him again, much less ask him for money. Do me a favour, Wally, drop it.'

His eyes turned back to the ceiling.

'Wally?'

He shrugged. 'You said you liked me and would like to have a relationship, but the first time I ask you to do something for me . . .' He shrugged again. 'What a relationship means is *doing* things for one another. I mean, all I want you to do is *ask* – '

'No!' The syllable escaped from her in a bark, abrupt and final. 'Don't come on with that bullshit!'

His broad handsome face closed down at once; animation blinked out of it as if a light switch had been pressed. And she was immediately regretful, moved by his vulnerability. She had touched some secret quick, and hurt him.

'I'm sorry, Wally. I'm sorry, darling.'

She put her hand on his cheek and tried to draw his face around to her. He stiffened his neck muscles; his head was immovable.

'Please look at me, Wally.' His face was set in irreconcilable rigidity. 'Won't you look at me, Wally?'

She tried again to turn his head, but he jerked away from her hand.

'Wally?'

He spoke upwards to the ceiling. 'I'm sorry. I just can't stand anybody who won't try to help. So you can just get your ass up out of this bed and get lost.'

The icy cruelty of his tone, as much as what he said, brought sudden tears to her eyes. Tears, Nella? For what? Haven't you been rejected before, and by some of the worst bastards in the Western Hemisphere, at that? She looked down at Wally. His face was set in a fixed, impregnable obstinacy.

'Wally? Please don't look like that.'

He lifted his hand and made a contemptuous, dismissive gesture. All right, Wally, that does it. Hail and farewell, and no more tears.

She got out of bed and began to put her clothes on.

'What do you think you're doing?' Wally was sitting up in bed, staring at her. She stood on one leg to pull on a shoe. 'What's the idea of getting dressed?'

She put on the second shoe and looked around for the shearling coat.

'Don't be a fool, Godssake. Come over here, Godssake.'

She remembered that Wally had hung the shearling in the closet in the entry hall. He was leaning forward, his expression wavering between bafflement and exasperation. She went out of the bedroom and through the living-room to the entry hall. She rifled through the garments in the closet until she found the coat.

'Don't you know a little joke when you hear one?' He was padding across the living-room, naked and graceful.

'What do you want to be so over-sensitive for?'

When she put her arm into a sleeve of the coat he captured the end and pinched it shut, imprisoning her hand. He circled her waist and drew her against him.

'So let's not make a big federal deal. Come on back, okay?'

He couldn't abase himself by making an apology in so many words, but he had chased after her, and his eyes were pleading. However inhibited, it was an *amende honorable*, and possibly, she thought, the first he had ever made in a lifetime of lording it over women. He must like me, he must truly like me . . .

She drew her arm back out of the sleeve. She turned into his nakedness and clung to him.

She was not prepared for his display of relief and pleasure. Laughing, he lifted her off her feet, and carried her into the living-room. He shifted his hands to her hips and raised her overhead, parallel to the ceiling. He walked towards the bedroom with her, his arms firm and straight under her weight, and for the first time she realised that his extraordinary physical development was not merely decorative, but awesomely strong. At the bedroom door he lowered her slowly, and her feet touched the floor without a jolt.

He watched from the bed as she undressed, smiling his one-sided smile, no longer patient but pleased. She tossed her clothes on to the chair and crawled into bed beside him.

'Tell the truth. Are you glad you didn't go?'

'Yes, Wally. That's the truth.'

He kissed her, and she threw her leg over his hip.

His smile narrowed down to slyness. 'I knew all along you would come back.'

'Because you knew I knew you wanted me to stay?'

'Hey, come on. You stayed because I didn't want you to go.'

There was a touch of annoyance in his tone. Wally, please don't start going macho again. Let's not lose paradise just when we've regained it. She said lightly, 'Well, isn't that what I just said?'

'It certainly isn't.'

So much for his penitence. 'Look, Wally, if I hadn't wanted to stay, there was no way you could have kept me here.'

'No?' His smile was insinuating.

'No. Not short of using brute force.'

'Well?' He stopped smiling. 'You think I couldn't have done it?'

Remembering how effortlessly he had lifted her over his head, she glanced at his stubbornly scowling face, and a caution ticked off in her mind: back off, Nella, it's time for an orderly retreat.

In a bantering tone she said, 'And then what – forced me to submit to your advances? You know there's no need for *that*.'

'Then what? Hold you for ransom, and make that stingy uncle cough up some bread to get you back.'

She began to tremble. She would not be able to say, later, what the temper of his voice was, or what expression his face wore. But she felt, immediately and profoundly, a sense of revelation, as if the edge of some curtain had been unexpectedly lifted, allowing her an unwanted glimpse into a terrifying future.

Chapter 6

Wally lay flat on his back, his arms folded across his chest, his eyes rolled back in his head. It's the position called 'laid out', Nella thought, I've finally managed to kill him. His skin was leached of colour, even his lips looked white. His pallor redeemed his face from its slight taint of commonness; he looked like a beautiful dead classical poet, the kind whose poems rhymed and scanned, who died of tuberculosis at a tragically early age.

She pressed her lips gently to the corpse's brow and a corner of his mouth twitched wanly upwards in his inimitable smile. She said, 'Wally, darling, there's nobody like you in the whole Western Hemisphere.'

A delicate spot of colour appeared in his cheek. Nothing like a compliment to raise the dead. His lids closed down over his eyes and, still smiling faintly, he turned slowly on his side and, in a seamless, effortless transition, fell asleep. His breathing was muted, even. He slept the sleep of the gorgeous. She lay on her side, facing but not touching him, content to let his sleep run its course. After a while she got up and went out of the room. The door to Richard's room was open. He hadn't been home for dinner, and was still out.

She went into the bathroom and lit a cigarette. She braced her hip against the sink and blew smoke at her image in the mirror. Her face was relaxed, almost serene. You're calm as a clam, Nella, that's what comes of acquiring a purpose in life. You've been a new woman for all of thirty minutes now. She dumped her cigarette into the toilet and washed her face. A suggestion of purple smudge under the eyes – the stigmata of passion, as honourable as Heidelberg duelling scars.

She went back to Wally's room. She shut the door noiselessly and eased back into bed softly. No cheap shots – let him wake up in his own good time. She lay on her back with her head pillowed on her arms and waited.

When he awakened it was as smoothly as when he had gone to sleep. No wrench, no struggle. He simply rolled over on his back with his eyes open, clear and alert, a half smile tugging up a corner of his mouth.

'Hi, baby.'

She said, 'Wally, do you know how old I was when I saw my first ballet performance? I was eleven.'

His brows drew together in a puzzled frown.

Came at you out of left field, I know, but you'll get the drift after a while. She said, 'It was a watershed.'

'A what?'

'My mother was supposed to go, but her horoscope reading declared it unpropitious, so my father took me.'

'What do you mean it was a watershed?' He was scowling, whether because she had pulled an unfamiliar word on him or because of the abrupt surfacing of her thoughts, she couldn't tell. 'I mean I know what a watershed is, but how come going to the ballet was a watershed?'

'I know you know what the word means.' It was in everyday usage at Yale, wasn't it, Wally? 'Five minutes into the performance I had a revelation – I was going to be a dancer. A revelation – different from the way a kid decides he's going to be a fireman or an airline pilot, off the top of his head. I mean that the concept of dancing possessed me, I could feel it take over my body, change my metabolism, turn me into something graceful and floating. It may sound ridiculous, but it's what happened. I was transformed, at the age of eleven. Sitting in my seat I had become a dancer.'

'Yeah,' Wally said, 'that's a watershed all right.'

'The experience was mystical, transcendent, but in the event it turned out that I was talented. Do you know how some kids are natural actors or natural athletes? Well, I was a natural dancer. That's an absolute fact. Do you accept that, Wally?'

He nodded eagerly. 'Sure. Like with me, when I was still in my teens I knew I had a great bahdy. I knew it still had to be developed – '

'Exactly,' Nella said. We'll get around to your story later, Wally. 'I got right after my father. I pestered him, besieged him, overwhelmed him, and he entered me in a neighbourhood dancing class. Not that he was really interested, or normally paid very much attention to me, but he had no defences against the kind of pressure I put on him. Julian – I have to tell you about this, because Julian is the key figure – Julian knew about the dancing class, but he didn't know it was ballet; he thought of it, I suppose, as something out of his own childhood, little ladies and gentlemen wearing white gloves, learning the social graces. I became the star of the class. Dancing was my element, Wally. All the others were kids taking dancing lessons. I was a *dancer*.'

'A natural,' Wally said. 'Just like me. It's God-given.'

'Thank you for understanding, Wally.' She kissed him lightly on the lips. 'The lady who taught the class, bless her, called on my father. She told him how good I was, and convinced him that I belonged in the American Ballet Theatre school. But that was a big decision, so my father naturally took it up with Julian. By then, of course, Julian couldn't help knowing something was in the wind. I didn't talk anything but ballet, I had rigged up a *barre* in my room and spent hours limbering up, I played nothing but ballet music on my record player, I went to see practically every ballet performance in the city. I was fanatically absorbed by dancing, it had become my entire life.

'Julian took the matter under advisement. He mulled it over for about four seconds and said no, that I couldn't go to the American Ballet school. Being a dancer wasn't up to the standards of his distinguished family. What Julian said was law, scripture. My father faded out of the picture. But I wasn't to be put off. I went at Julian like a fury. I hammered at him, I pleaded, pestered, chivvied, threatened suicide, didn't give him a minute's rest. I was desperate, I was a pain in the ass, and finally I wore him down and he agreed to let me try it. Joy, joy, ecstasy, but just for a little while. Keep your eye on Uncle Julian, Wally, keep your eye on that poisonous bastard.'

'Easy, baby,' Wally said. 'You don't want to get yourself all worked up.'

'I enrolled in the school, I was in heaven. True, I was no longer a star, because all the other kids were talented, too, but that didn't matter. I was dancing, I was being taught by the best, I was learning.'

'A good school, right?' Wally nodded wisely. 'That's what my physical culture school – '

'Right. It's an incubator for professional dancers. The most gifted of the kids, or those who don't drop out for one reason or another, end up in the corps de ballet, or even as principal dancers with the great American ballet companies. The regimen is demanding, almost cruel. It's a form of slavery, I suppose, but you don't question it because you're doing the only thing in the world you want to do. That first year was the most wonderful year of my life – before or since. I was almost as good as I thought I was, and I had better than an even chance to go all the way. And then I began to put on fat.'

Even now, in the worst of her dreams, she could visualise with absolute clarity the drawn features of that astringent, graceful old woman who had been a celebrated ballerina, chewing her out in her comical Russian-accented English, warning her that if she didn't lose weight she would be dropped. It was threat and advisory in one. While she stood there blubbering, Madame told her that she was fortunate, that she still had a chance at redemption, unlike this child who had been kicked out because she had grown too tall, that one because she lacked dedication, another because her face was ugly beyond the limit of what was permissible in a dancer.

'When I told Julian about it, his first impulse was to barge in and tell them off for daring to find his most prized possession less than perfect. I got hysterical. They wouldn't have stood for it. I finally persuaded him not to do it. But then he went into his old act, telling me how he disapproved of anyone from his family being a common dancer – a common dancer, Wally!'

'How did you get fat?'

'I was a child, barely into my teens. I worked hard all

day, and I ate like a horse. I suppose it was partially the exercise, partially the need a growing child has for food, partially – oh, hell, I don't know, pressures of one kind or another, biological change . . . Whatever, I simply began to put on weight.'

'The right food in the right amount is one of the most important factors there is to a healthy bahdy,' Wally said. 'I'm very particular what I eat.'

'The ballerina had put the fear of God into me – I couldn't stand the thought of not being a dancer. So I began to deny myself. I skipped meals, cut out starches and sweets, barely touched my food at dinner time. And I was starved. I mean that literally, Wally, I was *starved*, I craved food, I suffered physical pain, withdrawal symptoms, it was pure torture. Julian took note of all that, and he kept at me to eat, badgered me, threatened me, painted pictures of the horrible things that would happen to me if I didn't start eating.

'He couldn't move me. I resisted him. I was in agony, but the only thing that mattered was shedding weight so that I could go on dancing. I'll never know whether or not I could have made it, Wally, to be perfectly honest, even without Julian going at me, but at least I would have had a good chance.'

'What about your parents?'

'My mother was off in a world of her own, she wasn't interested. My father – ' She shrugged. 'It was Julian who orchestrated the life of our family. Come to think of it, Wally, I was probably doing fairly well, or Julian wouldn't have had to . . . Can you guess what he did next?'

Wally shook his head and muffled a yawn. Don't be bored, Wally, there's a real juicy part coming up.

'All of a sudden, temptations began to appear at the table. Normally, we ate fruit for dessert, but now Julian brought in pastries, gorgeous pastries, with whipped cream, heavy chocolate icing, rich butter crusts. I managed to pass them up at dinner, gritting my teeth, with tears rolling down my cheeks. But hunger pangs would wake me out of sleep at two or three in the morning, and all I could think of were these pastries stacked away in the refrigerator, and I almost went out of my head. But I resisted, until one night I came downstairs and ate a huge éclair, and the next night . . . Julian took to bringing boxes of candy home, too, and our dinner changed. There were suddenly a lot of frankfurters, hamburgers, french-fried potatoes – irresistible food . . . I wasn't a superwoman, Wally, I was a kid, with normal appetites, with physiological needs . . .'

'What a miserable character he is,' Wally said. 'I never heard of anything so rotten in my life.'

'I wasn't a superwoman. I began to eat everything in sight. I got kicked out of the school.'

Not a kind word from the former ballerina, just a tight-lipped homily to the effect that the essence of ballet was discipline, and that if one could not master one's gross appetites . . . 'But perhaps you will find another life's work which is not so demanding.'

'It's awful,' Wally said. 'No wonder you hate him. Torture is too good for that man.'

Not too good, Wally, just condign. 'It destroyed me. It took me a year to get back to something like normal life. I had a nervous breakdown, a real certified breakdown. At the age of twelve going on thirteen. And was introduced to the first of a long line of shrinks.'

Wally turned and took her in his arms. 'You poor kid.'

She felt his penis harden against her. As with housework, distress was a powerful aphrodisiac. She lay passively in Wally's arms while he pressed against her and nuzzled her neck. Sorry, Wally. After a while, sensing her lack of response, his caresses became undemanding, consolatory. Thanks, Wally, I truly appreciate your delicacy, and I promise I'll make it up to you later.

'It must have been a real ball-breaker,' Wally said.

Well said – a ball-breaker. There's lots more, too, but you wouldn't find it as immediately conclusive as the dancing episode. Anyway, it might be hard for you to relate to. Sure, your old man clouted you every once in a while, but you were free to duck, maybe even hit back. You just wouldn't be able to grasp the all-encompassing despotism of the Tsar Julian.

His reign had begun with her father as his vassal, with Poor Philip. Julian, who was almost twenty years older, ran Poor Philip's life the way he ran a motor car: Philip was a mechanism, Julian was the authority behind the wheel. Her father had wanted to be an artist. (After his death, when they cleared the closets and attic of his presence, she had seen his pictures. They were well composed, unassertive, perhaps too prettily coloured, but quite appealing.) He was not an overwhelming talent but he was gifted, and if he had been allowed to follow his bent and go to Paris to study as he wished to, he might very well have made a career for himself.

But Julian put his foot down – whether because, like dancing, art was common or because it was his whim, she didn't know. Julian decided instead that Philip would become an architect. He also decided that Philip would live under the same roof. He picked out Philip's bride, named Philip's child . . . Okay, her father was weak, he lacked character, but that didn't excuse Julian's tyranny. And in the end Philip had escaped in the only way open to him – by dying.

After her father's death her mother had disappeared into California and had become an astrologer. A few years later Nella had paid her a visit, in the forlorn hope of establishing an intimacy that had never existed. It had turned out to be a bloody mess. Her mother scarcely had an hour a day to spare for her daughter, what with reading horoscopes and holding tête-à-têtes with her clients. She had, however, offered to update Nella's astrological chart for her.

Wally was up on one elbow, frowning down at her. It had been a long, deep silence and he must have been feeling excluded. But he managed a faint smile.

'So what are you thinking about?'

'I was thinking about your school, Wally.'

'My school? Oh, my physical culture school. Yeah, well . . .'

'It's such a terrific idea. I just wish you could get it started.'

'You don't wish it any more than I wish it. But there's a little problem, remember?'

'You know how I would do the ads? I'd run your picture, and I'd say underneath it something like, "This is Wally Cornwall, he's his own best advertisement".'

He nodded, pleased. 'Except I would use my full name, Wallace. Wallace Cornwall, it's more dignified.'

'And in small type I would run your credits – you know Yale, '71, or whatever the year was, winner of such and such a contest, featured model for thusandsuch products . . .'

'That sounds great.' He paused, and the light in his face dimmed down. 'Sure, it's great, but there's one little problem – the little problem of a hundred thousand dollars.'

As though she had been preoccupied and hadn't heard him, she said, 'You know, I think you underestimate the start-up money. I don't think a hundred thousand is enough.'

'Well, thanks, that cheers me up a lot.'

'If you want to do a real elegant – classy – job, I think you'd probably need a lot more. You'll want wall-to-wall carpeting, for one thing, maybe marble sinks, and real thick towels with your monogram, and, oh, very good accessories of all kinds. I'm sure that's what you have in mind.'

'Exactly. I mean, I'd want the person who walked into my school to say right away, first thing, "This is class." That's always been my dream . . .' He stopped and shrugged his shoulders. 'There's just this one thing about it – how the hell do I get the money?'

'From Julian.'

His eyes widened in surprise, then narrowed down suspiciously. 'Your uncle? But you said he wasn't good for a penny.'

'He's good for a lot of pennies. The problem is to get him to shell out.'

She studied his face and realised suddenly why he had never gotten anyplace: for all his overwhelming good looks he lacked class, and probably character, as well. But

I can change all that, Wally, I know how to make a winner out of you.

'Remember what you said before, Wally, about kidnapping me?'

It took him an instant to recall it, and then he stared at her. 'Come on, Nella, I may have said it, but I was just joking around.'

'I know it was just a joke. But it started me thinking.'

He cut a laugh short and stared at her again. 'Besides, a guy as mean as that would never shell out.'

She thought, You're coming along fine, Wally, but she didn't say anything.

'Well, he wouldn't, would he?'

In the firmest tone at her command she said, 'Yes, he'd pay. Enough to start your school, and more.'

'I honestly don't think he would pay.'

'Look, Wally, take my word for it – he would pay out his last penny if he thought my life was in danger.'

'I'll be damned. He's a funny old geezer.'

Oh, yes, as funny as a flash flood. She looked him straight in the eye. 'Would you like to get the money to start your school, Wally?'

'Hey, Nella, quit it. Don't tempt me. It's a really crazy idea, you know.'

'Answer me, Wally. Do you want to do it? Do you?'

'It's stupid. It's a real stupid idea, Nella.'

He was shaking his head from side to side, and the emotions she read in his face changed form as rapidly as in a kaleidoscope: from fear to greed, to hope, to disquietude, to yearning . . . but not disbelief.

'You ought to have your head examined, baby.'

But not disbelief, Nella thought. He knows I mean it. 'Well, Wally, do you?'

She didn't know whether she had awakened because she had sensed Wally's absence, or because of an automobile horn somewhere in the distance, sounding a single, unvaried note. She lay quietly in the dark room, orienting herself: the outline of a chair there, the frame of the exercise pulley on the wall, and spaced around it the shaded polygons that were Wally's gallery of pin-ups. Her heartbeat was a heavy thud. The auto horn persisted: the indignation of someone hemmed in by a double-parker or else a short in the ignition. Somewhere, probably on Third Avenue, a truck shifted its gears, shifted again, and again, and still again.

Where are you, Wally? I'm frightened now.

She got out of bed and went to the door. She felt for the doorknob, and, holding it with both hands, turned it slowly, disengaging the latch with barely a click. She inched the door open. Across the short hallway, light seeped out from beneath Richard's door. She listened for voices but could hear nothing. She eased the door shut and got back under the covers. Her thudding heartbeat was discomforting. She stood her pillow up against the headboard and sat up. The auto horn was still sounding. She settled down for a long anxious wait, but after a minute or two the door opened. She slid down in the bed. Wally's shadow passed by, and then there was a little rush of cold air as he lifted the blanket and got into bed.

'Wally?'

'I thought you were asleep. How long you been awake?'

'Were you in Richard's room?'

'So what if I was?'

'Did you talk to him?'

'What if I did?'

She tried to gauge the tone of his voice. Annoyance? Confidence? The smug possession of a secret? Ah, yes, gotcha, Wally. Her heartbeat quickened, thumped.

She said, 'I thought we had decided to wait until morning.'

'I heard him come in, so I decided to go talk to him. What's the difference, now or the morning?' His voice became teasing. 'Besides, we could have been talking about something else, couldn't we?'

She said, 'What time is it?' Is that the big question of the moment, Nella?

'About four a.m.'

'Has he been working all this time?'

'No. He's been getting his ashes hauled.'

That's a hell of a way to describe the act of love, Wally.

'He pays for it. You know why? Because he says with a whore you always know where you stand.'

'What's so wonderful about always knowing where you stand?'

'I don't criticise him. If that's how he feels, okay. It's his right.'

'Yes.' She paused, and with a tremor in her voice said, 'What did he say, Wally?'

'"Why not?"'

'What?'

'He said – Richard said – "Why not?"'

'Oh. Is that all he said – just "why not?"'

Wally stretched his leg. It touched her and abruptly withdrew. 'Christ, your feet are cold.'

Why not. Richard said 'Why not?' and there it was, the die cast in two emotionally uninflected syllables. Well, what did she expect, memorable words, an elaborate salutatory oration? Richard wasn't one of your big talkers. Just why not. But that was enough, wasn't it?

She said, 'It's all right, Wally, they'll warm up.'

Part III

ROEHMER

Chapter 7

Roehmer was twenty-two years old, six months out of the Police Academy, when he met Mrs Margaret Parris. She would refer to their first encounter as a 'cute-meet' (she had to explain to him what the locution meant, as she did many other things in her vocabulary which represented new ideas to Roehmer). He had never much cared for the description; he was profoundly and earnestly in love with her, and the phrase seemed reductive of his feelings. He himself preferred the more portentous word *destiny*, though he never spoke it aloud a second time after Peggy laughed at it.

He had turned a corner of his beat on to Park Avenue one morning and seen a couple of kids on bicycles bothering a woman. Not mugging or threatening or robbing – those things weren't fashionable twenty-five years ago – just bothering. They were riding their bikes around her in tight circles, hemming her in, causing her to move in fits and starts for fear that they would run her down, though they had no intention of doing that; it was only a sort of playful intimidation. He moved towards the scene with a measured tread – the situation called for the law's majesty rather than its threat – twirling his nightstick, a purposeful display of the sceptre of his authority. One of the kids spotted him, and immediately wheeled away, yelling at his friend. The friend was slow in reacting, and Roehmer got close enough to make a lunge at him. He missed the kid, but collided with the woman and knocked her down. A package fell out of her hands and spilled a dozen books on to the pavement. He made a start in pursuit of the kids, but realised that he couldn't really catch them – they had already turned the far corner – and that, anyway, the woman he had knocked down had first call on his services. He apologised to her and helped her to her feet.

She got up scowling and angry, but when she saw the look of anxiety on his face, she laughed and said, 'I landed squarely on my ass. No damage.'

He had already determined that she was a lady of quality, and so he was shocked by her language; most of his assumptions about the upper classes were still naïve. He bent down and picked up her scattered books. Her package had split apart, and he offered to help her carry the books. She was wearing a lime-coloured suit that had been dirtied in her fall. She kept brushing at the soiled area as if it were a pesky insect.

He said, 'I could have chased after them, but . . .' But it wasn't worth the trouble.

'You could have shot the little bastards. What have you got a gun for?'

He was shocked again. 'Look, ma'am, they were just – '

She laughed. 'I know. I'm joking. They were just a couple of little creeps.'

They walked the rest of the way to her apartment building in silence. He had already observed that she was young and pretty and well dressed, and that she smelled good. But that was just something that registered automatically on the litmus of a young man's awareness in the springtime. It was purely a reflex, and he didn't entertain any fantasies.

Destiny – it was the right word – destiny was on the job when they reached the entrance to her building. The doorman, to whom he would have turned over the books, was busy helping a man in a wheelchair get into a car. He started to give the books to the young woman instead, but realised that it was a clumsy burden for her. Not that she couldn't have managed, but it wasn't gallant; men held such thoughts about women in those days, and women accepted them as a matter of course. He offered to carry the books upstairs for her, though he could have placed them on a table until the doorman returned. But even then he had no thought of an adventure in mind; he just didn't think of the simple alternative.

She started to tell him to put the books on the table, but changed her mind in the process of giving him her first direct look and sizing him up: she noted his powerful build, the suggestion of strength and masculinity in his carriage, his youthful good looks (well, good enough) and it was in *her* mind that a fantasy took shape. (Or so she told him, but that was later.) She thanked him and accepted his offer, and they moved on through the dark elegance of the lobby to the elevator. She had taken destiny by the hand and was guiding it.

'Among other things,' she had told him once, 'I had never been that close to a cop in my life, and I found it thrilling. As for the idea of a cop being in my apartment, it was as exotic as sitting down to dinner with a camel. No offence, darling. I knew I would ask you in for coffee. It was preferable to taking coffee alone, but that was as far as it went at that point. I had no sexual designs on you, it really hadn't entered my mind, though I was aware that you were a very attractive man.' A smile. 'But you were still a camel.'

Maybe it wasn't in her mind, but it certainly lay just underneath the top layer of her consciousness, and it made itself felt even before they sat down to coffee. While she was out of the room for a moment, he stood by the window. The view wasn't inspiring, just the buildings on the other side of Park Avenue, but the vantage point, the richly draped window of this spacious, opulent apartment, made it awesomely glamorous. She joined him at the window, just stood there beside him, and immediately the proximity generated a spontaneous sexual aura. 'Simultaneously horny' was the way Peggy put it in her somewhat self-consciously vulgar way.

It began with a mutual physical attraction, of course (sex at first sight, to quote Peggy again), but the consummation was sparked, for both of them, by deprivation. At the time, Roehmer had been engaged to Mary McManus for six months, with their marriage date still a couple of months away, and since Mary was a pious Catholic, there was no sex between them. He had undertaken to remain chaste himself through the period of their engagement, and, by biting the bullet, had managed to carry it off. But he was bursting with repressed libido, or, as Peggy inevitably put it, 'carrying a terrific load around.' As for Peggy, she was carrying a load around herself, although it was somewhat less sexual than it was the burden of a foundering marriage. She was lonely and discontented and her husband was on a protracted stay out of the country. In those days the options for a society girl (as Roehmer thought of her) in her state of mind were limited: she could take a lover – even a cop.

They were both a little short of breath and tremulous when they moved away from the window. By the time they were drinking their coffee, side-by-side on a sofa, served by a maid in tiny cups that struck Roehmer as being frighteningly fragile (so this was demitasse!) there was a palpable tension in the air.

When Roehmer got up to go – partly because he was a cop on duty and shouldn't have been off the street in the first instance, and partly because the charged atmosphere had begun to scare him (he knew how *he* felt, but wasn't sure about *her*; if she had been a girl of his own class he would have been able to read her like a book, he had good sexual antennae) – she walked out to the foyer with him. The maid showed up to open the door but Peggy chased her away. Awkwardness. She thanked him for driving off the kids on the bicycles. He said it was nothing at all, and he was sorry he had knocked her down.

She said, 'What time are you off duty?'

All right, he understood that. He said, 'Four o'clock,' and for the first time gave her the kind of look that he would long ago have given a girl of his own class.

'Will you come back then?'

'Yes.'

When his tour was over, he showered and changed into his civvies. He was so eager that he turned up at her door with his hair still damp. Two minutes later they were in bed. He was surprised, even shocked, by the abandonment and virtuosity of Peggy's lovemaking, and embarrassed to realise that, his enthusiasm and raw vigour to one side, he was something of a novice. But he was to catch up. Who wouldn't be an eager and willing student in such a school?

Whatever the combination of frustrations it started from, their relationship soon turned into a grand passion. It might have been an attraction of opposites, of different circumstances of birth, background, expectations. So that they were continually delighted by the discovery – however obvious it should have been – that their sensibilities touched at many points. What they didn't know, or at any rate denied admittance to their consciousness, was that they also diverged at many points. They were simply too dazzled by each other. Eventually, when it mattered, Roehmer was to acknowledge these differences, and act upon them. Perhaps Peggy, too, might have acknowledged them in time – maybe not all that *much* time, either – and by then it would have broken his heart.

Once, early in their relationship, Peggy had told him that, until he came along, her life was in ruins. But he didn't take her seriously; he couldn't believe that a life like hers *could* be ruined. In the end, the only one whose life was truly ruined was Mary, the innocent by-stander.

From the time of their first meeting, Roehmer saw Peggy every day, with the exception of his days off, when he spent his time with Mary, consumed by guilt but nevertheless making invidious comparisons with Peggy. He explained his absences with a vague reference to 'special night duty'. Because he was hopelessly in love with his 'society girl', and not yet the first-rate dissembler he was to become as a detective, he found it impossible to hide his feelings. Mary was at first bewildered by what she thought of as his having become a 'changed man', then, by degrees, worried, anxious, and, finally, demoralised. She dug herself deeper into the grave by taking to weeping. One night Roehmer deliberately brought about an ugly quarrel and walked out. He left her crying uncontrollably and spent the rest of the night with Peggy. He stopped seeing Mary.

Later, a few months after Peggy had sailed for Europe,

he patched things up with Mary, and eventually they were married. But the damage was irreversible. Peggy had spoiled him irredeemably for Mary, and before long, in confusion and desperation, Mary began to drink. They had been married for twenty-odd years now, and it had been a flop from the start. From what he had learned about himself – from what had emerged from the crucible of his affair with Peggy – it would have ended badly anyway, probably including Mary's problem drinking, but at least there might have been a year or two of passable contentment.

An affair as white-hot as his and Peggy's would undoubtedly have burned itself out anyway, give or take a few months, but it ended prematurely. Her husband was due to return from Asia, where he had been representing his banks for the past half year, and since they were irreconcilably finished with each other, she elected to clear out before his return. She had been educated abroad, in Switzerland, and had inherited a villa in Ouchy overlooking Lac Leman. They – meaning she and Roehmer – would sail for Europe, spend a few weeks in London and Paris, and then go to Switzerland. After her divorce came through, they would marry and live on in the villa.

It was an outlandish idea, but it seemed both brilliant and feasible to Peggy, and she had no patience with his objections: he had no money, he didn't speak any foreign language, he couldn't abide being a kept man. She had an answer for everything: she would finance a detective agency for him, she would teach him French, he could earn his keep by helping to manage her money . . .

But the most important thing of all to Roehmer, which Peggy simply overlooked in her enthusiasm, was their essential difference. Although it didn't show in bed, or matter in bed, or as long as they kept to the seclusion of her apartment, he knew that it would tell in the long run, maybe the first time they broached the outside world. Her refusal to acknowledge the problem was emblematic of those differences. She could afford to take a high hand, to sweep everything out of mind, but he hadn't her resources. His bank contained only deficits: hunger, deprivation, insecurity.

He tried to boil it down for her. 'I've never once met any of your friends.'

She was stunned. 'You're too damn *good* for them. You'd hate them.'

They argued – fought – for almost twenty-four hours. More than once his resolution flagged, but in the end he held firm. She threatened suicide but didn't mean it. He went home and chucked a round into the chamber of his .38 and pointed it at his temple. But he didn't pull the trigger, so he didn't mean it, either.

He came to see her off. She clung to him compulsively at the foot of the gangplank as the ship's officers averted their eyes, and pleaded with him. 'It's not too late, darling. You can still come.'

'I haven't got a reservation.'

The rationalisation was meant to let her down gently, to avoid punishing her with another brutal *no*.

'I can *get* you a reservation. I know the purser, he'll do anything for me.'

'I haven't got any clothes.'

'We can buy clothing. I can even get you the purser's uniform if you want it badly enough. Money can do anything.'

He saw that it wasn't a rationalisation but a weakening of his resolve, so he wrenched himself free of her and fled, losing himself in the crowd that had come to see the ship off.

The way he put it to himself, watching the ship inch away from the pier, was that if he had been on board with her, he would have become somebody else than the Roehmer he had known all his life. Young as he was, he was wiser than she. But it was more than a question of losing, or compromising, his identity. Painful as it was at that moment, watching the ship push into the river, he knew that he was protecting himself, looking after his own interests. He would have made a botch of running a business, the French language would have eluded him, he would never have acquired the polish to deal with her friends, or even to hold her interest after their passion cooled. They would have ended up despising each other.

He was a Bronx-born cop and she was a society girl. To understand that was to understand everything, and yet not everything. He also understood that her going, and his decision not to go with her, would leave him with a permanent feeling of loss and regret.

So that, after twenty-five years, his hand faltered when he wrote down Julian Massey's address.

Chapter 8

The squeal hadn't come through the 911 emergency computer, but was made directly to the precinct house. Which, Roehmer thought, showed a degree of deliberation well this side of panic. It meant that the caller, nervous as he was, had to thumb through the directory for the precinct phone number and then dial seven digits instead of the three for 911. The call was routed through to the squad room, since it was a matter for the detectives and not a uniformed cop. Roehmer would have preferred teaming up with Murphy on this kind of squeal, but Murphy was spending the day in Criminal Court, testifying in a case involving a fencing operation; he would have to make do with Passatino.

The day was brisk but pleasantly sunny, so they ambled towards Park Avenue. Passatino was excited about the squeal. 'A kidnap, that's pretty big stuff. I mean, after a lot of B and E, aggravated assault, and the usual crap, it's a little different. It's got some class.'

Passatino might be the bravest man on the squad, but he certainly wasn't the brightest. Roehmer didn't want him blundering around with dumb questions and screwing up the investigation. It might be a good idea to cool him down a little.

'You know, Pass, I haven't got any statistics on it, but a hell of a lot of kidnap complaints turn out to be phoney. So the first purpose of the investigation is to try to establish if it's a real kidnapping or not.'

'You mean somebody would deliberately fake it? Why would they do that – money?'

'Sometimes. More often to get sympathy, or draw attention to themselves, or even to punish somebody, a revenge motive. So the first thing we try to do is find out if there's bad blood between the alleged victim and some other member of the family.'

'Be damned,' Passatino said.

'The problem is that the family hates to talk about it – they're ashamed to admit that relationships are so bad that one of them becomes desperate enough to pull a fake kidnap.'

'People,' Passatino said. 'That's the trouble – people.'

'It's very delicate. The idea is to put pressure on them, so that they'll open up, but at the same time you have to be diplomatic. If it gets to be too much of a confrontation, they might get their ass up and file a complaint.'

'That's gratitude for you,' Passatino said. 'That's people for you.'

'Even if you're convinced it's a phoney,' Roehmer said, 'you still have to watch your step. You keep your feelings, your opinions, out of your reports, and you investigate exactly as if it was legitimate.'

'I can't see doing that,' Passatino said.

'Pass – what's the first rule of procedure for a detective?'

'Don't let your ass hang out?'

Roehmer nodded. 'Let's suppose you do a half-assed investigation because you're absolutely, one hundred per cent convinced you're dealing with a phoney, and then a dead body turns up. What happens to you?'

'It's your ass.'

'And your pension. Scratch a cop and ask him why he's a cop, why he puts up with all the shit of being a cop, and if he's levelling he'll tell you it's the pension. So the thing to remember – first, last, and always – is don't get caught out, cover your ass, protect your pension. The truth?'

'I guess.'

'Don't guess. It's the truth and the whole truth.'

But it wasn't really the whole truth. Cynicism was a vital ingredient in the average cop's make-up, but so was an inner conviction, a 'vocation', like they said of priests and ministers. Call it acceptance of responsibility, hatred of criminals, even a kind of vanity. Whatever it was, it made a cop take chances his sense of self-preservation should have rejected. Passatino was a little different. He was in equal parts braver and dumber than the average. These were the qualities, in combination, that had motivated him to get up off the pavement and pursue three goons with knives who had knocked him half unconscious and taken his piece away. And, eventually, in the words of his commendation, 'subdued them'. *Subdued* meant that he had fought on with a dozen slash wounds, never quitting, holding his own, until a ten-thirteen brought help. He spent three weeks in a hospital, where he received a visit from the PC himself, who gave him the NYPD version of a battlefield commission, the gold shield of a detective third grade, although it was well known that Passatino didn't have the smarts to be any kind of halfway competent detective. Well, all right, Passatino was all balls, and a believer, which wasn't such a bad way to be. It was a lot tougher to be like Detective First Grade Roehmer, a cynic and a believer at the same time. But Roehmer was convinced that you had to have those conflicting elements inside you if you were going to be a good cop, which was to say halfway between a true believer like Passatino and a hundred per cent gold brick like Murphy, who would watch thousands die before he let his ass hang out.

Waiting for the traffic light at Park Avenue, Roehmer looked upwards, counting floors to eight. What he saw was a row of windows, nothing more. No gold drapes, no Art Deco lamp, no small animated face . . . Well, the face had disappeared twenty-five years ago, and so had the furnishings. But Roehmer the rookie cop had disappeared, too, or, rather, worn away, eroded by domestic problems, disappointments, disillusionment, and the simple burden of the years. Yet, even the new – and maybe wiser – Roehmer had never been able to pass by that building without feeling a pang of regret.

'Shit.'

Passatino said, 'What?'

'Nothing. Just a twinge of the old arthritis.'

They crossed the street and went into the building. The doorman on duty, a Hispanic, took their names, but when he announced them over the intercom, merely said, 'Two men from the police.' Roehmer recognised the elevator operator, who appeared to be in his seventies now, as the one who had first taken him up twenty-five years ago. The car rose with deliberation – only parvenu buildings had high-speed elevators – and he watched the floor numbers go by. At the ivory-coloured number eight his eyes went out of focus and he felt a stirring in his groin. Christ, Roehmer, at your age. And at hers – if she's still alive, she's past fifty.

Julian Massey opened the door for them, and Roehmer made several unfavourable comparisons. In the first place, the maid would have answered the door; people like Peggy didn't do things like opening doors. The maid, he remembered, would also take his coat, make his drink, and then discreetly vanish, not to appear again until he was ready to leave, when she would help him into his coat. She would also pick up the telephone and take a message when he and Peggy were in the sack. He had sometimes wondered, in the old days, what secret thoughts the maid might have had about the affair between him and Peggy. After all, he was much closer to her social class than he was to her mistress's; so how come he was fucking Peggy Parris instead of opening doors for her?

Massey didn't offer to take their coats. He led them directly into the sitting-room – the same shape and vast size as the one on the eighth floor, but unlike Peggy's, with its cool, understated elegance, a hodgepodge of discordant styles and periods, freakish pieces. From his association with Peggy he had absorbed a little knowledge of interior decoration. Which probably made him the only cop in the whole NYPD who knew what the words *Biedermeier* and *Pleyel* meant – a terrific asset when you were kicking down a tenement door.

The three of them stood awkwardly in the centre of the room – Massey wasn't about to invite the hired help to sit down – with Massey looking at a loss and rubbing his temples. But then he reached into his pocket and took out an envelope.

'This is the letter.'

He handed the envelope to Roehmer, then drifted over

to the fireplace, where he picked up a framed picture from the mantel and began to study it.

Passatino, waving his hand to take in the room, whispered, 'Boy, isn't this some dump?'

Roehmer held the envelope so that Passatino could see it. The address was pieced together from letters clipped from a magazine. The back of the envelope was blank. Well, what did he expect, a return address? He checked out the post office cancellation: 11101 zip code; someplace in Queens. The date was smudged.

Massey replaced the picture on the mantel and returned to them. Roehmer said, 'When did you receive this, sir?'

'Tuesday. Yesterday.'

And waited twenty-four hours before getting in touch with the police? We'll come back to that in a while. Roehmer opened the envelope and took out a single sheet of paper. As with the envelope, its message was pieced together from cut-out letters.

> *I have your daughter Nella.*
> *Don't contact the cops*
> *unless you want her killed.*
> *Another letter will follow.*
> *I mean business.*

'All right,' Roehmer said. 'To begin, could we just get some basic facts down?' He took his notebook out of his pocket. 'Such as your daughter's age – '

'She's twenty-six years old,' Massey said, 'and she's not my daughter, she's my niece.'

'But the letter – '

'I can't help what the stupid letter says,' Massey said testily. 'Don't you think I know the difference between a daughter and a niece?'

'Certainly, sir. Could you describe what she was wearing when you last saw her?'

'Jeans,' Massey said. 'What else do they wear these days?'

Roehmer wrote *jeans* in his notebook. 'Blouse, sweater, hat? What kind of outer coat was she wearing?'

'She never wore a hat. I guess she was wearing a sweater. The coat was a navy blue cashmere. I bought it for her myself in England, cost me three hundred. Pounds, not dollars. Plus duty.'

Massey appeared to be expecting him to make another note, so Roehmer dutifully wrote *blue cashm coat*. He had a good memory, but note-taking seemed to give civilians confidence.

'Now then, sir – '

He stopped as a woman came into the room. She was red-haired, and wearing a green hostess gown. She said to Massey, 'Aren't you going to ask them to sit down?'

'Sorry,' Massey said. 'Will you sit down?'

'And take their coats?'

'It's all right, ma'am,' Roehmer said.

'And introduce me?'

'Agnes, my wife,' Massey said. 'Sit over there.' He indicated an oddly curved love seat covered in what looked to Roehmer like elephant skin. Roehmer nudged Passatino and they sat down.

'It comes from Arabia – right, Julian?' Agnes Massey said.

'Afghanistan. I bought it off a prince or a pasha or something.' Massey laughed. 'He was refurnishing his palace, and he held a garage sale.'

Roehmer watched the woman settle herself in an armchair. She looked to be about half her husband's age. Massey remained standing.

With his pencil poised, Roehmer said, 'Does Miss Massey reside here with you?'

'Yes.'

Agnes Massey pursed her lips. 'Oh, Julian.'

'Well, on and off,' Massey said. 'But this is her real home.'

'On and off,' Agnes said.

Keep an eye on Agnes, Roehmer thought, she'll tip you off every time the old man trims the truth.

'Well, she's been here the past two weeks or so, hasn't she?'

'That's true,' Agnes said.

With his gaze midway between Massey and Agnes, Roehmer said, 'Is there another address for Miss Massey?'

'No,' Massey said. Agnes nodded in agreement.

'Does she have an address where she works?'

'She's not employed.'

'Unemployed,' Roehmer said.

'Not unemployed, just not employed. There's a difference.'

I'll be damned if I can see any difference myself, Roehmer thought, but he nodded his head. 'When was the last time you saw her, sir?'

'Six days ago. Thursday night.'

'And you got the note in the mail yesterday?'

'That's what I said.'

'Can I ask why you waited until today to get in touch with us?'

Agnes said, 'I *told* him not to wait.'

'I had to give it some thought,' Massey said.

Passatino whispered, 'What the hell is there to think about?'

Roehmer nudged Passatino to silence him. 'What time did you last see her on Thursday night?'

'About eleven, I think it was.'

Agnes said, 'I got home from the movies at eleven, and she was gone. So it couldn't have been eleven.'

'So it was ten-thirty,' Massey said. 'Is the time to the exact minute all that important?'

'It might be helpful in tracing her movements,' Roehmer said.

'Ten-thirty,' Agnes said. 'You said you were laying there on the floor about a half hour before I came in.'

Massey turned on her furiously. 'Agnes, when I want your two cents' worth I'll ask for it. Till then, kindly keep your mouth shut.'

'For pity sake,' Agnes said, 'don't get so damn excited.'

Roehmer felt Passatino nudge him. He ignored it. 'Sir, did your niece mention any destination, someplace where she was going?'

'She's twenty-six,' Massey said. 'These days you don't

ask a girl of that age where she's going. If you did, she wouldn't answer, anyway.'

Passatino whispered, 'Picture?'

Don't worry about it, Pass, I'll get around to it. But he said, 'Would you have a picture, or a good clear snapshot of Miss Massey that you might give us, sir?'

'Got plenty of them. You can take your pick.' He gave Roehmer a sharp glance. 'You have any idea about giving it to the newspapers?'

'The primary reason is for distribution inside the police department.'

'I don't want her pictures in the newspapers. Is that clear?'

'A picture in the papers can be helpful. A lot of people see it, and someone might remember having seen her, and might come forward and give us a lead.'

'I won't have it. People like us don't get our pictures in the newspapers for this kind of thing.'

Oh, yes, they do, Roehmer thought, and for murder, rape, child abuse . . . He nodded noncommittally and changed the subject. 'I'll also ask you to give me a list of your niece's known associates. Friends, acquaintances, and so forth.' He paused. 'To your knowledge, sir, did she sometimes travel with a rough crowd?'

'So far as I'm concerned, except for some old girl friends of her college days, her friends were all shit. I don't know if you would call them rough or not, but they were certainly shit.'

'Julian,' Agnes said, 'such language.'

Roehmer said, 'Would you mind elaborating on that, Mr Massey?'

'There's nothing to elaborate. Don't you know what *shit* means?'

Yes, Roehmer thought, shit is what you're handing me, mister. 'Did your niece have any enemies, people who might want to do her harm? And yourself, sir, do you have knowledge of people who might want to do *you* harm?'

'Everybody loves him,' Agnes said, covering a yawn, 'so who would want to do him harm?'

'I used to have plenty of enemies,' Massey said,

grinning. 'People who envied me and wanted me to fall on my face. But that was quite a while ago. One of the advantages of a long life is that your enemies predecease you. As for Nella, with her kind of friends she didn't need any enemies.'

'You didn't like them, sir, right?' Roehmer put a sympathetic look on his face. 'But still, they weren't the type to go in for kidnapping, were they?'

Massey snorted. 'They knew how to get money out of her, out of *me*, without going to all that trouble.'

'Would you mind explaining what you mean, sir?'

'Never mind. That's all I'm going to say about it.'

'With all respect, sir, you shouldn't hold back on something that might help our investigation.'

'It won't help a bit.' Massey held his hand up peremptorily as Roehmer started to speak. 'And I'll be the judge of that. I've said the last word about it.'

Passatino, barely containing his indignation, said, 'You want us to try to find your niece, don't you?'

Massey stared at Passatino. 'Well, you don't think I would invite you up here on a social call, do you?'

Passatino shook off Roehmer's restraining hand. 'You have to give us all the information you can, Mr Massey. What did you mean, they get money out of you? *Who* gets it?'

'I won't be grilled,' Massey said. '*I'm* not the criminal.'

'Oh, tell him,' Agnes said. 'What the hell is the difference?'

'Don't you try to tell me my business, Agnes.' Massey pointed a finger at her. 'Before these men came, I said you could sit here provided you didn't say anything. But all you've been doing is shooting off your mouth. If you don't stop it, I'm going to ask you to leave the room.'

'Okay, Julian, okay, don't get yourself agitated.'

Agnes didn't look very agitated herself, Roehmer thought. She was either very sure of Massey – which the difference in their ages argued – or just placid by nature. He had seen women who reminded him of Agnes often enough, hanging out at bars, and they usually didn't let much get under their skin. She obviously wasn't in

Massey's league socially, but then he hadn't been in Peggy's, either.

Roehmer said in a soothing voice, 'I hate to add to your distress at a time like this, sir, but we need all the information we can get, even if it might seem unimportant to you. Believe me, I know how painful it must be . . .'

'We're just doing our duty,' Passatino added.

Agnes said, 'Julian . . .' Massey turned on her fiercely and she held up her hands, laughing. 'Okay, not a blessed word out of me.'

Massey wheeled abruptly and went to the fireplace, facing the picture he had been holding earlier.

'Some character,' Passatino whispered.

'He's the man,' Roehmer said, his voice low. 'His taxes pay your salary, and he may remind us of it any second.'

Massey came back. 'Go on to something else.'

Roehmer said, 'Your niece's associations, and her habits, can be vital, Mr Massey.'

'Habits? What do you mean by habits?'

'Well, does she drink, does she take drugs, has she been under psychiatric treatment?'

'She doesn't take drugs and she's a moderate drinker. As for psychiatric treatment, I hope that nobody in this day and age equates seeing a psychiatrist with being crazy.'

'To come back to Miss Massey's associates – are you aware of any of them who might have criminal connections or past criminal records?'

'It wouldn't surprise me in the least. But I can't say. I've rarely ever seen any of them, thank God.'

'Yes, well, we'll check it out ourselves.' Roehmer frowned at his notebook. 'When Mrs Massey came back from the movies last Thursday, she found you lying on the floor?'

Massey shook his head. 'Has nothing to do with anything. I fell and cut my hand. That's all there is to it.'

Roehmer was watching Agnes. Her face was bland, but he saw her lift her eyebrows. Thanks, Agnes.

'I'd like to come back to your niece's friends again,' Roehmer said. Massey started to protest, but Roehmer went on, overriding him. 'I'll explain why it's important. In most kidnapping cases, the kidnapper and his victim are acquainted. The exceptions are when the victim, or the victim's family, are well-known public figures.'

'Julian is a famous architect,' Agnes said. 'He used to have his picture in the paper a lot.'

'Never mind, Agnes. You know I don't like to blow my own horn.' Massey turned to Roehmer and, with a sly look, said, 'Tell me, if these kidnappers are acquainted with Nella, how come they thought she was my daughter?'

Everybody loves to play detective, Roehmer thought. But the old guy had a point. He made a meaningless notation in his notebook. Next to him, Passatino was stirring restlessly. Well, he was restless himself. Massey was a tough, arrogant old bird, but the truth was that you couldn't run a decent investigation if you were all that concerned about covering your ass.

Closing his notebook with a snap, Roehmer said, 'Mr Massey, what was the nature of your relationship with your niece? I mean, how did you get along?'

'What kind of question is that? She's my only niece, and I brought her up practically single-handedly. She's precious to me, she's the one thing in this world I really love.'

'Hey,' Agnes said.

'And Agnes, but in a different way.' Massey ran his hand through his sparse white hair. 'We had a difference of opinion every once a while, but that's only natural.'

'Did you have a recent difference of opinion? Within the last week or so?'

Massey's eyes darted towards Agnes. Then, after a slight hesitation, he said, 'We had a little tiff the night she left.'

Roehmer checked out Agnes. Her brows rose, then settled back into place. He said, 'Would you mind telling me the nature of the quarrel, sir?'

'It's a purely private matter and none of your business. And it wasn't a quarrel, it was just a little tiff that didn't amount to anything.'

'A little tiff! Now, Julian – '

'That's it, Agnes!' Massey turned on her furiously. 'I warned you! You're to leave this room at once!'

Agnes said, 'Oh, Julian, for God's sake, act your age!'

'Out!' Massey strode towards her. 'I want you out of this room at once. Come on, get out.'

'Don't yell, I'm going.' She stood up. 'You're behaving like an old fool.'

'Out!'

'You know what this is doing to your damn blood pressure?'

Massey stared at her, shaking with anger. She gave him an exasperated look, shrugged, and slowly walked out of the room. Massey, still quivering, turned to Roehmer.

'As for you, Detective, I've had as much of your dumb questions as I intend to take. You're entirely too personal, as if it's *my* fault Nella was kidnapped.'

Dead end. But when you couldn't get through an obstacle, Roehmer thought, you tried to find a way around it. If Massey wouldn't talk about his quarrel with his niece, he was sure Agnes would. The problem was getting to her without the old man being present.

He said, 'I realise this has been an ordeal, sir, and I won't ask you any more questions. But I would like that picture of Miss Massey, and also a list of her friends and associates.'

'Will you have to tell everyone Nella has been kidnapped?'

Was he concerned about his good name ('People like us don't get our pictures in the newspapers for this kind of thing'), or worried about the threat contained in the note? Give him the benefit of the doubt.

'You know, Mr Massey, kidnappers are smart enough to know that the police will be called in. Still, they always feel obliged to include a threat to – '

He stopped in astonishment as Massey broke into tears. They were the meagre tears of old age, moistening the eyes, brimming over the rims and into the corners.

'Please, please find my Nella before they kill her.' Massey clutched Roehmer's wrist in a strong, bony grip.

'Take it easy, sir. I'm sure we'll find your niece.'

Massey's grasp tightened, and his head darted forward. 'All that talk about quarrels and so forth – don't you think I know what you had in mind? You think it's a hoax of some kind. Well, you'd better get rid of those thoughts.'

His tears had miraculously dried, and his gaze was penetrating and fierce. The man was an emotional quick-change artist, Roehmer thought. He disengaged his arm from Massey's fingers.

'I was just following procedure, sir. Sometimes such things do happen – '

'They don't happen in this family. And you'd better get that through your head in a hurry. I'm acquainted with the police commissioner, and if I put in a call to him, believe me, you'll change your tune.'

Roehmer caught Passatino's eyes. Didn't I tell you so, Pass? He said solemnly, 'That's your privilege, sir.'

'Instead of making innuendos, you should be expending all your energy on tracking down the criminals and bringing Nella back to me safe and sound.'

Roehmer put his notebook away. 'Yes, sir. Could you give me those names and a picture of the young lady?'

He followed Massey through the sitting-room and into the corridor that led to the other rooms. He caught a glimpse of Agnes as they passed by. She was sitting on a leather lounge chair with her feet tucked under her, watching television.

The girl's room was feminine and simply furnished. There were a lot of pictures around, neatly framed, but Massey handed him a large album.

'You can look through this for what you want.'

Roehmer said, 'I'd better leave it up to you, sir. Any clear recent photo?'

Massey flipped through the album and pulled out a snapshot. 'This was taken less than a year ago. That's the cashmere coat I told you about. She's wearing it.'

She was standing in front of the entrance to the building, a slender, moderately tall young woman, hunched slightly against the cold, her hair tumbled over her forehead by the wind. Her face was unsmiling, sombre. She hadn't wanted her picture taken, Roehmer thought, she was submitting to it. She wasn't beautiful, but he knew that people would always look at her when she went by. She had a special quality, a style, that you recognised right off but couldn't define. Maybe it was the way she held her head, or some look in the eye. She reminded him of Peggy Parris.

Chapter 9

Agnes was half-reclining on the lounge chair with the TV screen framed between her feet. The wife was telling her best friend that her husband, the surgeon, had fallen for the beautiful star of stage and screen whose life he had saved by pulling off a terrific bypass operation. Why else, the wife asked, would he be paying her three visits a day at the hospital? Well, Agnes thought, in real life it would be to run up his bill. But that wasn't the reason, and neither was it what the wife thought it was. Actually, the husband's interest was purely professional. He had performed a brilliantly innovative operation and he wanted to monitor the recovery process in detail before writing the paper for the medical journal that would show up the chief of surgery for a jealous old fogey. But the truth was that the chief of surgery *wasn't* jealous of him, he was really trying to protect him from the important surgeon who *was* jealous of him. The best friend wasn't much help because she was sore at the doctor because he had refused to operate on *her*. *She* thought it was because *he* thought she was suffering from an inoperable disease, but the truth was that he knew she was an operation freak who could be cured by medication. If you could believe *that* coming from a surgeon.

Misunderstanding – that's what soap operas were all about. Somebody misunderstood somebody else, and the next thing you knew she was involved in a love affair with some rat with a lot of hair, or being mean to her kids, or crossing the street in a trance and getting tagged by a truck.

Nobody understood anybody else very well in real life, either, but they just didn't go ape about it. Take herself. She didn't understand Julian for beans – but did she let it blind her with tears so that she walked into a truck? Not on your life. She took things the way they came, she let problems roll off her back. Somebody else might have blown her stack if Julian had kicked her out of the room. Not Agnes. It didn't matter that much. *Nothing* mattered that much. Sure, she thought it was foolish of Julian to pretend there wasn't any bad blood between him and Nella. But that was Julian. Herself, she would have come right out with it. But then she just wasn't stiff-necked like Julian. She was a redhead from the working class, and Julian was the upper crust, so they acted differently. So be it. She might not understand him, but she didn't *mis*understand him.

A commercial came up on the screen. She doused the sound with the remote-control beeper and tilted her head towards the door. She could hear voices, so the cops were still there. Not that they would get any more from Julian than he wanted to give them. He was a stubborn old mule.

The commercial faded and she blipped back the sound.

Come to think of it, among the things she didn't understand about Julian was the dumb relationship he had with Nella. It seemed like a hell of a way to run a family. And carrying on the way he did about that picture of his. His attachment to that picture was honest-to-God weird. You'd think the finest moment of his life was acting in drag with Scotty. No, mustn't call him Scotty – Scott F. Fitzgerald. So he was a famous writer, but he must be dead for thirty or forty years, Godssake. Once Julian had given her one of his books to read, *The Great Gatsby*. Just a short little book, but it took her three whole weeks to get through it, and Julian had gotten sore when she told him she thought it wasn't too bad, but a little old-fashioned. He told her she was an ignorant biddy who didn't know literature when she saw it. Okay, so if that was what she was, why did he ask for her opinion?

Another thing was his family, what he called his lineage. Fine, so he was descended from a duke, and from druids, whatever *they* were, and her family was a generation out of the Irish bogs. Happens her father, the whiskey-sotted old dumbo, used to claim he was descended from Irish kings, but that was malarkey.

Maybe in Julian's case it wasn't malarkey, but it was still
. . . malarkey. So what if her old man drove a truck and his
father was a stockbroker or whatever, he married her
anyway, didn't he?

She heard footsteps in the hallway and saw Julian and
one of the detectives – the kind of tough good-looking one
– going by. In a little while they came back, but she didn't
pay any attention to them. The doctor's wife was standing
near the window and thinking of jumping out of it. Not
that she would, at least not today: it was time for the
episode to end. Personally, Agnes didn't think she would
jump. More likely she would be hit by a truck and become
paralysed, and get rushed to the hospital, where
everybody would act as if she was the only patient in the
whole place.

The show ended. When she clicked off the sound for
the commercials, she heard Julian's footsteps coming
down the hall. 'Have they gone, Daddy?'

He sailed past her. She shrugged and switched back the
sound. Sometimes he acted like a big dumb kid. Maybe
she shouldn't have tried to butt in with the cops, but why
shouldn't he have told them what the fight with Nella was
about? For all anybody knew, maybe it was Roland, the
Eau Boy genius himself, who had kidnapped her. Not that
she thought that was the case. He wasn't the type, in fact
he was probably a swish. Who else would come up with
that kind of an idea? Eau Boy Cologne, Godssake. And
who else but Nella would believe in it and hit Julian up for
a handout?

She remembered the night Nella had brought the
young guy to the apartment. Roland was his name,
Roland Something, a swish name if she ever heard one.
The two of them had put a hard sell on Julian – what a
terrific clever name it was for a man's toilet water, how it
couldn't miss being a hot item, and how Roland had to
have some cash to pay a chemist he knew to put the stuff
together, and an artist he knew to design a cute package,
so he could go around to the big stores and peddle it. It
sounded kind of dumb to her, but those two, Nella and
Roland, they raved like it was the greatest idea since the

Creation, trying to snow Julian, pleading with him, promising him half the profits . . . And Julian listening with that mean nose-in-the-air look of his, sniffing as if he could already smell Eau Boy and it smelled like shit.

Listening to all of it, she felt sorry for Nella, though Nella was pretty dumb to put any faith in a swish named Roland, or expect a hard nut like Julian to go for it. But Nella was shacked up with Roland – so maybe he wasn't a swish, though he sure did talk and look like one – and when Nella was in love there wasn't anything she wouldn't do for the guy, and all her brains went out the window.

Julian, with that stern face and cold eye, had them crawling and begging and sweating, and then, all of a sudden, out of the blue, he agreed to advance them ten thousand. She had been looking at Nella when Julian said he would pony up, and instead of bursting out with joy or gratitude, Nella reacted like she had just been told she had six months to live. But maybe that was the proper form for the descendants of a duke when somebody insulted them by giving them money.

Eau Boy didn't get off the ground, and Roland disappeared with what was left of the ten thousand. She had talked to Julian about it soon after he found out that Roland had taken a powder, three or four weeks ago.

'But Daddy, how could you do it? Even *I* knew that it was a fool-headed idea.'

Julian gave her his devilish grin. 'So did I. That's why I gave them the money.'

She said that it seemed rotten to encourage something he knew was bound to fail, and Julian got mad at her and told her she was simple, and that anybody with half a brain would realise that he had been motivated by considerations of Nella's *good*. Well, Julian was deep, all right . . .

For instance, that business of Nella's being kicked out of dancing school. It had happened before her time, but Nella had told her about it. It was funny how Nella would confide in her – at least about her grievances against Julian

– at the same time that she made no bones about disliking her. Agnes could see why Nella might be pissed off at her; after all she, Agnes, was a Johnny-come-lately, and now stood to inherit Julian's fortune. But even that was partially Nella's fault. When Julian had offered to settle a lump sum of money on her, she had snapped back that she intended to give his filthy lucre away. So it was hard to blame Julian for cutting her clear out of his will.

The way Nella told about her weight problem made Julian out to be a vicious bastard, deliberately tempting her with irresistible goodies. But Julian had a different slant.

'Certainly it was deliberate. I was testing her mettle. If she resisted temptation, I would know that she was seriously dedicated to being a dancer and was prepared to suffer and sacrifice for it. In that case I would have done everything in my power to help her realise her dream. But if she wasn't ready to stand the gaff, it was best to find it out sooner rather than later. My purpose was to spare her the agony of disappointment and failure. But to this day she doesn't comprehend it.'

'She sure doesn't, Julian.'

'That's the cross I have to bear. But one day she'll come to her senses and thank me for what I did.'

In the pig's ass she will, Agnes had thought, but didn't say it out loud.

'Meanwhile, I comfort myself in the knowledge that I acted in Nella's best interests.'

To listen to him, he had had the same motives with Philip, Nella's father. As for Philip's death, you had to say on Julian's behalf that it was never proved that he did commit suicide, much less Julian having driven him to it.

'Nurse!'

Oh Christ! Wouldn't you have thought, with all he was going through, that he would want to take a nap or something?

'Nurse, where are you?'

His voice echoed down the hallway from their

bedroom, fretful and demanding. Agnes sighed and sat up, but delayed switching off the set so she could catch the last bit of dialogue between the mother and her handsome son, who was bouncing the mother's best friend, who was at least twenty years older than him.

'Nurse! Nurse, I need assistance. Can you hear me, Nurse?'

'I hear you, Daddy,' she called out. She flipped off the remote-control button. 'Be right with you, Mr Massey, be right there, sir.'

'Hurry up, Nurse, it's serious.'

She went along the hall to the sewing-room, so-called, though she never set foot in it except to put the uniform on. She thought he was damn silly about all this, but if it aroused him, what the hell, she didn't mind. You'd think he would have dreamed up a fantasy that wouldn't remind him of the pain and discomfort of a gallbladder operation. But God knows, *she* had no reason to complain; after all, the hospital was what had led up to her becoming Mrs Julian Massey and living on Park Avenue and having all the money she needed and standing to inherit five or six million unless she predeceased him, which wasn't all that unlikely, considering the state of his vital organs and those famous genes of his. His parents, who had gone back to England to live, had died only five or so years ago in their mid-nineties. And not from natural causes, either; they had been hit by a car while they were walking on one of those English country roads.

Post-operative, he had hired around-the-clock private nurses, which was not strictly necessary but a sensible precaution considering his age. She was the night nurse, and he was a pretty sick old guy the first night she came on duty. He was an air swallower, so the doctor had inserted a tube in his nostril and a suction machine to keep him from getting too gassy. Between the discomfort of the tube and the normally attendant pain of the surgery, he was a nuisance the first couple of nights. She stayed wide awake and on her toes, and did everything she could to make him comfortable. He was a terrible patient – snarling and bitching and insulting her every time she tried to help him. The way he carried on, she was sure he would complain to his doctor and have her kicked off the case, but he didn't. By the third night he was feeling a lot better (just taking the tube out of his nostrils had worked wonders) and he surprised her by telling her that he appreciated her efforts and that, compared to his daytime nurses, she was worth her weight in gold. Which was reversing the usual order of things; most patients were nice while they felt rotten, and turned unpleasant when they started to feel better.

What *this* patient did when he started to feel better – not that *that* was unusual – was to get randy. On the third or fourth night he asked her for a bath and rubdown. From the sly grin on his puss she guessed what was coming, though she doubted he was up to it. But he was up all right – not for too long, but it was a promise of things to come. After a lot of childish dirty talk he dropped off to sleep and she settled down in her chair to get some shut-eye herself, taking off her shoes and loosening the neck of her uniform. She woke up when she heard him calling her. He was wide awake, which meant the old fox had probably palmed his sleeping pill.

'I need help, Nurse.'

'Does something hurt?'

His answer was so low that she couldn't hear him. She asked him to repeat it, and he motioned to her to come closer. When she bent over the bed, his hand shot out and plunged down into the front of her uniform, before she could react.

Having to cope with horny patients was an old story. In fact, the only male patient she could remember who'd never made a pass was a priest. She knew all the tricks, and she ran the gamut with Mr Massey: indignation and threatening to resign the case, threatening to tell his doctor, warning him that he was a sick man, that he could pop his stitches and start bleeding copiously, that over-exertion could prove instantly fatal; appealing to his better nature by telling him that if someone came into the room she would be fired and, what's more, lose her cap and her livelihood.

Nothing cut any ice with Julian Massey. He just kept grinning and ogling her, and she realised that he still had his hand on her breast. She removed it and went back to her chair, but Massey wasn't about to quit.

'Nurse, come here, please.'

'Go back to sleep, Mr Massey.'

'I need help, Nurse, I really do. Aren't you being paid to minister to the patient?'

He began to complain about a pain. She didn't really believe him, but she went back to the bed anyway and asked him where the pain was.

'Right here, Nurse.' He kicked off the blanket, grabbed her hand, and led it to his penis. 'Oh, what a terrible pain,' he said, cackling. 'Maybe you can heal it by a laying on of hands.'

By now she was laughing herself. She gave him a friendly slap and pulled the blanket back over him. But he wasn't about to call it quits. He kept nagging at her half the night, though she wouldn't go near the bed again. Finally they reached a compromise. He would shut up if she would just unbutton her uniform and let her breasts hang out. She settled for that, turning her chair around so he could get a good look at her. Eventually he fell asleep.

But the next night she had hardly come into the room before he kicked the blanket down and started waving his cock around. He had a pretty respectable hard-on too. She unbuttoned her uniform for him, but it didn't satisfy him tonight, so she came over to the bed and let him fondle her. One thing led to another, until, praying that nobody got the notion of coming into the room, she climbed on to the bed and gave him a blow job. After that, tickled pink, he went to sleep.

She figured that would be her nightly job for the few days longer the case might last – he let the other two nurses go the following day – but the very next night he demanded what he called 'the real thing'. He refused to let her go down on him.

'Get under the blanket, Nurse,' he whispered. 'I'm freezing, I need warming up.'

'You know I can't do that, you're not well enough.'

'Nurse, I need help.'

'I can see that. You want the same therapy as last night?'

'No. You have to get into bed with me.'

She had never met anyone before who could resist the offer of a blow job, but Massey was that man. Nothing would satisfy him but that she got into bed with him.

'Oh, well, all right,' she said at last, and started to peel back the cover.

'No,' Massey whispered. 'The uniform. Take off the uniform, Nurse.'

'It's bad enough I'm doing what I'm doing, without doing it naked,' she told him.

'Nurse, the uniform, take it off.'

It didn't really make any difference. If she got caught in the kip with him, it wouldn't matter whether she had her uniform on or off. So, while he lay there grinning and goggling at her, she stripped down and slipped into bed with him. But she was still concerned enough about the welfare of her patient – ethical, you might call it – to take the superior position so that he wouldn't have to exert himself too much.

After that they screwed every night – once a night, but that wasn't bad for a man of his age – until he was discharged. And she went home with him, theoretically for a week or so until he was back on his feet. It stretched out to a month, and finally she gave him notice. He really didn't need a nurse anymore – not for nursing, anyway – and she felt guilty about taking his money. He begged her to stay, but she had made her mind up.

He stood her absence for three days, then phoned her and entreated her to come back, not as a nurse, but as a sort of paid companion. She agreed, partly because she liked him, and partly because she was getting fed up with nursing, with being around sick people so much. They continued to hit it off real well, and after six months or so he asked her if she would like to get married. She wasn't swept off her feet – in fact she told him it was a dumb idea, he didn't have to marry her to get her to stay. He said he knew that, but that he wanted to get married anyway.

She asked him why, what was the big idea?

He grinned and said, 'I want to see what it feels like. I've never been married before.'

Maybe he was getting soft in the head – at least in that one respect if no other – but he was certainly serious about the idea, so she said, 'What the hell, why not?' and became Mrs Julian Massey. And although they were as different as any two people could be, it had worked out very well.

She stood naked in the sewing-room, her dress and bra and panties and stockings neatly folded on top of the sewing machine (might as well use it for *something*) and then slipped into the white uniform and white shoes and stockings. She went down the hall to their bedroom. Julian was under the blanket, only his face showing, with a scowl on it.

'What took you so long, Nurse? I could have passed away in the interim.'

'Now, Mr Massey, we mustn't get ourselves upset.'

'I could have died of sheer neglect.'

She fussed with his blanket and pillow. 'If we allow ourselves to be upset, it drives our blood pressure up, and that makes us susceptible to watchamacallitosis.'

'It hurts, Nurse,' Julian moaned.

'Well, we better have a look at it.' She folded back the blanket. Julian grinned, his eyes glinting mischievously. 'Oh, my, it does look bad, all swollen up.'

'Did you ever see one swollen that bad, Nurse?'

'Never.' She touched him lightly. 'Never in twenty years of nursing have I ever seen one swollen that big. We'll have to take emergency steps right away.'

'Yeah yeah yeah.' Julian laughed. 'Tell you what, Nurse, shut the door and then come back and get into bed with me. Okay?'

'Okay.' She started to unbutton her uniform.

'No, no, for Godssakes,' Julian said crossly.

'I forgot,' Agnes said. 'Oh, no, Mr Massey, it's out of the question, you're a gravely ill man.'

'Bend down here a second, Nurse,' Julian said. 'I want to tell you something.'

She leaned over the bed and he slipped his hand into the neck of her dress.

'Oh, Mr Massey, you mustn't do that.' She looked down at herself as he fetched her breasts out. 'We're a very bad boy, Mr Massey.'

Chapter 10

Roehmer checked in with Sergeant Tinney, the first whip of the Detective Squad, and told him briefly about his visit to Julian Massey. Tinney, sensing complications and covering his ass, told him to see Lieutenant Boyd. This was what Roehmer had wanted to do in the first instance, but, covering his ass, had taken care to go through channels.

While Roehmer told his story, the lieutenant leafed through a copy of *Who's Who* he picked up from his cluttered shelf. When Roehmer finished, the lieutenant read the entry on Julian Massey aloud.

'So even if he's retired, he's still a big wheel,' the lieutenant said, 'and got to be handled with care.'

'He told me he's a friend of the PC,' Roehmer said, 'and if we don't run the investigation the way he tells us to, or stop asking him dumb questions, he'll lower the boom.'

The lieutenant nodded warily. 'If he says he knows the PC, it's probably true. Not that I give a damn, I do my duty like I see it. But there's no sense making him mad.'

'He was mad right off the bat to start with. I spent a whole hour eating his shit like it was ice-cream.'

'A good detective knows how to get information without making people mad.'

'That's me, Lieutenant. Afterwards, Passatino said he never saw me act like that, like I was the guy's servant.'

'Oh, well, Passatino,' the lieutenant said. 'What's your off-hand opinion – does it look like a legit kidnapping?'

'Too soon to say, but it has a little bit of a funny smell. Problems in the family – you know what I mean?'

'Don't jump to conclusions. Whatever you think, this case has got to be investigated thoroughly.'

'Yessir.'

'At all times go on the assumption that the victim is in

138

danger of being killed. So if it turns out to be real, we've got our ass covered. You made out a report yet? Keep it straight, no innuendos. This Massey is an important citizen. How's your case load?'

'Medium.'

'Forget them, I'm taking you off the chart so you can run with this case, number one priority. You need help, use Passatino and Murphy.' The lieutenant picked up the ransom note. 'He doesn't seem in a hell of a hurry. He doesn't even mention money. He's working slow, so we got some time.'

'Mr Massey wants to keep it out of the papers, his kind of people don't like to be in the tabloids.'

'I've known better people than him practically lived on page five of the *Daily News*.' The lieutenant shrugged. 'We can try to keep it quiet for twenty-four hours, say, but you know the medias, sooner or later, they manage to get hold of a story.'

'He also doesn't want us to let on to anybody we interview that she's anything more than missing.'

'No problem. If we're not going to tell the medias, we can't tell anybody else, can we?'

'I guess not.'

'Would that hamper your investigation?'

'I guess not.'

'Yes or no.'

'At this stage, I don't see how it would make any difference.'

'All I'm trying to do is be helpful to a bereaved citizen. But if it's going to hamper your investigation . . .'

'I can't see it hampering the investigation.'

'It never hurts to show a little courtesy to good people. Okay, that's settled. You got a friend with the FBI?'

'I know a guy.'

'See if you can pick his brains. But no names. Tell him it's a hypothetical case.'

'I'll phone right away.'

'Start right in on the case. Use Passatino and Murphy as much as they can spare the time. Forget you think it smells. That way you don't bring disgrace down on the squad if it's a legitimate kidnap, which it could easily be legitimate.'

Roehmer went back to his desk and phoned Special Agent S. A. Jones at the New York office of the FBI on East Sixty-ninth Street. Jones was out. He left a message. You could never tell when you might pick up a pointer. The FBI had terrific resources, all kinds of computers and practically unlimited funds for snitches and informers. And they could walk in through doors that were usually closed to city cops. Kidnapping was really their bag. After forty-eight hours there was a presumption that state lines had been crossed, which automatically brought the feds in, so most kidnapping cases usually ended up in their laps.

Murphy came in, and Roehmer asked him to stand by until he made another phone call. He dialled the Intelligence Unit and after a careful exchange of names – cover your ass – he arranged to have Julian Massey's telephone tapped; Massey had given his permission, so no court order was required. The Intelligence cop said he would get in touch with the super of Julian Massey's building and tap into his line in the basement with a pair of alligator jumpers, and place a recorder in the basement with enough tape for about twenty-four hours.

Roehmer filled Murphy in on the case, and then, with Passatino sitting in, ran up a list of things to be done: check doormen and other personnel in Massey's building to see if they had anything to report on the girl and any possible associates; contact Missing Persons; get a lab analysis of the kidnap note and envelope; get dupes made and distributed of the picture of the girl; pass on description of the clothes she had been wearing when last seen; check out ex-husband; check out friends from list supplied by Massey; check taxi companies and bus drivers to try to trace girl's movements after leaving the house.

Some of it could be done by phone, but much of it meant shoe leather. It was a large order for three detectives, two of whom had other cases to handle.

Roehmer went out for a late lunch. When he returned,

he phoned Professor Laurence Adams, the missing girl's ex-husband.

Perfectly innocent people often became nervous when they dealt with the police. Roehmer's theory was that they started remembering – or even inventing – hidden guilts. So he didn't make anything of Laurence Adams's jitteriness on the phone, including dropping the instrument with a crash that made Roehmer wince. But Adams's insistence on coming down to the police precinct, innocuous as it undoubtedly was, had to be handled.

'I've finished with my last class, so I'm free,' Adams said. 'I've been meaning to go downtown to do some shopping, anyway, so I can kill two birds.'

He had a very light, cultivated voice, pitched in an upper register. Roehmer said that it was no trouble for him to come uptown – just hop a subway train. 'And I get a free ride,' he said in a jocular voice.

'But I really don't mind coming down,' Adams said. 'In fact I would prefer it. So if you would just tell me where to meet you . . .'

'Well, actually,' Roehmer said, 'It's a question of procedure. The regulation is that I *have* to go to your place.'

'Oh.' Adams was silent for a moment, and then, in a somewhat subdued voice, said, 'Are you telling me that you're obliged to come up here on the suspicion that Nella might *be* here?'

'If that's what I thought, I wouldn't have phoned first and warned you, would I?'

'No. Come to think of it, you wouldn't.'

On the ride uptown Roehmer reached into his pocket for the picture of Nella Massey before recalling that he had turned it in for reproduction. He tried to remember what she looked like, but drew a blank. All he had retained was the tilt of the head, the look in the eye that had reminded him of Peggy Parris. The failure of his memory irritated him, although he knew it wasn't important. If he opened one of Adams's closet doors and found a young woman hiding inside, he'd deduce that it was her – right?

Laurence Adams lived in an old apartment house off Riverside Drive – the Tudor style dated it back to the twenties. The nameplates under the bells in the vestibule contained the names of two, three, even four people. Students, who shared apartments. Laurence Adams's bore only the single name. Adams answered his ring and buzzed the door open. Two flights up, Adams was waiting in his doorway with his hand extended. His appearance belied the lightness of his voice: he was strongly built, with a square face and a luxuriant sprout of black hair showing in the open neck of his shirt.

They shook hands, and Adams ushered him inside. 'Can I offer you something – a glass of sherry?'

'Thanks, Professor, but I'm on duty, you know.' If the offer had been whiskey, he would have accepted.

'Please don't call me professor. Mister will do, or, if you prefer, Laurence.' He smiled. 'Or, even better, Larry.'

The living-room satisfied Roehmer's expectations for the lodgings of a bachelor college professor. It was disorganised, messy. The furniture looked new but dusty. There was a large stereo and a scattering of tapes, records, books, and magazines covering almost every flat surface in the room.

Adams motioned him into one of the pair of facing armchairs and they sat down. 'Typical bachelor's digs, I suppose.' Adams's smile was strained. 'It's really quite compact. This room, a bedroom, a study, a bath . . .'

He spotted me checking the place out with a professional eye, Roehmer thought. Well, what did I expect to find – a pair of panties hastily tucked behind a sofa cushion, with a frilly edge sticking out?

'If you'd care to look around . . .'

Roehmer shook his head. 'I just want to ask you a few questions that might give us a lead as to Miss Massey's whereabouts.'

'Certainly.' Adams's brow creased. 'You're sure that's all it is – I mean, she's just been missing a few days?'

'It's a routine matter. Mr Massey called us this morning – '

'I've been thinking about that since you phoned me,' Adams said. 'How long has Nella been missing?'

'Six days. Since last Thursday night.'

'And Julian Massey reported her missing? I find that very odd. Nella's on her own, you know. She just lives at Julian's apartment from time to time, and I *know* that she never bothers checking in and out with him. To my own certain knowledge, she's often been gone for five days, or much longer, without telling him.' He leaned forward anxiously. 'Are you sure that nothing's happened to her?'

'That's all it is,' Roehmer said, looking dumb and honest. 'Tell me, if Miss Massey doesn't live with her uncle, where does she live?'

'I honestly don't know where she's been living recently. I last spoke to her on the phone during the summer, it might have been August, possibly late July. So she *might* have been staying at Julian's. Julian could tell you, of course.'

'I must have gotten the wrong impression, that she lived with her uncle permanently.'

'Not at all. Only when she doesn't have a place of her own, or between – ' He caught himself, looked chagrined, then went on with an air of defiance. 'Or between relationships, when she would be living with someone else, at someone else's place. So, you see, although she might actually have been living at Julian's up until Thursday, she might at that point have moved in with a friend. If that's the case, she wouldn't necessarily tell him. In fact, the odds are that she wouldn't bother to, would simply leave without telling him where she was going.'

Laurence Adams was flushed and a little angry. Better try to cool him down, Roehmer thought. He said, 'Come to think of it, maybe I'll take you up on that sherry now.'

Peggy had introduced him to sherry, but he had never really learned to care for it. Sipping from a slightly smudged glass now, it was like transubstantiation: he was back in uniform, a rookie cop, an inexhaustible lover, a captive to passion, with one foot into a life that was glamorous and exciting and foreign, the other mired in reality.

Enough of that, Roehmer. He said, 'The relationship between Miss Massey and her uncle – how do they get along?'

'Not very well. But I assume you wouldn't have asked the question if you hadn't already guessed the answer.'

'They get along poorly?'

'Poorly.'

'But she lives with him, so . . .'

'Only when she can't live anyplace else.'

Come back to this later, Roehmer thought, and said, 'Is this feeling of dislike mutual?'

Adams sighed. 'It's a very complicated matter.'

Roehmer took out his notebook, and made a meaningless mark in it. 'Mr Julian Massey is very well-to-do?'

Adams smiled. 'He's loaded. He's a rich man. By my poor standards, an extremely, even excessively rich man.'

'Until his recent marriage, Miss Massey was his sole heir. Is that right?'

'It's right,' Adams said defensively, 'but the inference is wrong. Money has nothing to do with it.'

'When Mr Massey married, did his wife, Agnes, then become his heir?'

Adams studied his glass for a long moment. 'Detective Roehmer, do you mind if I make an observation?'

'Go right ahead.'

'Your line of questioning. It strikes me as being a little odd and a lot more personal than I would have thought necessary.'

Roehmer sipped his drink and said nothing.

'I would have guessed that your questions would have been directed to exploring her associations, to the end of trying to find out where she might be located. But you seem to be chasing after motivations, the *reasons* for her disappearance. Isn't that irrelevant since she *has* disappeared?'

Roehmer thought of invoking the 'procedure' ploy again, but discarded the idea. Laurence Adams wasn't a fool. He said, instead, 'We already have most of that information in hand, though I'll be asking you for more names later on. That's the simple part of a missing persons investigation, just routine gumshoe work. Sometimes it's all that's necessary. But with more sophisticated people, motivations and interrelationships give us an insight into the missing person and often give us important leads. The public doesn't realise it, but a lot of our training is in the psychology of a – ' He had almost said *crime*. 'Of a disappearance.'

Adams said, 'I guess you people are a lot subtler than I thought.'

Roehmer couldn't tell whether he was being sarcastic or not. Maybe Adams didn't know himself. He said, 'So . . . can we come back to the matter of the inheritance?'

'I suppose so,' Adams said without much conviction. 'What you're getting at is this: Has Nella disappeared to punish Julian because she resents his marriage and the loss of his money?'

'Exactly. You're right on the button, Mr Adams.'

'After I repeat that I'm not at all sure she has disappeared, the answer to your question is categorically *no*.'

'If you say so,' Roehmer said. 'But it's pretty unusual for someone to feel like that about money – about a *lot* of money.'

'Nella is a very unusual person.'

It was said with pride, with quiet certitude, and Roehmer thought, He's still in love with her. He studied Adams carefully, wondering what it was that the girl had seen in him. He wasn't a beauty, but he was certainly passable looking, although that high, light voice might be considered a drawback. He was cultured, educated, undoubtedly a very decent guy . . . Christ, Roehmer, what has this got to do with anything?

He made a scribble in his notebook. 'Has she got any money of her own?'

'Not a penny.'

Roehmer made another mark in his notebook and waited.

'I told you,' Adams said with a trace of annoyance, 'she's unusual. She simply doesn't give a damn about money. To be perfectly truthful, I regard her attitude as a bit heedless, although at the same time I find it refreshing and admirable. When we divorced, she refused to take a penny in settlement from me, though I offered it, or a penny in alimony. She said I didn't owe her anything. That's Nella, Detective Roehmer.'

'Still, Mr Adams, we're talking here about . . . you said Mr Massey was a very rich man.'

'Meaning how much could she have gotten from a poor schnook of a college professor?'

'No, sir, that isn't exactly what I meant.'

But Adams wasn't offended. 'It would have been no different if I had had millions, like Julian. She felt I didn't owe her anything.'

Roehmer said, 'But what about her uncle? Did she feel he didn't owe her anything either?'

Adams hesitated, then said decisively, 'Not money. Definitely not money.'

'Well, if not money, what?'

'It's hard to say.' Adams pursed his lips in thought. 'But whatever it is she might feel he owes her, it probably isn't collectible within the normal standards of the term.'

Too deep for me, Roehmer thought. It was hard for him to believe anybody could be as indifferent to money as Adams claimed for Nella Massey. It was against the laws of human behaviour. True, he himself had turned down a lot of money when he refused to go to Europe with Peggy, but there was an expensive entailment involved – the pawning of his life. Well, wasn't there *always* an entailment, even when he allowed the owner of a restaurant to murmur ingratiatingly, 'No check for my friend Detective Roehmer'? And might there not be an entailment with the girl and her uncle?

He said, 'Still, money to one side, did she resent the new Mrs Massey?'

Adams smiled and didn't say anything. It was a slightly sad smile, an appealing smile that made a claim on your sympathies, and, for the first time, Roehmer thought he could see what the girl saw – had seen – in the professor. Come on, Roehmer, what are you, a visionary, a marriage counsellor? And is it any of your goddamn business?

He said, 'Sir – you didn't answer my question.'

'Did she resent Agnes? Certainly. Was she justified?' He shrugged. 'Look, Detective Roehmer, don't expect me to be objective about all of this. I'm no longer married to Nella, but I have more than a lingering affection for her. Not that I think she's always been right with respect to her relationship with Julian.' He paused, and with a touch of asperity and challenge said, 'I think we're getting far too personal.'

Roehmer nodded his head gravely. 'I'm going to be absolutely candid with you, sir.' Meaning I'm about to snow you. 'In ninety-four cases out of every hundred, family problems are at the bottom of sudden disappearances. And in sixty-five per cent it's a profile of the missing person, drawn from conversations such as this one, that leads to a solution.'

Adams was following him closely, and he seemed to be impressed by the statistics, which Roehmer had just invented.

Adams said, 'I've certainly had to revise my perception of what detective work consisted of. I had always thought it was a lot of hard pavement-pounding.'

With a confidential air Roehmer said, 'It is. Shoe leather and snitches, of course, though we don't like it to be aired around how much we depend on snitches. Though snitches don't help in this kind of case.'

Watch your step, Roehmer, you're practically telling the truth. Snitches were rarely any good in a kidnapping case because most of the perpetrators were amateurs. He gave Adams a look with his open, tell-all face, and almost felt ashamed of how easy it was to take advantage of this nice man. Well, it was for his own good, for the girl's own good, wasn't it?

Adams, noting that his glass was empty, offered to fill it. The sherry tasted like liquid candy to him, but he nodded his thanks. You couldn't terminate an interview if you had just filled somebody's glass.

He said, looking at his notebook, 'According to my

notes, sir, you described the relationship between Miss Massey and her uncle as poor?'

Adams nodded'

'*Extremely* poor?'

Adams smiled his sad smile. 'I take your point. You made it before – postulating that Nella might have disappeared in order to punish Julian. The answer is still no. And, as I said before, I'm not convinced that it's a disappearance at all.'

'Well, as to that, that's what Mr Massey said it was, so that's what I have to go on.'

'It's happened before, I told you that, but he never called in the police before.' Adams looked at him sharply. 'Are you sure that's all that's involved?'

'To the best of my knowledge.' Roehmer flipped a few pages of his notebook and pretended to read from it, his lips moving silently. 'That's all it is according to my notes.'

'Well, it strikes me as being peculiar.'

'Human nature is peculiar,' Roehmer said. 'It's unpredictable. Human nature is what the detective business is all about, Mr Adams.'

'Yes, I suppose it is.'

Adams sounded fatigued, drained. 'I won't be much longer,' Roehmer said. 'What I'd like to ask – if there was such bad blood between Miss Massey and her uncle, could you explain why she returned to him, between, I think you said, relationships?'

'I can't see that that's pertinent.' He made a gesture of helplessness. 'But who am I to say? She goes back there – mind you, this is going to sound like cheap psychologising – she goes back there as a form of penance, to punish herself.'

'For what? I mean, penance for what?'

'For her failures, or for what she regards as her failures.'

'Failures?' But Adams's face had closed up, so Roehmer took another tack. 'When she comes back, Mr Massey takes her in?'

'He loves her – if that's the right word. In fact, she's his most precious possession, and that's really the story of Nella's life. But I think I'm talking too much.'

There was no point pursuing that angle, Roehmer thought; in fact, he had already been pushing too hard. He had confirmation of what he needed: the pattern of a possible fake kidnapping for revenge.

'Just one last final thing. About Miss Massey's men friends. Can you tell me anything about them?'

Adams stared at him. 'That's entirely too intimate and private. I won't respond to it.'

'It could give us a good lead to where she might be.'

'It isn't exactly a tactful thing to ask of her ex-husband, you know.'

Roehmer spread his hand. 'Try to help me, Mr Adams.'

'I don't keep tabs on her relationships,' Adams said curtly and stood up.

But when they were at the door, he suddenly said, 'I don't know what Julian has told you, or is likely to tell you, about Nella's relationships with men, but he's prejudiced, he doesn't even begin to understand her.'

Adams paused, his head lowered, his brow furrowed, as if struggling to decide whether or not to go on. Roehmer waited silently, with a neutral expression on his face.

Adams looked up. 'She's known a lot of men. But no matter what Julian may say, she's not – to use his own words – wayward. Yes, she falls in love too often and too easily. I could tell you it's because there wasn't enough love in her early life, but I'd be psychoanalysing again. She falls in love because love is the essence of her needs, her dependency.' Abruptly, Adams fell silent. 'I'm not going to say any more.'

Roehmer waited, but Adams's lips were pressed together obstinately. After a moment he put out his hand and said, 'You've been very forthcoming, Mr Adams.' It was a phrase he had picked up somewhere along the line, and used with a certain type of person. 'I appreciate your help.'

Adams held on to his hand. 'Will you let me know what develops?'

'Absolutely. The instant we locate her I'll give you a call.'

'You're sure she's all right? I mean, nothing has happened – '

'You don't have to worry, Mr Adams, it's just a routine case.'

After seeing Detective Roehmer out, Laurence Adams put his set of the six Brandenburg concertos on the record player. Bach was his 'worry music'. It had a soothing effect on him, or he thought it did, which came to the same thing. He weighed pouring Roehmer's barely touched sherry back into the bottle but instead, uncharacteristically, downed it in a single gulp.

Roehmer had said that there was nothing to worry about. But, of course, he *was* worried. While it was true that Roehmer had seemed to be quite open with him (he had been impressed by the man's style; it was his first contact ever with a policeman, and he had been surprised to find him not at all tough or authoritarian, but serious and intelligent), many of his questions had been disturbing, not only for their personal nature but because they seemed more deeply probing than he would have guessed to be routine in a missing persons enquiry.

The references to money and Nella's relationship with Julian and Agnes had struck him as being more concerned with motivations than with tracing her whereabouts. The questions about Nella's men friends had upset him in a different way. Actually, he had been less than candid in his responses, justifying himself on the grounds that the questions were an invasion of privacy – his and Nella's, both. The truth was that he didn't approve of her friends, those he had met as well as those he had heard about. If asked to describe them in a single word, he would have said that they were 'tainted'. But that opinion, self-serving as he knew it to be, was itself tainted. On a purely objective level, his only entitlement would have been to tell Roehmer that they were quite unlike Laurence Adams, who was responsible, respectable, and, doubtless, predictable and dull.

Or – much more to the point – that he disliked them primarily because Nella liked them better than she liked him. For better or worse, they were Nella's kind of man. He thought he knew what lay at the heart of her attraction to them. He saw it as a primitive form of rejection (and defiance) of Julian's notion of the right kind of man for her: respectable, responsible, essentially predictable and dull. And rich, of course – which was what had disqualified *him* in Julian's eyes.

That point had been established quickly enough in their first meeting.

They had accepted Julian's invitation to dinner at his own insistence and over Nella's strenuous objections. At that, he had been a little slow on the uptake. Learning that Laurence was a college teacher, Julian had said, 'A poorly paid profession.' Laurence had accepted the remark as being sympathetic rather than disparaging, although someone else might have assessed Julian's tone of voice more accurately. It was typical of his tendency – *weakness* was the word his friends used – to interpret an ambiguity in the kindliest possible light.

There had been a single fleeting moment of rapport, when Julian discovered that he, too, was a Princeton man. Julian had been delighted, and wasted no time in scuttling over to the mantel for his Triangle Show picture. Laurence had been appropriately appreciative. He wasn't certain that the man in the picture was really Fitzgerald, but just the thought itself had a degree of charm.

Julian, warming to his subject, said, 'It was always a source of regret to me that I didn't know Scott better. We might have turned out to be the best of friends if we had seen more of each other, especially if we had had the luck to belong to the same eating club. But I was Cap, and Scott, I don't recall, either Cottage or Ivy.'

Nella said, 'Laurence, tell Julian about the officers' rooms at Cottage.'

Julian was impressed. 'You were an officer at Cottage?'

Laurence gave Nella a reproachful look for her mischievousness. 'No. I didn't belong to Cottage. Or to any of the clubs. I used to tutor some of the Cottage officers in their rooms. That's what Nella was referring to.' He noticed that Julian had turned perceptibly cooler, but he pushed on, perhaps superfluously. 'I was a scholarship student.'

If he had simply reinforced Julian's contempt for him as an impecunious schoolteacher, and if any kind of halfway civil relationship had been closed off, that didn't prevent Julian from taking him aside, later in the evening, and urging him to use his influence to 'reform' Nella and instil in her a 'purpose in life'.

'She lacks ambition. She's beautiful, intelligent, and well educated, but she refuses to harness any of that to a useful purpose. Our family has always been what you people call achievers. But Nella just drifts, without a goal in life. She needs to be guided into some worthwhile profession or calling. She's much like her father in that way, but I was able to rescue Philip. I made an architect out of him.'

Aghast at Julian's insensitivity about Philip Massey, Laurence nevertheless managed to make a response. As tactfully as he could, he disavowed any interest in making Nella into something she didn't want to be. Of course, he refrained from adding that her ambitions had been consumed in the fires that destroyed her dancing career.

Those evenings at Massey's apartment, which for Nella were acutely uncomfortable, struck him as merely tedious. He avoided being drawn into arguments with Julian, although at times his normally placid temper was sorely tried. But he liked Agnes, whom he described to Nella as a 'dispassionate Molly Bloom'. Nella had reacted with vehemence: 'Damnit, you can't explain everything in life with a literary allusion.' Molly Bloom to one side, he found Agnes's earthiness and good nature highly agreeable; and her aimless chatter helped defuse antagonisms. It also interested him that Julian, despite his irritation with her babbling, seemed quite fond of Agnes, and that she returned the feeling.

At the end of one of those evenings he had told Nella that, although Julian was a difficult and perverse old man, he loved her very much.

'Love is no excuse,' Nella said forcefully. 'How often do people kill in the name of love? Love is no alibi for tyranny and wickedness.'

Without defending Julian, he tried to tell Nella that she was allowing her feelings about Julian to poison her life. Granted, she had ample grounds for her disaffection, but couldn't she see that she was punishing *herself*?

'If an assortment of shrinks couldn't do it,' she said coldly, 'what gives you the idea than an English teacher who knows more about a bunch of old dead Transcendentalist writers than about life can make an acceptable judgement in the matter?'

At that point their marriage was already sliding dismally downhill. That he loved her wasn't enough; that she loved him a little in return, and liked him more than a little, wasn't enough. The marriage had been a mistake in a very ordinary way: they simply weren't suited to each other, the metabolism of their union was out of kilter.

In the reception room of the municipal marriage bureau, waiting their turn to be joined by the clerk, he had asked, half in jest, half seriously, 'Why are you marrying me?' and she had answered, 'Laurence, I really don't know.' He had taken her response to mean that she didn't know why she was marrying him as opposed to simply living with him, though perhaps if he had been more perceptive – or less self-deluding – he might have seen that she was being literal: she simply didn't know.

In retrospect, he thought that there was a reason, although she probably wasn't aware of it. Her life had been at a particularly low ebb at that moment. Partly because of her problems with Julian, but also due to a recently collapsed relationship with a man. He was convinced that, without realising it, she hoped that marrying him – or marriage itself, which she had never before contemplated with *anybody* – would somehow apply a magical tourniquet to the bleeding away of her youth. In short, she had married him out of desperation. In short, he had caught her on the rebound.

He remembered now, quite suddenly and with an inward groan, the night he had asked her about the men in her life, that pathetic cliché betokening insecurity and a repugnant species of possessiveness. She had demurred, but in the end, worn down by his persistence, she had given in. As he should have known, and as Nella *had* known, he had been hurt and embarrassed by her recital. Had he been so stupid as to expect her to be a virgin?

After they had decided to separate and divorce, she had made an oblique reference to that night. Holding his hand, with a wash of luminous unshed tears in her eyes, she had said, 'You're too damn good, Laurence, that's the trouble. Listen, Laurence, there's a class of woman who, to their sorrow, choose Rhett over Ashley. They can't help it, and, oh, darling, I'm sorry, good-bye.'

The Brandenburg concertos were still running their course on the record player. He had hardly heard a note. The music hadn't soothed him, and he was still worried about Nella.

When he left the precinct house, Roehmer was bushed, but he braced up when he hit the cold night air. The city had a shine to it, and, approaching Massey's building, he recalled a night much like this one when he and Peggy stopped in for a few drinks at the Plaza and then walked home. In the sharp clarity of this night he could visualise them as they walked arm-in-arm: young, romantic, yearning – and randy as hell. They kept deliberately swaying against each other, fired up by the contact. Riding up in the elevator, they felt each other up outrageously behind the stiff back of the elevator man.

He paused on the kerb across the street and his eyes travelled up the building to the eighth floor, to the unfamiliar drapes, and then on the the fifteenth, where, behind the lit windows, he saw not Julian Massey or his red-headed wife but Peggy herself, watching for a glimpse of his arrival.

Let the dead past bury the past.

The doorman, Karl, gussied up like an ex-general in his maroon coat and peaked cap, didn't look all that much older than he had twenty-five years ago. He said he had been on duty the night Nella had last been seen, but continued to regard Roehmer with suspicion even after he flashed his ID. Roehmer wondered if he was trying to place him, if he recognised him from twenty-five years ago. More likely it was only the kind of superior look servants put on when they dealt with the lower orders.

Karl told him about Nella's departure on Thursday night with a mixture of German precision and outrage. He sat on the ornate bench in the lobby and pantomimed holding a bottle of milk when he told how Nella had berated him.

'Nobody else in this house would do such a thing, they know I have to eat. But that girl, that . . .' His lips moved, searching for an epithet, found none, but made a profanity out of *girl*, spitting it out with malice. 'Then she stood at the door and made me open it for her. Stood there like the Queen of England.'

He muttered something in German. Probably, Roehmer thought, the bad words he couldn't bring himself to say out loud in English.

'You didn't want to open the door for her?' Roehmer said.

'It's my job, I don't mind. But for that person, that *girl*, the terrible way she acted to me . . . And she didn't even live here. In and out, in and out, and never once an appreciation.'

Read *tip*, Roehmer thought. 'But her uncle owns an apartment here . . .'

Karl moved off to open the door for a brisk man who said, 'Good evening, Karl,' and swept by into the lobby. Karl returned.

'Mr Massey is a fine gentleman,' Karl said.

'Mr Massey and his niece get along well?'

The doorman's lips clamped together. The heavy folds of his face took on an obstinate set.

Roehmer said, 'How can you be so sure it was exactly ten twenty-seven when she left the building?'

With a show of contempt for the question Karl said, 'I looked at my watch.'

'What made you look at your watch just then?'

'I look at it all night, maybe a hundred times a night. I like to know what the time is.'

Fair enough, Roehmer thought, there were compulsive time watchers. 'Did she seem particularly upset? Angry?'

'With *me* she was angry. That girl.'

'Did you see which direction she went after she left the building?'

Karl snorted. 'Why should I care which way she went? Straight down, that's where she should have gone.'

'She didn't get into a taxi?'

'I didn't look, I told you.' Something like a smile flitted across Karl's face. 'She's in trouble, that girl? I'm not surprised.'

'She's not in trouble,' Roehmer said. 'Thanks for your help.'

'Not in trouble,' Karl said, snickering. 'That's why a policeman is asking me questions.'

Karl opened the door for him and Roehmer went out into the glistening street.

Part IV

THE SIEGE

Chapter 11

Waiting for the late evening news to come on, Nella tuned into an old movie with a plot as stunningly familiar as scripture. Then she remembered that some of the local channels put their evening news on at ten, but it was already fifteen minutes past the hour and the hard news had been supplanted by features. She switched back to the movie. When a commercial came on, she got up and stood to one side of the window overlooking the backyard. The two rear windows of the Pleasant Times Bar and Grill glowed with the dullest possible light short of no light at all. Probably a forty-watt bulb in each, barely enough illumination to enable an exigent beer drinker to locate the toilet bowl.

She tried to envision Wally and Richard at the centre of the bar, part of the huddle of the regular clientele, and, facing them, McGarry the bartender with his clean white shirt and handsome Irish face. It was the second time they had visited the bar since Thursday night. The first had been Saturday night, after they had sent off the kidnap note. McGarry had mentioned her. Specifically, he had asked Wally if he had 'scored with that chick the other night'. It was a casual, uninterested question, small talk, on a par with 'How's the wife?' Wally had replied scornfully (she had tested him on annoyance, on resentment, and on disgust, but finally settled on what he did best): 'Would you believe she asked me to pay for it? *Me?* That'll be the day.' Shaking his head: 'Until then, I admit, I didn't make her out for a hooker.' McGarry had said something to the effect that these days there were a lot of amateurs around who liked to pick up pin money. Wally said, 'Wally Cornwall pay for it? Maybe when I'm ninety. I said to her, "Look, lady, that way is the Bowery, maybe you can find some takers there." She took off

heading south, so for all I know she was taking my advice.'
A big laugh from Wally, a crisp nod from McGarry. End
of conversation. The bit about the Bowery had been an ad
lib, they hadn't rehearsed it, but he was so pleased by it
that she didn't have the heart to criticise him for departing
from the script. In his own considered opinion he had
carried off his role to perfection, and Richard agreed with
him. Well, Richard would applaud Wally spitting; still,
there didn't seem to have been any harm done.

But the acid test of his ability to be plausible would
come later, after the story broke, and especially when
McGarry saw her picture in a newspaper, as surely he
must. She was less concerned about Richard. He was
habitually silent and deadpan. But the combination of
Wally's vanity and talkativeness might pose a risk. When
the time came, she would have to warn him about the
dangers of ad-libbing.

She returned to the sofa and settled in. The movie was
plodding along predictably. She looked at her watch.
Ten-thirty, still a half hour to the news. Time was
creeping, as it had done all day long. She had begun to
worry seriously about the failure of the kidnapping story
to surface. She had even expected it to break yesterday,
Monday, although, to stretch a point by allowing for the
slowness of the mail, Julian might not have received the
letter. But he surely must have it by now. From noon on
she had been glued to the radio. When the early-evening
television news had come and gone, the uncertainties that
had been gnawing at her all day became oppressive. To
make it worse, she had been obliged to maintain a stance
of cool confidence in order to appease Wally's anxiety. It
was a relief when he and Richard had gone off to the
Pleasant Times.

That the story of the kidnapping wouldn't become
immediately public hadn't occurred to any of them on
Saturday morning, after they had decided to take the first
step. At breakfast she had played the professor, with an
attentive class of two hanging on her words as if she were
the final authority on kidnapping, which, in a way, she
was, learning, in the process of teaching, that she

possessed a practically flawless memory for everything to do with the subject that she had ever seen on television or in the movies, or read in books and newspapers. Wally and Richard had seen the same movies and TV shows, of course, which gave them the same background as she, and, in some ludicrously logical, self-fulfilling way, put the imprimatur on her expertise. We are, after all, she had thought, the sum of what we read on a page and view on a screen, and all that separated a real and a fictional kidnapping was the actual doing thereof. The difference between her and Wally and Richard – and her superiority – resided in her fluency and the surpassing purity of her motivation; their goal was merely money, hers was vengeance. So her passion took the lead and they followed, spurred on by greed.

She had awakened that morning feeling light-headed and eager, even frivolous, to the sound of Wally's grunting. My own personal cockcrow, she thought, and forgave herself the pun. She scampered to the foot of the bed and watched Wally doing his effortless push-ups. She wished him good morning but he was too preoccupied to do more than stare at her glassily. She slipped out of bed and went to the bathroom. She removed her underthings from the shower-curtain bar – if she knew she was to die the next morning she would still wash out her panties the night before – and stepped into the shower. She lathered herself with Wally's expensive soap-on-a-string, shampooed with Wally's expensive proteinaceous shampoo, and dried her hair with Wally's professional-type blower.

When she turned off the blower, she heard a knocking at the door. Wally was outside, sweating copiously, his skin a rosy glow, a scowl on his face.

'Man, you take all day. It's no good to cool down too much after exercise.'

'I'm finished. I'll get breakfast started, then we can talk. Okay?'

'Richard is making breakfast. You better put something on.'

From the bedroom, she heard kitchen sounds and smelled brewing coffee. Putting on her jeans and sweater, it occurred to her that she would somehow have to get some fresh clothes for the siege. Couldn't run a major kidnap operation smelling like a henhouse, could you?

Richard was busy at the sink in the tiny kitchen. She said good morning and he responded inaudibly. He was wearing grey slacks covered by an apron tied around his middle and a dark blue sports shirt with a red, white, and blue stripe on the collar. He was beating eggs in a large flat bowl – hadn't these two ever heard of cholesterol? – his thin face austere, even ascetic, in profile.

'Can I do something to help?'

He glanced upwards from the eggs and shook his head.

'Let me set the table.'

He gave her suggestion a moment's thought before saying hesitantly, 'Okay.'

She asked him where the place mats were and he pointed to the cabinet standing against the wall in the foyer. Talky Richard. He kept glancing at her worriedly while she placed the mats. Chrissake, Richard, it isn't all that difficult to do. But she lined up the mats precisely flush with the edge of the table. Behind her, she heard the bathroom door open and then the patter of Wally's bare feet.

As silent as Richard, she went back to the kitchen for plates, cups, and saucers. Foraging for flatware, she opened the wrong cupboard drawer. Richard pointed to the right one. The flatware was cheap stainless steel, faultlessly stacked in a compartmented plastic tray. Her eye was caught by an old cleaver with a rough wooden handle and a sharp heavy blade worn in the centre by long usage. It was the only implement in the drawer that was not of recent vintage, and the only one with character. She picked it up.

'This is a beautiful old thing, Richard. Where did you get it?'

'It was my mother's.'

'It's beautiful.'

He nodded, as if to thank her, and said shyly, 'It's one of the few things of hers that I have.'

Grendel loves his mother. Touched, feeling that she

had clumsily invaded his private sorrows, she returned the cleaver to the drawer. She carried the dishes and the flatware to the table and placed them with such finicky care that even Richard would have to be satisfied.

He was. He gave her a vote of confidence: 'You can put out the orange juice, if you want.'

She poured the juice, making sure that not a drop spilled on the table.

'You like French toast?' Richard said.

She nodded, and watched him butter a skillet and then place several slices of bread in the eggy mixture in the flat bowl.

'I'll get it started,' Richard said. 'Be done just when Wally gets here.'

'You know that, Richard – exactly how long it takes him to get ready?'

He looked at her in surprise. 'Certainly.'

He had dark brown impenetrable eyes that the spareness of his face made seem larger than they actually were. She watched him slide basted bread off the end of a spatula into the skillet.

'Aren't you driving your cab today?'

'Day off.'

Four pieces of bread in the skillet. Richard, using the edge of the spatula, squared them off with the precision of a fussy sergeant dressing up the awkward squad. She said, 'Did Wally speak to you last night?'

He gave her an impatient look. Did he hate the idea? But he had said *why not*. Ah, Nella, don't you get it? You're cluttering up the kitchen with unnecessary talk, right? You *knew* Wally had spoken to Richard last night, right? Only a fool asks a question he knows the answer to. Right!

But eagerness pushed her on. 'What do you think of it?'

He lifted an edge of a slice of bread with the spatula and peered at the underside. He shrugged.

Well, Richard, while it's conceivable that some people might equate the importance of a kidnap plot with a slice of French toast, still it rates more than a shrug, if only something like, 'Sounds okay.'

163

She said, 'Does it sound okay to you?'

'Sure.'

Okay, Richard, I know your type: hero's friend, strong, silent, true-blue, ready in a pinch to lay down your life for your pal. He became aware that she was staring at his spare, studious profile and he averted his head. Invasion of privacy again. Sorry, Richard. She redirected her gaze to the frying squares of bread, and applauded silently when he flipped each over neatly, and squared the lot over again.

Wally came in from the bedroom. He was wearing a Japanese kimono, and he was glowing with health and beauty.

'The toast is ready,' Richard said.

Bravo!

Wally ate more or less in silence, barring a few observations about the weather and the toast. She bottled up her anxiety – have to respect a man's morning habits – and made a brave show of enjoying her toast for Richard's sake, not that he would show his disappointment if she didn't. But when Wally had finished his coffee, he set the matter to rights, and without milking the suspense.

'Well, when do we get started?'

Ah, Wally, a thousand thanks, I could kiss you, I *would* kiss you except that now I have officially become an arch-criminal, a mastermind, and such a person doesn't kiss his co-conspirators during business hours.

Suppressing her excitement, she said crisply, 'Immediately. As soon as we clear the dishes away.' She saw Wally frown, and gravely amended the proposition. 'Right after you've been to the bathroom.'

Richard went to the kitchen for the coffee urn and refilled their cups.

She said, 'First item is a letter to Julian. It begins something like this: I have your daughter, don't contact the police or I'll kill her . . .'

She had thought of the first-person singular during the night, but 'daughter' simply popped out, a blessed improvisation.

'Daughter,' Wally said. 'I thought you said you were –'
He scowled with suspicion and she smiled at him
encouragingly, holding her smile until, at last, a light
dawned in his eyes. He turned to Richard, beaming. 'This
kid is a brain, Richard. You get the point?'

Richard nodded, but Wally told him anyway.

'First, saying *I* instead of *we*, which makes it look like
there's only one kidnapper, and throws them off the trail
of *us*, you and me.' He paused. 'But why should anybody
think it was us, anyway?'

'They won't,' Nella said firmly. 'It's just a red herring
to get them thinking in terms of a single kidnapper.'

Wally nodded. 'And the part about the daughter, to
throw them off *your* trail. Like, if you kidnapped yourself
you would know you weren't the daughter.' He laughed
gleefully. 'Richard, I think we're gonna be rich. Those are
two real clever bits – right?'

'Good,' Richard said guardedly.

Stop rolling around the floor in ecstasy, Richard. But
she realised that he recognised, correctly, that these were
just a couple of tangential details; the hard-core stuff was
yet to come.

'The note to your uncle,' Wally said. 'We write it with
letters we cut out of a magazine, so there's no handwrit-
ing. I got all these beefcake magazines – '

'No,' Nella said. 'Nothing that might be identified with
you, however remotely.'

'Right again,' Wally said. '*Playboy*. Richard has a stack
of *Playboys*.'

'Does he subscribe to it?' Nella said. God, I think of
everything. I'm an instinctive criminal, a deluxe nit-
picking Queen of Crime. 'Because if it's by subscription
. . .' Then it would narrow the field of suspects down to a
bare couple of million or so and that would be cutting it
too fine – right, Nella?

Wally assured her that Richard bought the magazines
on the news-stand. Okay, agreed, we go with *Playboy*.
They moved on. The next order of business, by popular
demand, was money. And it shook her sense of reality,
almost toppled the whole idea into fantasy. She had had to

cope from the start with the idea that, no matter how deadly earnest she was, there was a sense of game-playing about it. But mightn't there be an element of romantic diversion involved in the perpetration of any crime? Didn't the mugger view himself as Robin Hood, as a righter of wrongs (himself the wronged, poor and therefore oppressed), hitting back at a figurative Sheriff of Nottingham every time he put a bullet into the chest of his helpless victim? A lark – Wally, who hadn't the proverbial pot to piss in, tossing around hundreds of thousands of dollars like so much play money. No restraint, no sense of proportion, but maybe he was right: if the criminal was totally sober-sided about a crime, he would never attempt it.

She felt distanced from the discussion; after all, the reparations she sought were reckoned in another coin than money. But she knew better than to say so; waiving her share of the loot would make Wally and Richard immediately suspicious: Who was so weird as to spurn money? Nella the Avenger, that's who. But she would take her third, and disburse it for good works: anti-nuclear, antipollution, a lesser anti or two, a bit set aside to finance the unworthy ideas of unworthy young men.

The auction began with Wally setting a floor of half a million. When both she and Richard concurred, he promptly reconsidered. You had to take inflation into account. At a third of half a million, the price of everything being what it was, the best he could hope for was a dingy little health club without even wall-to-wall carpeting, much less monogrammed towels, and he wasn't about to settle for a no-class place like that. It had to be a half million apiece. Unamused by his pretensions, she played the skinflint, arguing that Julian might have trouble raising that much cash; wealthy people had their assets tied up in investments. They bargained spiritedly back and forth. Richard was silent for the most part. Richard was a realist, at least more of one than Wally – and than herself? – because he had been in prison, because having to put in a twelve-hour stint behind a wheel in traffic, he knew the value of money.

In the end Wally compromised. 'A million. The risk we're taking, we can't afford to take a penny less than a million dollars.'

She heard the figure with a sense of comic despair. It had the dull ring of cliché. Not worth getting out of bed in the morning for less than a million – right? Still, what possible difference could it make to her? Julian could *afford* a million.

'Okay, Wally, a million.'

Her sudden capitulation gave Wally pause. He said anxiously, 'He'll pay it, won't he?'

She was certain that Julian would do anything in his power to shield her from being hurt, at least in the physical sense. He cared for her deeply, with a fierce possessive passion, no matter what the turbulent state of their relationship. He had cared for Poor Philip, too, and had never been able to forgive him for the wasteful stupidity of his death, for depriving Julian Massey of a valuable piece in his collection. Julian's version of love, but it could be counted upon.

She said, 'He'll pay if he's truly convinced that I'm in mortal danger.'

Wally said explosively, 'If? You're not *sure*? Then chrissake, let's forget the whole thing.'

Richard nodded in agreement.

'You don't get money just for the asking,' Nella said. 'You have to make the victim's family believe that the victim is in peril, in actual danger of being killed. If we can do that, he'll pay the ransom, no question about it.'

Wally was relieved. 'If that's all you're worried about, I don't see the problem.'

She wanted to pursue the point, to impress Wally with the thought that it wasn't all a cakewalk, but just then she was suddenly stunned by an omission so chillingly obvious that the realisation of her own stupidity left her devastated. How could she have overlooked the fact that she had been seen at the Pleasant Times? It was either a wanton carelessness that put in serious question her own credentials as a kidnapper, or else she had been so eager to proceed that her subconscious had suppressed it. In either case, it seemed to put an end to the kidnapping before it had fairly begun.

Wally, reading the consternation in her face, said, 'Now what's bothering you?'

She told him, but to her surprise he dismissed her concern with a confident wave of his hand. 'No problem. They keep that place dark like a dungeon. No chance anybody could have seen or recognised you.'

'You saw me, didn't you?'

'I knew what you looked like – right? Besides, I halfway expected you to follow me.' He smirked. 'When you came in the door I recognised the way you walked, and more or less your shape. I *knew* it was you, even though I couldn't see your face at all.'

'I saw yours and Richard's.'

'We were in the light. The only light in the joint is where McGarry works behind the bar.'

I want to believe you, Wally, I really do. But she was still shaken. Careless, Nella, very careless.

'Take my word for it,' Wally said. 'Nobody came close to seeing you.'

'The bartender did.'

Wally was momentarily deflated, then began a rambling rationalisation that McGarry was no threat. At the far end of the bar, where she had been sitting, it was so dark that even nose-to-nose McGarry wouldn't have been able to see what she looked like; McGarry was a bartender, and bartenders only had eyes for people's money; bartenders were famous for minding their own business. Anyway, the fact that she left the bar in his company didn't mean he kidnapped her; *anybody* could have kidnapped her . . .

His reasoning was pathetic, but she wanted desperately to believe it. Wally seemed subdued. He didn't believe it himself.

Richard broke his silence. 'McGarry won't say nothing.' He paused for a long moment while she and Wally regarded him hopefully. 'Because if he talked it would bring the cops.'

Wally hit himself on the forehead with his cupped palm

and laughed out loud. 'Sure, sure – how could I be so dumb. Great thinking, Richard!'

'I don't understand,' Nella said, but she felt encouraged by Wally's renewed air of confidence.

Richard said patiently, 'If he recognised you that night, and if he talked about it after the kidnapping came out, it would bring the cops around. That's the one thing he don't want.'

'Why not?'

'He hates cops. Really *hates* them.'

'*Really* hates them,' Wally said. 'Tell her, Richard.'

'He used to be on the force,' Richard said, 'but they kicked him out. So he hates cops. It's the one thing you ever hear him say right out – how much he hates cops.'

'Why did he get kicked out?'

Wally, chortling, said, 'Tell her, Richard.'

'He claims they framed him. Raid on a bookie shop, and some of the money disappeared. McGarry said he never touched a penny, that the sergeant put it in his own pocket and then jobbed him.'

'Did he go to prison?'

'Departmental trial. They found him guilty, but his "rabbi" put in a word for him so they didn't get him indicted, just kept it in the family and booted him off the force and killed his pension. The pension part, that's what really burned him up.'

It was at least logical that a man who had reason to hate the police might go to any length, even take pleasure, in withholding information from them. But what convinced her was Richard's calm certainty. Your strong, silent man was by definition not a bullshitter. And so she put aside her doubts – because that was what she wanted to do, because she was hooked on going on.

A half hour later they began the composition of the kidnap note. While she cut the letters out of a copy of *Playboy*, Richard – who turned out to be the most manually dextrous of the three – pasted them into place on a sheet of paper, wearing thin rubber gloves.

'No prints,' Wally said. 'Great.'

Great, you're great, Nella, and you didn't even see it in a movie, but thought it up all by yourself. Oh, it's great, Nella, it's great, you may have found your true vocation at last. Even Julian would be proud of you if he knew. No effete nonsense like ballet dancing, no precious shot-in-the-dark like Eau Boy, but a real solid money-making proposition.

Wally was so deeply absorbed that he postponed his bowel movement until the letter was finished.

With a swell of banal music the banal movie finally ended. Nella sat fast during the spate of commercials that followed. They gave way, at length, to the appearance of the newscaster, who, just prior to another batch of commercials, read off the highlights of the news to come: President charges Congress with indifference to nation's interests. Two gangland-style murders in Gerritsen Beach. Longshoremen threaten to tie up East Coast shipping. Review of new Broadway play.

Where was the kidnapping of the Park Avenue heiress? Surely it was more important than the everyday slaughter of a couple of Mafiosi? Swallow your pride, Nella, it'll turn up.

But she knew it wouldn't. When the hard news was exhausted, and nothing was left but sports and the weather, she pounded the sofa cushions with her fists in rage and frustration. Julian was not rising to the bait. Damn you, Julian, damn you. She had expected him to run directly to the police, but somehow she had miscalculated. At one point Wally had suggested a phone call to Julian, because a letter took too long; he was in a hurry to get his million. But she hadn't been certain that either Wally or Richard could carry off a phone conversation convincingly. She had reckoned that a slower development, using the mails, might keep the story alive over a longer period of time, and increase the pressure on Julian. Thus far, Julian had not followed the script.

Take yourself in hand, Nella. No need to panic. She smoothed out the indentations her fists had made in the sofa cushions and pondered. It took only a short while to see the obvious solution. She turned off the television and got to work.

By the time Wally and Richard returned, a little before midnight, she had everything ready: the script printed in block letters so it would be easy to read, even the telephone numbers of the three daily newspapers.

Wally, who had reported happily that McGarry hadn't mentioned her again, turned despondent when she told him the story hadn't been on the TV news. 'He's screwing us. If he won't say anything, we're out of business. He's got us by the balls.'

She showed him the script. 'It's simple. If Julian won't tell, *we* will.'

Wally was tickled, but sobered up for a moment to worry about whether or not the calls could be traced.

That's an easy one, Wally, it turns up on the tube at least three times a week. 'It takes anywhere from ten minutes to more than an hour to trace a call. We'll be off the phone in thirty seconds.'

She made Wally read the script through twice, then dialled the number of the *Daily News* for him so that he could hold the sheet of paper in his right hand. The phone was answered on the second ring.

'City desk,' Wally said.

Nella couldn't hear what the operator said, but she was sure it was almost identical with what she had indicated in the script: *Do you have news to report?*

'Yes,' Wally said, and waited. Then he cleared his throat and said, 'Got a tip for you. Somebody snatched the daughter of Julian Massey, the architect. Check it out.'

Nella broke the connection. 'Did he say anything?'

'He said, "Who is this?" How'd I do?'

She kissed him smackingly on the mouth. 'You were terrific, Wally.'

'I wasn't nervous, not the least bit nervous.'

'You should have been an actor,' Nella said. 'Okay. *New York Times* is next. Ready?'

Chapter 12

'Leftenant Kojack wishes to see you,' Murphy said when Roehmer arrived in the squad room in the morning. 'Right away.'

'Not before my coffee,' Roehmer said.

'Before your coffee. He wants to tell you about the rings under his eyes.'

Roehmer tossed the copy of the *Daily News* on to his desk and went to the lieutenant's office. Boyd was talking on the telephone. There was a copy of the *News* on his desk. Roehmer waited patiently, thinking about coffee, until the lieutenant hung up.

'You want to see me, Lieutenant?'

'You have a good sleep last night?'

Fair, Roehmer thought, if you didn't count being wakened by Mary, who had been whimpering because of a drunken nightmare and had to be soothed for over an hour before she calmed down sufficiently to be able to go back to sleep. But maybe that was more detail than the lieutenant wanted to hear.

'So-so, Lieutenant.'

'Well, mine was a lot worse than so-so. I got three calls after midnight from the medias.'

Roehmer watched the lieutenant make a production of rubbing his eyes. Actually, the rings under his eyes didn't seem any worse than usual.

'They called the precinct house and some shithead gave them my number. They wanted to know if it was true that the Massey girl had been kidnapped.'

'Who gave them your number?'

'I'll find out, believe me, and I'll kick some ass.'

'That old man, Massey, is going to be pissed off.'

'Is he? Well, he can kiss my ass. The medias called him, and he told them to call the precinct house.'

'And you told them it was true about the kidnap?'

'What choice – lie to the medias when I would be caught out? What I want to know is, who called those newspapers in the first place.'

'In the *News* it says that the caller was an anonymous male voice.'

'See if you can't think of who that anonymous male voice might be.'

The lieutenant was leaning across his desk and staring. Roehmer said, 'The kidnapper. I can't think of anyone else.'

'Well, I can, and I didn't get a good night's sleep like you did. *Maybe* the kidnapper. But if not the kidnapper, who? You know what I mean, Roehmer?'

'I know what you mean, but you're wrong, Lieutenant. It wasn't me. What would I call them for, what's the sense of it?'

'The sense of it is that some cops have been known to tip off the medias in return for a consideration. You wouldn't do that, would you, Roehmer?'

'No,' Roehmer said. He looked directly into the lieutenant's eyes. 'I don't do things like that. Not *me*.'

'Not you.' The vertical vein in the lieutenant's forehead stood out in relief. 'But somebody else. You care to name who might do something like that?'

Roehmer shook his head. 'I don't know any cop who would do a thing like that.'

'Yeah, well . . .' Boyd leaned back in his black cracked-leather chair, his eyelids drooping. 'Jesus, after the third of those papers called I was wide awake, and so goddamn pissed off I couldn't get back to sleep. Okay, let's say it was the kidnapper who called. What motivated him?'

'I'll admit I was surprised when I picked up the paper this morning, but when I thought about it, I could see it was a smart move. He guessed we were holding up the story, so he tipped the papers off. It's a smart move.'

'That's how you figure it – a smart move?'

'It puts pressure on this Massey. If nobody knows there's a kidnap, he can be cagey, play a little hard to get. But if the public knows, he don't want to look cold-blooded about what happens to his kin. He feels the pressure and has to respond more.'

The lieutenant grunted. 'Now that it's out, we have to bring in the FBI. It's forty-eight hours.'

'I guess that's the law.'

'See that you co-operate with them. But I don't mean stop plugging. You got any leads?'

'I barely began checking out family and associations. The trouble is, Lieutenant, I don't have to tell you, Murphy and Passatino with their case loads – '

'And then the special agent comes in, and all he has to handle is this one case. Don't get bitter, Roehmer, that's the way the game is played. They're on the same side, just keep remembering that. They're here to help us.'

'I'll try to remember that they're on the same side.'

'Downtown will be calling about this, and I want to have something to tell them, so keep plugging. Jesus, if I get through this day without collapsing . . .'

Roehmer went out to the squad room and asked Murphy and Passatino if they wanted to discuss the case.

'The lieutenant show you his rings?'

'He wanted to know if it was me who tipped off the papers.'

Murphy threw his head back and shook in a pantomime of helpless laughter.

Passatino said, 'What's eating Murphy?'

'It's a very busy day coming up,' Roehmer said. 'You guys got anything for me?'

Murphy had zip. His case load was breaking his balls. He had hoped to find an hour or two to give it, yesterday, but then this battered child thing started to percolate, and by the time that was over he was so bushed he was dropping in his tracks.

'Yeah, you must have gotten rings under your eyes like the lieutenant.'

Murphy started to get sore, but changed his mind and smiled. 'Murphy makes the jokes around here, okay?'

Passatino had contacted the taxicab companies and they had promised to get back to him. He was checking out the Fifth Avenue, Madison, and Lexington bus routes. But if she had taken another bus line, or a cab driven by a driver-owner . . .

Murphy said, 'I'll try to get something going on it today, Rome. But it's like bailing out the ocean with a thimble. We could use another half a dozen men.'

Roehmer reviewed the details of his interviews with Julian Massey and Laurence Adams, and told them about the doorman.

'You can't ever be sure,' he said, 'but the whole thing smells a little fishy to me. Could be a phoney.'

Passatino shook his head. 'To me, something like that, a phoney, seems very far out.'

'I hate to ever have to agree with Passatino,' Murphy said, 'but I call your attention to the kidnappers calling the papers.'

'Yeah, there is that,' Roehmer said. 'Well, I got to get to work.'

But the only thing the call to the papers proved was that the kidnapper – *whoever* – wanted publicity. The inherent weakness of a phoney kidnap was that the threat of death didn't exist, so putting the pressure of public opinion on the family was essential. If his instinct was right, the case was a simple one to break – just refuse to pay the ransom. That is, if he was right. If he was wrong, the girl would die.

In the skin-tight surgical gloves Richard's hands seemed disembodied and vaguely science-fiction. His fingers were long and bony and efficient; they moved unhurriedly, patiently. Only his eyes were quick, scanning the pages of the magazine for an entire word or several letters in sequence that would fit the context of the note.

Nella sat beside him at the table in the foyer, helping him on occasion by collecting discarded bits of pages into a neat pile. Wally sat opposite them with the *Daily News* spread out before him, reading the story on page three over and over, poring over it as if something new might turn up that he had missed in previous readings.

It was a brief story, but it covered the essential points under the heading: PARK AVENUE HEIRESS MISSING:

KIDNAPPING SUSPECTED. The body of the story reported that she had been missing since last Thursday night and that a ransom note had been received by her uncle, the wealthy socialite architect, Julian Massey.

Wally had been put out that the story didn't contain a reproduction of the note, and he complained that her picture didn't do her justice. She remembered the picture; the police or the newspapers must have gotten it from Julian. She had posed for it unwillingly, and looked as grim and ungracious as she felt. Wally was wrong. It did her – or her mood – full justice.

Kidnapping *suspected* – that bothered her. It implied a certain degree of scepticism on the part of Julian, or the police, or both. Neither Wally nor Richard seemed aware of it, and maybe it was only a convention of headline writing. But if either Julian or the police were suspicious that the kidnap might be a fake, she could see rough going ahead.

Her eyes blurred, watching Richard's fingers painstakingly glue a tiny *s* to the sheet of notepaper. Suddenly restless, she got up and walked towards the window. She turned, walked back to the table, then returned to the window. When she came back again, Wally reached out and pulled her down on his lap.

'Relax, baby. There's nothing to be nervous about.'

She said, 'I'm fine, Wally. We're in business now, aren't we?'

'Because if you're nervous,' Wally said, 'I got a real good cure for it.'

He slipped his hand into her sweater – Richard's sweater – and fondled her breasts. She looked warningly towards Richard and stopped Wally's hands.

'Richard? You worried about Richard? Look, it's in the family, Richard don't mind.'

Richard didn't look up from his work.

'Let's go into the bedroom,' Wally said.

'No, not now . . .' Under the thin silk of the kimono his hardening penis rose against her buttocks. Yes, now. She got up and walked to the bedroom. Wally followed, smiling, and shut the door.

In bed, with Wally moving on top of her with his patented slow graceful rhythm, she heard the radio go on in the kitchen. To cover any sounds of passion from the bedroom?

'Ah, Wally . . .' She pressed her mouth to her shoulder to muffle her cries. 'Ah, Wally, now, now's the time for all good men to come. Now!'

Smiling up at her from the bed, Wally said, 'You sure fill out Richard's clothes real good, Nella.'

She hadn't wanted either of them going out to buy women's clothing – your true mastermind thinks of everything – and so she had had to make do with some of Richard's things: a pair of cheap double-knit trousers and a brown crew-neck sweater. Except for a slight snugness of the trousers around her hips, they fitted her well enough.

She pulled the sweater on over her head and combed her hair with her fingers. 'Aren't you getting up, Wally?'

'Soon as you kiss me, baby.'

She kissed his lips and then his limp penis.

'Nice,' Wally said.

He rose from the bed in a single flowing movement as she went out. The radio was droning away on a news station. Richard was sitting back in his chair, resting. The note was finished.

Richard said, without looking at her, 'It came over the radio.'

'It did? What did they say?'

Richard shrugged. 'About the same thing. You want to see the note?'

She bent over the table to read it. No fingerprints – right, mastermind? It was very neatly done; the cut-out letters ran across the page in straight lines, and all traces of glue had been eliminated.

> *These are her clothes –*
> *no charge. The price*
> *for HER is one million.*

'Very good,' Nella said. 'Thanks, Richard.'

He glanced upwards, but his eyes were focused at a

point on the wall past her right shoulder. 'What do you call that coat you were wearing?'

'It's a shearling.'

'The radio said you were wearing a cashmere coat.'

'But you *saw* what I was wearing – '

Wally came in from the foyer, wearing the kimono again. 'What's up?'

'The radio,' Richard said. 'They said she was wearing a navy blue cashmere coat.'

'How come?' Wally frowned. 'Are they trying to pull something?'

She had despised the cashmere coat, simply because Julian had given it to her. Four weeks ago, in a bar in SoHo, she had swapped it for the shearling with some spaced-out young woman who lived in the East Village. The cashmere was probably worth four times the shearling, but she didn't care.

She said to Wally, 'It's a break for us. The police will be trying to find somebody wearing a cashmere coat. So we won't mail the coat now – just the sweater and jeans.'

'Great,' Wally said. 'But how did they get it screwed up?'

'Probably because of Julian. He sees what he wants to see. He's not all that observant to begin with, and since he gave me the cashmere, he assumed I was wearing it.'

Wally beamed. 'I like it.'

'Me too,' Richard said. 'If we don't have to send the coat, we save a lot on postage.'

His caved-in face was expressionless, and so it took Nella a moment to realise that he had made a joke. His first.

It was to be one of the longest, most tiring, and, on balance, disheartening days of Roehmer's career as a detective. Not that he had any high expectations for it from the start: it would just be detective work at its most basic level – plugging, shoe leather, and hoping some lead might pop up.

Murphy had said he would try to check out some people in Massey's building and the help in the nearby buildings

178

on Park Avenue. Passatino would follow up on the taxi companies and bus lines. For himself Roehmer had elected to work the names Massey had supplied him with. It was a short list, consisting mostly of women whom Nella had known at college, which was to say about five years ago, so he didn't expect too much to come of it.

The name at the top of his list was Jane Henley Halworth, who had been Nella's room-mate at Radcliffe for a year. She lived on East Seventy-fourth Street in a handsome brownstone, and she was not in. Roehmer checked his list. One block east and two blocks south, Nancy Newton Carrier lived on the twentieth floor of a high-rise apartment house. After a long conversation over the intercom, with the doorman hovering suspiciously, she agreed reluctantly to see him. The entire interview was conducted at the door. Her cleaning woman was working inside and became sullen when there were visitors; she had, in fact, once walked out because of it. Did he mind?

Perfectly all right, ma'am. When he told Nancy Newton Carrier the purpose of his visit, she gave him a long stare and then threw her head back and laughed loudly and mirthlessly.

'You're in the wrong pew. I wasn't a friend of hers, even at school. Well, maybe I was a *sort* of friend for a *very* short time. I not only haven't seen or spoken to her recently, but I stopped talking to her after the first year at school.'

'I see.' Roehmer shifted his weight in the doorway and waited.

'You might as well know that I didn't *like* Nella. In fact, I detested her. I'm sorry she's been kidnapped, of course, but . . .'

Nancy Newton Carrier began to edge the door shut. She was a pretty young woman, beginning to run to plumpness, and her expression, like her cleaning woman's, was sullen.

Roehmer said, 'Would you mind telling me *why* you didn't like Nella Massey?'

He was prepared to pull back if she balked at the

question, but she surprised him. 'I disliked her because she was not a nice person. She was entirely devoid of a sense of decency about . . . Well, let's just say she had no sense of decency.'

'You were going to say *about* something. I'd appreciate it if you would finish that thought, Mrs Carrier.'

'I'm sorry, I really must go.'

'I appreciate that you don't like to bring up something that might be unpleasant, Mrs Carrier.' He tried a wistful smile. Bulldog Roehmer never quits. 'But if you would just try . . .'

'It's entirely too personal.' She looked at him resentfully, then said, 'Oh, why not? She was the most unscrupulous woman that I've ever met where men were concerned. To put it bluntly, she was a man-stealer. She put out shamelessly, if you know what I mean.'

Nothing here but spite, Roehmer thought. She's been pissed off all these years because Nella Massey took some boy away. He nodded understandingly and waited.

'I'm not a prude, God knows, but Nella went beyond the bounds of ordinary decency. I'm afraid that's all I have to say, in fact I'm sorry I've gone this far.'

Roehmer thanked her for her trouble and took out his list. 'Maybe you can give me some additional names, Mrs Carrier?'

She looked at the list. 'I see most of these people from time to time, and none of them is likely to be any more helpful than me.' She handed the list back to him. 'With the possible exception of Jane Henley, and I doubt that even Jane has seen her in the past few years. But at least she likes – *liked* – Nella Massey, which is more than I can say for any of the others.'

He thanked her again. She nodded curtly and shut the door, then opened it again and said, 'Please don't misunderstand me. I might not like her, but I certainly feel sorry for what's happened and hope she'll come out of it unharmed.'

On the sidewalk he studied his list, and decided on Sharon Weiss Kornblau, back a few blocks west and north. Sharon Weiss Kornblau was not at home. He cut over one street to Seventy-fourth, and this time he was in luck. A dark-haired young woman climbing the stoop with a load of bundles from the supermarket turned out to be Jane Henley Halworth.

Jane Henley Halworth had not heard about the kidnapping, and when he told her who he was and why he wanted to speak to her, her soft brown eyes filled with tears. He sat in her high-ceilinged living room while she put her 'spoilables' in the refrigerator, and then told her as much about the case as she would be able to read in the newspaper. She said she would be glad to answer any questions that might be helpful.

'I saw Nella sporadically for a year or so after college, but much more infrequently after I married. We were very close in college, although we were very different from each other. I was a cheerful kind of a dunce, and Nella . . . well, she had problems. She was a lot smarter than I, but she was unhappy. I felt badly for her. I liked her very much.'

'When did you last see her, Mrs Halworth?'

'Almost two years ago. You know, I was her third room-mate. She didn't get along with the others. But you mustn't read anything into that – it happens all the time at college.' She stopped and looked doubtful. 'But this can't be very helpful, can it?'

'You'd be surprised at how much stuff that seems meaningless turns out to be helpful,' Roehmer said gravely. 'During the period when you were seeing her, did you ever meet any of her friends? I mean *new* friends?'

'It's odd that you should make that distinction. Because actually her new friends were a lot different from the old ones.'

'Different in what way?'

'They were . . .' She looked up at the ceiling, and Roehmer thought: She means a different social class, and she's searching for a way to say it that won't offend me. 'They were different.'

'Did you meet any of them?'

'Just one or two. Oh, and Laurence, of course, her husband. Have you spoken to him, by the way?'

'Yes.'

'He's so nice, isn't he?' She waited for him to nod his agreement. 'And yet it didn't work. It was a mistake.'

'How long were they married?'

'Hardly any time at all. A few months – two or three months.' She hesitated briefly. 'Do you know what I think the problem was? I think the problem was that Laurence was simply too nice. That may sound peculiar, but Nella has never really been attracted to men who are basically nice. I hope you don't think I'm criticising her – it's just the way she was. She knew it too. She once said, half-jokingly, that she was searching for the Bluebeard of Happiness.'

'About those new friends of hers that you met?'

'I met one of them just briefly, and I honestly can't remember anything about him. But the second one, Nella brought him to one of my parties. This is going to sound snobbish, but he just wasn't our type. He was . . .' She wrung her hands. 'Different. We're all, oh, educated, and we move in certain circles, have certain habits, a certain set of conventions.'

Roehmer nodded encouragingly.

'What it adds up to, I guess, is that most of us turned out to be stuffy, more or less as stuffy as we always felt our parents to be. But not Nella.'

'She was different?' Roehmer said.

'She took a different path. After college we got into things like publishing, advertising, social work. Nella didn't want to do any of those things. She just rattled around, taking this odd job or that. When she was younger, she had wanted desperately to be a dancer. It didn't work out, and I think it burnt up her ambition. She didn't particularly want to do or be anything else.'

'Can you tell me about this friend she brought to your party?'

'He was a longshoreman, he worked on the docks, but that isn't the point. He showed up in a sweaty T-shirt, and with his baling hook, but that isn't the point, either. He strutted around, he was abusive, he boasted about people he had beaten up on the docks, about his criminal record.

He was just an all-around bastard, Mr Roehmer, take my word for it.'

'What sort of criminal record?'

She shook her head. 'It was quite a while ago.'

Roehmer took out his notebook. 'Can you remember his name?'

She shook her head again. 'I don't think I ever really knew it. Can I tell you something? In my opinion, Nella knew just how awful this man was, and was going around with him *because* of what he was, deliberately, to punish herself.'

'Punish herself for *what*?'

She looked helpless. 'I can't explain it, it's just a *feeling*.'

When he had asked why Nella Massey kept returning to the apartment of the uncle she hated, Laurence Adams had said it was a form of penance, a way of punishing herself. Meaning what? Too deep, Roehmer, go back to the facts.

'About this longshoreman. Do you think any of the people who were at your party might remember his name?'

'I doubt it very much, but I can phone around and ask.'

'I'd appreciate it.' He put his notebook away and stood up. 'Thank you for being so forthcoming, Mrs Halworth.'

He stopped at a deli on his way back to the precinct house and bought a couple of sandwiches. The squad room was nearly deserted; almost everyone was out working, including Passatino and Murphy. He found six phone messages on his desk. One was from Special Agent S. A. Jones, returning yesterday's call. Too late, forget it. One was from his wife, and one from an assistant district attorney, both with the notation 'want you to call'. Another was from Laurence Adams, phone number but no notation. A Special Agent Charles Fairborn had called and would call again. Julian Massey: the message, in Murphy's hand, read, 'Old guy is pissed off, wants to know how the papers got the story.'

While Roehmer was eating his sandwich, Special Agent Charles Fairborn called. He had been assigned to the

Nella Massey kidnap case, and would like to arrange a meeting to discuss the case. Roehmer said he was looking forward to co-operating with the Bureau, and they arranged to meet at three o'clock at the precinct house. Roehmer phoned the assistant DA, who was out to lunch, but whose secretary told him that an armed robbery trial, at which Roehmer, as one of the arresting officers, was to have appeared to testify, had been postponed. Good. A day in court postponed was a day saved, at least temporarily, maybe even permanently, if a plea bargaining was arranged.

Chewing the last bite of his sandwich, he dialled Laurence Adams's number. Adams's light voice was aggrieved. 'You misled me yesterday, Detective Roehmer.'

'I know,' Roehmer said. 'But I had to – those were my orders.'

'Although, from the line of your questioning, I *suspected* something more.'

Roehmer didn't say anything.

'You know, misleading people hardly helps build trust in the police force. I'm really upset that you felt you had to lie to me.'

'Don't take it personally, Professor, I was lying to everybody.' No, Roehmer thought, you're not entitled to be irritated. 'I felt badly about giving you the runaround. I apologise.'

'Yes, well, all right. But what about Nella? Do you have any clues? Is she in real danger?'

'We have some real good leads we're following up on.'

'I'm very concerned. I'm worried. Is there anything I can do?'

'I don't think so, but thanks anyway.'

'Anything I can do to help. *Anything*.'

For a moment he was tempted to test his theory about a phoney kidnapping against Laurence Adams's insight into Nella Massey's character, but caution held him back. Besides, Adams's feeling for the girl would probably compromise his judgement.

He said, 'Nothing you can do at the moment, but I

appreciate it, and I appreciate you not holding it against me for holding out on you.'

A few minutes later the phone rang again. The caller was the dispatcher for one of the large taxi fleets, and he wanted to talk to Passatino.

'I'm Detective Passatino's partner. You want to give me the message?'

The dispatcher had gone through the route cards the drivers had turned in the night Nella Massey had disappeared. Several of his drivers had picked up fares along Park Avenue at roughly the right time. 'But it's a needle in a haystack. You're going to have to talk to all those drivers personally and hope they remember. You know how many passengers they carry on a good night?'

Roehmer thanked the dispatcher and told him that Passatino would be in touch. Poor Passatino. It meant going down to the taxi garage and showing Nella's picture to a bunch of hackies who hated cops and were anxious to get out on to the street. And this was only one company. Well, that was police work, it was inconvenient.

He checked out his list of calls. Two left: his wife and Julian Massey. He dialled Julian Massey's number. He let it ring half a dozen times before hanging up. But Mary was at home, as he knew she would be. She hardly ever left the apartment except to replenish her stock of liquor.

'How are you feeling, Mary?'

'Much better. Listen, I'm sorry I woke you up last night.'

'Don't worry about it.'

'I wouldn't of, I know how bad you need your sleep, but this dream was terrible, it scared the daylights out of me. This morning I remembered it. You know what it was?'

'I'd like to hear about it, but I got another phone call waiting.'

'Oh.' After a pause she said brightly, 'I only had this one drink today, that's all, and I won't have another one until tonight. That's good, isn't it?'

'Great.'

'You going to be home for dinner?'

'I don't know yet. I'm working on a big case, and I may have to work tonight.'

'Oh.'

'I'll phone and let you know.'

'Phone early, so that if you're coming I can make dinner.'

'I'll do that.'

And he would, though it would make no difference. By the time he got home – whether for dinner or not – she would be sodden, maybe comatose, and he would throw a couple of TV dinners into the oven and try to force her to eat. One of these days she would probably die of malnutrition, the drunk's disease, and there wasn't a thing he could do about it. The time when he might have done something about it was twenty-five years ago, when he had been spending his nights in Peggy Parris's arms. But even then she would probably still have ended up as an alcoholic. It ran in her family.

Special Agent Charles Fairborn turned up just as Roehmer was putting the finishing touches to his report on the Nella Massey case to date. He had handled the kidnapping objectively, without casting any doubt on its legitimacy.

Fairborn was of medium height, handsome and enviably trim in that standard way that was typical of the Bureau. Roehmer recognised a bias in this judgement and, as if to make amends for it, put himself out to be cordial, even effusive, in telling Fairborn how pleased he was to have the Bureau in on the case, and how eager he was to co-operate.

'All I know about it is what I've read in the papers,' Fairborn said. 'Can you fill me in?'

Roehmer handed him the report and made a mild joke. 'You have to make allowances – like all NYPD typewriters, this one doesn't spell too good.'

Fairborn read through the report slowly, without change of expression or comment. When he was finished he said, 'You ought to have somebody change your ribbon for you.'

In addition to dignified salaries and superior resources, Roehmer thought, they even had people to change their typewriter ribbons for them. He said, 'The fellow who changes them is on sick leave, he should be back next week.'

Fairborn said, 'This business in your report about a family quarrel. You don't draw any conclusions. Not significant, in your opinion?'

He wasn't as dumb as he looked, Roehmer thought. Fairborn was gazing at him levelly across the desk. He was probably one hell of a sharp interrogator, with those piercing eyes that could probably go five minutes without blinking. Roehmer pulled at his lower lip thoughtfully before answering.

'Might or might not be. You know how it is.'

Fairborn nodded vigorously, as though Roehmer had said something decisive. But I'm not fooling him, Roehmer thought, he's just playing the game.

'To tell you the truth,' Roehmer said, 'I don't know whether it means anything or not. If those people were PR's or like that, you know, they'd be easy to read, spilling their guts, hollering for God to be their witness and so forth. But people like Massey, they keep it all inside. They don't want the world to spy on their problems, and that makes it tough on a police officer.'

'The kidnapper doesn't even mention a ransom in the note,' Fairborn said. 'He's a pretty leisurely fellow.'

We may be on the same wavelength after all, Roehmer thought. Kidnappers liked to move things along in a hurry. It was a strain to hold somebody captive, not to mention that it was in their interest to dispose of the evidence as quickly as possible, one way or the other. But speed wouldn't matter too much if the victim was a willing one.

He said, 'In one way it's an advantage, we don't have to panic at our end.'

'Do you smell drugs in this?'

'No idea,' Roehmer said. 'No sign of it so far, but you can never tell.'

Fairborn's lids flickered, and Roehmer knew that this business of answering every question with a firm maybe was beginning to annoy him. Well, I have to cover my ass, don't I?

Fairborn said, 'I hope there's nothing to do with drugs, so that we can expect him to at least be rational.' He looked at his watch. 'I'm looking forward to working on this case with you, Detective Roehmer.'

'Me too. You can count on me for a hundred per cent co-operation.'

'I'm due back at the office for a meeting. Why don't we get this thing rolling tomorrow?'

It's supposed to have *been* rolling, Roehmer thought. 'Can't be too soon for me.'

'I've got some paperwork to clear away in the morning. How about noon? My office okay?'

Sure, Roehmer thought, I'll come down to your nice clean office, and maybe if I'm lucky I can meet the ribbon changer. 'Your office at noon, fine.'

'Hey, Roehmer, I got some hot news for you.' The lieutenant was charging out of his office across the squad room. 'It'll make you piss – ' He spotted Fairborn. 'Oh, excuse me.'

'I'd like you to meet Special Agent Fairborn. Lieutenant Boyd.'

Fairborn stood up, and Boyd shook his hand. 'Don't get up,' the lieutenant said. 'Please sit down.'

Manners like a fucking grandee, Roehmer thought. 'He's been assigned to the Nella Massey case, Lieutenant.'

'Good. I hope you have assured him of our fullest co-operation?'

'Yes, sir, I did.'

'You can count on it, Agent Fairborn. Detective Roehmer is the squad's best detective, and he works smoothly with any other law-enforcement agency.' The lieutenant shook Fairborn's hand again. 'See me when you get a moment, Detective Roehmer?'

Certainly, Roehmer thought, just let me run home and put my tux on. 'Yes, sir.'

'I was just going,' Fairborn said.

'Don't let me rush you,' the lieutenant said. 'Look, my door is always open, and anything at all I can do to help . . .' He shook Fairborn's hand for a third time, smiled graciously, and went back across the squad room to his office.

'Pleasant fellow,' Fairborn said.

'A peach.'

Roehmer escorted Fairborn to the street and, not to be outdone, shook his hand twice. Then he went back upstairs and into the lieutenant's office.

'What's he like?' the lieutenant said.

'You know how they are,' Roehmer said. 'Looks dumb, but isn't.'

'They can be helpful. I mean that about being co-operative.'

Roehmer nodded.

'But don't eat his shit. Uphold the dignity of the squad.' Boyd leaned back in his chair and locked his hands behind his head. 'What I wanted to tell you – you got a date at five o'clock with the TV people.'

'Me?'

'We got a media press conference at five, and the TV channels will tape it. You're gonna be a big star, Roehmer.'

'So far as I'm concerned, that stuff is all bullshit.'

'Yeah, I know. But it grows on you, and next thing you know you get peeved if a day goes by without you're on the six o'clock news.'

'It's just a pain in the ass so far as I'm concerned. They ask dumb questions. Can't somebody else do it?'

'I'd take it off your hands,' Boyd said, 'much as I hate it. But the captain named you.'

So, Roehmer thought, I'm a pawn in a little power play between the commander and the lieutenant. He said, 'How am I supposed to handle it?'

'Play it by ear. Just be polite, make sure you don't say too much, and every once in a while throw in the word *perpetrator*. The public expects it.'

*

189

Julian Massey's strident old man's voice echoed unpleasantly in Roehmer's ear.

'Ah, Mr Massey. I'm glad you phoned, sir. I tried to get you earlier today but nobody answered.'

'You couldn't have tried very hard. I was only out for an hour or so.' Massey's voice became fainter as he spoke away from the phone. 'I said I'd do it, Agnes. Now let me alone.'

'About the papers getting the story,' Roehmer said, 'somebody phoned them, probably the kidnapper himself.'

'Those newspaper people woke me out of sleep, but I didn't tell them a thing, not a damn thing. I told them to call the police station, and you people spilled the beans.'

'We had no choice.'

'Why not? Why didn't you just deny it?'

Why didn't *you*, you old fart? 'Well, once the kidnapper phoned, it had to come out sooner or later.'

Massey's voice turned anxious. 'Have you got any news for me?'

'Nothing I can talk about yet,' Roehmer said. 'But there have been some promising developments that we hope will provide us with good leads.'

'What kind of developments?'

'I'd rather not say just yet, and raise false hopes.'

'By now you should have been able to raise some *real* hopes.'

'It's a slow process, Mr Massey, it takes a little time.'

'A slow process.' Massey's voice broke. 'You're taking your time, and meanwhile Nella is at the mercy of God knows what kind of a degenerate thug . . .' Off the phone: 'Please don't interrupt, Agnes.'

'We have a dozen men on the case, trying to track down leads. I assure you, Mr Massey, your case has number one priority in this precinct.'

After a moment of silence Massey cleared his throat and said, 'There's something I want to tell you. I don't think it's worth a damn, but Agnes – Shut up, Agnes, I'm telling him, aren't I?'

'Yes, sir?'

'You asked about some of her new friends the other day, and I said I didn't know any, but I guess I forgot – I do know one of them. His name is Roland Duffield.'

Roehmer asked him to spell it.

'Agnes didn't even know his last name. But I did. You want to know why? Because it was on the cheque I gave him.'

'What cheque would that be, sir?'

Reluctantly at first but with increasing vehemence, Massey told him that this Roland Duffield had conceived the harebrained idea of marketing a cologne called Eau Boy, and Nella had badgered him into lending him ten thousand dollars. Against his better judgement – because it was hard to deny his beloved niece – he had written out a cheque, and the inevitable had happened – the idea flopped, and after spending several thousand, Duffield had decamped with the rest of the money.

'Typical,' Massey said, 'He was typical of the kind of riff-raff my niece associates with.'

'Oh? Do you know some others?'

'He's the only one I ever met, but it isn't hard to guess that the others are just like him. I discouraged her from bringing them to this house.'

'But Duffield came? Can you describe him?'

'Certainly I can describe him – he looks like a fairy, and I'll bet my bottom dollar that's what he is.' Roehmer could hear Agnes's voice saying something off the phone. 'Agnes agrees that he's a fairy.'

'What makes you think he might be involved in your niece's disappearance?'

'I don't know if he is or not,' Massey said testily. 'You wanted to know about her associates, didn't you?'

'Do you know his address?'

Massey spoke off the phone. 'Agnes says he lives – or did live before he ran off – on Hudson Street someplace. She doesn't know the number.'

'Thanks, Mr Massey. I'd like to come by tomorrow afternoon for a fuller description of this Duffield, and also to ask a few more questions about him.'

'There's no need for questions. I've told you everything.'

Dealing with criminals was simple, Roehmer thought; it was the straight people who made police work a thankless job. He said, 'Also, I'd like you to meet Special Agent Fairborn of the FBI. He'll be working on the case with me. Can I bring him along?'

'I suppose so,' Massey said.

'Thanks. Thanks a million, Mr Massey.'

While the television cameras were setting up, Roehmer went out to the john. He combed his hair carefully with water and studied his face critically in the mirror. He closed the top button of his collar and pulled his tie up. The collar was so tight it made him gag. They hadn't yet made a collar that would fit a detective's neck. He went back to the squad room and put on his jacket. Somebody told him to stand with his back to the bulletin board, and somebody else turned on a blinding light.

Chapter 13

If she had suffered a loss of face when the kidnapping initially failed to appear in the news, and recouped after the midnight phone call to the papers, her stock soared to dizzy heights when the six o'clock news came on.

They were number one in the preview. 'Among the stories in the top of the news: A noted Manhattan architect's niece is reported kidnapped.' Wally let out a bray of triumph and gave her a series of unsolicited kisses on the mouth. Even Richard allowed himself a smile. Now the deed is official, she thought, now it's ratified. I am on the tube, therefore I exist.

The commercials ended, and then, with no warning, she was on the screen, the same photograph that had appeared in the newspapers. She felt exposed, naked.

Wally said, 'Jesus, right up there. Isn't that something?'

I'm a newborn media star, Nella thought, pinned up for the entertainment of millions. She found herself looking at the picture critically. Okay, a slender young woman, attractive enough, but the turned-down mouth and the cast of the face was sombre. Shouldn't a media star have the privilege of choosing the picture of her own preference? Julian, you're fired.

'You look great,' Wally said. 'Passionate and sultry.'

That's distemper, Wally, but never mind. 'If I had known I was going to be on the tube, I'd have combed my hair and brushed my teeth.'

'There it is!' Wally was at the edge of the sofa seat, pointing at the screen.

A disembodied hand, trembling slightly, held up the kidnap note to the camera lens.

'Will you look at that!' Wally was laughing with excitement. 'That's your work, Richard, take a bow, you're famous.'

Richard was watching the screen intently, too absorbed to respond.

'Earlier today, Julian Massey, barricaded in his luxurious Park Avenue co-operative, refused to see or speak to reporters.'

A camera focused on the entrance to the building, then climbed upwards to the fifteenth-floor windows.

'So that's the building,' Wally said. 'It's like a fortress.'

In the outer lobby a crowd of clamorous reporters and photographers milled around a doorman, who kept shaking his head and saying that Mr Massey wasn't at home to them.

Julian's picture flashed on the screen. It was an old newspaper photo, black and white, grainy. It had been taken twenty years ago, before his hair had turned completely white.

'He *looks* like a mean old bastard,' Wally said. 'I don't like his looks.'

The announcer accompanied the picture with a thumbnail biography: '. . . distinguished socialite family . . . wealthy architect . . . Cosgrove Building, Bronson Arcade . . .'

Abruptly, on a diapason of noisy voices, the camera shifted to the Eighteenth Precinct, where a pair of large men stood at bay before a pressing mob of microphones and cameras. 'Captain Peter Lafferty, commander of the Eighteenth Precinct, and Detective William Roehmer.'

In the questioning that followed, the captain was silent. After a while the cameras focused mainly on Detective Roehmer.

'Will you look at the jacket on him?' Wally said jovially. 'Checks and stripes both, what a clown.'

Detective Roehmer, his expressionless face trickling sweat under the TV lights, answered all the questions that were thrown at him with economy and what seemed to be candour. Nella watched him with interest. He was her antagonist, an impersonal partner, now, with Julian. He didn't seem to be the least bit clownish, despite the ridiculous sports jacket that was far too tight across his chest and shoulders. His features were heavy, his skin rough, his nose broken just below the bridge. But his eyes redeemed the face from brutishness. They were large, intelligent, and, she concluded, stained with sins and regrets.

Yeah, sure, Nella, you're a pushover for eyes with regrets in them – and how many of them seduced you into misplaced affection and eventual sorrow? Well, in this instance she was safe enough: Detective Roehmer was the enemy.

A reporter asked if Nella was in the hands of a professional kidnapper.

'I don't know. Usually kidnappers are amateurs.'

'You have any idea why the kidnapper called the newspapers himself?'

'Maybe he figured you fellows needed some help in getting the story.'

The camera flashed to the captain, scowling at Roehmer's levity.

The man who had asked about the kidnapper's phone call demanded to know if the police had been suppressing the story.

Roehmer shook his head. 'No, sir.'

'Since Nella Massey is not a famous person *per se*, or widely known to be wealthy, does that suggest that the kidnapper might be someone she was acquainted with?'

'It's possible. We're looking into her associations.'

'Any leads?'

'Nothing solid yet, but the investigation has just begun.'

'Any idea why the kidnapper didn't mention ransom money?'

'I guess they're not in a big hurry.'

'You said "they". Does that mean you think there's more than one kidnapper?'

Roehmer shook his head. He was sweating more heavily now; a series of droplets, like beads on a string, hung on his cheeks. 'We haven't got any information to that effect.'

'Do you *think* there's more than one?'

'Change the subject,' Wally said.

'In a kidnapping it's probably harder for a single perpetrator to handle the victim. He'd have to sleep, for instance, but he could tie her up. It's been done.'

'In the Getty case, and some others, there was a question as to whether the kidnapping was legitimate or not. Does that question arise here?'

Wally prodded Nella with his elbow. She said, 'Don't worry. They're just fishing.'

Roehmer dabbed at his face with his handkerchief. 'Far as we know, it's legitimate.'

He wasn't looking at the camera, Nella thought, but through it, beyond it, and with an expression that seemed to combine at the same time challenge and appeal. And even after his image had faded out, a beat-up middle-aged man with a demotic New York accent and an intelligence that hid itself under a layer of professional stolidity, she couldn't quite shake off the impression that he had been reaching out to her: *Roehmer to Nella: Is it really a kidnapping?*

At five minutes past six Roehmer stood on the west side of Fifth Avenue at Sixty-eighth Street with the park at his back, waiting for MTA bus number 1988. It wasn't due for another fifteen minutes, but bus schedules weren't all that precise. So, because he was anxious not to miss it, he was obliged to endure the cold, biting wind that rolled up leaves, grit, and people before it. Across the street a doorman, warm and secure in the lobby of his building, was sneaking a smoke, cupping his cigarette in his palm and opening his glass door every once in a while to push the smoke out into the street.

Roehmer jogged in place to keep warm. He was still damp from the press conference, although it had taken place an hour ago. He had sweated as if he had been in a sauna, a combination of stage fright and the heat of the TV lights. Afterwards the TV people told him he had come across very well. Boyd, who had watched from the sidelines, had told him kiddingly – but with an undertone of envy – that he was on the road to stardom.

A steady stream of traffic was flowing southwards on

Fifth, but he couldn't spot anything in the distance that looked like a bus. He checked out his watch – ten minutes past six – and then checked it again to make sure it hadn't stopped. He made a sound of disgust. He was over-anxious. It would probably add up to nothing. Still, it was a promising lead and, coming this early in the case, could turn out to be a real lucky break.

The MTA dispatcher had phoned about ten minutes after Passatino had left for the day. Passatino would have felt honour-bound to follow up, so Roehmer was glad he was gone. He preferred to handle it himself.

'There's this driver, Carter Robinson,' the dispatcher said. 'He's sure he had the girl on his bus.'

'What time?'

'Around ten thirty or forty, thereabouts. He recognised her from the pictures your partner gave me.'

Too easy, Roehmer had thought. 'Is he sure? Hundreds of people ride his bus.'

'No, they don't on Fifth Avenue in the Sixties at that time of the night. Besides, he had a particular reason for remembering her. She gave him a hard time.'

'What kind of a hard time?'

'Listen,' the dispatcher said, 'what are you grilling *me* for? I didn't see her. Talk to Robinson, that's what you want to do.'

'How can I get hold of him?'

'Walk over to Fifth Avenue and catch him on his southbound run. He's due at Sixty-eighth Street at six twenty, give or take a few minutes.'

Roehmer had phoned Mary before he left the precinct house. The phone had rung eight times before she answered in a slurred, slow-motion voice.

'I have to check out a lead before I can get home. Figure an hour or so. Okay?'

'Okay?'

'Pay attention,' he said sharply. 'Listen to me, Mary. I have to work for another hour and then I'll be home. You got that?'

She began to sob.

'Don't cry, Mary. Chrissake, there's nothing to cry

about. I'll be home at seven thirty. Listen. I'm going to be on the television at six o'clock.' He waited for a response, but she went on sobbing. 'Don't you want to see me on the TV?'

She began to babble. He couldn't make any sense out of what she was saying.

'I'll be home about seven thirty. Stop crying. And for Godssake, don't have anything more to drink.'

He slammed down the receiver and left. By the time he had walked a block or two, he realised that he should have stopped to take a leak. In this cold weather he could get caught short. He thought of going back to the House, but he didn't want to take a chance that the bus might show up ahead of schedule. By a quarter past six he was hurting, so he climbed over the retaining wall into the park and peed, bending his knees so that he couldn't be seen, meanwhile watching the street. If he saw the bus coming, he could cut himself short if he had to, zip up, and get over the fence before the damn thing passed him by. But it was another ten minutes after he got back to the kerb before the bus showed up. He flagged it down and read the number: 1988. He got on. The bus was about three-quarters full, and it was nice and warm.

'Mr Robinson?' He leaned against the coin box and looked behind the partition that protected the driver from the distracting lights in the interior of the bus. 'Carter Robinson?'

'That's me,' the driver said, steering into the flow of traffic. 'Who might you be?'

'Detective William Roehmer.' He flipped open his ID. The driver looked at it and nodded. 'Your dispatcher told me I could pick you up.'

'Pick me up? What you think I done?'

'It's about Nella Massey – the kidnapped girl?'

Robinson said, 'Knew her the instant I saw that picture.'

'Are you sure, sir?'

A buzzer sounded in the bus. Robinson eased towards the kerb. A passenger hopped off, and the bus swung out into the traffic again.

Robinson nodded his head vigorously. 'Damn girl made such a unholy fuss, be a year before I forget her.'

'What kind of fuss?'

'Who kidnapped her must got his hands full with that girl.'

'What kind of fuss?'

'Surprise me if anybody pay any money to get *her* back. How much they asking for that piece of trash?'

'What did she do?' Roehmer said.

His pleasant face creased in anger, Robinson told him how she had first stood in front of the bus, then, when he had let her on, opened up a big mouth.

'Either that girl was crazy or high on something.'

'Did you see her eyes? I mean, did they look funny, as if she might have been shooting up or something?'

'Eyes were mad, that's how I saw her eyes.'

'What made her stand in front of the bus?'

'So she could get on. I was already out of the stop, I was on my way, and she come charging across the street in front of me. Coulda been killed, I didn't stomp on the brake.'

'What did she do when she got on the bus?'

Robinson pulled the bus into the kerb at Grand Army Plaza, where the park ended. Several passengers got on. The bus moved on past Fifty-ninth Street.

'When she got on the bus,' Robinson said, 'she reamed me out, then sat down and never said another word until she got off.'

'Where did she get off?'

'South of Thirty-fourth. Either it was Thirty-second or it was Thirtieth.'

'Will you let me off where you think she got off?'

'Sure.'

Roehmer took the picture out of his pocket and handed it to Robinson when the bus stopped for a red light. Robinson looked at the picture. 'That's her, all right.'

'No mistake about it?'

'No mistake. You don't forget that kind so soon.'

'She was dressed differently from this picture. Can you describe what she was wearing?'

'One of them shearlings. Heavy thing with a collar. Shearling.'

'Shit,' Roehmer said under his breath. 'What colour was it?'

'Yellow-like. You know that colour of shearling? Yellow.'

'Not dark blue? Navy blue? Blue cashmere?'

Robinson's eyes turned upwards to him, showing an expanse of white. 'I know blue from yellow. Couldn't swear I could tell cashmere, but I know yellow when I see it, and shearling when I see it.'

'Mr Robinson, try very hard to remember. Could it have been a navy cashmere coat?'

'No.' Robinson shook his head decisively. 'My own daughter got one just like that, I bought it for her. Shearling.'

At the next red light Roehmer gave the picture back to Robinson. 'Just once more, please. Is that the girl? Take your time.'

Robinson held the picture close to his face. 'That's her, mister. That's the very same person.'

Roehmer put the picture away. Civilians were notoriously unreliable about making identifications, but even the least observant of them could distinguish between yellow and blue. He would have gotten off the bus right then, but it had begun to move. He said, 'Did you happen to notice where she went after she got off?'

'She was standing by the kerb after I pulled out, so maybe she wanted to cross over to the east side of Fifth, but maybe not. I was glad she was getting off my bus, it made no difference to me where she went.'

'Thanks,' Roehmer said. 'I'm much obliged to you. Can you let me off at the next corner?'

'Realise you wanted me to say navy blue cashmere,' Robinson said, as he pulled up to the kerb. The door hissed open. 'I *realise* that. But I had to say what I saw – yellow shearling.'

Wally and Richard sat down by themselves, midway between the centre of the bar and the entrance. McGarry served them without saying anything, and returned to his work place. It was a slow night at the Pleasant Times with just a sprinkling of regulars at the bar. Most of them left early so that, by ten o'clock, Wally and Richard were practically alone at the bar.

'Maybe we ought to move down,' Wally said, nodding to the centre of the bar where McGarry was polishing glasses.

Richard shook his head. 'Stay here. If he's going to say something, he'll come to us.'

'It's like waiting for the dentist,' Wally said. 'You can't wait to get it over with, but you also hope he'll get a heart attack before it's your turn.'

'It won't hurt like the dentist,' Richard said.

When McGarry started to walk towards them, springing on the duckboards, Wally's mouth got dry. For a second his mind went blank and he couldn't remember what the hell he was supposed to say. It was Nella's idea, at first, that Wally should bring up the subject himself – it would be 'disarming', she had said. But he had argued that if McGarry hadn't made the connection himself, they would be making him a gift of it. Nella saw his point.

What McGarry was doing now, leaning with his elbows on the bar, was making small talk. A slow night, Wally said, and McGarry said that it was due to it being near the end of the month – most of the regulars were holding tight, waiting for payday. Which certainly wasn't news. Then the subject shifted to football talk until McGarry had to go back to one of the booths to take an order.

Wally said, 'I don't think he knows.'

'McGarry,' Richard said, 'you know how he is, always sliding around things.'

'I hope he missed the connection,' Wally said.

'He don't miss too much.'

After filling his order for the booth, McGarry returned to his work place and polished a couple of glasses. But then he reached down under the bar and came towards them, unfolding a copy of the *New York Post*.

'You see this?' McGarry turned the paper around and placed it on the bar in front of them.

'The kidnapped girl?' Wally wondered if his voice was a little louder than usual. He was sweating under the arms. He glanced at the paper and said, 'You noticed it too?'

'It looks a little like the bimbo who was in here the other night,' McGarry said.

'It looks a *lot* like her,' Wally said. He felt Richard's leg press warningly against his own, but he paid no attention to it. All of a sudden he was feeling fine, not the least bit nervous any more. 'Moment I saw that picture I told Richard it looked like her. But Richard don't think so.'

'To me, it don't look like her,' Richard said.

'I was real close when I served her,' McGarry said, 'but up front where she was sitting, you can't really see too much. Looks something like her, though.'

'That's what I told Richard,' Wally said. He smacked Richard on the back and said jovially, 'Jesus, wouldn't it be funny if it really *was* this Nella chick?'

'Her name was Marilyn,' Richard said.

'So couldn't she give a false name? I mean, if she was a high-class broad who was slumming?'

'Slumming,' McGarry said. 'Thanks a lot.'

'Well, look, McGarry, you don't get all that many heiresses in here.'

'I guess it *would* be funny,' Richard said, 'but it wasn't her.'

'The coat was wrong,' McGarry said. 'They said she was wearing a navy blue coat, and the girl in here, this . . .'

'Marilyn,' Wally said, prompting him.

'She was wearing one of them yellow shearlings.'

McGarry picked up his paper and walked back to the centre of the bar.

Wally winked at Richard. 'Okay?'

Richard said, 'With McGarry, you never know what he's thinking.'

Wally smiled confidently and, looking down the bar, called out, 'Hey, McGarry.'

'What're you doing?' Richard said.

Wally winked. 'Watch me.'

'Let it lay,' Richard said.

McGarry came back to them.

'I was just thinking,' Wally said, 'on the off chance that Marilyn was this Nella – should we call the cops and tip them off?'

McGarry's face closed up. 'Up to you, what you want to do.'

Wally said thoughtfully, 'Except I would feel like a jerk if it was a bum steer, which it's probably a bum steer.'

'Bum steer,' Richard said.

'Maybe *you* ought to call them, McGarry.' Wally felt Richard give his leg a nudge.

'Me?' McGarry poked a finger into his chest.

'Sure. You saw her too. I mean, if a responsible citizen like the owner of a gin mill calls them – '

'Horseshit,' McGarry said, reddening. 'Those sonofabitches, I wouldn't give them the sweat off my balls if they paid for it by the drop.'

'On the off chance it was her,' Wally said, 'it would be our duty to tell the cops.'

'Duty is horseshit,' McGarry said vehemently.

'Well, I don't know about that . . .' Wally snapped his fingers. 'Oh, no. No. I forgot. Richard's record, you know? Guy has a record, even a little one, right away the cops start hassling him. Forget it.'

'You don't have to give your name,' Richard said. 'You could call anonymous.'

Wally covered up a smile. 'That's right, Richard. All I have to do is call anonymous and say where I saw her.'

'Hey,' McGarry said. 'You want to bring them in *here*?'

'Well, I gotta say *where* I saw her, don't I?'

'Look.' McGarry leaned forward over the bar. 'I don't want them blue fuckers anywhere near here, I don't want them stinking up the place. So forget the whole thing.'

'Don't get excited,' Wally said. 'I'll forget it. It's just that I feel it's my duty – '

'I told you, that's horseshit.' McGarry's face was only a couple of inches away, and he was glaring. 'You think you owe them bastards anything?'

'McGarry's right,' Richard said. 'There's no sense stirring things up, especially since it wasn't her.'

Wally sighed. 'I guess you're right. I certainly don't

want them hassling you, Richard. Or you either, McGarry. Forget it. Forget the subject ever came up.'

McGarry straightened up. 'Thanks, Wally.'

'Anytime,' Wally said.

They left soon afterwards. They held themselves back until they had turned the corner of Third, then burst into laughter. Wally doubled up on the sofa when they got back to the apartment, laughing so hard that it was up to Richard to tell Nella what had transpired at the bar.

'He thanked us,' Richard said. 'McGarry thanked us for not calling the cops.'

Chapter 14

Roehmer received a standing ovation when he arrived in the squad room. He took a bow and accepted a bouquet made out of old newspapers from Murphy. He pretended that he hadn't taken the trouble to watch the TV clip the night before, although he had, in fact, caught it on the late news. He had been impressed at how much like a detective he looked – 'Christ,' he had said aloud, 'I've got a size fucking twenty-two neck' – and how copiously he had sweated.

After the joke ran its course, he held a coffee-cup meeting with Murphy and Passatino. Passatino was still checking out taxi companies, but so far had drawn a blank. And if the girl had taken a driver-owned cab, they were up the creek unless a driver recognised her from her picture and came forward.

'You been asking about a single girl, alone,' Roehmer said. 'But if the kidnapper snatched her and took a cab, you would have two – the girl and somebody else.'

Murphy said incredulously, 'You expect a kidnapper to take a taxi with a struggling victim?'

He might, Roehmer thought, if she *wasn't* struggling, if she went willingly. He said, 'I guess it's a dumb idea.'

Murphy said, 'I checked out some of the help and a few tenants at her house, and the doormen in the nearby houses. Zilch.'

Roehmer said that he was expecting a lab report on the kidnap note later in the day, but that the chances of there being fingerprints on it were remote, and the paper and envelope would probably turn out to be cheap five-and-dime stuff, untraceable.

He told Murphy and Passatino about the bus driver, Carter Robinson. 'He was so goddamn positive about the identification. I really believed him. And then he told me about the coat and killed it.'

Murphy said, 'You know yourself, Rome, civilians like to tell you what you want to hear. Also, it makes them important, it puts them in the limelight.'

'This Robinson was a very solid citizen, and he had plenty of reason to remember her, but . . .' He shrugged. 'But she was wearing a yellow coat.'

'You best forget it,' Murphy said.

'I'm trying to,' Roehmer said.

Roehmer was fifteen minutes late for his appointment with Special Agent Fairborn at the FBI offices on East Sixty-ninth Street. Fairborn didn't mention it, but he seemed a little tight, so Roehmer felt obliged to go into more detail about the reason for his tardiness than was really called for. Passatino had gotten a telephone tip from the girl friend of a wanted man – a Colombian who had cut up his brother-in-law in an argument over the brother-in-law's treatment of his wife, the assailant's young sister – and since Murphy was out, he had no choice but to go along with Passatino to make the arrest.

Fairborn was listening with an air of polite attentiveness. Already bored, Roehmer thought, but he went on anyway, although he knew that it wasn't an unusual or especially interesting story.

The girl-friend had met them on the corner of Lexington and Eightieth Street and taken them to her third-floor apartment. She opened the door with her key and led them to the bedroom. The Colombian was snoring away, half-naked, on a rumpled bed. Roehmer and Passatino snapped a pair of cuffs on him before he woke up.

'He was something, his eyes were all washed out,' Roehmer said, 'and meek as a lamb. He didn't even cuss out his girl-friend for giving him away. But then, when we got out on the street, he suddenly went ape. He didn't try to run away, just turned on us and began to scrap. Kicked, butted with his head, took a bite of Passatino's ear. All of this without a word, which is unusual for a Hispanic. Drew a little blood out of Passatino's ear. Nothing much.'

'What happened?' Fairborn said.

'Nothing. He had to be subdued. And we took him in.'

'Yes, well, to the point,' Fairborn said crisply.

'Right,' Roehmer said. 'Two new things have come up since you read my report.'

He told Fairborn about the bus driver, and Fairborn seemed interested, then let down when he mentioned the shearling coat. But he perked up when Roehmer told him about Roland Duffield.

'Hudson Street, eh? We ought to be able to track him down. If he's a homosexual, as Mrs Massey intimates, we can look into gay hangouts down there, and over in SoHo, where he's likely to be known.'

Which, Roehmer thought, means that he has an informant down that way, probably a fag, who he can brace for information.

Fairborn said, 'Have you had lunch?'

They went to a small French restaurant, where both the food and the prices were too rich for Roehmer's taste. He had eaten in such places with Peggy, but since then his taste buds had readjusted to TV dinners, ham sandwiches, heroes, hamburgers, pizzas. They each had a glass of white wine before lunch, and another with the meal. Maybe special agents could put in an expense account for a business lunch?

They discussed the case as they ate. There wasn't much to say until Roehmer tentatively advanced the theory that it might be a put-up job.

Fairborn swallowed a bite of his veal cordon bleu, and washed it down with a sip of wine, before saying, 'What makes you think so?'

'I don't actually think so, I'm just trying out a supposition that seems to hang together a little bit – the bad relationship between the girl and her uncle, his marriage to this Agnes and the girl's being cut out of his will, her not having any money of her own or even a job, the trouble with this Roland Duffield, her associations with some seamy characters . . .'

'From similar circumstances,' Fairborn said, 'various people suspected a plot in the Hearst and Getty kidnaps, but they turned out to be legitimate.' He waved his fork in the air. 'You're playing a hunch?'

'I wouldn't call it a hunch. More like, say, a notion.'

Fairborn smiled knowingly. 'How many crimes are ever solved through a hunch?'

Not many, Roehmer admitted to himself. 'Still, I have a special feeling about it.'

'Mind you, I don't put down intuition,' Fairborn said. 'But "special feeling" – well, it just isn't very concrete.'

He looked across the table with languid challenge. Okay, Roehmer thought, you win the point, because I damn well can't tell you – or anybody else, for that matter – that I feel the way I do because I have an affinity with a girl I've never seen or spoken to, because twenty-five years ago I had an affair with a woman who is totally unlike this one except for a tilt of the head and an address. Because, in short, Special Agent Fairborn, I'm a sentimental asshole.

'Good food,' Roehmer said.

Any idea he might have had that Fairborn would put the meal on an expense account was dispelled when the check came. Fairborn looked it over carefully, added up the figures, and told Roehmer that his share, including tip, came to nineteen dollars. It was about seven times the cost of his usual lunch.

They walked briskly through the streets under a leaden sky to Julian Massey's building. The elevator glided by eight and Roehmer watched the number until it disappeared. Agnes Massey opened the door. Roehmer introduced Fairborn.

'Something came in the mail,' Agnes said. Roehmer looked at her questioningly. She said, 'You'll see. Don't tell Julian I told you.'

In the sitting-room Massey was standing over an open package on a long, narrow marble table. 'Her clothes. They came in the mail just fifteen minutes ago.'

Massey grunted when he was introduced to Fairborn. The table held a paper wrapping with Massey's address spelled out in letters cut from a *Playboy* magazine, a note, and the clothing itself – a pair of worn jeans and a cashmere sweater with a Harrods label.

'You identify this clothing as your niece's?' Fairborn said.

'It's hers,' Massey said. 'The nerve of those bastards – a million dollars.'

Roehmer read the note carefully. *These are her clothes – no charge. The price for HER is one million.* There was a sort of playfulness about it, not like the usual ransom note, which tried to sound menacing. It wasn't hard for him to imagine the girl composing it.

Massey and Fairborn moved away from the table. Roehmer lingered for a moment. He placed his palm flat against the sweater's softness. Peggy had had such a sweater. Yeah, well, she must have had half a dozen of them, in different colours. And so had a lot of other women, if they could afford it.

He joined Massey and Fairborn. Massey was raving about the demand for a million dollars and Fairborn was trying to soothe him.

'It's one thing to ask for it and another to get it, Mr Massey. Ransom requests are invariably negotiable.'

'Negotiable! Am I expected to haggle with a criminal?'

'Meanwhile, it's helpful that he's proceeding slowly, which indicates that he's disciplined and not likely to do anything rash. It also gives *us* time – '

'Time! *Meanwhile*, you say. *Meanwhile* Nella has been in this pervert's hands for eight days. God knows whether she's being fed or not, or given a decent place to sleep, or what hellhole she's being kept in. And what unspeakable torture he may be inflicting on her. She's just a little girl. Oh God, poor Nella . . .'

Fairborn said patiently, 'We must proceed with discipline, too, Mr Massey. In the first instance, we require definitive proof that the kidnapper is holding her.'

'Proof!' Julian Massey waved his hand towards the package. 'Isn't that proof enough?'

'Not necessarily,' Fairborn said.

'How can they have her clothes without having *her*?'

That's the tough one, Roehmer thought. Let's see how you field it, Special Agent.

Fairborn avoided a direct answer. 'With so much money involved, we have to be sure that they have the goods.'

Roehmer saw Massey's eyes glaze over, and he knew that the old man had grasped what Fairborn was implying – that the kidnapper might have the girl's clothes, but not the girl herself, in which case she might be dead. Massey shook his head from side to side, not so much in denial, Roehmer thought, but as if to dislodge the implication. He retreated to safer ground.

'A million dollars. If he thinks I'm going to hand him a million dollars, he's got another guess coming.'

Fairborn said, 'We can't entirely eliminate the possibility of paying a ransom, if everything else fails.'

'You hear that, Agnes? He's telling me to give in to extortion.'

Through tight lips, Fairborn said, 'I'm certainly *not* advising it, except as a last resort.'

'What about a *first* resort? I don't see you people accomplishing *anything*.' Massey's gaze shifted to include Roehmer.

'Perhaps you're not aware of what we're attempting to do. To settle your mind, I'd like to take you into our confidence. I think you're entitled to know how we go about our work.'

'I don't care about your tricks of the trade, all I want you to do is bring my Nella back to me safe and sound.'

Agnes said, 'Let him tell you, Julian. You know how you always feel better when the doctor explains things?'

'Doctor,' Massey said. 'There's no analogy whatsoever.'

'I used to be a nurse,' Agnes said to Roehmer.

'At this stage,' Fairborn said, 'we must rely on two techniques. First, to pursue an intensive investigation of the victim's friends, associates, habituations. Second, to get a line on the criminal by listening in on his telephone calls.'

But the third, Roehmer thought, was the best bet. During the delivery of the ransom a kidnapper was most vulnerable; he had to come out into the open. But

Fairborn knew that, of course, so maybe, like doctors when they got confidential, he told the patient only what he wanted him to know.

Massey said, 'But he hasn't called. The only thing you've listened in on so far is my personal calls, and I don't mind telling you that I resent it.'

'He'll call,' Fairborn said. 'He's obliged to use the phone to make arrangements for delivery of the ransom.'

'Well, I wish he'd hurry up.'

Right into our hands, Roehmer thought, exchanging a glance with Fairborn. Now they could make the pitch they had decided on at lunch.

'Exactly how we feel ourselves,' Fairborn said. 'There's a way of doing it – of getting them on the telephone soon, and at the same time, perhaps, establishing for certain that they have your niece.'

Massey glowered suspiciously but said nothing. Agnes spoke up. 'How can you do that?'

'Very simply – by conveying doubt on your behalf that Miss Massey is truly being held, and asking for further proof.'

'I saw a movie once,' Agnes said, 'where the kidnappers sent a picture of the kidnapped person holding a newspaper so the date could be read. To prove they had the victim and that he was still alive?'

Massey rounded on Agnes, and there were in his eyes two species of anguish – at the suggestion that his niece might be dead and at Agnes's innocent brutality – which, Roehmer thought, blended together into pure outrage.

'Oh, I didn't mean – ' Agnes covered her open mouth.

Fairborn said quickly, 'It's a challenge the kidnapper will have to accept. We hope that he'll put Miss Massey on the telephone. Do you agree, Detective Roehmer?'

'I do,' Roehmer said.

'All right,' Massey said. 'You can put it out that I'm asking for more proof.'

'Very good,' Fairborn said. 'Thank you, sir. I believe that does it for now. You have any questions, Detective Roehmer?'

Roehmer shook his head, but then, on impulse, said,

'Does the area east of Fifth Avenue in the thirties mean anything to you, Mr Massey?'

Massey shrugged his shoulders. 'What could it mean?'

'I'll admit it isn't very specific, but does that general area suggest any friends or associates of your niece who might live around there?'

'I told you I don't know any of her friends or associates, and the area doesn't mean a thing to me. East of Fifth in the thirties? I haven't been down that way in years. I used to own a house down there, on Thirty-first between Lexington and Third. Why are you asking?'

'No particular reason,' Roehmer said. 'Is there any reason why your niece might go there? Old friends, maybe, who still live there?'

'She never had any friends there. She was just a kid then. I sold the house fifteen years ago.'

Massey started to ask again why he was interested in the neighbourhood, but Fairborn diverted him.

'I'd like to give you some advice about what to say if the kidnapper calls, Mr Massey – say as little as possible, let *him* do the talking.'

'But if he puts Nella on?'

'The same. We might be able to get some information from what she says. We'll be monitoring the call – '

Fairborn cut himself off as Massey suddenly slumped over, burying his face in his hands, and began to sob. Agnes got up and put her arms around him.

'All right, Julian, it's all right. I think we'd better lie down until it passes over.'

Roehmer gathered up the clothing and the note and packed it loosely in the paper it had been wrapped in.

'It's bad for our blood pressure to get so worked up, Daddy.' Nodding goodbye over her shoulder, Agnes started to lead him across the room. 'We'll just take a few minutes' rest . . .'

Fairborn and Roehmer let themselves out.

Jane Henley Halworth phoned a few minutes after Roehmer got back to the precinct house. She had gotten in touch with several of the people who had been at her party the night Nella had brought the longshoreman. With a little prodding they managed to remember him, but not his name or, except vaguely, what he looked like. Roehmer thanked her for her co-operation, and asked her to call him again if anything occurred to her that might be helpful in his investigation. But he didn't think he would learn anything more from Jane Henley Halworth or, for that matter, anyone else on the list Julian Massey had given him. It was the wrong list, it was out of date.

Before leaving the House, he stopped at the lieutenant's office. 'You're sharing top billing with the G-man today,' Boyd said, 'unless your old pal the Chief drops in, which he may, if he's taking an interest in the case, and then you and the G-man both are just spear carriers.'

Twenty-seven years ago Roehmer had been a Police Academy classmate of the present chief of detectives, who, even as a rookie cop, had shown sure signs of being a winner. They weren't really old pals. What it amounted to was that the Chief remembered him by name and, on the rare occasions when their paths crossed, would pass the time of day with some brief reference to the good old days at the Academy. But it was just the superficial, transient camaraderie of one old grad with another. Roehmer knew that the Chief wouldn't give a second thought to lopping his head off if he screwed up. Still, it didn't do any harm to let the lieutenant think that the Chief was his 'rabbi'.

He rode the Lexington Avenue subway to Thirty-third Street. Walking eastward on Thirty-first, he remembered how his fingers had tingled when they had touched Nella Massey's sweater, as if they could feel the warm living flesh beneath the strands of wool. At Lexington he realised that he didn't know the number of Julian Massey's old house. And if he did? Well, maybe if he saw the house, it might tell him something. Yeah, it would tell him loud and clear that he was full of crap. Although there was a tenuous link between the bus driver's strong identification of the girl on the bus as Nella Massey – except for that fucking shearling coat – and the fact that she had once lived on this street, the truth was that what he really wanted was to get close to the girl's past because in some dumb mixed-up way he was half in love with an *idea* of Nella Massey. Face it, Roehmer, you're wasting the taxpayers' money.

Still, checking out the neighbourhood was logical procedure – provided it was the right neighbourhood. Well, it would fill up the hour and a half before he was due back at the House for the news conference. He walked back to Lexington. The avenue had changed since Julian Massey had last lived here, fifteen years ago. So what else was new, in a city that seemed to be built on social quicksand? But on the whole it still wasn't too bad an area, at least in the daytime. Late at night an army of whores turned out to work passing cars at the stoplights.

He went into a small fruit and vegetable store that looked as if it had been there for fifty years. Nobody opened up that kind of store these days and tried to buck the supermarkets. The people who remained were survivors, existing marginally at the old stand because they were too old to try anything else, and they didn't have to worry about rising rents because they owned the building above the store.

The owner of the fruit and vegetable store was a very short, very dark Italian in his middle seventies. He studied Nella's picture. 'Who's this girl? What she do?'

'Did you ever have a customer, about fifteen years ago, named Massey, lived on Thirty-first?'

'She don't look like no criminal, but today who can tell? Fifteen years ago – you kidding?'

Roehmer tried to jog his memory. He described Julian Massey as he might have looked fifteen years ago, and said that he might have been accompanied by a little girl.

The proprietor shook his head. 'I can't remember so far back.' He cut off a tiny bunch of purple grapes. 'Take it. You look sad, maybe eating a good grape make you feel better. Anyway, they're getting ready to spoil.'

Sad, Roehmer thought, this student of human behaviour thinks I look sad. What do I have to look sad about? Nothing, you sweet dumb little guinea, absolutely nothing except my whole life.

He plodded on, from one dusty store to the next. A few

of the owners recognised the picture from television or a newspaper. Some of the storekeepers were pleasant, others were annoyed at being asked to do something for nothing. *The cops gonna pay my rent?*

In one place he took some abuse. The owner of a yard-goods store, with a sick-looking, sour face, opened up a big mouth: What the hell are you taking up the valuable time of a hard-working honest guy when the streets are full of murderers with sawed-off shotguns? Go on, take a walk, flatfoot. Roehmer turned away without a word and left the store. Three to one that behind the grimy curtain that separated the front of the store from the rear, the bastard was running a numbers drop. And he was on somebody's pad, so that if Roehmer rousted him, he would stir up a terrible fuss in this precinct.

A shoemaker's shop was next, a mare's nest of dust, scraps of leather, nails, rusted taps, a package of soles, old placards advertising rubber heels so springy you'd think you were flying, a lathe with belts that were worn white, thin and frayed with use. The proprietor examined the picture of Nella Massey. When Roehmer asked him if he had seen the girl, the shoemaker stared at him without answering. Roehmer repeated his question; the shoemaker ignored it. Roehmer got sore, and told him he was a fucking shithead, and then suddenly realised that the man was stone deaf.

He apologised. 'I'll make everybody in the One-Eight bring his sole and heel work down here. You'll get rich.'

The shoemaker stared at him blankly.

On the street Roehmer checked his watch. Time for one more. He went into a cluttered hardware store. The owner looked at Nella's picture and shook his head. But when Roehmer asked him about Julian Massey, he snapped his fingers decisively.

'I remember him! Massey. He used to buy paint and a few things from me. Massey. Tall, skinny geezer. Nose in the air, thought he was King Shit. Always complained about this or that, always tried to beat the price down, charged everything and took months to pay his bills. That's how I knew he was rich – he was slow pay.'

Roehmer said, 'The girl in the picture I showed you is his niece. Try to remember if you've seen her around here recently.'

The hardware man looked at the picture with interest now, but shook his head again. 'That's who she is? I would never of guessed. I remember her when she was a child – blonde, pretty. A few times Massey came into the store with her, and sometimes I saw them walking on the street, holding hands. I used to think, See, he can't be such a bastard if he loves his little daughter so much. I thought she was his daughter. Her uncle, eh? Old bastard was a damn pain in the ass.'

The hardware man didn't remember where Julian Massey had lived, other than it was 'in the neighbourhood'.

Detective Roehmer was wearing the same loud sports jacket. Special Agent Fairborn, by contrast, was smartly turned out in a sharkskin suit, a light blue shirt, and a darker blue silk tie with a tasteful grey figure. He spoke quietly, with a self-control so profound that it bordered on menace. Roehmer faced the cameras head-on, stolid and expressionless.

For Nella, curled up on the sofa facing the TV set, cheek resting on Wally's wonderful chest, the first moments of the newscast were without surprise. Earlier a radio news bulletin had announced the receipt of her clothing. When the cameras closed in on her jeans and sweater, displayed on a table, Wally, massaging her stomach with a lazy proprietary motion, said they looked real glamorous.

At the start of the newscast he had criticised the editorial judgement of the programme's producer for leading off with a spectacular riverfront fire instead of the kidnap story. 'One of those crappy old piers burns every week. You've seen one, you've seen them all.'

Old ground was covered with expert concision – the story up to now. Her picture was put up on a split screen. Julian's apartment house was shown (yesterday's shot, with the milling reporters), 'where the famous architect remains in seclusion, still declining to talk to the media.' Then the camera closed in on her picture until it filled the entire screen (Wally's hand tightened on her stomach, reacting to some emotion she couldn't quite identify – maybe pride), while a voice called attention to a special police number, shown at the bottom of the screen, for anyone who had information about the missing girl.

'Let's jot the number down,' Wally said, 'in case we get some information.'

Special Agent Fairborn, in answer to a question, said that although the clothing had been positively identified by Mr Massey as being his niece's, it didn't constitute definitive proof that Miss Massey was alive and well.

Wally laughed. 'If he could see you in bed, he wouldn't say that.'

'Are you suggesting that she might *not* be alive?'

'No, sir. All I'm suggesting is that this is Nella Massey's clothing, not Nella Massey. Mr Massey would appreciate some further communication proving that the writer of this note is indeed holding Nella Massey, and that she is alive and well.'

'Have there been other communications from the kidnapper besides the two notes? Any phone calls?'

Fairborn said, 'We hope there will be further communications so we can establish a rapport.'

'Does this mean Mr Massey has agreed to pay the ransom?'

'What Mr Massey wishes is to establish a mutual faith and trust with the writer of the note. Then he can proceed from there, once he is satisfied that his niece is in this person's hands.'

As the sequence came to a close, Roehmer, who had been silent throughout, narrowed his eyes and intensified his gaze, focusing beyond the lens into some finite distance. And again, as she had the night before, Nella felt that he was trying to reach her in some shared secret code.

Wally said, 'It was too short. It wasn't even as long as the thing about the fire.'

'It's only a million-dollar snatch, Wally. These are inflationary times.'

'You like the part about how they hope we'll com-
municate so we can learn to trust each other? Well, they'll
have their wish tonight.'

'No. We'll wait until tomorrow.'

'I thought we decided to phone him tonight.'

'That's when *they* want us to do it.'

'They didn't say so. Anyway, what's the difference?'

'I don't want us to seem to be doing anything they ask
us to do. I want *us* to call the turns.'

'But we decided to do it *before* we heard them talk about
it.'

'They don't know that. We'll do it tomorrow.'

'All that does is delay it another day.' His face
darkened. 'Anyway, what are you – a dictator or
something?'

Wally understood beginnings and endings, and nothing
in between. She said, 'Wally, darling, you're beautiful
when you're angry.'

His distemper vanished; a smile tugged his lip upward.
Snuggling against him, she thought, Us dictators move in
mysterious ways our wonders to perform, Wally.

Mary was semi-sober when Roehmer got home, and
almost childishly eager to please him. She had made a
salad to go with their frozen dinners, but the lettuce was
limp and discoloured at the edges, and the prepared salad
dressing had gone rancid. In order not to disappoint her,
he forced himself to eat some of it. As usual, she barely
touched her own food. She watched him drink his beer,
and ostentatiously sipped at her own glass, which
contained water. He commended her. Her eyes filled with
tears of gratitude, and she told him that this was the first
day of a new life without drinking. She probably hadn't
had a drink for two hours.

She broke a dish when she was cleaning up, and burst
into tears. He put his arm around her and said it didn't
matter, but she ran out of the kitchen. He finished up the
dishes, and then turned the television to a college
basketball game. After a half hour or so he went to see how
Mary was. She was in the bathroom, and the shower was

running. There was an open bottle of whiskey standing on the dresser. He put the cap on the battle and went back to the basketball game.

He was unaware of Mary's presence until her arms encircled his neck from behind his chair. She was wearing a pink nightgown and a filmy negligee, both of which had become too large for her since she had bought them. Her hair was neatly combed off her forehead. She was wearing shakily applied make-up and had doused herself in perfume.

He patted her arm and asked her if she wanted to sit down and watch the game.

'I'm going to bed. Do I look nice?' She touched his cheek with her dry lips. 'Don't you want to come to bed?'

She arched her spare, bony pelvis against his shoulder. He leaned forward, away from the pressure of her body, and said, 'You go ahead, Mary, I'll be in in a little while.'

She made a sound of disappointment; it was like a child's whimper.

'Just until this quarter is over. It won't take long.'

Obediently, as if she feared he might rescind his promise if she lingered, she went away. At the door she glanced over her shoulder flirtatiously and said, 'I'll be expecting you, honey, don't be long.'

When he looked into the bedroom a half hour later, she was asleep. The whiskey bottle was uncapped. He went back to the living-room and watched the basketball game to its end. Although he was yawning and his eyes were half shut, he decided to watch himself on the late news. What he saw shocked him: an overweight man, beefed up by rotten food and careless habits, a neck strangling in its collar, sad eyes. Peggy Parris would have been revolted by the man on the TV screen, he thought, remembering how she had doted on the whiteness of his skin, the keenness of what she had called his 'shocking blue eyes', the charged power of his body. Nella Massey, if she was watching, would know nothing of what he had once been, only what he had become.

Christ, he thought, the man on the screen wasn't even an individual but a stamped-out type. One good look and you would know that he was a detective, that his feet had a sour smell, that he always bought the first suit off the rack, that he hadn't been to the dentist in five years.

He snapped the television set shut, turned off the lights, and went into the bedroom. Mary had barely moved since he had last seen her. He undressed and got into bed. He fell immediately asleep and woke to Mary's negligible weight pressing against his back.

Oh Christ, dear Christ.

'Mary . . .'

She was tugging at him, trying to bring him around on top of her.

'Mary, go on back to sleep.' This isn't your real need, Mary, you need only the bottle; and whatever I need is unattainable, it requires the undoing of twenty-five years. 'Go back to sleep, Mary.'

But she persisted, babbling in the darkness, her strength astonishing. He lay on top of her without moving, while she clasped her arms around his back clumsily, her nails gouging his skin. She was dry and abrasive, but – dear God, I can't help myself – he began to thrust into her. He shut his eyes and thought of Peggy Parris and then, to his astonishment, of Nella Massey, and they merged. Peggy disappeared into the mists of a quarter century, and it was Nella beneath him, straining to match his quickening pace. He gasped out her name in his mind and thrust into her deeply as Mary groaned under the pressure of his weight.

The cement floor of the cellar looked freshly swept, and yet its pores held dust that sifted upwards, unseen until it settled on Fairborn's suit. Almost ritually he had changed into a dark suit simply because, on balance, it was rule-book appropriate for night work. But it was the wrong outfit for sitting in a cellar, however clean. Detective Pittman, the electronics expert from the NYPD Intelligence Unit, was wearing grey slacks and a pepper-and-salt jacket, neither of which showed any sign of dust. Fairborn had been ushered in by the building super-intendent, and after shaking hands with the electronics detective, asked him if he had done a recent check of his equipment. The detective looked surprised and didn't answer, just pointed to the two jumpers hooked into Julian Massey's telephone line.

Five minutes of desultory conversation was enough to convince Fairborn that silence was preferable. Pittman must have thought so, too; he went to sleep. It occurred to him that Roehmer might have been a more agreeable companion – he seemed quite intelligent, and he could undoubtedly help pass the time with anecdotes about sordid murders, cheap robberies, brutal knife fights, crimes of passion among his low-life clientele, tales of arson, confidence tricks, stakeouts. But he had told Roehmer he could go home if he wanted to, that he would cover the phone alone. It didn't require two of them – three if you counted the electronics man – to listen to a phone tap.

By one o'clock he was convinced that there wouldn't be any call, but he hung around for another hour anyway, trying to make himself comfortable on the straight-backed chair the super had supplied (undoubtedly salvaged from the discards of one of his tenants), collecting dust and listening to Pittman's noisy sleep sounds.

At two o'clock he got up, stretched, slapped half-heartedly at the fine silting of dust that covered him, nodded to the sleeping detective, and picked his way through the labyrinth of the cellar to the freight elevator and then up to the lobby of the building. Waiting on the sidewalk while the doorman whistled for a taxi, he bent back to look up at the façade of the building. The windows of Julian Massey's apartment were dark. Massey had agreed to stay up past his bedtime in anticipation of a call, but even his deadline had obviously been reached. Victims of crimes, Fairborn thought with some bitterness, got more sleep than fighters of crime.

Chapter 15

'Mr Massey? This is your friendly neighbourhood kidnapper.'

Richard's hand, circling the phone tightly, looked bloodless. Nella nodded encouragingly. Reading from the script he held in his right hand, Richard went on.

'Just keep your mouth shut and listen. I'm going to put Nella – '

'No, Richard,' Nella said. 'Wait a bit and see if he replies before you say you're going to put me on.'

'Right.' Richard pointed his chin at the script. 'It says to pause.'

'And if he does answer, no matter *what* he says,' Nella said, indicating the notation on the script, 'you say, "Shut up. Just listen, and listen good".'

'People don't talk like that,' Wally said with a snort. 'It's phoney.'

How could it be phoney? Hadn't it been vouched for by a hundred movies and television shows? And didn't life imitate cheap art? But she said to Richard, 'How would you say it, in your own words?'

Richard made a noncommittal gesture with the telephone. '"You better listen to me."' He shrugged. 'Something like that.'

'Right,' Wally said. 'That's natural, that's how people talk. It's wrong to write everything down like that, and besides, it's insulting. It's like saying Richard is stupid.'

'Hang up,' Nella said to Richard. 'We'll do the dishes and then try again.' She turned to Wally. 'Look. This is our first direct contact with Julian and it's crucial. It has to be right to the point. We have to assume that the police will be listening in, and we have to be quick, so there's no chance of their tracing the phone call. Now didn't we all agree about that?'

She sensed that her tone was pedantic, and Wally's face confirmed it; it had turned obdurate. But instead of picking up the argument, he reverted to an earlier grievance. 'I still think we should let me do it. Richard, in some things, in *most* things, he's terrific, but this, I can do this better than Richard.'

Richard said, 'Wally can do it if he wants to.'

'The way Richard reads it,' Wally said, 'he loses the humour of it. "This is your friendly neighbourhood kidnapper" – it's supposed to be humorous, but Richard says it straight, without humour.'

They had set out with the idea that Wally would make the call, but he had botched it. He was self-conscious, and his voice came out stilted and elocutionary. Richard's level, uninflected monotone was more convincing.

She said, 'You do the humour much better, Wally, but Richard sounds more sinister and that's what we want – we want to sound scary.'

'I didn't *try* to be scary,' Wally said. 'I can be scary if I *try*.'

'You sound too cultured, Wally, too high class.'

His resistance collapsed, and he preened with pleasure. But having to make the egregious compliment irked her, and she felt put upon. Her annoyance persisted as she and Richard washed the dishes.

It was Richard's day off. He had awakened early, anyway, and prepared breakfast. Now, working at the sink, he seemed withdrawn, and she made no effort to break the silence.

When the last of the dishes were put away in their cupboards, they went back to the living-room. Wally was slouched in a chair, riffling through one of his muscle magazines. He looked out of sorts again. The effects of her flattery had worn off. Have to increase the dosage next time? She handed Richard the script, imitated the sound of a ringing phone bell, and said, 'Hello?'

Richard cleared his throat. 'This is your friendly – '

'Hold it, Richard. Try clearing your throat *before* the phone rings.'

Richard nodded and cleared his throat. Wally laughed.

As Richard began again, Wally flipped the pages of his magazine furiously.

'Wally, would you please stop that?'

'Stop what?'

'You know what I'm talking about. Stop it.'

He glared at her. She glared back. He raised the magazine in front of his face, only his eyes visible, hot and insulted.

'Go ahead, Richard.'

'This is your friendly neighbourhood . . .'

Wally was riffling the pages, without even a pretence of reading, staring at her challengingly.

'Oh, you fool, you goddamn fool!'

He rose from the chair in a single purposive flow, and she thought he was coming at her, but he veered off and, sending the magazine sailing, strode into the bedroom and slammed the door.

Life imitating bad art: thieves fall out. She said, 'I'm sorry, Richard.'

He shrugged. She couldn't see his face. 'Wally is very sensitive.'

Wally is a bloody peacock. 'Let's try it again, okay?'

His face still averted, Richard said, 'Maybe you ought to go in to Wally first?'

'I will, Richard, as soon as we finish. Will you start again?'

He raised his head, and his pale blue eyes studied her, as if to gauge her sincerity. He nodded.

On the fourth try he was letter perfect. Then, as he sat quietly across the table, she read her own piece. She was nervous, her voice quavered, but that was all right, it was appropriate.

'Sound okay?'

'Fine,' Richard said. He stood up. 'I got some things to do. You going in to Wally?'

'Yes.'

But she remained seated after Richard went to his room. She wasn't ready yet; she had to simmer down before she could make the effort to placate Wally. She had been in the apartment for nine days now, and she had begun to feel the strain. Nine days of sequestration, of tedium and the tension involved in intimacy at close quarters with strangers. Even the purely physical restraints had begun to tell: she couldn't look out of a window except sidelong through a slit in a drawn curtain.

Richard wasn't a problem. He was out of the house much of the time, and was reclusive by nature anyway. But Wally was impatient and mercurial, with no tolerance for waiting or taste for detail. And her own patience with his petulance and poses had begun to wear thin, which made the situation potentially explosive. It troubled her that in considering pressure and stress she had thought of it only as it applied to Julian, and overlooked its effect on themselves. Hadn't she seen enough television and movies – the *vade mecum* of her expertise – to know that waiting was corrosive? There was so much time to kill, such long intervals between periods of activity, and so little real companionship. Diversion in this household – and after all it was the boys' domain, not hers – consisted mainly of watching television, which distracted Wally, and, so far as she could read his silences, Richard, too, but not herself. Her only real diversion was the bed. Although the frenzy of the first few days had subsided somewhat, Wally's stamina was still something to marvel at, and there was no abatement of her own fierce absorption in the wonders of his body.

But her overriding interest, and her chief source of pleasure, derived from the kidnap plot itself. If her habits had been casual and sloppy before, they had now become fanatically disciplined. She paid ferocious attention to details. She insisted that everything they sent to Julian must be mailed from distant post offices (she had dispatched Richard to The Bronx to mail the package containing her clothing). Wally had protested that she was being over-finicky, and even Richard, echoing Wally, had objected mildly. But she had insisted, and won her point, as she had also insisted and also won when she made Wally get her cigarettes from a store where he wasn't known (since he didn't smoke), and buy four rather than three pork chops. It was scripture, wasn't it, that criminals were invariably tripped up by the most insignificant details?

It was Nella's show. She was its author and its leader. She had found a métier. She had invented it – and invented herself. And she had uncovered in herself a taste for danger. It was different from the recklessness that had characterised her father, whose first and last decisive act had been to invite suicide. If she had been like Poor Philip, her failures would have plunged her into depression, instead of angering her, and she would have been dead by now.

Time to mend fences, Nella. The kidnap's the thing, and your true mastermind comprehends that the end justifies the means. She went into the bedroom. Wally was lying with his head cradled on his hands, staring moodily at the ceiling. She sat down on the edge of the bed.

'Wally, I want to apologise.' He gave no sign of her presence, not even the flicker of an eye. 'Wally, I'm truly sorry. Forgive me?'

He turned to face the window, putting his back to her.

'Wally, please?'

He didn't budge. Not a tremor in those massive shoulders, that sculptured back. Work to be done, Nella. She got into bed and lay down. Snuggling against him, she put her hand on his waist. Slowly, lightly, she trailed her fingers down over his hipbone, at the same time pressing her pelvis gently against his tight buttocks. Her hand moved slowly along his flank to his knee, then back. It paused for a moment before lapping over to the inside of his thigh, rested briefly, then edged closer to his groin, retreated upwards to his stomach, fluttered downwards, and then, betrayed by her own rising desire, plunged suddenly.

He seized her hand and flung it away from him, and at the same time heaved himself around on his back. His face was red with anger. 'I don't want you touching me.'

'Oh, Wally, I want you so much.'

'Fucking don't settle anything.' His face was stern, ungiving. 'You want to have everything your own way.'

He started to turn his back to her. Terrified, she threw

herself across him, pinning him down. 'But I don't, Wally, I don't. That's what I came in to tell you. You were absolutely right. We're going to let Richard do it his own way, without the script. I came to my senses, Wally. I really and truly did.'

'You really changed your mind?'

She nodded vigorously. 'Yes, yes. I remembered how well you both handled McGarry, and I realised I was terribly wrong. Won't you forgive me, Wally?'

'You mean it?'

'I mean it, Wally, I came to my senses.'

It was true that they had handled McGarry well, and it was undoubtedly wrong of her not to allow them a more responsible hand in the game. But she knew that that was secondary, an afterthought. What truly mattered was that she couldn't tolerate rejection. Her abiding weakness was that she needed people more than they needed her.

'Wally? Oh, darling, you're bewitching.'

His face softened, the corner of his mouth twitched in the start of a smile. Wally had his weakness, too: he couldn't resist being adored.

'Okay, Nella, you don't have to get so upset.'

He smiled – ah, Wally, you're smiling, even if it's just half a mouth's worth – and pushed her head downwards, pressing her face into his crotch.

All's right with the world, Nella, reason has prevailed.

Roehmer took a call from Fairborn around noon. Fairborn sounded out of sorts, and complained about having gotten to bed at three o'clock after leaving the cellar of Julian Massey's after two. Roehmer made sympathetic sounds but Fairborn wasn't appeased. He went on at length about what he called 'insidious' dust in the cellar, and the 'unconscionable' snoring of Detective Pittman.

Roehmer listened with a pretence of patience until Fairborn got down to business.

'Our St Louis office tracked this Roland Duffield down.'

'Good work,' Roehmer said. He meant it. The Bureau could move like lightning sometimes.

'He's staying at his mother's house. Been there for almost two weeks, at least two or three days before the girl disappeared.'

'Are you sure?'

'Two of our agents went down to see him,' Fairborn said.

Considering the time difference in St Louis, they must have barged in on him at dawn. 'I mean are you sure about how long he's been there?'

'Our men interrogated him,' Fairborn said huffily. 'We're pretty good at that, you know.'

'So I've heard. Well, I guess that eliminates a Roland Duffield conspiracy theory.'

'*I* haven't had any conspiracy theory.'

But it didn't eliminate a conspiracy theory *per se*, Roehmer thought.

'Duffield still has a few thousand of Massey's money left,' Fairborn said. 'So far nobody's brought any charges against him, but if we put a little pressure on, he might cough up the money.'

'The money doesn't matter to me,' Roehmer said.

'Nor to me,' Fairborn said. 'It isn't in my brief. But we can stretch a point and squeeze this fellow if you want us to.'

'I suppose we can check it out with Massey, see how he feels about it.'

He suggested to Fairborn that they get together sometime during the day. Fairborn said it was a good idea, but he couldn't make it until late in the afternoon, too much to do. Roehmer didn't ask him what the too much was. He told Fairborn he would be going back to Nella Massey's old neighbourhood.

'Seems a little flimsy to me,' Fairborn said. Roehmer didn't say anything. 'Well, see you at the press conference.'

I'm ready for it, Roehmer thought, I'm wearing a clean shirt.

★

The Pleasant Times Bar and Grill could just as well have had a sign outside reading: Our Clientele Are Losers. It would cater to the rear guard of a once all-white working class – Irish, Germans, whatever – who had planted themselves stubbornly to resist the changing tide of neighbourhood, and stuck it out where they had – many of them – been born. That, Roehmer thought, was what the Pleasant Times was; what it wasn't was a place a girl like Nella Massey would frequent or even consider for a drop-in.

He had come directly down to Massey's old neighbourhood as soon as the news conference was over. It hadn't taken very long; there was nothing new. But the newspapers, wire services, and television crews had turned out in force. The Massey case had glamour, and they would keep following it up until it was resolved or simply withered away. He had stood under the light and let Fairborn carry the ball, such as it was: Yes, they were following some leads; no, the kidnappers had not been heard from; yes, Massey was still awaiting further proof from the kidnappers that his niece was alive and well.

Roehmer showed his picture of Nella Massey in a dry-cleaning store without results. That was all there was time for; everything closed at six o'clock. He walked aimlessly along Third Avenue and paused in front of the fly-specked posters in the window of the Pleasant Times. He found himself wondering with what amusement or blank incomprehension Peggy Parris would have regarded it. Or Nella Massey. Asshole! They were two different people, their similarities existed only in his fucked-up mind. Or they were the same person, inhabiting different times. If Peggy were Nella's age today, would she have married a college professor, brought a loud-mouthed dockworker to a party? But his imagination failed him; he couldn't transport her through a quarter of a century. She was Peggy Parris in her own time, and she didn't exist in any other. Nella was now, so immediate that he had been able to feel her warmth in an empty sweater. He couldn't visualise either of them in the Pleasant Times Bar and Grill. But a beer, he thought, pushing open the door, a beer might wash the bitterness out of his mind. At worst, it would taste good.

It was so dark inside that he thought the bar was closed, that someone had forgotten to lock the door. After a moment he made out a glow of light at the centre of the bar, and the faint movement of something white. The whiteness took shape as the shirt of a bartender, who was braced on his elbows on the bar, poring over a racing form, though Roehmer couldn't guess how he could see well enough in this skimpy light to read. The bartender glanced at him as he sat down on a barstool, and then went back to his racing form. There was nobody else at the bar. He cleared his throat. The bartender didn't look up.

'Are you open for business?'

The bartender, still reading, nodded his head.

'In that case,' Roehmer said, 'I'll have a beer.' The bartender didn't move. 'If it isn't too much trouble.'

The bartender straightened up lazily and stared at him. A big, handsome Irish stud, Roehmer thought, and if he doesn't draw me a beer in thirty seconds, I'm going to shoot him between the eyes.

'A beer,' the bartender said. He moved slowly, picking up a glass, holding it under the tap, levelling off the foam. He placed the beer in front of Roehmer.

Roehmer put a dollar on the bar. The bartender turned to the register, rang up the sale, and slapped the change down on the bar. Roehmer stared at him. What in hell was eating at this turkey?

He said, 'You have some kind of problem, fella?'

'I got no problem. You got a problem?'

Just a little leprosy. 'Maybe we ought to start over. Good evening, bartender. Nice evening, isn't it?'

'Up till now, yeah. I don't like it so much any more.'

Twenty-five years ago, Roehmer thought, I would have thrown my beer into your face and maybe hauled you clear over the bar and worked you over. But cops didn't do that kind of thing any more, they lived up to a different image these days. He took out Nella Massey's picture and placed it face down on the bar.

He said, 'I'm a police officer, a detective.'

The bartender shrugged.

'You want to see my ID?'

'Don't bother. I can smell one a mile away.'

Cop hater, okay, Roehmer thought, no more mystery. He took a sip of his beer and then picked up the picture and handed it over. The bartender tilted it to the light, looked at it, and flipped it back on to the bar.

'You want to know if I seen her?'

Roehmer nodded.

'I seen her. In the paper. Okay?'

Roehmer put the picture back in his pocket. He drank some of his beer, picked up his change, and put it in his pocket. 'Thanks for your hospitality.'

The bartender took his beer glass off the bar and emptied it into the sink.

Roehmer took a couple of steps towards the door and stopped. 'You ever been in trouble with the police?'

'Straight ahead is the way out,' the bartender said. 'Don't hurry back.'

No good seeing red, Roehmer thought, you can't do anything about it. Like he had told Passatino, that's police work. He walked the length of the bar and through the door.

In a stationery-candy store on Third Avenue, one of the few stores still open, the shopkeeper, a hollow-faced old man with a two-day growth of white beard, told Roehmer where Julian Massey had lived. For more than ten years, until Massey moved, he had delivered newspapers to his doorstep. He couldn't remember Massey at all, but the house and the number, when you threw a newspaper at a stoop for so many years at six-thirty in the morning, *that* you didn't forget.

Roehmer found the house midway up the block between Third and Lexington. He stood across the street from it. It was a nice house, but it wasn't giving off any special messages. He wasn't able to populate it with a younger Julian Massey whom he had never known, or transmute a pretty little girl into a young woman who might or might not have engineered her own kidnapping.

It was already dark. Dimly, through curtains in the downstairs quarters, he saw figures moving around inside. He crossed the street, entered the little courtyard, and rang the bell on a massive cross-hatched iron gate giving into a small vestibule two steps down. After a while a scrolled wooden door inside the vestibule opened and a blond young man wearing a cream-coloured T-shirt stepped out.

'Hello,' Roehmer said. 'I'm a New York City police detective. I'd like to – '

From just behind the inner door, a voice whispered, 'Ask him if he has a warrant.'

The blond young man, who was slender and well built, and who didn't seem to feel the cold, bare arms or not, turned to the door and said, 'Oh, Freddie, for heaven's sake.' He faced back to Roehmer. 'What can I do for you?'

'I'm investigating the kidnapping . . . Sir, don't you want to see my credentials?'

'I suppose.'

Roehmer handed his ID through the tesselated bars of the iron door. The young man took a casual glance at it and handed it back. From behind the inner door, the voice, identifiably male now that it was no longer whispering, said, 'Those things can be faked, you know, Peter.'

A puff of smoke came through the open door, and the aroma reached Roehmer's nostrils. Pot. So what else is new? He said, 'I'm investigating the kidnapping of Nella Massey. Are you familiar with the case?'

Peter nodded. From behind the door, Freddie, giggling, said, 'Tell him we're a case ourselves.'

'Oh, shut up, Freddie,' Peter said, smiling. 'What can I do to help you, Officer?'

'Can I come inside? I won't be more than a couple of minutes.'

'No,' the voice behind the door squealed. 'He can't come in, I haven't got a thing on.'

'Can't we just do it from here?' Peter said. 'We don't know word one about it, you know.'

'Sure,' Roehmer said. 'What I'm doing, interested

in knowing, is whether Miss Massey might have been in this neighbourhood last Thursday, a week from yesterday.'

'Around here? Whatever would she be doing around here?'

'There's reason to believe that she may have been in the general area. She used to live around here, in fact in this very house.'

'*Really*. How intriguing. Freddie, did you hear? That Massey girl once lived here, in our house.'

There was no response from behind the door.

'Freddie, did you hear what I said? Isn't it marvellous?'

A puff of smoke wafted from the doorway, but Freddie remained silent.

'Freddie, I know you're there, so stop playing games.'

There was another puff of smoke, and then Freddie said, 'I saw her. She was standing across the street looking up at the house. A girl. I happened to be looking out the window, and I saw her.'

'Freddie,' Peter said, 'this is serious. This man is a police detective.'

'I didn't know it was her, of course, but it was last Thursday, I remember that distinctly, it was the night we went discoing with Harlow and Francis. It must have been about eleven or so, and I watched her for a little while. She didn't look like a hooker; there was something quite mysterious about her, something fetching.'

'Don't go on so fast,' Peter said excitedly, 'and don't swallow your words so. This may be terribly important.'

'It's all right,' Roehmer said. 'Tell it your own way. Did you see her face?'

'Of course I didn't see her face, silly. It was eleven o'clock. Pip emma.'

Peter broke out laughing. 'You're *something*, Freddie, honestly you are. One doesn't say *silly* to a detective, silly. One doesn't say *pip emma*, either.'

Freddie said, 'She kept looking at the house, sort of studying it, in a sort of sad way, I think.'

'How could you judge that in the pip emma?' Roehmer said.

'Oh, good,' Peter said, and smiled at Roehmer. 'That was really quite good.'

'*Sad* might not quite be the word,' Freddie said. 'Perhaps wistfully, or even yearningly. I could see *that* much quite clearly, even in the dark. Bodies say things, you know. Attitudes?'

'Was she there very long?' Roehmer said. 'And did she do anything except look at the house?'

'Just a few minutes. And then she sort of sauntered off. I watched her until she was quite out of sight, going towards Third. It was really a fascinating little vignette.'

'And you never told me a word about it,' Peter said reproachfully.

Freddie puffed smoke. 'I can't think why I didn't. Just forgot it, I suppose. Don't *you* ever simply forget to tell me things?'

'Damn you, Freddie,' Peter said. 'It was her. I know it was. Don't you think so, Detective?'

'It might be,' Roehmer said. He looked past Peter to the door. 'Did you happen to notice – even in the dark – what she might be wearing?'

'How delicious,' Peter said. 'The kidnapped girl, here, maybe just a tick before she was snatched. Wait until I tell everybody.'

'Oh,' Roehmer said, 'I'm afraid you won't be able to talk about it. Privileged communication, you know.'

'Oh damn,' Peter said. 'Couldn't I just tell it to a *few*?'

Freddie said, 'I saw her glide under the streetlamp, it was terribly romantic, and I could see that she was wearing slacks, no hat, brownish hair. Yes, and a coat, of course.'

'A navy blue coat?' Roehmer siad.

'No, dear, it was one of those clumsy yellowish things – a shearling?'

The telephone was on the table at Agnes's side of the double bed. When it rang, around ten-thirty, Julian dropped the book he was reading and flung himself across his wife to pick it up.

'Yes? Hello?'

234

'This is your friendly neighbourhood kidnapper.'

'What? Who? Is this a joke?'

'Just keep your mouth shut and listen.' The voice was toneless, sterile. 'I'm putting Nella on.'

Julian stared wildly at Agnes, pinned beneath him and trying to free her arm, which was caught awkwardly under his body. His eyes were wide and he was trembling.

'Hello? Where is she? Where – '

'Julian? It's Nella.'

Julian made a spastic movement, punishing Agnes's arm, and she let out a cry of pain but lay still. His breathing was heavy, and she knew that his heart was labouring.

'Julian, it's me, Nella . . .'

'Oh my God. Are you all right? Nella – '

'Oh, Uncle Julian – '

She was cut off abruptly, and the monotone voice said, 'You'll be hearing from me.'

'Send her back to me,' Julian said. 'I'll do anything you say. I'll pay what you want. Just send my Nella home – '

'He hung up,' Agnes said. 'I heard the click.'

'Oh my God . . .'

Agnes felt Julian's heart thumping against her abdomen. She heaved upwards and dislodged him. He fell back on the bed, still holding the phone. She rolled over to her knees and began to haul him backwards, propping him up against the headboard in a sitting position. He was pale and his lids were fluttering. She put her fingers to his pulse. It was rapid, but already beginning to slow down. Man had a heart like a diesel engine.

'Let's just stay there like that, Daddy, while I get us a little Valium. Okay?'

He nodded his head.

As soon as Richard hung up, Wally started to glide around the living-room in a swooping, clumsy waltz, singing aloud to an improvised tune: 'I'll do anything you say, I'll pay what you want, do what you say, pay what you want . . .' Richard was smiling in simple pleasure at Wally's antics. Wally sailed towards her and tried to draw her into his dance. She ducked under his outstretched arms, ran into the bedroom, and slammed the door. She stood trembling in the darkened room for a moment, and then flopped down on the bed. She cradled her head on her clasped palms and stared emptily at the ceiling. She didn't stir, didn't blink an eye, when she heard the door open.

'Hey, what's the matter, baby?'

Wally was standing beside the bed, looming massive and top-heavy. She rolled away from him on to her side, facing the shaded window.

'Baby?' He sat down on the edge of the bed. 'You all right?'

She shrugged his hand off her shoulder. Am I all right, Wally? I don't think so, or I wouldn't be lying here, instead of dancing a joyous *pas de deux* in the living-room.

'Jesus – you're not crying, are you?'

Why would I be crying – simply because an old man invoked the name of God, a cry of convenience rather than belief? Because of the quaver in his voice? Because, through the telephone wires, I glimpsed the bloodlessness of his hand clasped around the telephone? *Hand that once held mine.*

'You think I'm crying?' She rolled over on her back. 'Touch my eyes.'

'What do I want to touch your eyes for?'

'I want you to touch my eyes and see if you can find a trace of tears.'

'I take your word for it. So what did you run out of the room for?'

'Touch them. Touch my eyes.' She found his hand and led it to her face. 'Well, are there tears?'

'Okay, chrissake, no tears.'

He tried to withdraw his hand, but she clutched it tightly and led it to her mouth. She bit down on his fingers. He tried to withdraw them but she held on tightly, softened her mouth, and began to suck on them.

Still partially dressed, their clothes twisted, they lay panting on the bed. Her eyes were accustomed to the darkness now, and she could make out the shapes of

Wally's pulleys and weights, the frieze of pinup pictures on the wall. She was propped up against the headboard, Richard's sweater rolled up under her chin, Wally's head resting on her breasts.

His breathing back to normal, Wally said, 'Seriously, what was that all about – that act you put on?'

'I wasn't crying, was I?'

'Okay, you weren't crying. But you were feeling sorry for him, weren't you?'

Okay – a fair question. Had the mastermind, the chief executive of the kidnap plot, shown an uncharacteristic sign of weakness? It was a legitimate concern of the rank and file.

I felt his pain, I felt his pain. 'Not exactly. I was just trying to accommodate to the fact that I was every bit as much of a shit as Julian.'

'Come on, baby,' Wally said in disbelief. 'What he did to your father, making him kill himself? Marrying that woman and cutting you off without a penny? And the dancing – only a fucking monster would do what he did, deliberately getting you fat . . .'

And those were just the highlights, Wally. 'Let's talk about something else, okay?'

'Sure, baby. What do you want to talk about?'

'Well, let's see. Money?'

'Right.' A corner of his mouth quirked upwards in a smile. 'Money.'

Chapter 16

In the morning Nella awakened early and slipped out of bed without disturbing Wally. Richard's door was open, his bed neatly made, as usual. This was to be his last day on day shift. After a day off he would switch over to nights. When she returned from her shower, Wally was on the floor, doing his effortless push-ups, his eyes glazed, lost in the ritual of celebrating his body.

She turned on the kitchen radio as she prepared breakfast. An all-news station was at the tag end of its cycle, presenting odd features, marking time until the hour, when it would again begin its cycle of hard news. After a set of interminable commercials, the announcer gave a preview: OPEC meeting starting today in Vienna; terrorists still occupying embassy in Cyprus; two wounded in attempted supermarket robbery; mayor flying to Washington to plead for federal funds. Where was kidnapped girl phones wealthy architect? Maybe it wasn't important enough, and would come in the next, second-tier batch of news. Not as important as a commonplace holdup?

Wally came into the kitchen, radiant, fragrant, eager. His smile disappeared when he saw her face. 'What the hell are they trying to pull?'

She tried to cheer him up. 'Nothing to worry about, Wally. It's still early times.'

But who cheers up the cheerer-up?

Wally dressed and went out for the newspapers. He came back with the *Times* and *News*, both in disarray, and flung them down on the table.

'They're fucking us around,' he said. His cheeks were tinted a rosy pink. 'And don't tell me it takes time, that's bullshit.'

'Relax, Wally, it isn't the end of the world.'

'Bullshit. We're finished.'

238

If you say bullshit once more, Wally, I'll pour bacon drippings over your gorgeous head. 'Look, if you collapse every time something doesn't go according to schedule, you can kiss your money goodbye. We can handle this, it isn't serious.'

'Bullshit.'

'Listen to me,' she said, her voice rising. 'Where did you get the idea kidnapping was a picnic? If you wanted to get rich painlessly, you should have tried something else, maybe let some rich fruit blow you. It can't make all that much difference whose mouth it is, you know.'

He wheeled and walked out of the kitchen.

Wonderful, Nella, you've done it again. The witch of the whole wide world. You can't *have* a quarrel a day. How can you control Wally if you can't control yourself? She poured a cup of coffee and took it to the table. Wally wasn't in the living-room. She glanced through the newspapers on the table without interest until she heard Wally's footsteps. He walked by, his eyes straight ahead, and marched into the kitchen. He poured himself a cup of coffee and stood there drinking it, glowering.

She followed him into the kitchen. 'I'm sorry, Wally, it was uncalled for.'

He was silent, his lower lip jutting stubbornly.

'It was a stupid thing to say.'

'Damn right it was stupid.' He glanced at her resentfully. 'Especially because you know how I feel about fags.'

'I don't know what came over me. I beg your forgiveness.' She moved a step closer and looked up at him pleadingly. 'What I said about it not mattering whose mouth it was? It does matter.'

He quirked his shoulders in a neutral shrug.

'Wally dear?' She looped her thumbs in his belt and lowered her eyelids. 'Can I show you that it matters? May I, Wally, please?'

The beginning of a smile fluttered at the corner of his lips. 'Well, I'd like to have my coffee first.'

As a rookie policeman, the chief of detectives had been

239

thin and wiry, with a concealed strength and agility that made him more than equal to his huskier classmates at the Academy. He didn't look like a cop but an athlete in a noncontact sport like tennis. He was olive-skinned, with a long intellectual nose and alert black eyes. His instructors thought he was a know-it-all and didn't like him very much, but they, like everybody else at the Academy, knew that he was a winner. He might have been better liked if he talked like a cop; faultless grammar seemed like an affectation.

Twenty-seven years later, the Chief's command of grammar was intact, but, Roehmer thought, he had grown into looking like a cop. He hadn't put on much flab, except for a puffiness around the jaws, but the profession had put its stamp on him. He had acquired a weightiness of movement where once he had been catlike, and his eyes were now suspicious rather than alert. As a rookie his toughness had lain under the surface, something to be sensed rather than seen; now it was right up front, partner to his air of authority.

He had always been a bit of a dude, and growing sophistication and a high salary had refined his taste. His suit was well tailored and discreetly patterned, and he wore a dark, immaculate chesterfield with a velvet collar and a Borsalino hat which, according to rumour, he had made for him in Rome, a new one every year.

His unannounced appearance at the One-Eight precinct house at eight-thirty in the morning created a stir; it made everybody nervous, especially in the detective squad room. He made a point of coming over and shaking Roehmer's hand before disappearing into the lieutenant's office. The handshake, Roehmer reckoned, was good for about three days' worth of envy from his colleagues in the squad room (including Murphy, who made a predictable joke about not washing the hand that had shaken the Chief's). It would reinforce their belief that the Chief was his rabbi.

In a few minutes Boyd came out of his office and beckoned. Murphy winked and said, 'For personal valour he's gonna give you one of his old hats.'

There were no seats left in the lieutenant's office. Boyd sat behind his desk, the Chief was in one of the two chairs, and the captain in the other. So Roehmer stood. The captain ignored him, the Chief regarded him neutrally, and the lieutenant, on his best behaviour in the presence of the Chief, was polite and formal.

'Detective Roehmer,' he said, 'tell the Chief the details about the telephone call last night.'

'I intercepted,' Roehmer said. 'Special Agent Fairborn and me, we intercepted the call on the telephone cutoff in the cellar. You want to hear the tape, sir?'

The Chief shook his head. 'Just describe it.'

'The kidnapper said something like, "This is your friendly neighbourhood kidnapper. Here's Nella." And then a girl's voice – '

'The kidnapper's voice,' the Chief said, 'what colour?'

'What *colour*? Oh. Far as I could tell, white. The girl's voice said something like, "Uncle Julian, it's me, Nella." And then Massey said something, and she said, "Uncle Julian," again, and then the kidnapper's voice, male, white, said, "You'll be hearing from me," and hung up. But Massey didn't know it. He said, "Send her back, I'll pay what you want," and then his wife told him the phone was dead.'

'You try to trace the call?' the Chief said.

'Yessir. The phone company's Annoyance Calls Unit was patched in from their district office, but the call was only about thirty seconds long, so there was no way. The least they need is ten to fifteen minutes, up to an hour or more.'

Pittman, the electronics detective, had told him that the Annoyance Calls Unit could set a successful trap for a suspect whose phone number was known, but not for a local call made at large.

'After the phone call,' Roehmer said, 'the special agent and me . . . and I – ' The captain looked at him for the first time – with irritation. 'We went upstairs to the apartment of Julian Massey, but he denied us entry.'

Smiling, the Chief said, 'That means he wouldn't let you in?'

Roehmer waited stolidly while the captain and the lieutenant had their laugh, then went on. 'His wife came to the door, and when we said we wanted to talk to him, she asked us to wait outside. When she came back, she said he couldn't talk to us, he wasn't feeling good. We said it was important, we had to talk to him about the phone call. So she went back in again, and then came back and said Massey told her to say he didn't want anything more to do with us. All he wanted was to get the girl back, he was ready to pay the ransom, and so forth. That scared us. We wouldn't go away. We kept Mrs Massey running back and forth, and finally, I guess, she wore him down, and he agreed to see us this morning.'

'That's it?'

'Yessir, that's it.'

'He was quite an architect,' the Chief said. 'Did you know that at one time he was considered to design Number One Police Plaza?'

The lieutenant said, 'Whaddya know!'

Roehmer said, 'Special Agent Fairborn is going to run a check on the tape through their voice-print bank.'

The captain made a derisive noise. 'Those fellas think they can run their whole operation by remote control. Armchair detectives.'

The Chief said to Roehmer, 'All the white male voice said was that they'd be hearing from him again? No instructions? Nothing else?'

Roehmer shook his head.

'And it's been nine, ten days since the girl disappeared? It's the most leisurely kidnapping I've ever heard of.'

'Slow motion,' the lieutenant said.

'What do you make of it?' the Chief said to Roehmer.

'If I was a kidnapper,' Roehmer said, 'I would want to get it over as fast as possible. Must be a lot of strain. Especially if it's just one kidnapper. Putting myself in his place, I don't see how it's possible, unless he ties her up and gags her so he can sleep, go to the john, buy food . . .'

'You think it's more than one?' the Chief said. Roehmer hesitated. 'You're the man, Roehmer. Speak up.'

'It *figures* to be more than one, but I don't know.'

Roehmer paused. 'As for the girl's voice, sir, I think it was legitimate. I think it was the voice of Nella Massey, age twenty-six, white female.'

'You've heard this girl's voice before, of course, in order to come to that conclusion?'

'No, sir, I never heard her voice, but it sounded just right, like the voice of a girl who was brought up on Park Avenue.'

'Mr Massey will tell us whether it was her voice or not – he's better qualified.' The Chief's tone was glacial. 'Are you riding some kind of a hunch on this case?'

'I have a theory on the case, sir.' He stressed *theory* slightly, just enough to make his point without seeming to be insubordinate. 'My theory is that it's a setup with the girl involved.'

'It's a workable theory, I guess.' The Chief smiled. 'But haven't you been around long enough to have learned rule one – don't hang your ass out on the line?'

The captain said, 'Fake or legit – either way we got the same exact police work to do.'

Not quite the same, Roehmer thought, but he wasn't about to irk the captain by saying so. So he stood by silently and waited to see if the Chief would pick up the ball. He did.

'If it's a fake, nobody's going to get hurt, which gives us a great deal more time to operate, and in a much bolder way.' The Chief paused and, with an appeasing nod at the captain, said, 'But we don't make policy on hunches.'

Back to hunch again, Roehmer thought. In his years as a detective he had made the discovery that what was called a hunch – he called it that himself – wasn't a magical bolt from the blue but an accretion of details and inductions, based on experience and observation, that his mind couldn't quite put together, but that leaked out as a *sense* of something, a *feeling* . . . well, a hunch. Of course in this particular case there was something else: the special insight to Nella Massey he thought he had inherited from knowing Peggy Parris. Now *that* was hunchy.

'I'm not trying to knock you down,' the Chief said. 'You're a smart detective, and sometimes a hunch is useful. But I don't want you to let it run away with you and distort the way you handle the case. Make sure you don't let Massey get wind of it. He's still the girl's uncle, and even if it *is* a phoney, he wouldn't want to admit it.'

'Exactly what I been telling you,' the lieutenant said.

'Yes, sir,' Roehmer said to the room at large.

Fairborn phoned to say that he had been delayed, and would meet them in the lobby of Massey's building. The Chief told Roehmer a little exercise would do them some good, so they walked, with the Chief's car, chauffeured by a sergeant, trailing a little behind them and screwing up traffic on the side streets. The Chief chatted briefly about the good old days at the Academy.

'Remember what they taught us about being objective? Don't let your thesis lead you around by the nose.'

'Yessir. I'll try not to.'

'Not that I'm saying it's not valid. In the light of the relationship between the girl and her uncle, and the money going to the new wife . . . You know what impresses me?' The Chief paused, but Roehmer guessed that the question was rhetorical, and remained silent. 'What impresses me is all the time they're taking, which might indicate that it's a fake.'

'You said *they*. You think it might be more than one?'

'They – the kidnapper and the girl. That's one theory. Another one is that the kidnapper – they or he, whichever – doesn't issue an ultimatum because he hasn't got the guts to kill the girl if the ultimatum fails. Have you thought of that?'

'I guess it's possible.'

'One way or another, as I said back at the House, we seem to have some slack. I'd like to exploit it. But that requires the co-operation of Mr Julian Massey, doesn't it?'

'He wasn't too co-operative last night. In fact he sounded like he was kicking us out.'

'Hysteria,' the Chief said. 'He just finished talking to the girl on the phone. Don't worry, he'll come around. We'll *bring* him around, we'll make him see the light.'

'Make him?' Roehmer said.

'You think I'm trying to play God?' The Chief scowled. 'Just keep this in mind – there isn't a thing I can do if he won't allow me to. He has the last word.'

'Yessir.'

'I'm not going to risk the girl's life,' the Chief said. 'But I'm not going to lie down and die, either. Understood?'

On Park Avenue, waiting for the traffic light to change, the Chief waved his arm at Massey's building. 'Those old houses – they build them like fortresses. Solid, like the people that live in them.'

Yeah, Roehmer thought, solid like that old fart Julian Massey, like his troubled niece, like Peggy Parris, who slept with rookie cops and, without meaning to, fucked up their lives.

As they were crossing the street, a taxi pulled up in front of the house. Fairborn got out and hurried into the lobby.

'That was the G-man,' Roehmer said.

'Which reminds me,' the Chief said. 'Don't let him hog the ball on those TV interviews. Assert yourself, speak up.'

Massey and the Chief hit it off right from the start. It was a case of power acknowledging power, authority recognising authority. But the Chief was not emotionally involved, and that gave him an advantage. He exploited it – ruthlessly. What he had in mind was persuading Massey to do what was best for the concerns of the police rather than his own. It was the way cops were. They hated criminals, they hated to see them get away with anything, they wanted to nab them. It was an article of faith, and even corrupt cops subscribed to it.

The Chief took the floor and held it – there was no room for Roehmer or Fairborn to edge in. It was clear to Roehmer where he was heading. He wanted to strengthen Massey's resolve, to keep him from panicking, from giving in, to let the police direct his responses to the kidnapper. His plan was to test the nerves of the kidnapper by prolonging negotiations, so that, eventually, he would either be smoked out or driven to quit in despair.

He struck a snag when he challenged Massey's contention that the voice he had heard over the telephone was Nella's. 'People have a way of hearing what they expect to hear,' the Chief said. 'We see it happen all the time in our work.'

Massey showed a flash of temper. 'Don't try to tell me I don't know my own niece's voice. I know it better than I do my own. It was Nella's voice.'

A stone wall. The Chief backed off and tried an end run. 'In our recent experimentation with voices and tones we've made two valuable discoveries. The first is . . .' He paused, his eyelids flickering, and Roehmer knew that he was improvising all the way. 'The first is that human voices under extreme stress have a tendency to lose their individual characteristics, and to resemble each other as a category. The second is that the telephone lends itself to easy imitation of a voice. Something to do with the levelling effect of electronic vibrations, plus the psychological boost inherent in the absence of a face and body – the listener reflexively supplies the details of body and face when the name is said.'

Fairborn was making an effort to conceal his annoyance at the Chief's bullshit. No appreciation, Roehmer thought, it's first-class bullshit, befitting his high rank. But Massey wasn't entirely taken in.

'How could anyone imitate Nella unless he knew her voice very well. And why *would* he do it unless . . .'

He gave Agnes a stricken look. His logic had opened up a terrible insight for him, Roehmer thought: it had occurred to him that the only reason the kidnapper had to imitate Nella's voice was that she couldn't speak for herself. The Chief took note of Massey's sagging face and tacked violently.

'I think you've misunderstood me, sir. I do believe the voice you heard was your niece's. I've been laying everything out for you to show you that it's plausible to *deliberately* raise doubts about it.'

Massey looked relieved. He didn't appear to have been

aware of the Chief's abrupt about-face – probably, Roehmer thought, because he didn't want to be, didn't want to pursue the unthinkable thought. The Chief explained his position more or less truthfully: the longer it could be dragged out, the better the chances that the kidnapper would make a mistake, the more time the police had to track him down.

'But if I keep putting him off, he might . . .' Massey couldn't complete his sentence, but the thought ran on into the silence as if it had been shouted.

'Trust us,' the Chief said. 'You can bank on our not allowing anything to happen to your niece. If the time ever approaches when the kidnapper might be prepared to carry out his threat, we'll know it. When that time comes, if it ever does, we'll pull out and advise you to co-operate with the kidnapper.'

'You mean pay the million-dollar ransom?'

'It's one hell of a lot of money, and we'd hate to see you lose it.' The Chief managed to look grim and sympathetic at the same time.

Actually, as Roehmer knew, the police didn't care all that much about the victim losing money, they just didn't like to see criminals *get* it. There was a difference.

'Well, I certainly don't *want* to give a million away if I can help it. I worked hard to earn my money.'

'And contributed to the beauty of the city at the same time,' the Chief said earnestly. 'Our optimum goal is the recovery of your niece unharmed without the payment of money, *and* apprehension of the kidnapper. Isn't that the way you feel too?'

'Of course,' Massey said. 'But the first priority is the return of my niece. If I have to, I'll pay to get her back, little as I like the idea.'

'Exactly,' the Chief said. 'We're in total agreement, Mr Massey.'

'It's the worst thing that's ever happened in my entire life.' Massey's voice was suddenly tearful. 'Living with the knowledge that someone dear to you is at the mercy of some vicious monster . . .'

'Excuse me,' Roehmer said, getting to his feet. The

Chief frowned at him. 'Sorry. Excuse me.' He crossed the room to Agnes Massey. Bending towards her, he whispered, 'Mrs Massey, could you please tell me where the bathroom is?'

'I better show you or you'll get lost,' Agnes said. 'I'm going to show this fella the john,' she said to Massey. 'Be right back.'

As he followed Agnes out of the room, Roehmer heard the Chief's voice pick up again, assuring the old man that, having beloved nieces of his own, he could well understand the depths of Massey's anguish . . . Partway down the corridor Agnes stopped and pointed to a door.

'There's the john. We got four more – would you believe it?'

'Thanks, Mrs Massey.' Roehmer struck his forehead with his hand. 'Oh, I've been meaning to ask you something about the blue cashmere coat Nella was wearing.'

'It wasn't – ' Agnes Massey stopped herself and made a wry face. 'I better be getting back. I don't want to miss anything.'

'What about the coat, Mrs Massey? Was it a navy blue cashmere?'

'Well . . . does it make that much difference?'

'Yes. It might turn out to be very important.'

Agnes sighed. 'She wasn't wearing a navy cashmere coat. I haven't seen her wearing that coat in over a month.'

'What kind of coat was she wearing?'

'A shearling. You know what that is, a shearling?'

Roehmer kept his voice low. 'Are you positive?'

'Come on – can't I tell the difference between cashmere and shearling?'

'But Mr Massey described the coat as a navy blue cashmere.'

'Julian!' Agnes's voice was filled with humorous scorn. 'That man never knows what a person is wearing. *Never*. I can be wearing a dress for six months, and he might say, "When'd you get the new dress?" Honest, that's the way he is. A man of his intelligence, a college graduate,

Princeton, and he might as well be stone blind so far as knowing what somebody is wearing.'

'But why did he say she was wearing the blue cashmere?'

'He didn't know *what* she was wearing. But a few years ago he *gave* her the coat, so he said that was what she was wearing. But it must have been the shearling. The last month or so it was the only coat she ever wore.'

'Mrs Massey – I hope you don't mind my asking – why didn't you tell us about this earlier?'

Agnes grimaced. 'Because Julian hates to be wrong. I *told* him she was wearing a shearling, and I *told* him to tell the police, but he said to mind my own business. He just can't stand looking dumb. But men aren't supposed to notice what women are wearing, so where's the shame in admitting you're wrong?'

'I'm much obliged to you, Mrs Massey.'

'Listen – you're not going to tell him I tattled, are you? He'll skin me alive.'

'We always respect confidences, Mrs Massey. He'll never know. Trust me.'

'Okay.' Agnes cocked her head and grinned. 'I'll bet you didn't have to go to the bathroom – it was an excuse to get me to one side.'

'Well,' Roehmer said, smiling, 'as long as I'm here.'

By the time he returned to the living-room, it was all settled. 'Detective Roehmer,' the Chief said solemnly, 'you'll be pleased to know that Mr Massey has agreed to co-operate with our game plan one hundred per cent.'

'I'm certainly pleased to hear that, sir.'

'Yes,' Fairborn said. 'Yes, indeed.'

In the afternoon, after Wally decided to take a walk, Nella ranged through the apartment restlessly. Cabin fever. She had been confined for ten days now, and there were moments when the little apartment made her want to scream. Not that the apartment itself was at fault, nor Wally, either – she would have felt no differently if she had been sequestered for ten days with some impossibly ideal man: Wally's body plus intelligence plus tenderness. The problem was simpler than that. Except for a prolonged illness when she was a child, she had never been pent up indoors for so long a period, and she was suffering from an acute physical yearning for open space, even such grimy, gritty, illusory space as the city streets provided.

She was still shaken by her quarrel with Wally. Aside from her inadmissible loss of control, the fact remained that Wally had a valid point. The story of her phone call to Julian should have been aired – unless it was being deliberately suppressed. Unless, as Wally put it, they were being fucked around. Whoever was responsible for withholding the story – she was convinced it was Roehmer, the bleary-eyed detective who pleaded with her earnestly through the TV camera in silent code – it brought home the extent to which they danced at the end of a string. It was almost as if the other side suspected their basic weakness – that she wouldn't be killed – and was testing them. Wally had suggested calling the story into the newspapers, as they had after the first note to Julian, but it didn't feel right to her: it advertised their dependence on the other side.

Wally returned after five o'clock. His shoulders sagged when she told him that there had been no report on the radio. She set herself the task of diverting him, but he resisted her most blatant efforts at seduction.

'I don't feel like doing it.'

'You will,' she crooned, touching him. 'I'll make you feel like it, darling.'

He held her off. 'I'm not in the mood.'

'What do you feel like doing?'

'Nothing.' He shrugged. 'I'd just as soon talk.'

Man does not live by bed alone. 'All right. But we might as well lie down and be comfortable.'

He shook his head. 'I'll make us some tea.'

They sat at the table and sipped tea and talked. The subject was of Wally's choosing, and as always it was of money and the life of the rich. He no longer spoke much about his physical culture school. In a way, she was responsible for the shift in his viewpoint. She had warned him that he would have to lie low after he got his share of the ransom, not make a splash for fear of attracting attention. She also pointed out that the money would have to be laundered – he couldn't walk in and buy a school with a bag full of cash. Now he told her that he had been having thoughts about not working at all. He could live very well from the interest on a third of a million. Travel, buy new threads, a nice Mercedes, anything he wanted to do. He might fly to Switzerland and open a numbered account, no questions asked. Or live in Brazil so, in case anything went wrong, he couldn't be extradited.

As for the rich, he was endlessly fascinated by details of Julian's life-style, going as far back as his days as a Princeton undergraduate and his friendship with Scott Fitzgerald, 'the man who wrote the movie, *Great Gatsby*.'

Six o'clock. Time for the news. The kidnap story was the lead item.

Almost from its start, Nella sensed that there was something contrived about the newscast, as if it had been orchestrated in advance. And one of the newspeople, a woman television reporter with a beautiful, elaborately remodelled nose, seemed to have been rehearsed in detail.

There was a new presence on the screen along with the familiar faces of Roehmer and Fairborn – the chief of detectives of the New York Police Department, a dark, suave, handsome man with star quality. Even the reporters seemed to acknowledge his pre-eminence; they addressed their questions to him with an edge of respect. He announced that Julian Massey had received a phone call purporting to be from his niece, and gave a word-for-word description of it.

'You said "purported",' a newsman said. 'Does that mean there is a doubt that it was Nella Massey?'

Almost immediately another man said, 'Did Julian Massey recognise his niece's voice?'

The Chief said, 'Mr Massey identified the voice as that of his niece.'

'Is he absolutely sure of it?'

The Chief frowned and pointed his finger at the woman

reporter, who said, 'Chief, could the voice, Nella Massey's voice, have been taped?'

The Chief flicked a glance at Fairborn and Roehmer before replying. 'We have no sure way of knowing that.'

The reporter – the bitch is acting up a storm, Nella thought – frowned thoughtfully. 'If it *was* a tape, then it might have been recorded days, even a week, ago.'

'It's conceivable.'

'In that case, there's no assurance that the Massey girl is still alive.'

'What the hell are they talking about?' Wally said.

The Chief glanced at Roehmer and Fairborn again. Fairborn gave a slight nod. Roehmer, sweating in his checked jacket and too-tight collar, was impassive.

'I can't hypothesise about that,' the Chief said.

Someone shouted, 'Can't or won't?'

The Chief raised his brows and ignored the question.

The woman reporter said, 'Can we assume that you – and Mr Massey – would like the kidnapper to come forward with some evidence that she's still alive and well?'

The Chief produced a thin smile. 'I never tell criminals how to run their show. But there is an open question here.'

Someone shouted, 'What would you accept as evidence?'

The Chief ignored the question. He made a little bow and started to move out of camera range. Then he stopped. 'I have nothing else to say except this: Mr Massey is bereft and suffering deeply. In the name of human decency we appeal to the kidnapper to reunite this sorrowing man with his beloved niece.'

Nella threw her slipper at the television screen. It missed, sailing by harmlessly across the living-room.

'What do you want to do that for?' Wally said indignantly.

She was furious with herself. She was sure they knew her voice had not been taped; nevertheless she had presented them with an opening to express their reservation. It was inexcusable not to have anticipated it. The mastermind had slipped up.

'We're going to make another phone call to Julian,' she said. 'Turn that damn thing off.'

By the time the phone had rung three times, Nella was certain that nobody was home. But suddenly, on the sixth ring, it was picked up.

Her voice breathless from tension, she said, 'Uncle Julian, it's Nella, please listen and don't interrupt – '

'Nella? How are you?'

Oh God, the Creepy Housekeeper. 'Agnes, put Julian on, hurry.'

She heard Agnes's voice off the phone. 'It's her – ' and then a scuffling sound, and Agnes protesting, 'don't grab like that.'

'Nella?' Julian's voice was excited, eager. 'Is it you, Nella? Are you all right?'

'Please, Uncle Julian, don't speak. I haven't much time. Listen. This is from the front page of today's *Times*. "The Senate today rejected the President's foreign aid package legislation by a vote of seventy-two to twenty-five" – '

'Nella, I want you to tell me how you are – '

' – "the bill, sponsored by Senator" – '

Wally snatched the phone from her hand. It thudded against her cheekbone as he slammed it into its cradle.

'Hey,' Wally said, 'did I hurt you?'

'It was beautiful, Wally,' she said, touching her tingling cheek. 'Exactly how your average vicious kidnapper would do it.'

Chapter 17

Dim lighting in a bar was meant to be sexy, but its effect in the Pleasant Times, Roehmer thought, was to conceal its own sleaziness and the decrepitude of its clientele. The darkness hid them from one another, from the mirror image of each other's face, a chronicle of petty disasters: the monthly scramble for the rent money, the deadening job, the hunt through the supermarket freezer for the cheapest cuts of meat, the incessant juggling to pay off this bill and stall off that one, the ageing, worn-out wife (who surrendered all points but the weekly donation to the church; to hold on to that piety she would even suffer blows without conceding), the children turning their backs on their parents in their scramble to move a notch up the ladder . . .

At a quarter past six there was a handful of men at the bar. Roehmer took a seat that left a gap of empty stools between him and the nearest patrons, who were discussing the football season in heated agreement over the poor quality of the local teams, the stupidity of the coaches, the ineptitude of the linesmen, the pathetic incompetence of the quarterback . . .

'Bartender.'

The bartender spent a full thirty seconds inspecting a glass for motes before edging along the bar towards him. 'What's your order?'

'I was in here yesterday. Remember me?'

'You had a beer. Bud. That what you want?'

'I asked you about the kidnapped girl, Nella Massey. Remember?'

'I told you I didn't see her. Remember?'

Roehmer nodded. 'But I forgot to tell you she was wearing a shearling coat.'

There was no movement of the bartender's eyes, no

lifting of the brows, no sudden start. He just shrugged. So much for taking him by surprise.

'Was there anybody in here a week ago Thursday wearing a shearling coat?'

The bartender shrugged again. 'Not that I know about.'

'What does that mean? Were you on duty all night?'

'All night.'

'And you didn't see her?'

'That's what I said.'

Roehmer took the picture out of his pocket and handed it across the bar. 'She was wearing a shearling coat.'

The bartender barely glanced at the picture before sliding it back across the bar. 'I told you I didn't see her. Stop hassling me.'

Roehmer tucked the photograph away in his pocket. 'You own this place?'

'What's that got to do with anything?'

'I'm just asking.'

'And I don't have to tell you.'

'It's not that much trouble to find out.'

'So go find out.'

A customer called, 'Hey, McGarry,' and held his empty glass up.

McGarry, okay. 'You got a first name?'

'No.'

The customer waved his glass in the air. 'Hey, Pat, how's about a little bit of service?'

'You want a chance to change your story?' Roehmer said.

McGarry stared at him with contempt and walked away.

Strikeout, Roehmer thought. Maybe if I'd lit a match when I first popped the question about the shearling, I might have seen him flush. A man could control his muscular reactions but not the colouring of his face. He turned up his coat collar and groped his way to the door. Outside, he braced against the bite of the wind. Now what? Home to Mary? Well, he had reports to write up first. And after that? Well, the reports would take half the night, so maybe he ought to count on sacking out on a cot in the precinct house and then, first thing in the morning, check out Pat McGarry.

Another hunch? Well, it was something to do, wasn't it?

He stopped in a coffee shop for a bite to eat. When he got back to the precinct house, he learned that Nella Massey had made another phone call to her uncle, and that the chief of detectives and Fairborn had gone to see Massey at his apartment.

They were coming out just as Roehmer arrived – he met them in the outer lobby of Massey's building – the Chief, Fairborn, and a third man. The doorman held the outer door open.

'I guess I'm too late,' Roehmer said. 'I heard she phoned again.'

'That's the trouble with perpetrators,' the Chief said jovially, 'they work after hours.'

Fairborn introduced the third man. Special Agent Neal Rakisch. They shook hands.

'I wasn't in the House,' Roehmer said, 'but I was working.' Why do I have to explain? I'm not being paid to work twenty-four hours a day. 'What was the phone call about?'

'She read something from today's paper,' the Chief said. He pointed his finger at the doorman. 'Shut the door, it's getting cold in here.'

'Was that all, sir?' Roehmer said.

The Chief shrugged. 'She read her piece and then, it sounded like, somebody grabbed the phone and hung up.'

Fairborn, speaking to the Chief, said, 'Look, I don't want to keep him waiting, we'd better be getting along. If you'll excuse us?'

They shook hands all around. The Chief held on to Fairborn's hand and said, 'I want to hear him tonight – if it works out.'

'It'll work out,' Fairborn said, and Rakisch nodded in agreement.

Fairborn and Rakisch left. Outside, fighting the wind, holding on to their hats, they flagged down a taxi.

'Those people . . .' The Chief shook his head, bemused. 'Still, I guess they know their stuff.' He turned to Roehmer and, with a satisfied little smile, said, 'Mr Massey thinks it isn't the girl's voice.'

'Is that what he said?'

The smile disappeared from the Chief's face. 'I just told you so, didn't I?'

'Yessir.'

'Which puts a slightly different complexion on it. Either we've got some kind of a scam going or – ' He looked at the doorman. 'Can you find something to do inside, old fellow?'

The doorman mumbled and went inside.

'Ears on him like a donkey,' the Chief said. 'Or she's dead, and they're using a ringer. That would explain the change in the old man – I mean, thinking now that it's not the girl's voice, when last time he was so sure of it.'

Roehmer didn't say anything.

'That would explain it, wouldn't it, Roehmer?'

No, sir, Roehmer thought, what *would* explain it is that you fed the old man a line of bullshit, and worked on him like the expert con man you are, and in the end got him to say exactly what you wanted him to say.

'Yessir,' Roehmer said, 'that would explain it.'

'Say it as if you meant it,' the Chief said. His voice was harsh. 'Remember who I am.'

'Yessir,' Roehmer said.

'You got any objections, let's hear them.'

'No objections,' Roehmer said.

'If *he* says it's not her voice, that's definitive. It's not her voice.'

It's her voice, Roehmer thought, she's alive and well and she rose to our bait.

'I played the tape back for him a few times, and he swore it wasn't her. I don't want you doubting me.'

The extenuating circumstance, Roehmer thought, was that you couldn't pull off anything with intelligent, educated people unless they were ready to meet you halfway. Besides, who am I to take a holier-than-thou attitude? I'm just as much a con man as the Chief, only not as good at it.

'Sir,' Roehmer said, putting some conviction into his voice, 'I don't doubt you. What would I want to do that for?'

'You're a good man,' the Chief said, 'and I'd like to see you bust this case, which is why I haven't sent any men up from the Major Case Squad yet.' He patted the velvet collar of his coat. 'We're going on the eleven o'clock news with the old guy's denial.' A smile. 'That should give the kidnapper something to think about.'

'Yessir.'

'Any questions?'

The hard edge was back in the Chief's voice. I'd better watch my step, Roehmer thought. Old school tie or not, he wouldn't waste a minute sending me to Siberia if I crossed him.

'No, sir, no questions. And I appreciate your holding off on the Major Case detectives.'

'Okay, Roehmer. Let's call it a day.'

'Just one thing, sir. I've placed the girl in her old neighbourhood, and I think it might be worth tossing that area. I'm working on it myself, some of it on my own time, but one man can't do much. If I had some real help, I mean like a half-dozen detectives . . .'

'Not a chance,' the Chief said. 'We haven't got the manpower. I don't say you're not on the right track, but it's too tenuous. You got the idea that if somebody rings the right bell, she'll come out and answer the door?'

You know I don't mean that, you shit. And you know that a hell of a lot of cases are solved in just that way. 'Maybe if I could use the other detectives in my team, exclusive . . .'

'Talk to Lieutenant Boyd about it. You can say I think it's a good idea – if he can spare the manpower.'

The Chief walked to the door and waited. Just in case I don't remember who he is, Roehmer thought. He reached around and opened the door for him. Outside, the Chief raised his hand, and his car, double-parked near the corner, started to back up.

'Can I drop you some place?'

Roehmer shook his head. 'I'm going back to the House and finish up some reports. I'd rather walk, clear my head a little.'

The Chief moved across the pavement to the open door of his car. 'You don't think I'd go just on the say-so of a shell-shocked old man, do you? Fairborn and the other guy are meeting this Laurence Adams at their office to play the tape back to him.' He waved his hand peremptorily as Roehmer started to speak. 'No, I don't need you there. It's the feds' show.' The Chief started to get into his car. 'Catch the eleven o'clock news. This Adams may be on – live.'

Yeah, he'll be on, Roehmer thought as the Chief's car pulled away, he'll be on if he says the right thing. He turned up the collar of his coat, lowered his shoulder to the wind, and headed back towards the precinct house.

Fairborn said, 'We'll play it through for you as often as you like, it's quite short, so there's no need to rush to a conclusion on the first go-round. Okay?'

Laurence Adams nodded his head soberly. His eye was fixed on the cassette Fairborn held in his hand.

'Let it go to the end,' Fairborn said. 'Don't comment until you've heard it through.'

He gestured with the hand that held the cassette, and Laurence Adams kept following it with his eyes, as though, Fairborn thought, it were the girl herself, as though the cassette were a bit of her substance.

They were seated at an oval table in a conference room in FBI headquarters, Fairborn and Rakisch on one side of the table, Laurence Adams on the other, and the cassette player on the table between them. Fairborn inserted the cassette into the player, put his finger on the *play* key and held it there for a moment, his head cocked to one side as if he were examining some sudden thought, then removed his finger amd scratched his ear. Laurence Adams was leaning forward over the table, his brow furrowed, his breathing irregular.

He'll fold, Fairborn thought. He removed his finger

from his ear. 'Well, here we go,' he said, and pressed the *play* key.

'*Uncle Julian, it's Nella, please listen and don't interrupt –* '

'*Nella? How are you?*'

In a whisper, Laurence Adams said, 'That's Agnes Massey.'

Fairborn frowned at him. Adams ducked his head apologetically.

'*Nella? Is it you, Nella? Are you all right?*'

'*Please, Uncle Julian, don't speak. I haven't much time. Listen. This is from the front page of today's* Times. "*The Senate today rejected the President's foreign aid package legislation by a vote of seventy-two to twenty-five*" – '

'*Nella, I want you to tell me how you are –* '

' – "*the bill, sponsored by Senator*" – '

The voice on the tape was cut off abruptly by a crash. Fairborn let the tape run on for a moment before pressing the *stop* key.

'It's Nella's voice,' Laurence Adams said. 'No question about it.'

Fairborn pressed *rewind* and the tape whirred briefly. 'I'll play it through again.'

'It's unnecessary,' Laurence Adams said. 'It's Nella.'

Fairborn started the tape. '*Uncle Julian, it's Nella, please listen . . .*'

Twice during the second playing Fairborn frowned as Laurence Adams started to speak. When the tape finished, Adams blurted out, 'Look, Mr Fairborn, there isn't the slightest doubt in my mind. That voice is Nella's.'

'Fine,' Fairborn said. 'We're glad to have your spontaneous reaction.' Rakisch nodded in agreement. The tape whirred as it rewound. 'All right, let's have another try.'

'What for? There's no point to it. I *know* the voice. It's Nella's voice.'

Fairborn tapped his finger lightly on the *play* key. 'We want to be *absolutely* sure of it. This time I'm going to request that you listen from the point of view that it might be somebody trying to imitate Nella's voice. Can you put yourself in that frame of mind? Do you understand what I'm asking you to do?'

'I understand,' Laurence Adams said, 'but it's futile. I'm not going to change my mind no matter how many times you play it.'

But he would, Fairborn thought. By the time it had been played a half dozen times, a dozen, a hundred if necessary, he would begin to have his doubts. He might not come around 180 degrees, but he would at least be so uncertain that he couldn't contradict the old man with any assurance.

When the tape finished, Fairborn said, 'Well, Mr Adams? Is it conceivable that somebody is imitating Nella's voice?'

Laurence Adams shook the question off. 'Look, I'd like to point something out to you. Julian Massey, on the tape, during the actual phone call, accepts the voice without qualifications as Nella's. He talks to her *as* Nella, he *knows* she's Nella.'

'That would seem to have been the case – *at that time*.'

'I can't fathom why, having accepted the voice unequivocally as Nella's *during* the phone call, he would change his mind later.'

Fairborn pressed the *play* key. Laurence Adams opened his mouth as if to protest, but instead, brow knit with effort, he concentrated on the tape. When it finished, Fairborn, rewinding at once, said, 'I'm going to play it back immediately. I'd like you to tune in for nuances, for anything that might be foreign to Nella's style.'

Adams listened the tape through, then said firmly, 'It's either Nella or it's an absolute perfect, flawless imitation of Nella.'

'Oh?' Rewinding the tape, Fairborn exchanged a glance with Rakisch. 'Then you're suggesting that it *might* be an impersonation?'

'Of course not. What I said was its exact opposite. I put it that way to show you how *certain* I am that it's Nella's voice.' He gave a short, exasperated laugh. 'I'm sure you're aware that the usage is a very common way of expressing a dead certainty in an ironical, humorous way.'

Looking at him blankly, Fairborn said, 'I don't see the point of the joke.'

'It wasn't said as a *joke* . . .' Laurence Adams made a gesture of helplessness. 'Look, please, forget what I said, and just revert to my earlier statement – that it's Nella. Just that – it *is* Nella.'

'Relax,' Fairborn said. 'Special Agent Rakisch and I have no intention of holding a slip of the tongue against you. We realise how difficult this is. All right. Unless you'd prefer to take a little rest, to clear your mind, I'll play the tape again.'

Laurence Adams's shoulders sagged.

'Would you like a break?' Fairborn said.

Laurence Adams shook his head wearily. 'No. Go ahead.'

'Try to make your mind a perfect blank,' Fairborn said. 'Which is to say, clear it of all preconceptions – whether in terms of your certainty that it's Nella's voice or of any doubts you might have, such as that it's a perfect impersonation.'

'But I just explained . . .' Adams subsided, and made a dismissive motion of his hand.

'Pretend that this is the first time you've heard the tape, and that you'll be making the first judgement of any kind about it.'

'I'll try,' Laurence Adams said, 'but I question that such a detachment is at all possible.' He looked at Fairborn sidelong. 'You're not *trying* to get me to change my mind, are you?'

Fairborn said quietly, 'I think you know better than that, Mr Adams. What possible motive could we have for such an approach?'

'I keep coming back to the fact that Julian accepts the voice on the phone without question as Nella's, and only later, perhaps after he has talked to you people, expresses doubt about it. Could he have been influenced by you?'

'I'm sure we couldn't have influenced that man if we wanted to,' Fairborn said with a smile. 'I can only theorise as to the reason for his change of heart. It's possible he accepted the voice as Nella's because he *expected* it to be her, it fulfilled his expectations. And, of course, we have to keep in mind his highly agitated state – he was in no condition to detect nuances in the voice he heard. Later on, when we played the tape back to him, when he listened to it without being under the extreme pressure of the actual call, when he was more in possession of his faculties, he had serious second thoughts about it.'

'Yes,' Laurence Adams said. 'But I'm not under the same kind of pressure . . .' His voice trailed off and he smiled sheepishly. Fairborn smiled back at him. 'It's true that I'm not exactly *calm*, but I *do* – honestly – believe that the voice is Nella's.'

'Good,' Fairborn said. 'Let's give it another whirl.' He played the tape and listened to it as intently as Laurence Adams. When it was finished, he said, 'Same reaction, Mr Adams?'

Adams paused for a long moment. 'I'm still certain it's Nella, but I can no longer be *certain*. That sounds ridiculous. May I explain what I mean? More lucidly, I hope?'

'By all means,' Fairborn said, and Rakisch smiled sympathetically.

'To be truthful, at this point I can't say *anything* with certainty. I've heard the damn thing so often, and listened to it with such fierce concentration, that I find it very difficult to form an objective judgement.'

'You can't?' Fairborn looked at Rakisch, who pursed his lips with an air of gravity.

'How can I? It's become so repetitive that I've begun to *hear* things, subliminal things. Actually, it has ceased to make sense. It's like . . .' He paused, groping. 'It's like saying a word over and over again, over and over again. It loses its meaning, simply becomes gibberish.'

'What word did you have in mind?' Fairborn said.

'Any word. *Constitutional*, let's say.'

'Constitutional?'

'*Any* word. If you repeat the word endlessly . . . Try saying *constitutional* over and over again and I think you'll see what I mean.'

Rakisch said, 'Constitutional, constitutional, constitutional, constitutional . . .'

Fairborn looked at him sharply. 'Shall we play the tape again, Mr Adams?'

Adams let out a sigh. 'Must you?'

'I know it's an ordeal.' Fairborn's finger hovered over the *play* key. 'Here we go. You're to try to tell us if it's Miss Massey's voice, absolutely, unequivocally, without a shadow of a doubt.'

'That's exactly what I did do at the start. I suppose I could do the same now. But without a shadow of a doubt?' He shook his head wearily. 'Go ahead and play it.'

'*Uncle Julian, it's Nella, please listen . . .*'

His face glistening with a slick of sweat, supporting himself on his trembling arms, Adams leaned halfway across the table towards the machine. Another half hour at most, Fairborn thought, and I could have him barking like a dog if I wanted him to.

Chapter 18

And once again, as though hours hadn't elapsed, they sat on the blue sofa facing the television set. Actually, they had been sitting there for the past two hours, watching Wally's favourite programmes run by, so seamlessly like each other that if your attention wandered, you might never know that one had ended, another begun. The characters, handsome young men and women barely distinguishable from each other, performed modestly, as if aware that they were subordinate to the twists of the plot, the clipped dialogue, and, above all, the screeching of cars making turns on two wheels or less.

Over the past week her entertainment (aside from sex) had consisted almost exclusively of television drama. Wally and Richard listened to music only sporadically and then it was pop, which she had never been able to cultivate much of a taste for. At times she had tried to divert herself by reading one of the paperback books from the shelf over Richard's bed. They were mostly crime thrillers, which didn't strike her as having much in common with the real thing, assuming that her own limited criminal career made her a valid judge. Their television counterparts, Wally's fare, had an advantage over Richard's books: they eliminated the labour of turning pages.

At ten o'clock she turned the dial to one of the independent channels which put on its news broadcast an hour earlier than the networks' stations. The programme began with the usual fanfare of commercials and a teaser about the coming attractions. Item three was the kidnap story: Missing girl phones uncle.

'Beautiful,' Wally said. 'Beautiful.'

But it was a reprise of the six o'clock news; a summary of the first phone call to Julian. There was no mention of a second call.

'They're fucking us around again,' Wally said. 'It's the same old shit.'

But it wasn't. There was a surprise. 'We present an exclusive interview with Iris Massey, mother of the kidnapped girl, living in Pasadena, California . . .'

'Oh, dear Jesus,' Nella wailed, 'not that.'

A newswoman, photographed from the rear, walked up a pathway leading to a neat white house. She pressed a bell, and while she waited the camera focused on a shingle to the left of the door: IRIS MASSEY. ASTROLOGIST.

'What do you know?' Wally said.

The door opened, and Iris Massey, freshly groomed, peered out. The reporter asked if she might come in, and Iris, with a bright smile, said, 'By all means.' It was all arranged, of course. The cameras were already stationed inside the house, and Iris had had ample time to select her dress, fix her hair, renew her make-up; even, Nella thought bitterly, practise her smile in the mirror. The reporter followed Iris into the living-room. It was furnished in bright Sun Belt style – wicker, rattan, cheerful fabrics – with the exception of the drapes, which Nella recognised as the heavy wine-coloured drapes of her childhood, cut short to fit the more modest proportions of these windows. One wall of the room was dominated by a large intricate zodiacal circle, its cabalistic symbols and stylised animals handsomely worked. There was a desk, covered with papers and holding a portable typewriter, against another wall.

As the reporter broached the matter of Nella's kidnap, the camera closed in on Iris's face. She had put on some weight, but her face was unlined, still ingénue-pretty. Her fluffy blonde hair was artfully dyed. It was one of her few genuine talents that she had always been able to find a good hairdresser.

'I have thought much about my dear Nella.' Iris's voice was as even and dispassionate as ever. 'I have consulted the heavenly bodies, their situations and conjunctions, seeking to penetrate the curtain and, hopefully, to forecast her immediate future with reference to her predicament.'

Dear God, Nella thought, if *I* could have penetrated the

curtain and seen this lunacy, I might never have done any of this.

'I have recast her horoscope, drawn up a new chart.' Calmly, with the camera following, Iris moved to the desk and picked up a sheaf of papers. 'This is it. Shall I read it?'

The reporter's eyes flickered. 'Perhaps it would be better if you just told us your conclusions, Mrs Massey?'

'Well,' Iris said, 'the details are quite interesting. Nella was born under the sign of Leo on the cusp of – '

'Oh, God,' Nella said.

'Quiet,' Wally said, 'I want to hear it.'

Iris was going on in her soft, placid voice. The moon was in the house of Jupiter. This signified that –

The reporter broke in smoothly. 'What our viewers want to hear, Mrs Massey, is whether Nella will be released unharmed, or – '

'No harm will befall her. She will be released.'

Nella threw her slipper. It plopped softly against the screen. Iris's face had faded out.

'I told you not to do that,' Wally said. 'You want to break the damn thing?'

'Yes.'

'Well, break your own goddamn set, not mine. Jesus, you're flipping, I swear.'

He glared at her with disgust, then got up and switched the channel. For the next hour they sat in brooding silence and watched a square-jawed young hero with beautiful hair drive his car through an unending series of hairpin turns, while, beside him, the heroine with equally beautiful hair and a lovely jawline stared through the windshield with wide lapis lazuli eyes.

The show ended at last, and Nella went to the kitchen for a glass of water. She returned to the living-room at the precise moment that her voice, or a metallic, dehumanised version of it, was issuing from the television set.

'. . . *Julian, it's Nella, please listen and don't interrupt . . .*'

Wally was turned away from the set, looking back at her with bewilderment. She stood behind him, leaning on the back of the sofa.

'Is this the voice of Nella Massey?' The camera drew

back from the anchorman to show him gazing studiously at a tape recorder. 'You have been listening to an excerpt from a recorded conversation between Julian Massey and – perhaps – his kidnapped niece. We'll have all the details right after this.'

She came around the sofa and sat down. Wally was leaning towards the television set, his face brooding.

When the commercial was finished, Nella's picture appeared on the screen and the taped conversation was played through. The anchorman reappeared and read from a sheet of paper. 'Mr Julian Massey said, quote, "I think I was speaking to my niece but I can't be one hundred per cent certain," unquote.'

'They're playing fucking games,' Wally said. 'With the first call they said it might be taped, and now they're saying it wasn't your voice. Fucking games.'

Right, Wally, they're playing fucking games. Not the least of which is admitting that they're tapping Mr Massey's telephone by brazenly playing their tape of the conversation on the air.

The anchorman announced that they were going, now, to a conference room at FBI headquarters in midtown Manhattan.

'Damn them,' Nella said. 'Damn them.'

Seated at a table facing the cameras were two FBI agents, Fairborn and a second man whose name Nella didn't catch, and, between them, Laurence Adams. Laurence looked rumpled, and his voice was reedy with fatigue. In answer to a question from Fairborn he was saying that, although the voice on the tape *seemed* to be Nella's, he wasn't convinced, *entirely* convinced, after hearing it many times, that it wasn't a remarkably skilful impersonation.

Wally said, 'Oh, Jesus,' in a soft wail.

'Specifically, Mr Adams,' Fairborn said, 'what caused your doubts?'

Laurence ran his fingers through his hair distractedly. Where was Detective Roehmer? Nella wondered. The second FBI man looked calm, almost detached. She preferred Roehmer with his sweaty face and ratty jacket, his appearance of verging on being asphyxiated by the knot of his tie, the unexpectedly tormented eyes.

'Nothing,' Laurence said. 'That is, nothing specific. Just, well, it's hard to articulate a feeling, a received perception . . .'

'Would you describe it, perhaps, as a *gut* feeling?' Fairborn said.

Laurence nodded. 'Perhaps that's as good a way as any to put it.'

Fairborn faced the camera. 'Like Mr Massey, Mr Adams has reservations as to the authenticity of the voice.' He cleared his throat before continuing in a weightier tone. 'I am authorised by Mr Massey to request the kidnapper of his niece to produce more concrete evidence that the voice is indeed Miss Massey's. In other words, proof that Miss Massey is alive and well . . .'

Laurence was blinking his eyes in bewilderment. Oh, God, Laurence, Nella thought, the bastards have misused you, damn them. You should have spat in their bloody eyes. But I'm going to use you myself. Oh, Laurence, what have I done to you?

She jumped up and switched off the set.

'You know what I think?' Wally was looking up at her from the sofa. He was pale, and his hazel eyes were washed out. He was speaking slowly, momentously. 'You want to know what I really *think*?'

I know what you think, Wally, you're not all that hard to read. She shook her head.

'They're fucking us around,' Wally said.

'You said that before. Please stop saying it, Wally.'

'They're fucking us around. And you know what else I think?'

She walked past the sofa, not looking at him. She had almost reached the turn into the hall before he spoke.

'Hey – where the hell you going?' He was shouting. 'Come back here, you. I got to talk to you.'

She continued on into the bedroom and shut the door. She sat on the edge of the bed in the darkness. Wally was in the hall now, she could hear him muttering just outside the door. He slapped the door with his hand but didn't open it. After a while she heard the solid, reverberant slam of the heavy outer door.

Wally didn't especially want to go to the Pleasant Times, but he wasn't about to hang out in the cold streets. Tell the truth, he wasn't so much sore at Nella for walking away as he was surprised. He would have sworn that she would have had an answer for everything. They were up shit creek, and Nella must have known it as well as he did, which was why she didn't even try to con him. They weren't being taken seriously – first saying that the voice was taped, then that it wasn't her voice . . . Bullshit – they were playing games. The cops, or Julian Massey, or whoever, they were stalling, giving them the runaround.

What it was – they were up against the power. In one way or another he had run up against it before in his life. The power – the cops, the TV, everything – they could always crush the little guys. So what kind of a chance did the three of them have? The smart thing would be to call it quits while they were at least in the clear. But a third of a million dollars – God, how beautiful. If only they weren't going up against the power.

His feelings as he walked into the Pleasant Times were mixed up. In the past ten days he had seen himself moving up to another level in which the Pleasant Times would disappear from his life. With his share of the ransom he would be doing his drinking at uptown places – the Plaza, the St Regis, the plush singles bars. Well, the way things looked now, the Pleasant Times would be his saloon for a long time.

He was greeted noisily by the regulars, and almost at once found himself falling into the old ways – relaxing, swapping jokes, teasing Martinez, who kept touching the scar on his head self-consciously.

'Martinez, you got to realise that it was two weeks ago that you got hit on the head. It's ancient history.'

Martinez said it was still an open case; if the cops ever picked up those four *Puertoriqueños*, he would be the star witness against them.

Wally laughed and said the cops would never track them down, and that they had seen the last of them.

'You never can tell,' Martinez said. 'If they knock this place over two times, they maybe come back again for number three.'

'And you get knocked on the head again?'

Martinez got all excited, but Wally had lost interest, and he hardly paid any attention as the other regulars got into the act. McGarry served him a beer, then carried a tray of drinks back to the booths in the rear. When he returned, he gestured at Wally with his head and moved a distance away along the bar. Wally hesitated before getting off his stool and joining him.

McGarry leaned towards him and said in a low voice, 'That cop was in here today.'

'Cop? What cop?'

'If you watched the TV news, you saw him. Roehmer something. The kidnapping? Second time he's been here.'

'Here? What's he doing here?' His heart had begun to thump, but he stared at McGarry without blinking.

'Christ, I don't know, I never could figure out how detectives worked. He wanted to know if she was in here, the kidnapped girl.'

Wally's mouth was suddenly so dry that he couldn't speak. And even after he had taken a sip of beer, the most he could manage to say was, 'Be damned.'

'What I want to tell you,' McGarry said, 'he claims the girl was wearing a shearling coat.'

'Oh, yeah?' Wally took another sip of his beer. 'I thought they said it was a blue coat. How come they changed it?'

'How the hell do I know? But that chick in here that night – what's her name? – she was wearing a shearling.'

'Marilyn.' Wally paused and looked thoughtful. His heart was still thudding, but he tried to sound offhanded. 'It's quite a coincidence. But this Marilyn was just a bimbo. What I'd like to know is how that cop got steered into this place.'

'Could be the coat. Somebody spotted a girl in a coat

271

like hers in the neighbourhood and tipped the cops off, so they come down on a fishing expedition. Whatever, I wish they'd keep the hell out of here.'

Wally said, 'Yeah, that's probably it. They spotted Marilyn or something. What'd you tell the cop, McGarry?'

McGarry smiled sourly. 'I told him I never in my life seen a girl in a shearling coat inside the Pleasant Times.'

Wally let out a relieved breath. 'You told a fib, McGarry. Marilyn was wearing a coat like that. I think it's my duty as a citizen to tell the cops about it.'

'Don't be smart,' McGarry said. 'Just keep your mouth shut.'

'But suppose it *was* her, and suppose . . .' Wally felt daring. He winked at McGarry. 'And suppose I'm the kidnapper?'

McGarry grunted and started to move towards the centre of the bar.

'You realise what that makes you, if I'm really the kidnapper? Accessory after the fact.'

'Don't think it didn't cross my mind,' McGarry said. 'For all of about one and a half seconds. But you haven't got neither the brains nor the balls.'

'Thanks,' Wally said. 'Thanks a lot.'

'Don't mention it,' McGarry said, and walked away.

So I overreacted, Nella thought, after Wally slammed out of the apartment. If I'm not careful, I can push him over the brink; he's teetering dangerously. I promise to reform, Wally, to take your feelings strictly into account from now on. Promise. First thing, when you get back, I'll apologise humbly. I'll make it up to you, Wally, you'll see.

All right, now that I'm cool again, Wally, in total possession of my awesome faculties, let's get back to business. I'm going to level with you, Wally, heart-to-heart, man-to-man, strictly above-board. Call me Honest Nella. Wally, I'm not going to insult a first-rate mind like yours by denying that we've been put in an awkward position.

Why did I refuse to listen to you before, Wally? I'm

glad you asked that question. Like I said, I'm going to
level with you, straight from the shoulder. But not on this
particular point. It wouldn't help anything to tell you that
I was terrified that you were going to say you wanted out.
I couldn't bear to hear it. I simply can't tolerate the idea of
failure. Failure has been the recurring theme of my life,
Wally, but I've reached the saturation point. The very
thought of failure is insupportable, so I'm telling you here
and now that *I will not fail*. Whatever the odds, I'm going
to win over Julian because I can't afford to lose. I'm a
desperate woman, Wally, and determined beyond all
reason. So I hereby tell you, in capital letters, that
THERE IS NOTHING I WILL NOT DO TO WIN,
NOTHING!

Very well. To show you how candid I am, nothing up
my sleeve, Wally, let me agree with you that they are
demonstrably fucking us around. Amend that, Wally:
trying to fuck us around. They're testing us, probing our
resolution and resourcefulness. Is that any reason to be
fainthearted? No, no, no, *no*. Viewed in the proper
perspective, it provides a healthy challenge, adds a dash of
zest to the game.

Bear this in mind, Wally: they don't know our one
weakness – that I am in no danger of being killed – but we
know theirs: that they don't know ours. They're taking a
risk, true, but a cautious one, and they'll pull back if we
apply a countervailing pressure. The most convincing
way to do that would be to kill me, but I reject that
solution on a point of high personal privilege. Failing that
– you're entitled to ask, Wally – how are we going to
impress them? Here, Wally, I must plead for your
patience and trust. Look at my track record. I'm
inventive, right? A master criminal, right? All I ask is a
little time to come up with the answer. The other side has
the momentum temporarily, but I'm already working on a
bold initiative to wrest it away from them.

Meanwhile, no sweat. We've got lots of time, we're in
no danger whatsoever of discovery. One favour, Wally –
yes, I know I promised, but you must help too – while I'm
planning our next move, I'd appreciate it if you didn't

distract me by whining. Divert yourself by thinking about money. You'll find it very soothing, and a good spine-stiffener too . . .

She got out of bed and went into the living-room to wait for Wally to return. In ten minutes or so she heard him at the door. She jumped up from the sofa and ran to meet him with open arms. But before she reached him, he blurted out the news about Roehmer.

No matter where she sat – the sofa, an armchair, a straight chair in the foyer – a tremor ran through her legs and thighs. But it disappeared when she was on her feet, so she began to walk about, establishing a route that she followed without deviation: from the foyer to the left wall of the living-room, behind the television set, past the curtained windows, towards the sofa, a right turn back to the foyer, where she started the pattern over again.

On her second circuit she began to take notice of the long rectangular painting over the sofa: the black log cast up on the sunny beach. Thereafter it became a focal point as she made her turn towards the sofa, and it irritated her increasingly with each circuit. By reason of faulty perspective, the log was implausibly long, stretching towards infinity. It was hideously misdrawn, but she had never been bothered by it until now. She couldn't take her eyes off it. Foyer, behind the television set, past the windows, picture – log!

As well to think of the log as anything else. It was more attractive than Wally's collapsed face when he had told her about Roehmer's two visits to the Pleasant Times. The news had taken her aback, and at the same time given her a perverse little thrill – the *joli-laide* detective with the guilt-ridden eyes had somehow narrowed down the pursuit. But she had been prepared to rationalise it for Wally.

Wally had cut her off abruptly. 'I don't want to talk.'

He hung his jacket away in the closet and brushed by her. She followed him into the bedroom, but she didn't say another word. She knew that Roehmer's appearance had pushed Wally over the precipice. He was ready to quit. She watched silently as he undressed, got into bed, and turned away under the covers. She went back to the living-room.

She didn't want to go to bed yet. She couldn't abide the thought of lying beside Wally and becoming contaminated by his fear and despair. She decided to wait up until Richard came home. Was this his night for getting his ashes hauled? Richard? It was futile. Richard's principal commitment in life was his loyalty to Wally, and under that rubric he accepted whatever Wally said. Still, if he heard about Roehmer from her, rather than Wally . . .

And so she paced, making her mindless circum-ambulancy, centring her frustration on the black log on the sunny beach. The picture would be at least tolerable if the log was cut down to size. One slice, about a third of the way from the right margin of the picture, would do the job nicely. One sharp blow with Richard's mother's cleaver. Two circuits later she broke her pattern and went into the kitchen. She pulled open the cupboard drawer. The cleaver was lying there, old-fashioned and distinctive among the mass-produced banalities of the stainless steel flatware. She shut the drawer and went back to the living-room. On the next circuit she stopped in front of the picture. She raised her hand and brought it down sharply towards the log, a third of the way from the right margin. As she moved on, an unformed thought beat away at the edges of her mind.

She decided not to wait up for Richard. In the bedroom, Wally was sleeping soundlessly. She undressed and slipped into bed. She lay as far away from Wally as she could, and thought about the thought that pulsed just outside her grasp. She fell asleep knowing that it would be there when she needed it.

Roehmer rose groaning from the cot in the precinct house with the first light, shaved and showered, and went back to the cot for another half hour. In drowsy half-sleep he remembered how, at the beginning of his affair with Peggy Parris, before he started spending the night, he would leave her apartment in the early-morning hours and walk through the empty streets to the House, where he would sack out on a cot before reporting for duty. He had done that several times a week, walking his tour on three hours' sleep and never feeling it. He had been young and in love. Now he woke groaning with a bladder full of piss.

He put in a call to Intelligence and had breakfast at his desk – coffee out of a Styrofoam cup and a large soggy Danish. Coffee and Danish, cop's food. When he began to stay the night in Peggy's bed, her maid would prepare and serve him breakfast. Eggs, bacon crisply done and drained of grease, jellies in little pewter pots, coffee in delicate china that was weightless and that you could practically see through, linen tablecloth, napkin bound up in a filigreed silver ring. Peggy would join him for breakfast, but after he left, she would go back to bed and sleep until noon.

He watched for the lieutenant's arrival, but the Intelligence Unit man called back first.

'Got your information. This McGarry, Seamus P., was a police officer.'

Of course. He had the look of one. 'NYPD?'

'Right. He was kicked off the force in seventy-four.'

'Kicked off? What for?'

'He had a departmental trial and they found him guilty, but there was some kind of technicality involved, so strictly speaking he wasn't kicked out but forced to resign. Lost his pension, though.'

Roehmer winced. Without pension: that was cruel and unusual punishment for a cop. 'What'd he do?'

'His hand stuck to some money in a bookie-parlour bust. One of the perpetrators sang, and he denied it, naturally, but they investigated and got him dead to rights. He wasn't all that smart.'

'Any record after that?'

'That's it. He's been clean since then, running this bar, as you know.' The Intelligence man paused, then said in a peculiar tone between sympathy and apology, 'It happens, you know, a cop gets greedy, and it makes him stupid. It don't necessarily mean he's a crook.'

That was exactly what it did mean, but cops stuck together. 'Yeah, I know, it happens,' Roehmer said. 'Well, thanks a lot.'

Roehmer went into the lieutenant's office and made his pitch.

Boyd leaned back in his chair with his hands clasped behind his head and said, 'Okay, she used to live there a long time ago, and these two faggots allege they saw a girl with a coat like hers on the block, but it's too thin. You want to follow up on it, go ahead, but don't expect me to put any army into it.'

'I'll do what I can, but you know how it is – one man alone can't get any place on a house-to-house canvass.'

'If some poor old woman got her head bashed in in her room by an intruder, that's different, it's homicide, and you'd get an army tossing the area for witnesses. That's where the crime was committed, and that's where the perpetrator and the victim were, so that's where the investigation would have to be. But with this girl, all we got is a coat which there's thousands of coats like it in the city, and we don't know whether any crime was committed there or not. She could have – assuming it was her in the first place, which the identification is weak – she could have gone from there to any place in the city, or outside of it, and got herself snatched. There's no real connection.'

Roehmer said that at the least there was a circumstantial connection: she had once lived there, she had gotten off the bus near there, and the fags had placed her – or somebody who might have been her – at the scene.

'Ain't solid,' the lieutenant said.

Roehmer was willing to concede that on the face of it Boyd wasn't wrong. But the lieutenant didn't have *a hunch*. In a way, there wasn't all that much left of the hunch. He had a strong instinct that McGarry had seen the girl and was covering up. Yet McGarry's peculiar attitude could be explained: defrocked cops hated cops. But he still wouldn't accept it at that. The hunch persisted, shaken by what he had learned from Intelligence, but still hanging on stubbornly, still talking to him in its own mysterious language.

He said, 'You know, Lieutenant, it isn't all that big of an area. If I could just have, say, half a dozen – '

'How do you *know* how big of an area it is? Half a dozen detectives, you're off your fucking nut.'

'Then maybe just Murphy and Passatino – '

'You can have them on the basis we said you could have them, between their other investigations. This kidnap isn't our only case, you know, we got a whole houseful of crime to handle.'

Well, Roehmer thought, it had been a lost cause from the start. All he had accomplished was giving the lieutenant a chance to make speeches.

'How come,' Boyd said, 'you didn't go to your rabbi, the Chief, about this? He got it in his power to give you the whole entire detective division if he wanted to.'

'I didn't want to go over your head.'

The lieutenant smiled. 'Bullshit, Roehmer. You knew he'd think you were off the wall. Why don't you hit up the FBI guy? You tell him yet about the coat, and the two fags? They got all kinds of manpower when they feel like using it. Did you talk to him?'

'Not yet.'

'Don't hold out on him. I want to see you co-operating.'

'I'll tell him today.'

'Do that. I don't want to have to tell you again.'

'Yes, sir,' Roehmer said.

Nella was alone in bed when she awoke. The bedroom door was open, and she could hear the sound of muted voices. She wrapped herself in the blanket and went out. Wally and Richard were sitting at the table in the foyer, speaking softly.

'Good morning.'

Wally gave a start and flushed. Richard said, 'Good morning.'

Wally said, 'Richard bought the *Daily News*. Look what it says.'

He turned the paper towards her. A headline read:

She said, 'They both know it's me.'

'That ain't what they said,' Wally said. 'You know what I think? Your uncle don't give a shit if you get knocked off.'

She shook her head. 'It's not Julian. It's the police. They've *made* him say it.'

'A rich, important character like your uncle? People like him don't take orders from cops.'

A valid point, Nella thought. At the very best, Julian was an equal partner of the police. It was possible that Roehmer or somebody like him was the tactician, the technician, planning the day-to-day moves, but Julian's sanction was behind it.

'I hate to tell you this, Nella – he don't care if anything happens to you.'

'He does care,' she said calmly, 'and I can prove it.'

Wally shrugged. 'And if that's not bad enough, there's this cop, Roehmer, smelling around. So you know what I think?' He looked at Richard, who nodded. 'I think we're dead.'

Don't argue, Nella, don't challenge him – you've got the goods. But first you have to neutralise the threat of Roehmer. 'Can I ask Richard a question?'

'What's the use?' Wally looked at Richard, who gave a slight nod of assent. 'Richard and me, we've been talking it over. We want out.'

'Richard,' Nella said, 'you know a little bit about how cops work, don't you?'

Richard shrugged, admitting nothing, denying nothing.

'Forget it,' Wally said. 'We already made up our mind. We're pulling out.'

'Tell me if I'm correct, Richard. The police found out from Julian that we used to live around here, and as a matter of standard procedure – and because they didn't have any real leads – they checked out the neighbourhood, which would include the local bars. Does that sound reasonable?'

'I guess.'

'I told you McGarry said he was in the Pleasant Times twice,' Wally said. 'That don't mean anything?'

'The second time was after they found out about my coat. But when McGarry denied seeing anybody in a shearling, that was it. He won't be back again. Right, Richard?'

'Possible.'

'What's the difference?' Wally said. 'We made up our mind. We're quitting.'

'Richard, do you think Roehmer represents a real threat?'

Richard glanced quickly at Wally. 'Maybe yes, maybe not.'

'Okay, so he's not,' Wally said. 'But it don't matter. We can't win anyway.'

Okay, Roehmer sort of neutralised, even if mostly by default. Move on to the main point. 'We're agreed that the key factor is Julian. If Julian shifts his viewpoint, the cops have to follow his lead. Correct?'

'One of the things about life,' Wally said wearily, 'is to know when you're licked. We can't do anything. They got the power.'

'Only because Julian isn't sure that I'm in danger. But suppose I can convince him that I am?'

'How? We kill you? I got to admit that might work.'

Into my trap. Thank you very much, Wally. I can always depend on you, you beautiful fool. 'I'll show you how, Wally.'

Tucking the blanket in firmly under her arms to anchor it, she walked behind Richard's chair, past Wally's disaffected stare, and into the kitchen. She opened the cupboard drawer and took out the cleaver. With her back to the foyer she held it for a moment, fascinated by its heft and balance, by the cold line of light glinting off its cutting edge. She walked back to the foyer and, reaching over Wally's back, placed it on the table.

Old Chinese proverb – one cleaver is worth a thousand words.

Chapter 19

Extract from the unwritten journal of Nella Massey, gentlewoman, descendant of dukes, druids, and dunces: 'On the eleventh day of my captivity I did cause the severing of the third (ring) finger of my left hand. It was no simple matter.'

She awakened, lying on the blue sofa, wrapped in a blanket. It was dark inside the room, but there were streaks of daylight lining the edges of the drawn drapes. She was alone in the apartment and content to be so, cuddled and contained (and fractionally reduced) in the cocoon of her blanket.

The pain had throttled down from a high breathtaking urgency to a persistent ache. Orders from the doctor: Don't move the hand. But how else could she know what time it was? She sent the message to the hand, and slowly, not very willingly, it began to crawl out of the blanket, probing, inching its way cautiously through the folds. It found an exit through a flap near her left hip. She didn't look at it until it rose to eye level, impinging itself on her vision, a bulky whiteness. Gingerly, she drew back the sleeve of Richard's sweater to peek at her watch. Quarter of six.

The hand began to crawl back to its hiding place without her bidding. She stopped it. Who's managing things around here, anyway? With infinite slowness she extended her arm to the limit of her reach, then rotated it at the wrist, bent her elbow, and held the hand up vertically against the background of the grey television tube for viewing. In that theatrical context it struck her as being a baggy pants comedian.

Three fingers, a thumb, a fat foreshortened stump splinted and hugely bandaged, leading to an intricate cat's cradle of palely bloody gauze entwining the other fingers and then trailing upwards, anchored to her hand by strips of adhesive tape. The tip of the missing finger throbbed with pain. Not *my* finger but *the* finger, a third-person finger, neatly packaged, travelling solo through the orderly channels of Uncle Sam's mail: scooped out of the box on the street and tossed into the carrier's leather pouch, carried to the branch post office, its zip code read and deciphered, tossed into the appropriate bin, thence trans-shipped by truck to another post office, tossed again into a cubbyhole, stacked for a second carrier who would place it in his leather pouch with the cards from distant relatives, the bills, the business letters ('replying to yours of the eighteenth'), the love letters ('I miss you, miss you, miss you, hon'), the appeals of charitable organisations, the direct-mail offers ('A once-in-a-lifetime opportunity') . . .

In the whole leather bag, in the entire city – perhaps, on this particular day, in the whole world – it was the only severed finger in the mail anywhere. Take pride, Nella's finger, bask in your uniqueness!

The pain was causing her to suck in her breath between her clenched teeth. She lowered her arm and let the hand find its way back into the folds of the blanket. The pain ceased somewhat with the hand at rest. She was concerned with the pain, not with the finger. She had accepted its loss without a qualm. It seemed a tiny price, in relation to the entirety of her body, to pay for turning a losing enterprise into a winner.

Nobody had questioned that premise. No need for long-winded explanations. It was clear to one and all that the finger would revive, in fact reinforce the original death threat. But after the first burst of enthusiasm, Wally felt obliged to demur.

'Hey, wait, I can't let you do it. I would sooner blow the deal than have you mutilate yourself.'

It's not as if I'm undoing perfection, Wally, I'm not you. 'I won't miss it,' she said gravely. 'I hardly ever use it for anything important.'

'The suffering, the pain of it,' Wally murmured.

Which, Nella thought, is already a strategic retreat from his first position.

'It's going to hurt,' Richard said.

'Forget it,' Wally said. 'It's too much of a sacrifice, even though it would work.'

'One little finger,' Nella said. 'Is it worth a million dollars or isn't it?'

'Well, it's certainly logical when you put it like that, it makes sense. But still . . .'

'It's worth *more* than a million dollars to me, Wally.'

'I know just what you mean – the way you feel about your uncle and all. I don't want you to do it, but I see your point – I would be standing in your way. What do you think, Richard?'

Richard shrugged. 'It's up to her.'

'Think of it as doing me a favour, Wally.'

Wally let his hands drop helplessly. 'If that's what you want, much as I don't like it, I got to go along.'

'Fine. Thank you for your understanding, Wally.' She touched the cleaver lightly. 'Let's get on with it. Will you do it for me, Wally?'

'Me? You expect *me* to do it?'

'Yes, please.'

'You gotta be kidding.'

'I can't do it myself, can I?'

'Not me.' Wally shook his head vigorously. 'I won't do it.'

'I'll do it,' Richard said.

'No. I want Wally to do it.'

'He don't know how,' Richard said. 'I was the doctor – in the joint, I mean.'

Wally brightened. 'That's right. Richard knows all about it.'

'You were a doctor, Richard?'

'That's what they called it. I worked in the prison hospital, helping the doctor.'

'Even if I know as much about it as Richard, which I don't,' Wally said, 'how could I do such a thing to somebody I . . . like, love?'

Well, Wally, *like love* is the point. In some way – I can't be sure whether it's romantic or perverse – I thought you would show your feeling for me by cutting off my finger at my request.

She said to Richard, 'Did they let you perform amputations?'

'Just assist, but I learned a lot that way. I know about wounds, how to treat them.' His pale eyes wandered off into a distance. 'Some character, a snitch, they hacked off his hands . . .'

'Tell her what the doctor told you, Richard,' Wally said. 'How if you only had an education, you would have made a terrific doctor?'

Richard ducked his head and mumbled a protest.

Nella looked at Wally and then back to Richard. She nudged the cleaver along the table towards Richard. 'All right, Doctor, go ahead and do it.'

Richard shook his head. 'You just don't go ahead and do it. It's not that simple.'

'That shows you how much I know. I thought you just picked up the cleaver and chopped.'

Wally got up, pale, and made a half-turn away from the table.

'You want to do everything just right,' Richard said seriously.

Wally was out in the entry hall. She heard him open the closet. 'Of course, Richard. You're the doctor.'

The outer door opened and then closed.

Richard brought her a scratch pad and a ballpoint pen. She discovered that the cleaver had somehow vanished from the tabletop. Neither of them had made any reference to Wally's departure.

Richard said, 'You can take your time. I got some things to do.'

'What kind of things?'

'You know – preparations.' His hand was behind his back, concealing the cleaver.

She said, 'Richard, are you one of those doctors who makes a dark mystery of what he's doing?'

'If you want, I'll tell you.'

'Yes.'

He eyed her appraisingly. 'All right. First thing is to sharpen the cleaver on a sandstone.'

Her hands were in her lap, the fourth finger of her left hand enclosed tightly in the fist of her right. She nodded, and Richard went back into his bedroom. When he returned, he was carrying a shoebox, which he placed on the table.

'This is what they call the *materia medica*. I sneaked it out of the joint.'

He took the lid off the box. She saw in it a neat array of gauze, adhesive tape, small bottles, absorbent cotton, several pairs of scissors, some unidentifiable things. Richard rummaged, and brought out a dark brown bottle. He read the label carefully, then shook out two white tablets.

'Swallow these. I'll get you some water.'

'What are they?'

'Codeine. Two thirty-milligram tablets. To kill the pain.' He paused. 'A little.'

He brought a glass of water from the kitchen and watched while she swallowed the tablets, then went back to the bedroom. By the time she finished the note, after two or three false starts, Richard was back again.

She said, 'Here's the note, Richard – "This is Nella Massey's finger. Only nine left. We are not fooling around. Pay up or else." Okay?'

'Okay.'

'I want it sent to Detective Roehmer, at the Eighteenth Police Precinct.'

'Instead of your uncle?' Richard pondered for a moment. 'If he got it himself, he might have a heart attack?' He nodded, satisfied with his reasoning. 'And if he has a heart attack and dies, we're in the soup.'

Julian has an armour-plated heart, Richard, but let's leave it at that. Nothing to gain by admitting that I'm deficient in cruelty. *Hand that once he held.*

'Or you could send it to the FBI guy,' Richard said.

Ah, but I have a secret understanding with the attractive, over-weight detective, Richard; there's an element of flirtatiousness involved. Can't tell you that, though, it's too kinky. 'Let's send it to Roehmer.'

Richard nodded agreement. He rummaged in his

shoebox and took out a green plastic bottle. 'Next, we have to scrub. Hexachlorophene. Kills all the bacterias.'

He led her to the washbasin in the bathroom, instructed her to wet her hands, and then poured a liquid from the green bottle into her cupped hands.

'Keep scrubbing for five minutes. I'll use the kitchen sink. It'll seem like a long time, but don't ever stop, keep washing.'

After Richard left, she began to feel nauseated. Bracing her thighs against the cold porcelain of the sink for support, she bent over the basin and gagged. It seemed to relieve her. She stood upright again, her throat aching, her eyes watering. Richard was standing beside her, his sudsy hands making circular motions.

'You okay? Keep scrubbing.'

'I'm fine. Something I ate, no doubt.'

'You can vomit if you have to, but don't stop scrubbing.'

'Isn't it five minutes yet?'

He shook his head. 'I'll let you know.'

She shut her eyes and tried to blank out her mind, keeping her hands moving, washing each other endlessly. Eventually Richard came back.

'You can stop now. Rinse your hands. Don't turn the faucet off, let the water run. Don't dry your hands.'

She saw that he was waving his hands in the air to dry them. She followed him back to the foyer. There was a flat block of wood on the table. He motioned her to sit down, took her left hand, and began to twist a rubber tightly around her finger, just below the large knuckle.

'You want to take the ring off?' Richard said.

'It won't come off. What's the rubber band for?'

'Tourniquet. To control the bleeding.'

She had suppressed the thought of blood. 'Will there be much bleeding?'

'Not much.'

Without warning, she turned queasy again. Her head drooped and she started to sweat.

Richard's voice came to her from a distance. 'Put your head down, way down between your legs.'

She followed his orders and in a few moments began to feel better. She straightened up.

'You don't have to do it,' Richard said.

'Who, me? I'm looking forward to it.'

He studied her for a while. 'All right. Not much longer.'

He got up and went into the kitchen and turned on one of the gas burners. Before he turned his back to her, she caught a glimpse of the cleaver. Thorough Richard. He was sterilising the blade of the cleaver over the flame. When he came back to the table, the cleaver was hidden. He lined up the slab of board evenly with the edge of the table and told her to put her hand on it.

'Curl the other fingers off the board, under the edge of the table.'

Her fingers felt as wooden and unresponsive as the board they rested on. Her thumb refused to obey, it kept edging up to the rim of the table. He helped her. He pushed her thumb downwards and tucked it in under her index finger.

'Just hold it that way,' Richard said. 'Don't move.'

'You're real cool, Richard,' she said. 'I appreciate it.'

He seemed surprised. 'It don't help to get excited.'

Right, Richard, let's all keep cool. Let's not chicken out, like a certain gorgeous creature who shall be nameless. Cool's the word, and victory is just around the corner.

'You all right?' Richard said.

'Right as ruin, Richard.'

'Close your eyes. Don't look.'

She squeezed her eyes as tightly shut as she could, but when she felt Richard's touch, they opened involuntarily. He was covering her hand with his own, his little finger lapping over the large knuckle of her hand, and she thought: If he botches it, he's going to slice a piece of his own hand off. She shut her eyes again, but not quickly enough, and she caught a glimpse of a blurred shape in downward motion.

The blow surprised her. It was dull, as if she had been pounded by something blunt and heavy, and she wondered if he had, unaccountably, used the wrong side of the cleaver. But when she opened her eyes she saw the severed finger lying on the board. It looked unreal, like one of those gruesomely unfunny objects one might buy in a novelty store. Beneath Richard's protective hand a bleeding stump showed, with a glossy whiteness in its centre that she knew must be bone. There was no pain now, only an odd, tingling numbness.

She heard Richard say, 'You did real good.'

His voice sounded filtered through a distance. She didn't think she had blacked out, but there must have been some kind of lapse in her concentration, because, somehow, without her being aware of it happening, everything had disappeared from sight – board, finger, red-tinged cleaver. The stump was hidden, enveloped in a heavy wad of gauze.

She said, 'I'm all right. It doesn't hurt.'

'It'll start to hurt soon. You don't want to look down.'

She focused on Richard. It might have been the first time she had truly looked at him; who saw the firefly when Apollo rode the sky? His skin was sallow, drawn tight over the bone. He had pale blond eyelashes, the colour of his hair. His long, thin, almost skeletal fingers applied firm pressure on the gauze pad. They were bloodstained.

She said, 'I'm beginning to feel sleepy.' A wary look came into Richard's eyes. 'Just tired. I'm not going to faint or anything.'

'You want to lie down?'

She shook her head. 'Tell me what you're doing now.'

In a grave, measured voice – a physician's voice, she thought – he said that he was ready to bandage the finger. He would put bacitracin ointment on the wound; it was an antibacterial agent, and it would also help prevent the bandage from sticking. He drew in his breath sharply, anticipating her pain, and she whistled through her teeth when he touched the stump. He worked methodically, speaking only once, to tell her that he would splint the wound with a tongue depressor to protect it. When he was finished, he led her to the sofa and told her to lie down. He covered her with a blanket.

'Get some sleep. Try not to move your hand.' He was silent for a moment, looking down. 'About Wally, you got to understand – he's very sensitive.'

She had slept, and waked drowsily, thrown back momentarily to her childhood, when some mild illness would have confined her to bed. At such times, Julian would fret over her – more so than her parents – and would pamper her outrageously. But that was a different Julian, and a different Nella, in a different time.

She rose slowly to a sitting position. Richard was bent close over the table; he was pasting up the cutout letters of the note. Her head was throbbing, but the pain, at least for the moment, seemed tolerable. She let herself down again and tried to place herself back in the room of her childhood; instead, she fell asleep.

She woke to the clatter of crockery. Pain was persistent and assertive. She reached under the blanket towards her left hand but stopped herself before touching it. She heard voices speaking softly. She levered herself up and peered over the back of the sofa. Wally was seated at the table, his chin propped on his hands, turning the pages of a magazine. Richard, carrying a plate of sandwiches from the kitchen, spotted her.

'You like to have a sandwich?'

Wally didn't look up. He was concentrated on his magazine, his brow knit with absorption.

She nodded to Richard and got up cautiously, as an invalid might. She went to the bathroom and, as she washed awkwardly, with one hand, studied herself in the mirror. Circles under the eyes, the haggardness of the presence of pain, perhaps a hint of lingering terror, but otherwise no significant difference from the ten-fingered Nella she had once been.

Wally glanced upwards fleetingly as she came to the table, then back to his magazine. Before she sat down,

Richard made her put on a sling fashioned out of a white scarf.

'The less you move it around the less it'll hurt.' He looked at his watch. 'Another couple of hours you can have some more codeine.'

They ate in silence. Wally continued to pore over his magazine, every once in a while fastidiously flicking a crumb from it. Poor Wally, Nella thought, in disgrace with fortune and men's eyes, reassuring himself with the power and beauty of his presence on a printed page.

Richard went into the kitchen for coffee. Without looking up, Wally said, 'I would like to say something.'

'No need to say anything, Wally.'

She meant it. He had let her down, but she had been wrong to feel betrayed. It wasn't a genuine betrayal because it hadn't surprised her, and surprise, after all, was the essence of betrayal. She had asked too much of him – he was meant merely to be decorative, not heroic.

He glanced up from the magazine. His eyes flicked quickly to her bandaged hand, then away from it. 'Why I walked out?'

He looked humble, and suddenly she felt sorry for him. A deflated Wally was a sin against nature. 'It's all right, Wally, I understand. Forget it.'

Richard brought the coffee pot and a plate of cupcakes to the table.

'Because I couldn't stand seeing you be hurt,' Wally said.

'That's right,' Richard said. 'He's very sensitive.'

Wally said, 'I couldn't stand that you were actually going to lose a *finger*.'

'Don't worry about it,' Nella said. 'I've still got all the things that matter – my head and my heart and my cunt.'

Tough Nella, foul-mouthed witch of the whole wide world. Wally was looking pained.

'I mean vagina, Wally.'

She spent the afternoon in a twilight of half-sleep, waking fully only when Wally and Richard came and went. She

290

had thought to make some appropriate mock ritual when they went off to mail the package – after all, it wasn't every day that you sent a bit of yourself out into the world – but she lost interest in the idea, and was concerned only that sufficient postage was affixed to the package and that they weren't observed slipping it into the mail drop.

They returned at two-thirty. Her wound was throbbing, and her teeth ached from clenching against the pain. Richard reminded her that it was time to take her codeine. He brought her the pills and a glass of water. Wally sat on the edge of the sofa and stroked her shoulder, but she turned away from him. His glowing health affronted her misery. She preferred looking at Richard – his hollowed-out face and sallow skin made him seem sympathetically ravaged.

After a short while they left to go for a swim at the Y, where, Wally told her, he expected to do his customary hundred laps. Richard, he said, would be lucky if he did five. His tone was bantering but affectionate, and Richard responded with pleased laughter.

They were whispering above her, and it was only after she noticed that Wally's hair was damp that she realised that they had returned from their swim. Wally told her that – if she didn't mind – he and Richard intended to have a drink at the Pleasant Times and then have dinner out. He offered to fix something for her to eat, or else bring something back for her. Did she like Chink's? She said that she wasn't hungry, and Wally said earnestly that she had to keep her strength up.

Richard brought her dosage of codeine and said she could have them at about six-thirty, or a little earlier if the pain got too bad. She thanked him and turned her face inwards to the sofa. She dozed off, and woke at a quarter of six.

At six o'clock she turned on the TV news. The report on the Nella Massey kidnapping was a brief recapitulation of last night's story. The only fresh news was Detective Roehmer's announcement: it had now been definitely established that the missing girl had been wearing a yellow shearling coat the night of her disappearance, instead of, as first thought . . .

Very boring, Nella thought. But don't get discouraged, all you good folks out there in televisionland. Tune in tomorrow for a sensational new development. And a cheery good night to you, too, Dear Enemy.

Wally and Richard came home at ten o'clock, waking her from a dream in which she was walking to school with Julian (although they were both their present age), their joined hands a pair of jagged stumps dripping large spots of blood on the sidewalk to mark their trail.

'How are you, baby?' Wally stood above her; Richard was just behind him.

'I'm all right, but my dreams are terrible.'

Richard stepped forward and put his hand on her forehead. His palm was dry, rough. 'Cool, no temperature.'

Wally sat down on the sofa. He bent forward and kissed her. 'You got a lot of guts, baby.'

Not really, Wally, I'm just strongly motivated. If Poor Philip could give his life in the war against Julian, surely I can spare a finger.

'You have something to eat?'

She had made herself some tea and some toast. 'Yes. How was your dinner?'

'Great,' Wally said. 'I mean, if I could have eaten it. Thinking of you here alone, with the pain and all, I couldn't really enjoy it.'

Richard reminded her to keep the bandage dry, to take her codeine in another half hour, and to keep a pillow under her hand when she slept. 'I think I'll say good night.'

'Don't you want to watch some TV?' Wally said.

'I'd rather read in bed for a while.' Richard left for his room.

'That Richard, he's terrific,' Wally said. 'Where would we be without him?'

'That thought has occurred to me, Wally.' She started to get up. 'I think I'll go to bed.'

Wally helped her off the sofa. 'I'll just watch a couple of shows, and then I'll be in in a little while. Okay?'

'Sure. Enjoy yourself, Wally.'

She went to the bedroom, took her pillow from the bed, and then crossed the hall to Richard's room. She went in without knocking.

He was propped up on his pillow, reading. At her entrance his pale eyes widened. He started to lift his blanket to cover himself, but then, as if in belated realisation that it was just a male chest, subsided. He closed his book but kept his finger between the covers to mark his place.

She moved closer to the bed. What did one say in the circumstances? 'Okay if I crash here tonight, Richard? I want to give you a little token of thanks for your kindness.' Or, with a leer, 'Kinda small bed, Richard, but that's all to the good, right?' One said nothing, Nella, one acted. Awkwardly, hampered by her bandaged hand, she began to take off her – Richard's – sweater. There was a slight flicker in the steadiness of his gaze when she slipped out of the sweater and stood before him with her breasts exposed. He put his book down on a bedside table. She began to work at the trousers, looking at him steadily. He was very thin, his chest flat, his ribs as sharply defined as the striations on a washboard. There were two tattoos on his left arm, etched in a faded blue and red: on the forearm a heart crossed by the word MOTHER; on the upper arm a coiled snake with wide-open mouth and threatening fangs.

'Richard, would you help me with the zipper?'

He nodded. 'Did Wally say it was okay?' He didn't look at her breasts but at her face.

'*I* said it was okay. Okay?'

For an instant she thought that he would balk, that he would refuse her without Wally's sanction, but after a brief hesitation he reached out and undid her zipper. She stepped out of the trousers and worked her panties down over her hips. Richard reached behind him and switched off the bed lamp. She slipped into the bed beside him.

He was shy, almost withdrawn, in the preliminaries,

which consisted of his massaging her breasts briefly and clumsily, after which he climbed on top of her. In the act itself he was fierce, intense, and silent throughout, and he finished long before she was ready. There were no kisses, and immediately afterwards he rolled off her.

She cried softly, in sexual frustration as much as anything more complicated, and Richard spoke for the first time since she had entered the bed.

'Did I hurt your finger?'

Sometime in the night she teased him awake, and tried to hold him back, to make something of it, but it was no different from the first time. It occurred to her that his entire sexual experience might have consisted of sleeping with whores. You paid your money and you got your ashes hauled. Where was the gentleness and solicitude he had shown in cutting off her finger? Ah, but that was different, Nella, that was *personal*.

Part V

DELIVERY

Chapter 20

Nella awakened as she had for most of the previous eleven mornings to the smell of coffee, Western man's universal reveille. She was alone in Richard's bed and, for the moment, enjoying the luxury of being able to sprawl. The bed was three-quarters size, and she had slept in a cramped position for most of the night, although Richard had crowded up against the wall in a gallant – or virginal? – attempt to give her adequate room.

Wally and Richard were at the table, both of them frowningly preoccupied with their food, neither one speaking. She felt a sudden pang of conscience. When she had gone to Richard's room, it had been to exact a penalty from Wally, to mete out a form of rough justice. Only the brave deserve the fair – right? But she had not realised – or not taken the trouble to think about it – that she would be driving a wedge between them.

Taking her seat, she said, 'Good morning, Wally. Good morning, Richard.'

Both of them mumbled, and after a silence Richard asked her how her hand felt. She told him that it was sore and achy but much better.

'The first ten or twelve hours are the worst,' Richard said. 'Just make sure you wear the sling and don't move it around too much.'

There would be no problem between herself and Richard. A sexual transaction had taken place, cash on the barrelhead, with no emotional debts incurred. This sale is final.

Wally looked up suddenly from his plate. 'Tell me something – okay? Is that how they do it on Park Avenue?'

His voice was light, but he was glowering. She helped herself to coffee and said nothing.

'I'm only a poor Uke from over on First Avenue,' Wally said, 'so I don't know the customs on Park Avenue.'

She sipped her coffee. Wally's head was thrust towards her now, and his eyes glittered with anger and hurt.

'She don't know what I'm talking about.' He was addressing Richard, possibly for the first time all morning. 'The reason she don't understand is because they talk a different language on Park.'

'I presume you mean fucking Richard last night?' The witch of the whole wide world! 'It didn't mean anything, Wally. I just wanted to be fucked properly for a change.'

She saw his hand sweep across his body on an arc towards her face, but she didn't draw back, and, finally, it wasn't much of a blow. He had tried to abort it, to recall his arm, but momentum carried it forward, and the tips of his fingers brushed across her mouth, wetting themselves on her parted lips. She barely felt it.

'You wouldn't dare do that if I had two good hands.'

She would realise, later, that she had dredged up her boffo comedy line out of some deep-seated, spontaneous instinct for self-preservation. To have taken it seriously would have put her in the order of women Wally might have struck, and she would have lost her immunity. What she would have done if he had hit her a solid blow was something else again, and she preferred not to dwell on it.

And even yet the issue hung in a delicate balance. Wally's face was still dark, angered, and it was not until she smiled broadly, forcing her smile on him, that he began to understand that she had not challenged him but made a joke. He acknowledged it, finally, not with a smile but a grunt.

Nevertheless, if the confrontation was over, an air of tension persisted. When Richard left for the Laundromat with a bundle of wash, Wally went off to the bedroom, and she heard him doing exercises. She cleared the table and washed the dishes awkwardly with one hand, listening to an all-news radio station, although she knew it was too early for a report on the finger.

She heard Wally showering, then returning to the bedroom. Eventually he appeared, heavily doused with cologne, dressed in a silky striped shirt and powder blue pants. He tied a scarf around his neck, put on his leather jacket, and left without a word.

Richard returned at one-thirty with the laundry neatly washed, dried, and folded. He toasted cheese sandwiches for their lunch and, when she sat down at the table, spoke for the first time.

'What about the finger?'

She started to tell him that there wasn't anything on the radio yet, then realised that he was asking her how she felt. She told him that the throbbing was steady and unpleasant, but not intolerable, and that she had taken her dosage of codeine a half hour before.

He nodded. 'Won't hurt as much if you keep it in the sling.'

Guiltily, she slipped her hand into the scarf, which had been hanging loosely from her neck. 'Funny thing, the pain seems worst at the tip of the finger.'

'Happens. People who have a leg amputated, they complain their toes hurt.'

'Richard – would you mind if I asked you a question?'

His sallow face coloured, and a wary look came over it. 'What about?'

'About all of this – the kidnap. I've never been sure how you felt about it.'

'Well, I thought it would be tough. It was a very high crime – know what I mean?'

Unlike Wally, he didn't harbour delusions of grandeur; in the matter of crime, he knew his place. 'Then why did you agree to do it?'

'I knew Wally wanted to do it.'

'Do you always do what Wally wants you to do?'

'If he wants to bad enough, sure.' He paused. 'Because I trust him.' He paused again, thoughtfully. 'We like each other a lot.'

The word he couldn't bring himself to articulate in terms of a male relationship – or any other? – was *love*. He was meeting her eyes squarely now across the table; where his feelings about Wally were concerned, he was on solid ground.

'Wally is the finest person I know.'

'Yes?'

Her single word was meant to be neutral, but it might have reflected her astonishment that anyone could say anything like that of Wally.

Flushing, his flat voice taking on contours she had never heard in it before, Richard said, 'Wally saved my life.'

Without prompting, carried along by conviction, he told her of Wally's role in his life after his parents had burned to death in a tenement fire. Even before that he had been a troubled child, constantly in and out of scrapes, in difficulty with the kids on the block, the school authorities, the police. Wally's parents, who had taken him in, were good people, hard-working and God-fearing, but they had little patience with him. But Wally . . .

His eyes turned moist, inward-looking, and he hid his face in his coffee cup before going on.

Wally stood as a buffer between his parents and Richard, and always defended him. Wally, who was popular on the block, took him everywhere, demanded and won acceptance for him with the other kids, helped him with his shyness, with the fierce touchiness that embroiled him in fights with other kids, built his confidence in himself.

'Some combination – Wally, like a God, everybody looked up to him, and me. Some combination. But we were always together, like partners. If anybody didn't like me, Wally wouldn't have nothing to do with him. Then, when I went to the slam – '

'Did you steal something?'

He shook his head. 'I beat somebody up – real bad. This guy, he jumped Wally, he had a knife.'

It didn't seem at all incongruous that Richard, with his hollow chest and stringy body, had come to the rescue of Wally, the incarnation of male strength and virility. (No wonder Wally had refused to discuss the fight that first night in the apartment – his vanity wouldn't stand for it.) Listening to Richard, she could sense the terrible ferocity, the intensity his loyalty and devotion produced, the disregard of his own pain, his determination to smash the attacker of his sponsor, his samaritan, his saviour. He had tried to kill the man, and almost succeeded.

'Wally hired me a lawyer, he wasn't about to let one of them Legal Aid characters defend me. He spent every cent he had, and borrowed too.' He shrugged. 'I got a bullet, but if it wasn't for that lawyer that Wally paid for, I might have gone up for five or even more.

'When I was in the joint, Wally came up to see me every weekend, and he always brought me something – food, butts, books, magazines. He didn't miss one single weekend. Then, when I got out, he looked after me, and supported me until I could get a job. He looks after me all the time.'

He fell silent; his confession was finished. She realised that she had been witness to a harrowing event: an emotionally inhibited man baring his soul. Deliberately, she changed the subject. 'What will you do with the money, Richard?'

'If we get it?' He almost smiled. 'When we get it? Buy a medallion and run my own cab.'

'What about the rest of it?'

'Give it to Wally, I guess.'

I'm sorry I came between you and Wally, Richard, I'm truly sorry.

Before Richard left, she suggested that he take along his small battery radio, but he said that he couldn't concentrate on driving with a radio in his cab. Instead he would check in by telephone from time to time to see if the story had broken.

She had offered to rehearse him, playing the role of Julian herself, but Richard had complained that it would only confuse matters if what Julian actually said followed a different line. He agreed to let her draw up a list of salient points, but balked at taking the list with him. He said he had a very good memory. She insisted on testing him, and after studying the list for a couple of minutes, he was letter perfect.

He left for work a bit after five o'clock. She swallowed her 60 mg dosage of codeine and lay down on the sofa. She slept fitfully over the next few hours. Each time she woke, she could hear the radio burbling in an undertone in the kitchen, but she lacked the energy to get up to listen to it, and instead nestled under her blanket in the dark living-room and slept again.

A shout penetrated her sleep, and she came awake with her heart thumping in alarm. There was a light on in the kitchen. She propped herself up on the sofa and saw Wally, his arms upraised, his fist pumping up and down like a running back who had just made a touchdown. He shouted again, and came trotting out of the kitchen.

He saw her, or her shadow, and yelled, 'It's on the radio, Nella, the finger! They got it!'

She switched on a lamp. Wally was still wearing his jacket. 'What did they say?'

'That the finger came in the mail, and that they checked out the fingerprints, and that it's Nella Massey's finger.'

He came across the room, smiling with his entire mouth, and sat down on the sofa beside her.

'Did they say anything about Julian?'

'Not yet. It was just a flash, and they'll have more details later.' He pumped his fist. 'Hey, baby, we're a winner.'

He put his arms around her and drew her close to him. Good news transformeth the man – right, Wally? She lowered her head to his chest. He smelled a little rank. She sniffed delicately, and a medley of odours sorted themselves out – his familiar cologne, a sweeter perfume, and the humid, earthy scent of a woman's body.

'Oh, God, would you look at that!' Agnes spoke aloud as the strip of letters crawled across the bottom of the screen. 'Oh, God, the brutes.'

The strip seemed to run on leisurely, interminably, although its message was short and terrible: Nella Massey's severed finger had arrived in the mail. Agnes half-rose from the longue, then settled back. What was that old saying about the messenger who brought the bad news being put to death? After dinner she had asked him if he wanted to watch the TV with her, but, thank God, he had said he wasn't interested in bushwah for serving girls, and instead had gone to take a little nap. But, Jesus, he had to be told, didn't he?

She got up with a sigh and went back to their bedroom. He was lying in the darkened room with a blanket drawn up to his chest. She stood in the doorway, trying to get her courage up to wake him, when the intercom buzzed. She turned away in relief and hurried down the corridor to answer the intercom. The doorman said Mr Fairborn was in the lobby. The FBI man – he must be here to tell Julian about the finger. Okay, then she could play dumb. She told the doorman to send Fairborn up, and then went back to the bedroom.

Julian was awake, lying with his head cradled on his hands, looking up at the ceiling.

She said, 'Better get up, Julian. Company's coming.'

'I'm not ready to get up yet. If it's that detective who was here today, tell him to go away.'

'He's on his way up, and it isn't the detective, it's the FBI.'

'Who said he could come up without my permission?'

'Me. I gave him permission.' She turned on the bedside lamp.

'Damnit, Agnes . . .' He sat up. His hair was dishevelled. 'Couldn't you have asked me first if I wanted to see him?'

'I didn't want to wake you up.'

'But you just woke me, didn't you? God, you're dumb, Agnes.' He rubbed his eyes with his knuckles. 'What does he want, anyway, this time of night?'

'It's only eight o'clock. How do I know what he wants? You think the FBI tells the doorman what they want, and the doorman tells me? Please, Julian, get up.'

'Do you think they have some news about Nella?' His voice quavered.

The doorbell chimed. Oh, God, what a scene it was going to be! She said, 'I'll go let him in. Throw some cold water on your face, and comb your hair, you look like the wild man of Borneo.'

She opened the door for Special Agent Fairborn and a

second FBI man, whose name was Rakisch. Both of them carried hats. Who wore a hat these days? Smart crooks probably spotted FBI men by their hats. The way these two dressed, they made that Detective Roehmer look like a Bowery bum. She invited them to sit down and said that Julian would be out presently. She thought of offering them a drink, but they were sure to say, 'Sorry, Ma'am, we never drink on duty.' She was pretty sure that Roehmer, duty or not, wasn't one to turn down a drink.

They both stood up when Julian started into the sitting-room. She got out fast. This was one time she didn't want to hang around. But she had hardly settled in front of the TV when she heard an anguished outcry. It was barely recognisable as Julian's voice, hoarse and screeching at the same time, like an animal in terror, if she had to make a comparison. She decided that if she heard it again, she would go to him. It wasn't repeated, so she stayed put. But after a few minutes she got up and tiptoed down the corridor until she could hear voices without being seen. Mostly she heard Julian's voice. He sounded mad as hell, and the FBI men seemed hardly able to get a word in edgewise. Julian was telling them off, and he was the one to do it. He thought everyone who worked for the government was his servant, and, the taxes he paid, who was to say he was wrong? She wouldn't have minded knowing what was going on, but Julian would skin her alive if she tried to barge in, so she went back to her TV.

Later she thought she heard the apartment door slam. She waited a few minutes and then edged down the corridor again. For a second she couldn't hear anything at all, but then a kind of spooky chanting sound began, eerie and monotonous. She edged up and peeked around the corner into the sitting-room. At first she thought the room was empty, but then she saw Julian. He was sitting in that crazy Viking chair with the horns, rocking back and forth and making that strange keening sound.

As she moved up behind the chair, his chanting turned into words. 'Ah, Scott old man, who would have dreamed when we were in our golden youth that this would be our sorry end. Ah, if you could have seen the perfection of that little hand, Scott, that little hand . . .'

Agnes went around the chair and stood directly in front of him but he wasn't aware of her; he seemed to be in a trance. He was holding his Princeton picture and he was talking to the damn thing.

'She would place her little hand in mine, Scott, tiny and delicate as a bird, and now it is ruined, Scott, like a crushed bird . . .'

She leaned over the chair towards him. He wasn't crying, but the rims of his eyes were red and they had a crazy faraway look to them. 'Daddy. Daddy? It's Agnes.'

'That hand, Scott, that trusting young hand . . .'

She took hold of the picture and eased it out of his grip. 'Let's get up, Daddy, and put some cold water on our face.'

He looked up at her, and gradually his eyes came back into focus. In a perfectly natural voice he said, 'I have to get dressed, Agnes.'

'You *are* dressed. Do you mean *un*dressed?'

'I want to get *dressed*. With a tie and jacket and so forth.'

Except for the nonsense about getting dressed, he seemed perfectly calm now. 'Anything you say, Daddy. You want Nurse Agnes to get you undressed and then help you get dressed?'

'No, you fool, I don't want to play games.' A bitter little smile twisted his mouth. 'I have to make myself presentable, I'm going to be on television.'

Richard had called at nine-thirty, a half hour after the radio had flashed the announcement that Julian Massey would appear on television to make a personal plea to the kidnappers of his niece. They told him to phone again at ten past eleven. Now they were waiting for the newscast to begin. How had people ever managed to do a kidnap in the horse-and-buggy days before television? Wally, sitting beside her on the sofa, kept glancing at his watch every ten seconds.

'You ever notice how fast time goes when you're having

305

a good time, and how slow it goes when you're waiting for something to happen?'

Eureka, Wally, you've just invented the theory of relativity.

When the newscast began, the anchorman briefly recapped the story of the receipt of the finger, which 'forensic and fingerprint tests have conclusively established as being that of the kidnapped girl.' He used the word *grisly* twice.

'Earlier this evening, at his Park Avenue apartment, our cameras taped a statement by Mr Julian Massey, the noted architect and uncle of the kidnapped girl . . .'

A long shot of the sitting-room, closing in quickly on Julian sitting in his ridiculous Viking chair, erect, motionless, his eyes focused on the camera, or perhaps on some television functionary behind it. Agnes was seated beside him in another chair. She was wearing a black dress; her red hair looked orange on the tube. Julian was wearing a tweed jacket and an orange and black tie – his Princeton colours. He seemed to be waiting for a signal to begin.

'It's a beautiful room,' Wally whispered, 'very tasteful.'

Julian cleared his throat deafeningly and said, 'I am addressing the kidnapper of my niece, Nella.'

He paused and glanced at Agnes, who nodded encouragingly. He cleared his throat again. 'Whoever you are I beseech you not to inflict any further harm upon my beloved niece.'

What the camera did, Nella thought, was to soften the hard edge of reality, to scale it down to the dimensions of theatre, to transform human beings into performers. The Julian on the screen was nobody she could either despise or feel sorry for. He was merely an actor improvising a melodramatic monologue for the entertainment of a vast audience whose thirst for diversion could sometimes be slaked but never thoroughly satisfied.

'He looks exactly like I expected,' Wally whispered. 'He thinks he's the ruler of the world.'

Wally was an actor, too, the offstage star. She made a *shushing* sound.

'. . . you have harmed her enough.' Suddenly Julian's tone changed. It was no longer the voice of a bewildered, piteous old man, but harsh, almost imperious. It was Julian the descendant of dukes and druids, dealing with the lesser ranks. 'Do not inflict any more pain upon her.' It wasn't a plea but a command.

The camera shifted to Agnes, who leaned towards him and whispered in his ear. Julian seemed confused, but then nodded.

'I appeal to you to give me back my niece. I will do what you say. I will pay what you ask . . .'

The camera showed Agnes nodding approvingly.

Julian's eyes were blinking. 'Please return my Nella. Here is my message to you: Send Nella back. I will pay what you ask. Spare her any further cruelties. I beg you to get in touch with me as soon as possible. Will you do that for me?'

Agnes reached out. The camera closed in on her plump hand patting Julian's long-fingered, gnarled one.

That's my hand, Creepy Housekeeper, keep your hand off it. That's the hand that once held mine.

The camera drew back, savouring the room, with Julian and Agnes at a distance, then faded out.

'You have just heard Mr Julian Massey appealing to the kidnapper of his niece, asking him not to hurt her again, offering to meet his demands . . .'

Television left nothing to chance, Nella thought. It told you what you were about to see, let you see it, and then proceeded to tell you what you had just seen.

Wally clapped his hands exultantly. 'He's going to pay, he said he would pay! We're in, baby, we're in!'

'How many times in your life do you get to see yourself on TV?'

But Julian flatly refused Agnes's urging to watch the eleven o'clock newscast. He chased her out of the bedroom and lay down on the bed, fully dressed. She threw a blanket over him and hurried to the TV room. When she came back, Julian was propped up in bed, reading some kind of architecture book. She told him that he had looked just fine, very distinguished, but that her hair had come out terrible, they would have to call a repairman to adjust the colour.

She didn't try to persuade him to get undressed and go to sleep. He was convinced the kidnapper would call, and she didn't want to upset him by starting an argument. He seemed calm enough, but you could never be sure with Julian. Earlier, he had scared the bejesus out of her, the crazy way he had been talking to that Princeton picture after the FBI told him about the finger. She noticed that from time to time he would doze off, but never for long. He would just open his eyes and start reading again.

The telephone rang a little after midnight. It sounded, Agnes thought, like the chimes of hell. Julian lunged for the phone, so excited that at first he put it wrong end about to his ear.

'You got a pencil and paper?'

Julian recognised the flat, sinister voice, and it threw him into a dither. 'Pencil and what? What did you say?'

'Get a pencil and paper. Hurry up.'

'Pencil and paper. Agnes, get me a pencil and paper, hurry up.'

'Is it him?' Agnes said.

'Never mind that,' Julian shouted. 'I want a pencil and paper.'

'There's one in that drawer, for Godssake.'

Julian put the phone down on the bed. He fumbled in the drawer and finally found a ballpoint pen and a small scratch pad. But he dropped the pad, and had to scramble for it on the floor, and would have fallen out of the bed if Agnes hadn't grabbed him. He shook her off and picked up the phone.

'Hello, hello, I've got it.'

The line hummed emptily. He said hello several times more and then slammed the phone back into its cradle.

'What'd you hang up for?' Agnes said.

'I didn't,' Julian said. '*He* did.'

'What did he say?'

'To get a pad and pencil.'

'And then he just hung up?'

Julian put his hand on his chest. 'My heart! I think I'm having a heart attack.'

Agnes picked up his hand and held it by the wrist. He tried to jerk away.

'Stop that. Hold still.' She looked up from her watch. 'It's running like a Rolls-Royce. You'll live forever with a pump like that.'

'Well, it's pounding. You know what I would do to that sonofabitch if I ever got my hands on him?'

'Calm down,' Agnes said. 'Maybe he had a bad connection.'

The phone rang. Julian snatched it up. 'Hello?'

'You got a pad and pencil.' The tone was dead level; it didn't rise as voices did when they asked a question.

'Yes. It's a pen.'

'Write this down. Number one – go to the bank tomorrow and get one million dollars.'

'I haven't got that much money in cash,' Julian said. 'I don't know if I can put my hands on – '

'Get it. Are you writing this down?'

Agnes was holding the pad steady on his lap. He wrote: *$ one million*.

'Write this down: ten thousand fifties and five thousand hundreds, all old bills, mixed-up numbers on the bills. And don't try staining the money with methylene blue. I got one of those black lights, so I'll know if you stain them. If the bills are doped, I'll kill Nella.'

'No, no,' Julian said. 'Don't hurt her.'

'You got that all down?'

'How do you spell methylene blue?'

'Write it like it sounds. Number two – get this Adams, the girl's husband – '

'He's her *ex*-husband.'

'Shut up and listen, you silly old bastard.' The voice was furious. 'Get this Adams and have him at your apartment tomorrow to handle the delivery.'

'How do I know he'll do it?'

'Just tell him we'll kill Nella if he don't do it.'

'Don't say that!'

'Number three – no cops. If we find out there's cops, we'll kill her. No cops, if you want to see her again.'

Julian wrote *no cops* and nodded dumbly.

'Number four – I'll call you tomorrow night to give you instructions for delivering the money.'

'What time tomorrow night?'

There was a thump in Julian's ear. He lowered the phone and held it pressed against his chest until Agnes took it from him. She held it to her ear for a moment and then replaced it in its cradle.

In the basement, Fairborn and Roehmer were staring at Pittman, the electronics detective.

'No dice,' Pittman said. 'He hung up.'

'Shit,' Fairborn said.

'It was a pretty long call, comparatively, but nowhere near long enough.' Pittman took his earphones off. 'He's smart. He knew it was going to be a long call, so he hung up when Massey started looking for a pencil. So we wouldn't have the extra time to trace him.'

'Tomorrow night,' Fairborn said. 'Probably late at night, but he could fool us.'

'Where do you think he found out about methylene blue?' Pittman said.

'They read crime books and go to the movies a lot,' Roehmer said. 'They know more about that stuff than most cops do.'

'In a way, I welcome it,' Fairborn said. 'He has to come out into the open, and we'll have a shot at him.'

'He said no cops,' Roehmer said.

'Who's a cop? I'm a special agent of the Federal Bureau of Investigation. That's not a cop.'

Fairborn made a comical face, but there was something about the tone of his voice that clashed with it. He might be joking, Roehmer thought, but at the same time he was pointing up a snobbish professional distinction.

'Yeah,' Roehmer said. 'For a minute there I was a little confused.'

After Richard phoned to report on his conversation with

Julian, Wally wanted to celebrate with a drink, but Nella said she was tired and wanted to go to sleep.

'Come on, baby. It's no fun drinking alone.'

She shook her head. 'Is it all right if I sleep on the sofa?'

'You want to sleep out here?' He looked disconcerted. 'Well, if you want to.'

He stood still, watching her, as she walked by him to the linen closet.

'You want me to help you put the sheet on?'

'I can manage. Good night, Wally.'

He went out, and presently she heard the shower running. She made up the sofa and turned out the lights. An hour later she was still awake, standing at the window and peering out at the edge of the blind. The street was empty until a taxicab shot by, accelerating, shooting out a wake of blue exhaust smoke. When a light went on in a window across the street, she dropped the blind and stepped back.

She returned to the sofa and straightened out the rumpled sheet. She lay down on the sofa, but got up again almost immediately. She picked up her pillow and blanket and crossed the living-room. She hesitated for an instant before going into the bedroom. Wally was a still, amorphous shape on the bed. Sleeping the sleep of the just. Well, it wasn't *his* uncle.

She laid the blanket on a chair, walked to the bed, and put her pillow in place against the headboard. When she slid under the blanket, Wally stirred but didn't wake. She lay on her back for a while, then turned towards Wally and placed her cheek against his shoulder. He smelled warm and slightly perfumed with the fragrance of his expensive bath soap. The shower had washed the trace of the other woman down the drain.

She opened her lips and pressed them against his shoulder. He woke without a sound and turned towards her. She opened her arms to him, and he climbed on top of her.

Chapter 21

When Roehmer came into the squad room carrying his morning coffee and Danish, Murphy and Passatino were at Murphy's desk, talking. He sat down and unwrapped the Danish. It was so soft and soggy that when he brought it to his mouth, it broke in half and splashed into his coffee container. He swore and fished it out with his fingertips.

'You got your hoodlum clothes in your locker?' Murphy was standing beside his desk.

'These fucking cakes,' Roehmer said.

'We're doing a stakeout this morning,' Murphy said.

'You and Passatino both? What's the matter with the Anticrime Unit?'

'They're busy on other stakeouts. So it's me and Passatino. And you.'

Roehmer stared upwards, suspecting one of Murphy's jokes, but Murphy wasn't smiling.

'Yeah. The whole team. There's this bank on Seventy-second. Knockoff artists have been picking up citizens coming out – '

'It's one of your terrific jokes, right, Murphy?'

' – following them home, and robbing them in broad daylight. They find out which ones make a withdrawal . . .' Murphy's face reddened. 'Well, shit, Rome, I don't make the assignments around here.'

'The first whip, or the lieutenant?'

'Himself.'

Roehmer threw his Danish on his desk. He shoved back his chair and stood up.

'Easy, Rome,' Murphy said.

Roehmer walked across the squad room. The lieutenant was seated behind his desk, feet up, reading a report. Roehmer knocked on the door.

Boyd, without looking up, said, 'Come in.'

Standing in front of the desk, Roehmer became aware

that his hands, hanging at his sides, were clenched into fists. He opened them before he spoke.

'Murphy says you want me to stake out a bank this morning.'

Still reading, or giving the appearance of it, the lieutenant said, 'It's an epidemic there. We got a chance to make some nice collars.'

'Tonight could be the big night on the Massey kidnapping.'

Boyd looked up with an air of innocence. 'That's not until tonight, is it?'

I'm being sandbagged, Roehmer thought. His hands had tightened into fists again. With effort he forced them open. 'Are we just going to sit by and let the perpetrator get away with a million?'

'Oh, no, nothing like that,' the lieutenant said. 'The feds are setting up a net. That okay with you?'

'It sure ain't, Lieutenant.'

'Well it ain't okay with me either.' He brought his feet down to the floor with a bang. 'And you know why they got the ball? Because you fumbled it, that's why.'

Roehmer stared at him dumbly.

'You were pushing this theory it was a fake, and that the girl couldn't get hurt – right?'

'I'm being blamed because the finger was cut off?'

'For something a lot worse – you made the department look bad.'

So it's all coming down on my head, Roehmer thought. They need a patsy, somebody to take the flak if anyone charged that the case had been mishandled, resulting in the girl's finger being cut off.

'You made a mistake, Roehmer, and we lost the case to the feds. The Chief is real unhappy about that.'

Policy had come down from upstairs; so much for the old school tie. You're in the shit, Roehmer. He said, 'Is it okay if I call Fairborn?'

'I don't see what for. They're gonna have twenty, thirty men mustered for it. If you think he needs you with that army, go ahead and call him. But I expect you to do the stakeout. You're back on the chart again. If Fairborn wants you to help, which I doubt it, you'll do it on your own time and under his orders.'

'Yessir.'

'One other thing.' The lieutenant smiled slyly. 'Mr Massey wants your head because you didn't say anything about the finger yesterday afternoon.'

'How could I? I didn't know it was her finger yet.'

'Yeah, well, we'll see what we can do. We try to take care of our own even when they make big mistakes.'

Roehmer went back to his desk. Murphy and Passatino were waiting for him, wearing their hoodlum outfits. Passatino looked great, like a Mafia heavy. Murphy looked too bright to be a small-time bum.

Roehmer said, 'I'll suit up in a couple of minutes. I have to make a phone call first.'

Murphy and Passatino withdrew discreetly. He dialled Fairborn's office. Fairborn came on the phone, sounding brisk and hurried. Offhand, he couldn't see where Roehmer could fit in. Right now the table of organisation was very tight . . .

Feeling like somebody begging for a handout, Roehmer said, 'I'd appreciate it if you could work me in somewhere.' He thought of adding that he had always co-operated, a hundred per cent, but decided not to because it might remind Fairborn of the way he had hogged the finger to himself yesterday.

'Listen, I'm sorry, they're signalling for me,' Fairborn said. 'A million things to attend to. Can you ring me later? I'll try to think of something.'

'Sure. I'll do that. Thanks.'

He went to his locker and put on a pair of ragged denims and a soiled leather jacket, and then went back to the squad room. Murphy made a pretence of being terrified by his appearance, but his heart wasn't in it.

The team made no collars, but they did almost manage to get themselves arrested.

Around eleven-thirty a young woman came out of the bank blithely holding a handful of money in plain view before stuffing it into her bag. The team had been hanging out nearby, doing a lot of smoking and spitting and ogling women. When they saw a young Hispanic walking about twenty paces behind the young woman, they peeled off and followed.

The young woman turned left at Second Avenue, and the Hispanic did too. She seemed to be enjoying the nippy weather, moving along at a brisk gait, swinging her bag by its strap in a wide arc. She paused once to look at some vegetables on a sidewalk stand, and at the same time the Hispanic stopped to check out the window of a haberdashery store.

Stopping to light a cigarette and spit, Murphy said to Roehmer, 'I think we got ourselves a perpetrator.'

Roehmer grunted. Across the street, on the west side of Second, Passatino was tying a shoelace, his foot propped up on a fire hydrant. The young woman moved on. The Hispanic moved on. Roehmer and Murphy and Passatino moved on.

The young woman crossed Seventieth Street and headed east. So did the Hispanic. Roehmer, Murphy, and Passatino followed. The block was empty. The Hispanic picked up his pace and began to gain on the young woman. She looked over her shoulder for a long moment, then broke into a run. She turned suddenly and pounded up the steps of a brownstone. She opened the door hurriedly with a key, went inside, and pulled the door shut behind her. The Hispanic paused in front of the brownstone and scratched his leg. Looking behind him, he spotted Murphy and Roehmer and took off.

'Come on,' Murphy said.

'What for? He hasn't done anything.'

'I need some action or I'll freeze to death,' Murphy said.

He started running after the Hispanic, who immediately picked up his pace. But Passatino, who had been front-tailing across the street, came charging back to cut him off. The Hispanic reversed his path, but he was surrounded. He covered his head with his hands and began to plead with them in Spanish.

Then he said in English, 'Don' hurt me, please. You can take my money, but don' hurt me.'

'We're police,' Murphy said, flashing his badge. 'So you can stop the act.'

They spread him over a car, tossed him, and discovered that he lived on the street, three houses down from where the young woman lived, that he worked nights in a provisions warehouse, that he was a contributor to the Police Athletic League, and that he was studying to be a CPA at the Twenty-third Street branch of the College of the City of New York.

'Still,' Murphy said, returning the Hispanic's documents, 'you were following that girl.'

No, the Hispanic protested, he lived here, he had made a deposit in the bank – if they looked in his wallet they would find the deposit slip – and then he had walked home . . .

'All right,' Murphy said, 'We'll let you go this time. Go on, beat it.'

Indignant, but too intimidated to protest, the Hispanic went into his house. Murphy, Roehmer, and Passatino started back towards Second Avenue. A squad car came roaring down the block with its siren going, and ran up on to the sidewalk. Both doors opened at the same time, and two uniformed cops jumped out with drawn guns.

'Oh, Jesus,' Murphy said. The car was from the Nineteenth Precinct.

The young woman they had been trailing appeared at the top of her steps and yelled, 'That's them, Officer, they're the men who were following me.'

'Freeze,' one of the cops said. 'Don't move a muscle or I'll blow your heads off.'

'Christ,' Murphy said, 'will you listen to that there?'

'Police officers,' Roehmer said, 'on the job.'

It was straightened out, but first they had to submit to the indignity of draping themselves over a car. By that time a small but enthusiastic crowd had gathered.

'If you could see the way you guys look,' one of the cops said by way of apology. 'And after all we did have a squeal about three suspicious-looking characters . . .'

'Ah, go fuck yourself,' Murphy said.

They went back to the bank and took up their posts again, but by then they were marked as cops; the muggers, if any, had gone elsewhere.

'So if we didn't catch anybody,' Passatino said as they headed back to the precinct house after the bank closed, 'at least our presence was a deterrence, right?'

'Right on, Pass,' Murphy said.

Roehmer phoned Fairborn from his desk. Not in – any message?

'Would you ask him to call Detective Roehmer, please?'

'Agent Fairborn is very busy,' the voice said doubtfully. 'Can someone else help you?'

'Just leave a message that I called and would appreciate him calling me back.'

'Well, I'll write it down, but it happens to be an extremely busy day . . .'

This is the worst day of my life, Roehmer thought. Well, no, the day Peggy Parris walked up that gangplank was much worse. But that was twenty-five years ago. This was the worst of modern times.

The money was brought in about two-thirty. It was delivered by armoured car in a canvas sack, and signed for by one of the two FBI men who were stationed in the anteroom of Julian's apartment. Agnes said that it looked kind of puny to be a whole million dollars.

'How much does it weigh?'

The FBI man hefted the sack and said he thought it might go somewhere between twenty and twenty-five pounds.

'Can I hold it? I'm curious to see how it feels to hold a million dollars in my hands.'

The FBI man gave her the sack. She hefted it, grinning, until Julian shouted, 'Agnes, damnit, this is no time to horse around.'

She returned the sack to the agent, who gave it to Fairborn, sitting beside Julian. Fairborn opened it and took out a few stacks of bills. The stacks were about two inches thick, bound with heavy rubber bands.

'We'll count it and then stack it in the valise,' Fairborn said.

'I made that money with brains and talent,' Julian said, 'and now some criminal pervert – ' His voice choked.

'Now, now, Julian,' Agnes said, 'easy does it.'

Fairborn spoke to the agent: 'Josephs, take this into another room, count it, and then put it into the valise.'

'I'll show you where,' Agnes said. She led Josephs into the TV room and told him he could work at the table.

Josephs said, 'Thank you, ma'am.'

The television set was playing. 'You want me to leave that on? Or I can turn it off.'

'Off, please, if you don't mind.'

Agnes sat down and watched Josephs pile blocks of bills on the table.

'You ever seen that much money before?'

He shook his head. He was riffling through one of the blocks of bills, his lips moving silently.

'You going to count every one of those bills in there?'

'No, just enough to – Damn!'

'Lost your count?'

Josephs began to count again, aloud.

'That's the best way,' Agnes said. 'Out loud, so you can hear what you're doing.'

Josephs turned red. 'Mrs Massey, please don't talk while I'm doing this. I keep losing the count.'

'I'm sorry,' Agnes said. 'I won't say anything. Will it bother you if I sit here if I keep quiet?'

Josephs said, 'I would appreciate it if I might be alone, Mrs Massey, so that I can concentrate.'

Agnes got up. 'Well, if you want anything, coffee or like that, sing out.'

She went into the bedroom and stood at the window looking down at the avenue. It was getting wintry-looking. Another few weeks and they'd have those Christmas trees up in the centre. She yawned. It had been a long morning, and she would be glad when it was all over. She hadn't realised how much was involved in getting a million dollars in cash. The doorbell and the telephone had hardly stopped ringing since the morning. There were calls to and from brokers and bankers and lawyers, people bringing papers to be signed, and FBI men popping in and out as if it were their own house, though she had to admit that they were very polite. But she didn't like their eyes. To a man, they had eyes that looked through you.

Fairborn had been at the apartment practically the whole morning, and he never seemed to stop talking to Julian. Julian looked worn out. Actually, he hadn't been himself ever since he had found out about the finger. He really loved her, Nella, she was very precious to him, no matter how badly she behaved towards him. Not that Julian wasn't difficult, though if you handled him right he could be a pussycat. Nella was kind of mean to her too – Creepy Housekeeper! – but she really didn't bear the girl any ill will. Actually, she felt sorry for her, she was her own worst enemy. Right from the start, she had been prepared to go halfway to meet her, but that wasn't Nella – she never went halfway to meet anybody.

She went out of the bedroom. As she was passing the TV room, she saw that Josephs had the lining of the valise pulled away from the back. He looked up, and their eyes met.

'It's a little torn,' Josephs said. 'I'm trying to put it back in place.'

'You want me to get you some glue or something?'

'Thanks, I've got some right here.'

She moved on down the hallway. She didn't remember the lining of the valise being torn, but they hadn't used that particular one in some time. Still – he brought his own glue? They were doctoring it! Putting a bug in it, or a poison gas that would shoot out when the valise was opened, or a self-destruct mechanism. Poison gas – come on, Agnes. But who travelled around with a bottle of glue?

She went into the sitting-room. Fairborn was still talking, and Julian looked tired and confused. Fairborn stopped talking when he saw her. She stood behind Julian and rested her hands on his shoulders. Fairborn kept looking at her. She paid no attention, but massaged Julian's shoulders gently. He felt like he was all bone.

'Mrs Massey, if you don't mind . . .' Fairborn's mouth was pursing.

'I've already been thrown out of my TV room, and if you think I'm going to be thrown out of my sitting-room, too, you have another guess coming.'

'Sir?' Fairborn looked at Julian.

'Let her stay,' Julian said. 'She's my wife.' He shrugged his shoulders irritably. 'But for God's sake, Agnes, stop leaning on me.'

'Very well,' Fairborn said, sighing. He looked pretty worn out himself, Agnes thought. 'Try to look at it this way, Mr Massey: because of our expertise in the field of kidnapping crimes – we're specialists, you know – you're receiving the benefit of the most informed advice in the world.'

Julian snorted. 'I took your damn advice once, and that brute cut off Nella's finger.'

Fairborn said, 'Sir, I don't usually make a practice of criticising a brother law enforcement agency, but I'm bound to tell you that the game plan you're referring to was the idea of the police department.'

'But you went along with it. Don't try to tell me you didn't.'

'The ball is in our court now, sir.'

'He said no police,' Julian said. 'He threatened to kill her if we brought in the police.'

Fairborn lowered his voice. 'There's one argument I've been reluctant to use up to now, sir. It's this – dealing with a conscienceless criminal, as we are, we have no assurance whatsoever that the kidnapper will release your niece even after he has gotten the ransom money.'

'Christ!' Julian said. 'Why would he do something like that if he collects the ransom?'

Agnes said, 'He might worry she could identify him, or give some other kind of clue.'

Fairborn nodded. 'I don't say he *wouldn't* release her, but it's always a possibility. As I've told you, the payoff situation is the most favourable for apprehending the criminal. And if we catch him, we *know* Miss Massey will be free.'

Julian looked around him helplessly, plucking at his meagre hair. Poor Daddy, Agnes thought, they've been at him half a day, how can he be expected to think straight. They're mean bastards at heart, hammering away like that.

'I'd like to remind you, sir,' Fairborn said, 'that our first priority, above all, is the safety of the victim.'

'Don't say that,' Julian said, flaring up. 'I won't have you calling her a victim. It makes her sound dead already.' He tilted his head up to Agnes. She patted his shoulder. 'Why is it up to me? Why do I have to make such a terrible decision?'

'Because without your approval, sir, we couldn't take any measures. We require the prior agreement of the family.'

Liar, Agnes thought, remembering the bug, or whatever it was, that Josephs had put into the valise. She started to say something about it, but Julian was speaking.

'All right,' he said hoarsely. 'All right. But God help you if anything happens to Nella.'

Laurence Adams took the subway at about five-fifteen, calculating that, adding in a crosstown taxi ride, he would reach Julian Massey's apartment a few minutes before six. The less time he spent with an hysterical Julian the better; not to mention the less time Julian spent with an edgy former son-in-law. Although they both loved Nella, it could hardly be called a tie that binds. The richest advantage of being divorced from Nella was that he no longer had to have anything to do with Julian. Another, though he was reluctant to admit it, was that his life was reasonably serene again.

As the train rattled southwards, he read from Kafka's *Parables*. He had chosen it because the pieces were short, and he knew his attention span would be limited during the wait at Julian's apartment. Not that the subway was ideal, either: between the noise and the sway of the cars, and the need to keep a wary eye out for possible assailants, he did very little reading.

The FBI agents had offered to send a car for him, but he had declined. He hadn't liked them a bit, and rejecting their offer was a mild way of showing his disfavour. They had arrived in the morning, two well-spoken and polite men whose civility was compromised by eyes that could best be described as opaque, impregnable, and unforgiving. Whatever their mood – and there were times when they were friendly – the eyes never changed. Their souls, or what passed for souls, were in their eyes; the rest was cosmetic.

At first their questions tended towards drawing a biographical picture of him. It didn't strike him as being particularly relevant, but it wasn't onerous, either, until one of them asked him to describe his politics. He was about to say that he was a registered Democrat, but it occurred to him that the question was impertinent.

'I'm sorry, I won't answer that.'

The agent who had put the query said, 'Do you find my question objectionable?'

'Yes.'

'In that case I won't pursue it. You're perfectly free not to answer it if you have a reason not to.'

'My reason for not answering it is that it's none of your business.'

The two agents exchanged a look. 'You're right, Mr Adams. Your politics are your own affair – even if you were a member of the Communist party. After all, it's a legal party.'

'Oh, for Christ's sake,' Laurence said, 'you're being nonsensical.'

'We respect your right to withhold an answer,' one of the agents said. 'Let's just drop the subject.'

'You fellows are really something,' Laurence said. 'I vote Democrat. Is that kosher?'

Smoothly, they went on to something innocuous, but before long the interrogation took another turn, and Laurence realised, with astonishment, that they were trying to find out if he was in league with the kidnapper.

Why did the kidnapper choose you? Well, yes, we understand that he might have gotten your name from Miss Massey, but why should they have *accepted* you? Is it possible that the kidnapper knows you personally? As her ex-husband, it's conceivable, isn't it, that you bear a grudge against Miss Massey? Or against your former father-in-law? Didn't you, at one time, teach a short-story course for inmates at Sing Sing prison? Did you form any associations, as a result, that continued outside of prison? Do you, currently, see any of your former students? Would you mind stating what your salary as a professor is?

From seething anger Laurence passed on to an appreciation of the ludicrousness of the situation. He burst out laughing.

The two agents, their eyes as hard as steel balls, waited for his laughter to run down, and then one of them said, 'Do you find this funny, Mr Adams?'

'I had a narrow choice between laughter and tears. You guys are – well, you're fantastic.'

As smoothly as though his line of questioning had not been interrupted, the agent said, 'Why do you think Miss Massey chose to offer you as intermediary?'

'Well, you're granting that Miss Massey chose me, that's a concession, isn't it? She probably chose me because she knew that she could trust me. It's as simple as that.'

'You've been seeing her lately?'

'You asked me that before. No, not for at least six months.'

'Have you been in touch by telephone?'

'No, alas. Listen, can I tell you fellows something?' He waited for a signal, but the eyes remained steady, saying neither yes or no. 'I'll tell you anyway. Your problem is that, although you're undoubtedly terrific at sniffing out villains, you have absolutely no capability for recognising an honest man when you see one.'

'Why did you say "alas"?'

'Because Nella is still quite dear to me.'

In some way that he couldn't fathom, he must have

allayed their suspicions, or, at least, convinced them that they weren't going to ferret out his crimes in so short a session. They turned to the night's work.

'Have you had any previous experience in acting as an intermediary?'

The question called for more hilarity, but he simply said, 'No. This is my debut. And I'm nervous about it.'

'You'll be all right if you just follow instructions.'

'What *are* the instructions?'

'The *kidnapper's* instructions.'

'Then I won't know what I'm supposed to do until the very last minute?'

'Most likely.'

'Something like going to a given phone booth – is that it?'

'What makes you say that?'

'Hell, I don't know. Isn't it always something like that?' He saw the agents exchanging looks again. 'I mean, in the movies, and in books?'

'It's best not to anticipate. Just follow your instructions to the letter and you'll be all right.'

'Will it be dangerous? After all, I'll be wandering around the city, presumably late at night, with a million dollars in cash. Wouldn't you call that dangerous?'

'What makes you think you'll be wandering around the *city*?'

'Oh, God,' Adams said. 'Well, I ought to know, I'm the mastermind, aren't I?'

'There's no call for facetiousness, Mr Adams.'

It was another concession to their belief that he was an innocent bystander.

He climbed up the subway steps and landed in the street in the middle of the rush hour. It was impossible to find a cab. He spent ten minutes frantically waving from the kerb before deciding to walk. Two blocks further, he jumped into a cab that was discharging a passenger; two blocks after that, because the cab was barely moving in the heavy traffic, he paid off the driver and walked again. He arrived at Julian Massey's building at five minutes past six, panicky at the thought that the kidnapper might already have phoned.

The doorman eyed him with distaste and moved very slowly to the intercom. He was probably suspicious of his clothing: corduroy trousers, a flannel shirt, half boots, a sheepskin jacket. He had thought it advisable to dress that way – surely intermediaries didn't wear a business suit and a tie? The doorman passed him into the lobby and the elevator man took him up and let him off in the anteroom of Julian's apartment. He pressed the doorbell.

'You're late,' Julian said.

It was almost six-thirty by the time Fairborn called. 'You phoned me?'

Roehmer quirked his lips in a sour smile. You phoned me? Only eight or ten times during the afternoon and early evening to the increasing annoyance of Fairborn's office, hanging around after his tour had ended, waiting for a phone call the way a lovelorn kid hopes for a ring from a girl who has already promised to go to the prom with the high school quarterback.

'I'd like to know what I can do. Tonight?'

'Tonight. Well, you see, we've got everything very tightly organised, and we've worked as a team before, of course. Do you follow me?'

'Yeah, I think I follow you. But there should be *someplace* I could fit in. I mean, I know the case better than anybody. I mean better than anybody else but you. Anyway, I don't think the NYPD ought to be shut out.'

'They're not,' Fairborn said. 'Your chief sent down a couple of detectives from the Major Case Squad.'

'Oh,' Roehmer said. 'Is that right?'

'Not that I can see where they can fit in, either. Listen, I have to run, got a hundred things to attend to.'

'You can't expect him to call this early,' Roehmer said. 'It doesn't figure.' Fairborn was silent, but his breathing sounded impatient. 'I hate the idea of not doing anything.'

'I sympathise, but . . . tell you, you can help monitor the phone call in the basement. Would you like to do that?'

'That would be just dandy,' Roehmer said. 'Thanks.'

He put on his topcoat and walked over to Park Avenue. He paused for the ritual glance up at the alien drapes at the eighth-floor windows before crossing the street.

In the basement Pittman introduced him to another man. 'This is Special Agent Heimlich, he'll be helping to monitor the calls tonight.'

And I'll help the monitor-helper, Roehmer thought. He shook hands with Heimlich.

'Take a load off your feet,' Pittman said.

But there were only two chairs. The electronics detective was sitting in one, and Special Agent Heimlich was sitting in the other.

'I'll buzz the super and get him to send another chair,' Pittman said.

'Don't bother,' Roehmer said.

'No trouble. Might as well be comfortable.'

And to think, Roehmer said to himself, if I had said yes instead of no, I might today be sitting around in bikini bathing trunks on the beach at Antibes with Peggy Parris, drinking cognac and swapping bon mots with the bon ton. In French, yet.

Chapter 22

At twelve-fifteen Richard let out a fare in Riverdale, just off the Henry Hudson Parkway. He lit up his OFF DUTY sign, got back on the parkway, and crossed into Manhattan. He took the first exit off the West Side Highway, Dyckman Street, and cruised north along Broadway until he spotted a pay phone near 207th Street. He started dialling Julian's number at exactly twelve thirty.

Julian was alone in the sitting-room when the phone rang. Agnes was in the TV room watching Johnny Carson, and Laurence Adams had fallen asleep in a leather chair in the library.

'Hello . . .'

'You got the money? Is this Laurence Adams there?'

At the sound of the flat, sinister voice Julian began to tremble. 'Yes, yes, I have the money. I'll get him, I'll get Laurence right away.'

'No, stay put. Write down what I tell you. Don't say a word. Just write. Ready?'

'I'm trusting you to let Nella – '

'Shut up.' The voice became louder, rasping. 'Write this down: Tell him, Laurence Adams, to take the money and go out and take the first taxicab that comes along to a phone booth at Thirty-seventh and Fifth, north-east corner. You got that?'

'Phone booth at Thirty-seventh and Fifth Avenue . . .' Julian saw Laurence come into the room. His hair was rumpled, his face creased. 'Yes, I've got it.'

'Tell him to pay off his cab and go into the booth and wait for another call.'

'Go into the booth . . . Can't you even tell me that Nella is all right? Please – '

The line went dead. He jumped up and ran towards

Laurence, waving his pad. 'Get going. Where's your jacket? Where's your damn jacket?'

Laurence Adams's hand was shaking as it took the pad.

The FBI agent who had been stationed in the anteroom was pressing the elevator button when Adams appeared, carrying the valise in one hand, trying to button his jacket with the other. Julian was pushing him, shouting at him to get a move on. Agnes was trying to calm Julian down, but he ignored her.

The elevator doors opened. 'Take him down,' the FBI man said, 'and don't make any stops.'

The elevator was halfway to the lobby before Adams, remembering that the FBI agent had been holding a two-way radio, understood how he had been able to anticipate his appearance. The phone was being monitored, and news of the kidnapper's call had been transmitted to him by radio. Yet Julian had assured him that they were obeying the kidnapper's injunction to keep the authorities out of it.

He felt agitated, and, at the same time, not quite awake. He had wanted to throw some cold water on his face, but Julian had run to get his jacket and the valise, and started shoving him towards the door. When he stepped out into the lobby, a man wearing a leather coat and a sporty little motoring cap fell in step with him.

'Just follow their instructions to the letter and you'll be all right,' the man said. 'They'll probably direct you to a second phone booth.'

Adams said, 'The police weren't supposed to be involved.'

'There's no reason for you to be nervous,' the man said. 'Just hang on tightly to that valise. It's a lot of cabbage.'

'That's why I'm nervous. Weren't you supposed to stay out of this?'

'Just keep calm and follow their instructions.'

They had reached the inner door. The man patted Adams on the shoulder and stepped back. The doorman was holding the outer door open. Adams stepped out into the street and the doorman followed. A taxi pulled up to the kerb. Adams got in, and the doorman shut the door. The cab driver turned a sharp nutcracker profile towards him, his head cocked enquiringly.

'Thirty-seventh and Fifth Avenue.'

The driver nodded.

'Northeast corner.'

The cab shot away from the kerb. Adams was sitting at the edge of the seat and he was shivering. When the cab made a sharp U-turn, before heading downtown on Park, he almost fell off the seat. He sat further back, placed the valise on the floor between his legs, and buttoned up his jacket to the neck. He picked up the valise, set it on his lap, and held it with both hands. The taxi proceeded southwards, rapidly and smoothly. At Thirty-seventh Street it turned west. Their destination was a commercial area, and bound to be deserted at this hour. The thought that he might be robbed, that losing the money might endanger Nella's life, turned Adams cold with fear.

The taxi pulled up just short of the corner, alongside the phone booth. As he was paying the fare, and adding a dollar tip, Adams was tempted to ask the driver to wait for him, but instead said good night and got out of the cab. He watched the taxi move off, and then he stepped into the booth. He placed the valise between his legs and leaned his weight against the folding door to secure it against being pushed open. The booth was cold and damp and smelled of various unpleasant odours that he preferred not to try to sort out. There were a few figures passing by, but none of them looked into or even at the booth. He realised that there was no light in the booth – it had been broken or stolen – and he was grateful for the sheltering darkness.

There was a moderate sprinkling of traffic going by on Fifth, including taxis. He wouldn't have any trouble finding a cab if he had to go to another phone booth. *Ring, ring, for Godssake, ring*. Something made him turn his head, and he saw a man looking in, with his face almost touching the glass. His heart lurched and he braced his body hard against the booth door.

Suppose it was just someone wanting to use the phone?

He reached into his pocket and mimed taking out a coin and dropping it into the box. But he kept the connecting bar down as he mouthed nonsense words into the transmitter. Ring, oh God, ring! The man outside the booth gave him a grin, then staggered off down the street. A drunk. Just a drunk.

The phone rang.

From midnight on Wally had been practising his Richard voice almost constantly, paying no attention to Nella's insistence that it wasn't important, that Laurence had never heard Richard speak, and therefore wouldn't know that he was listening to someone else's voice. His efforts made her finger hurt – or so it seemed. She went into the bedroom and lay down, and presently the pain eased, although, in the dark, she was beset by flashing images of Julian (a blend of agony, outrage, and anxiety), Laurence (the don miscast as go-between), Detective Roehmer (his conspiracy theory about her part in the kidnap – assuming it existed other than in her own mind – confounded by the severed finger) . . .

When the phone rang, she got out of bed and hurried to the kitchen, but Wally was just hanging up.

'Richard,' Wally said. 'They got the money and your ex-husband is there. Richard says he's sure they're gonna do it. He says to phone in about fifteen or twenty minutes.' Wally massaged his forehead. 'I'm a little nervous.'

Thanks for telling me, Wally, I'd never have known.

He sat down at the table in the foyer and, improvising a phone with his fist, began to rehearse his lines again. Nella sat down.

'What I like you to do,' Wally said, 'is listen and tell me if I'm doing it right.'

'Give you an honest critique?'

'Right. Here goes.'

Her finger began to hurt again.

When it was time to make the call, she told Wally to take a drink of water. He took a shot of whisky instead. She stood close to him while he dialled the number of the phone booth, then lifted up on her toes to bring her ear up to the level of his. She heard the phone ring, and then a faint voice responding.

'Who is this?' Wally said. His voice was constricted by nervousness, but it didn't matter. Only the message mattered. Indistinctly, she heard Laurence identifying himself.

'Okay.' Wally took a deep breath. 'Take the first taxicab and go to the pay phone on the south-east corner of Eighty-sixth and Lexington. When it rings, say who you are.' Wally hung up. 'How was it?'

'Beautiful, Wally. I swear, if I closed my eyes, I would have bet that it was Richard speaking.'

Wally's lips quivered upwards in a full-mouthed smile.

Laurence Adams picked up the valise and took a firm grip on it. There was no one nearby except the drunk, who was swaying at the kerb halfway down the street. As he pushed his way out of the booth, a cab glided towards him and stopped. He got in quickly and slammed the door shut.

The cab driver tilted his head back. 'Where to?'

'Eighty-sixth and Lexington, please.'

The cabdriver nodded, and Adams, leaning forward, recognised the nutcracker profile. His hand reached for the door handle, but the cab was already in full forward motion.

'Let me out,' Adams said, his voice rising. 'I changed my mind.'

The driver's head was solidly fixed to the front. At Thirty-sixth Street he turned left.

'Let me out. I'll pay you. You won't lose anything. Stop this cab.'

He began to shout and then, in a panic, reached for the door handle. The door opened slightly, but the slipstream slammed it shut. The cab was speeding down the street.

'Let me out,' Adams screamed. 'Stop this cab!'

The cab shot across Madison Avenue, then slowed as it approached a red light. The driver spoke over his shoulder. 'Don't get excited. You're safe.'

'Let me out!' Adams pushed the door open, but the light turned green and the cab sped across the avenue.

'Better shut that door, Mr Adams. I'm an agent of the Federal Bureau of Investigation.'

Adams stared at the profile. 'How do I know that?'

The driver's hand came back holding a small leather folder. Adams took it. It was the man's ID. He was Leonard Hubert; his photograph had been taken full face, but he was unmistakably the owner of the nutcracker profile.

'I'll take that back now,' Hubert said. 'Pull the door shut, please.'

Adams obeyed, then fell back against the seat, drenched with sweat.

At one-fifteen, after dropping a Chinese couple at a Mott Street address, Richard turned on his OFF DUTY sign. He cruised slowly north and west for a few minutes, then turned south again into the deserted courthouse area of Foley Square. He found a pay phone, double-parked, and dialled. The phone was answered on the third ring.

Speaking softly, evenly, Richard said, 'You miserable old sonofabitch, you had the cops in.'

'No, no.' Julian's voice was hoarse. 'No, no, you're wrong.'

'I *saw* them, you lying bastard.'

'No, I swear – '

'I *saw* them. I'm so fucking mad I could kill her right now.'

'No, please, please . . .' Julian's voice turned shrill. 'Give me another chance.'

Richard said, 'I'm going to take one more shot at the money. Just one, the last one, and that's the limit.'

'Yes, yes, thank you. I promise – '

'Tomorrow night, then I'm quitting. I won't go past tomorrow night. You hear? If there's cops tomorrow night, that's it, Nella is going to fucking die.' He held the phone away from his ear for an instant as Julian babbled into it. 'Keep quiet, old man. It's up to you. You have cops again, I'll kill her.'

Richard hung up. He waited briefly, then dialled again. 'All set,' he said when Wally answered.

'Great. Did he admit there were cops?'

'He didn't have to. He was scared shitless.'

Wally laughed. 'I'll phone the professor.'

'Give it about five more minutes.'

Richard got back into his cab. He turned off the OFF DUTY sign and began to cruise uptown, keeping an eye out for fares.

In the basement, Special Agent Heimlich was speaking to Fairborn in the command-post truck. Pittman was lighting a cigarette. Roehmer sat stiffly in the hard wooden chair the superintendent had brought down for him, his eyes red and itching, his head beginning to ache.

On the radio, Fairborn was shouting. Roehmer understood how he felt. Here he had laid on an elaborate surveillance set up, and it had unaccountably failed. Now, though it burned his ass, he had no choice but to dismantle his apparatus – taxicab driver agents, make-like-drunk agents, agents in delivery vans (the command post was set up in a carpet delivery van), agents in private sedans; send all of his army of twenty-odd agents home to bed and go home himself, wondering where he had made some vital slip up, wrestling with a loss of confidence and a growing feeling that the kidnapper had resources in terms of manpower and know-how that they hadn't guessed at.

Heimlich signed off. 'All of that fucking work for nothing.'

Pittman, shaking his head in disbelief, said, 'They made us. Can you imagine that – making us?'

'How the devil did he do it?' Heimlich said. 'Where did we give ourselves away?'

'There must be more than one of them,' Pittman said. 'Or how else could they have made us? You agree?'

'I don't see any other answer,' Heimlich said.

'How many of them would you figure?' Pittman said to Roehmer.

'No less than fifty,' Roehmer said. *Or none.*

★

Julian kept talking into the dead phone until Agnes came across the room and took the instrument away from him.

'He's gone, Daddy.'

'He's the devil. God, he sounded so vicious, Agnes, I really think he might have killed her right then and there.'

Agnes massaged the corded back of his neck, murmuring softly.

'I begged him to give us another chance. If you could have heard his voice, Agnes, it was inhuman, cold as ice.'

'There now,' Agnes said. 'There now, Daddy.'

'He promised me,' Julian said wildly. 'That Fairborn, that great FBI man, he promised me that they wouldn't be found out.'

Julian struggled out of his chair, his face twisted in rage. Agnes tried to restrain him but he pushed her away and ran towards the door.

'You lousy bastard!' He started shouting even before the door was fully open. 'Get out of my house, out of this building!'

Startled, the FBI agent got up off the Malaysian chest that served as a bench.

'Get out of here and never let me see your face again, you and the whole lot!' Julian ran past the agent and poked at the elevator button. He kept his finger on it, twisting it.

'Sir,' the agent said. 'What's the trouble?'

'Get out of here, you bullshit artist! You realise you almost got Nella killed? You gave me your assurance – oh, that's worth shit.'

'What's the matter?' the agent said to Agnes.

She went to Julian. 'Julian, come on, you're going to break that button. The elevator's on its way, I can hear it. Let's go inside and lie down.'

'I'll lie down when this bastard is out of my sight.' The elevator door opened. Julian shoved the grille back. 'Get in, you, get the hell out of here.'

The agent, still bewildered, started into the elevator. Julian put his hand against his back and shoved.

'Take him down,' Julian yelled at the elevator man. 'Take him down and see that he gets the hell out of this building.'

He continued to glare at the door even after it had shut, and the elevator had begun its descent.

'Can we go inside now, Julian?' Agnes said.

Julian kicked out savagely at the elevator door.

'No sense being mad at the door,' Agnes said. 'The door didn't do anything to you.'

Like the West Village, like Third Avenue north of Bloomingdale's, Eighty-sixth and Lexington, the heart of the Yorkville area, was one of those Manhattan localities that never seemed to go to sleep. The pay phone was one of the three-sided, half-length boxes. He wedged the valise tightly into the space between the phone and the plastic side panel of the booth, and pinned it there firmly with his right shoulder. He would have felt more secure with a door at his back, but there was some comfort in the presence of the lively crowd flowing by. He lifted the receiver from the hook, mimed dropping a coin in the box, and pretended to be carrying on a conversation.

The phone rang. He released the connecting bar and said, 'Hello?'

'Who is this?'

'This is Laurence Adams.'

'Okay, Adams. Go back to Massey's place now.'

'What? What do you mean?'

'Go back to Massey's apartment, you jerk. That's all.'

A taxi drew up to the kerb. Hubert, the agent with the nutcracker profile, beckoned to him. He picked up the valise and edged out of the booth. The rear door of the cab swung open.

'I'll take you back to Massey's apartment,' Hubert said. 'We won't be working any more tonight.'

Chapter 23

When Nella and Wally heard Richard come in, they got up and joined him for breakfast. It was a bit after seven-thirty. Richard was pale and fatigued, but at Wally's urging he recapitulated his two conversations with Julian.

'There was cops, all right,' he said. 'That was a great idea you had.'

All in the day's work for Nella Massey, famous throughout the underworld as the criminal's criminal. But she was pleased by Richard's compliment. 'It figured,' she said modestly.

Wally told of his calls to Laurence Adams. 'I swear, Richard, I sounded more like you than you do. Ask Nella.'

'With my eyes closed,' she said, 'I never would have known the difference.'

When they had finished eating, Richard pulled out a roll of bills. He had made sixty-three dollars in tips last night.

'Best night I ever had.' His pale cheeks were flushed with pleasure. 'I got two twenty-dollar tips, and one of them was for a three-dollar ride.'

'You made sixty-three dollars last night?' Wally was solemnly awed. He winked at Nella. 'You're putting me on, Richard.'

'On the level. One of them was a trip way out on the Island. Fourteen dollars on the meter and a twenty-dollar tip. The three-dollar ride, the guy was drunk, I mean he was really bombed. I guess the Long Island one was a little drunk too.'

'Sixty-three dollars,' Wally said. 'Richard, you're a wealthy man.'

Wally burst out laughing. Richard seemed puzzled, even a little put out, but when Wally pointed out the irony – how could he get so excited about sixty-three dollars when he was on the verge of acquiring a third of a million – Richard laughed.

Wally ruffled Richard's hair affectionately and told him to get to bed. 'Tonight could be the big night, buddy, you need your sleep.' He winked at Nella. 'Better put that money under your pillow so nobody can heist it.'

Nella helped Wally clear the dishes from the table. He was solicitous of her finger, and pleased when she told him it was feeling a great deal better, no worse than a dull ache.

'Richard,' Wally said, 'he knows his stuff.'

After washing the dishes, Wally went off to do his exercises. Nella turned on the radio and leafed through the morning newspaper Richard had brought home.

A little after ten o'clock the radio announcer broke in with a bulletin: Mr Julian Massey would be holding a press conference at noon at the offices of his attorney, to make an important statement with respect to the kidnapping of his niece, Nella Massey, missing for two weeks . . .

Wally was in the shower. She burst in on him to tell him the news.

No one was supposed to have heard about last night's abortion, but when Roehmer arrived in the morning, the squad room was buzzing. Most of the detectives drifted over to his desk. He told them that he didn't know any more about it than they did, and couldn't guess how the kidnapper had made the agents. There was a lot of sly amusement at the thought of the feds having fallen on their faces.

One of the detectives said, 'The way I heard it, they had twenty-five or thirty G-men on the job. That's too *much* manpower. A crowd like that, the kidnapper would have to be blind not to make them.'

Another said, with some resentment, 'They got manpower to burn. Christ, if we had half of their manpower . . .'

'And all the vee-hicles they used,' Murphy said. 'I hear they made a traffic jam outside the Massey place and had civilians in cars backed up three blocks, all blowing their horns and waking up the upper classes.'

Passatino said, 'I heard two things – they used a fed to drive the taxi that picked up this Adams, and also another crouched down on the floor in the back seat.'

'Where'd you hear that?' Roehmer said.

Passatino spread his hands. 'Rumours, rumours. Is it true?'

'You didn't hear it from me, because I don't know,' Roehmer said. 'The Chief sent down two detectives from the Major Case Squad. Maybe *they* said so. If *they* knew.'

Most of the detectives shared the belief that there had to be more than one kidnapper – possibly four or even five. How could one man have spotted the feds?

'You agree, Rome?'

With a touch of anger, Roehmer said, 'Jesus Christ, don't ask me. I wasn't on the operation, I was scratched. Don't you guys know that?'

There was a murmur of embarrassment mixed with sympathy. There might be competition between teams, but there was also a bond of loyalty and solidarity that united the men of the One-Eight's Detective Squad. Roehmer felt sorry for his loss of temper.

He said, 'Suppose he never did make the feds. Suppose he planned to abort the pickup from the start, from the word go, on the theory that there *had* to be cops of some kind around.'

Most of the detectives disagreed: perpetrators didn't have that kind of brains. Cops, himself included, Roehmer thought, held a universally low opinion of criminals, especially of their intelligence, or lack of it. But what if it was no ordinary criminal, but a bright young woman? If she was smart enough to organise a fake crime and gutsy enough to cut off her own finger (ride that hunch, Roehmer, ride 'em, cowboy), then she was certainly sharp enough to dope out that the law-enforcement agencies weren't going to pass up an opportunity like last night. He kept his thoughts to himself.

The discussion broke up when Boyd came storming out

of his office. What were they, a bunch of fucking stenographers having a taffy pull? Get to fucking work, chrissake, or you'll be out pounding a fucking beat.

After the detectives scattered, Boyd leaned over Roehmer's desk. 'You glad we didn't let you join the feds? So now, at least, you weren't a member of the fiasco.'

'Yeah, I'm very grateful, Lieutenant.'

The lieutenant eyed him suspiciously, sifting his tone for traces of insubordination, then walked off. Roehmer applied himself to paperwork until ten thirty, and then he phoned Fairborn.

'What can I do for you, Roehmer?' Fairborn sounded out of sorts.

'I'm just keeping in touch. Anything new?'

'Don't you believe in listening to the radio over there, or checking your Teletype once in a while?'

'Something up?'

'Julian Massey is holding a press conference at twelve o'clock. Old bastard – do you know he laid hands on an agent last night?'

Roehmer coughed to suppress a laugh. 'You mean attacked him, hurt him?'

'He didn't hurt him, but that's not the point. He was out of order to lay hands on him. Goddamn rich people think they can . . .'

Fairborn's voice trailed off, and Roehmer grinned at the thought of an eighty-year-old bag of bones assailing a G-man. He said, 'Any indication what he's going to say?'

'I hate to think about it. My best guess is that he'll blame us for last night's fuck-up and claim he didn't have anything to do with it.'

'He'll be talking for the benefit of the kidnapper?'

'It sure as hell won't be for *our* benefit. It's going to be held in his lawyer's office, so we can expect the worst.'

'I'll ring you later,' Roehmer said.

Murphy came over. 'This Hispanic girl says her father wants to snitch where her mother's boyfriend has got an apartment full of stolen radios and televisions and cameras and like that. Want to catch the squeal?'

What I want to catch, Roehmer thought, is Nella

Massey. What I want to handle is McGarry, the failed cop, and interrogate him for what he knows about the girl, and satisfy a theory that he's a weak sister who would sweat bullets and sing under pressure. What I want is help to toss the girl's old neighbourhood where that faggot saw her, not to mention McGarry, and the bus driver . . .

'Yeah, sure, I'd love to,' Roehmer said.

The law library of the firm of Harwood, Thompson, de Bergh, Stanley & Roux was unusually spacious, but at twelve noon it was untidily crowded by a large number of representatives of the press, radio, and television who had gathered there to hear Julian Massey. Roger de Bergh, the senior surviving member of the firm, and a Princeton classmate of Julian's, sat beside his client at one end of the long library table, the benignity of his old man's face barely concealing his dislike of the mob he faced.

Although some members of the press were still straggling in, he ordered the doors shut at precisely noon. He rapped on the table with his knuckles, and the room quieted. Blinking, shading his eyes against the glare of the television lights that outraged the calculated gloom of the library, de Bergh spoke briefly.

'Mr Julian Massey will read a statement he has prepared with the help of this office. There will be no questions afterwards.'

He nodded to Julian, who rattled a sheet of paper and then read from it slowly. 'Last night, against my express wishes – I repeat, against my express wishes – various law-enforcement agencies attempted to intervene in the delivery of ransom money to secure the release of my beloved niece, Nella Massey, from the toils of her kidnapper.'

He paused as a swell of rustling bodies and whispers arose. Roger de Bergh rapped his knuckles on the table and the noise subsided.

'In some way, the kidnapper became cognisant of this unauthorised intervention, and abruptly terminated the proposed exchange of money for Nella's freedom.'

A murmur rose again, but died away before de Bergh could rap the table.

'The kidnapper, upon his discovery that the law-enforcement agencies were involved, informed me that he would give me one more chance to deliver the ransom, and that, if the police or FBI were again involved, he would, without further ado, kill my niece.'

Julian's voice failed. His eyes moistened and began to blink very rapidly. De Bergh whispered to him and patted his hand. Julian nodded, touched his handkerchief to his eyes, and spoke again.

'I wish to make two declarations of intent. First, to the kidnapper. Whoever you are, please accept that I will undertake to convey one million dollars to you in accordance with your instructions, and that I shall sternly forbid any interference by any and all law-enforcement authorities.

'My second declaration is addressed to the New York Police Department and the Federal Bureau of Investigation. Do not attempt to interfere in this matter. I have only one goal – the safe return of my niece. If you attempt to intervene in any way, shape, or manner, I shall hold you fully responsible for any harm that may befall Nella Massey.

'That is all.'

The word had been passed: there would be no intervention from the NYPD or the FBI in any delivery of ransom money that might be attempted by Julian Massey.

The squad room was buzzing with the news. Roehmer said nothing, but went to his desk and started to write up a report on the Hispanic who had accused his wife's lover of being a fence. He and Murphy had found the apartment bare of stolen goods, containing only an angry middle-aged Cuban who swore that he would square accounts with his accuser with a knife. He was halfway through the report when somebody said the lieutenant wanted to see him. In his office, Boyd was in his favourite position, tilted back in his chair, hands clasped behind his head.

'You hear that we're laying off the Massey case?'

341

'They told me.'

'That's some mean prick, that Massey. Fairborn swore up and down that he agreed to last night's operation.'

'I guess he's worried about the girl. It's only natural.'

The lieutenant pointed a finger at Roehmer. 'You call it natural to blacken the name of the police and threaten them?'

'It was an FBI operation,' Roehmer said, shrugging.

'Well, they're police, sort of. Besides, the public don't know it was an FBI fiasco, so we get tarred with the same brush. I tell you that old man is a miserable shit.'

'I'm not defending him,' Roehmer said. 'He isn't my uncle.'

'I wasn't accusing you, but you could at least show a little emotion.'

'It sure is tough to knuckle under to a perpetrator.'

'That's a little better. You sure you understand the policy? Hands off. Don't get any fucking ideas.'

'How can I? I'm off the case.'

'That means no free-lancing on your own time, like detectives do in the movies. You understand me?'

'Yessir.'

'Okay. You turn anything up on that Hispanic fence?'

'It's a washout. I'm writing up a report. You want me to tell you about it?'

'I'd rather read the report,' the lieutenant said. 'I enjoy good writing.'

Wally said, 'I got a feeling of déjà vu.'

The phrase was delivered with such overreaching casualness that it instantly gave away his self-conscious pride in its use.

'You took the words out of my mouth, Wally.'

They were sitting on the sofa, waiting for the six o'clock newscast to begin. It could serve no practical point, since they had heard Julian's speech in full on the radio, as well as the joint statement of the FBI and the NYPD to the effect that they would respect Mr Massey's wishes and not intervene. But Wally had insisted. Television was The Word.

342

'Real déjà vu,' Wally said.

'Wally, you have a beautiful French accent.'

'Kidding me?'

'No, I mean it.' She rested her cheek against his biceps, bulging beneath the short sleeve of an apricot T-shirt.

'I took French in high school and I got like eighty-five in it.' She felt his biceps quiver. 'And in college I got around eighty-five too.'

Boola boola, Wally. She pressed her open lips gently against the smoothness of his skin. 'Oh, Wally, what am I going to do without you?'

'Look, baby, it'll just be for a little while, until everything quiets down, right?'

She felt a wave of sadness. It was coming to an end. Afterwards, it would be dangerous for them to meet. More to the point, she knew that, having served his purpose, he would no longer interest her. It would be true for Wally, as well. With money, he wouldn't regard her as something special. Money was class.

'We'll have to be careful and all,' Wally said, 'but we'll find a way.'

'Wild horses couldn't keep us apart.'

After the television clip (she had averted her eyes from Julian's display of emotion, as she might at an unpleasantly bloody scene in a film), they both lapsed into silence, as if in mutual acceptance of the fact that they lacked the resources to maintain civility for the next seven or eight hours of waiting. Earlier in the day they had been relaxed, basking in the feeling of triumph and catharsis engendered by Julian's surrender. When Richard awakened and joined them, they had discussed the question of her release. Richard had formulated a simple plan: she would leave the apartment shortly after 6.00 a.m., when the guard in the lobby had gone off duty. Richard would drive her into Brooklyn in his cab and drop her off. She would then phone the police.

She had already worked out a scenario for her interrogation by the police. She had been snatched off the street by two men in a private car – there would be no great risk in admitting that there had been two kidnappers

– blindfolded, and driven some distance. She would say that they had crossed one of the bridges into Brooklyn (she recognised the distinctive sound of the tyres on the metal road-bed), and taken her to a small apartment. In the one glimpse she had had of her captors in the car before they blindfolded her, she had noted that both were short dark men, and that one wore a moustache. After that they were always masked. They had treated her well up to the time of the amputation of her finger, except that they had forced some kind of medication on her each day which kept her dazed and befuddled. So, being drugged, she could remember very little of her ordeal . . .

In the early afternoon she had sent Wally out to a sporting goods store on Forty-second Street. When he returned, she had put his purchases – a dozen pair of sweat socks, two sweat shirts, swimming trunks, a couple of jockstraps – together with a sales slip, in one of two large identical shopping bags. She had put a sweat shirt in the second bag and folded it up in a flat package so that Richard could conceal it under his sweater until he drove his cab out of the taxi garage.

When Richard left at five-thirty, they shook hands solemnly all around.

On his way home the lieutenant made a detour to Roehmer's desk. 'The Knicks game is on TV tonight. You gonna watch it?'

'Maybe. Yeah, I guess I'll watch it.'

'I was you, that's what I would do – watch the Knicks play.'

Subtle as a fucking trip-hammer, Roehmer thought as Boyd left. Well, the lieutenant didn't have to worry – he intended to stay home tonight, but not necessarily to watch the Knicks play. Yes, he would be home, thinking about what he really wanted to do, which was to drop in on McGarry and try slapping the truth out of him, and if that failed, prowling the neighbourhood to try to sniff out the girl's presence with his infallible detective's sixth sense. But you weren't allowed to beat anybody up on suspicion these days, and if he got spotted on the street, he would get hung up to dry in the South Bronx. So he was going to go on home and watch the Knicks.

He put on his topcoat and then sat down again and looked up a number in the phone book and dialled it.

A voice said, 'Pleasant Times.'

Disguising his voice, making it nasal, he said, 'McGarry?'

'McGarry ain't here. Be back at eight o'clock. Tell him who called?'

'Yeah, his bookie.'

And what would he have said or done if McGarry had been in? Shaking his head in wonderment at himself, he left the precinct house and went home.

Chapter 24

Laurence Adams arrived a few minutes before six. After some drinks, Agnes served dinner, which consisted of a patently costly but badly overcooked steak and a salad garnished with a store-bought dressing. The cocktail hour, as Julian called it, had been distinguished by a ridiculous literary discussion. It had begun after Julian brought out his supposed picture of Scott Fitzgerald in drag. Laurence had admired it as though it were the first time he had seen it, instead of the hundredth, and murmured something to the effect that it was an interesting and charming bit of literary memorabilia.

'It's probably worth a small fortune,' Julian said. 'After all, it's a hitherto unpublished picture of America's greatest writer.'

Laurence agreed that it might have some value, but then made the mistake of saying that he couldn't quite agree with Julian's ranking of Fitzgerald as the country's *greatest* writer.

Bristling, Julian said, 'I defy you to name a better one.'

It was too late to retreat, so, after a moment's thought, he said, 'Mark Twain.'

'Mark Twain? I mean in modern times.'

'Faulkner.'

'He doesn't even write English, he writes Southern. Scott reads as smooth as silk and his meaning is always clear.'

'That's true about Fitzgerald,' Laurence said, looking for a way out of what he now regarded as a self-made dilemma. 'He wrote a lovely prose, and he had a marvellous ear.'

'What do you mean by "lovely"?' Julian said suspiciously.

Agnes appeared to announce that dinner was ready. Julian brought his picture to the dining-room table, and chomped away at his thesis like a bulldog. In the end, to save wear and tear, Laurence wearily conceded everything. Hereafter, he vowed to himself, he wouldn't contest a single syllable that Julian uttered, no matter how it outraged him. Unless, of course, he started sounding off on Nella, as he had done so often and so embarrassingly when they were still married. He simply wouldn't tolerate any animadversions towards Nella – not from anyone, and especially not from Julian.

After dinner Julian sat down at the telephone with a pad and three sharpened pencils ready on a table beside him. Laurence wandered into the library. He browsed through the shelves and ended up with a copy of *Tender Is the Night*. Well, Julian to one side, he *did* admire Fitzgerald.

A half hour after he walked through the door, Roehmer knew he wouldn't stay. He didn't even do much thinking about it; the decision just surfaced and took over his mind. Mary was about three-quarters under. He knew the signs, he could read them as fluently as he could a newspaper. She babbled on about how happy she was that he had come home so early, and how, after dinner, they would watch television for a while, and then, when they got tired, maybe fool around a little . . . Her eyes, flirting with him over the rim of the glass, were bleary.

He sat in the cramped living-room, listening to Mary fumble in the kitchen, dropping things, swearing at her own ineptitude, a few minutes away from tears. He thought: Although God may pardon me for violating the temporal rules of the NYPD and flouting the simple law of survival – not sticking your neck out – He will never forgive me for what I am about to do to Mary. He'll remember that forever, and, however long it takes, punish me for it. The punishment of the NYPD would come much sooner, if he was found out.

Roehmer wasn't all that big on God, but he did believe in Him, so, for a few minutes, he wrestled with his conscience. But in the end he followed where his demon led. He went into the kitchen and said jovially, 'Well, honey, I'm going to have another. Join me?'

347

A drink and a half later Mary was out to the world. He undressed her and put her to bed and kissed her penitentially on the lips. He tossed out her food and fried some eggs, which he ate with a bottle of beer, thinking that if God didn't get him first, a ruined stomach would.

He watched about five minutes of the Knick game, as a sort of dumb joke, then put on a Windbreaker and an Irish tweed hat. He checked out his .38 with the two-inch barrel, and stuck it in his belt. He went into the bedroom and tucked Mary gently into her blanket. She was tossing in her sleep and sweating. He dried her face with his handkerchief, gave her a long stricken look, and left the apartment.

He paid twenty-five dollars a month to park his car in the garage of a high-rise apartment up the street. The regular fee was a hundred and twenty-five, but he had once broken up an attempted holdup of the night attendant, and the garage management, in a show of gratitude (or because they liked the idea of a cop being around the premises), let him keep his car there at the special rate.

Not that it would matter if he was caught, but because conning people was intuitive to him, he informed the attendant that he had to run up to The Bronx to bring some hot soup to the missus's mother, who wasn't feeling too good. The attendant, who was watching the Knick game, barely listened.

He drove downtown slowly. It was a few minutes past ten, but he doubted that the kidnapper would phone before midnight, at the earliest. Perpetrators had their routine, too, though they probably weren't aware of it; if they were, there wouldn't be so many MO's in the files of the Bureau of Criminal Identification. And if he was wrong, so be it, he would go back and watch the Knicks. He cruised down Park Avenue, drove past Julian Massey's building, made a U-turn at the corner, and pulled up in front of an apartment house on the opposite side of the avenue, about thirty or forty feet north of Massey's. From the lobby he would have a clear view of the entrance to Massey's house. He double-parked and got out of his car. He had a sign that read *Police Business*, but he didn't want to advertise his presence by putting it in the windshield. The car would probably be all right where he left it; Park Avenue had more double-parking than any street in the city.

The doorman was one of the old-timey ones who was doubtless drawing Social Security in addition to a part-time salary. Roehmer showed him his ID and told him what he had in mind. The doorman said that it might look funny if there was a man hanging around the lobby. He gave the doorman a twenty-dollar bill.

'If anybody asks any questions, tell them that you're breaking in a new doorman.'

'You're kinda young,' the doorman said. 'I mean, being an American. The only young ones these days are the Spanish.' The doorman lifted the skirts of his greatcoat and tucked the bill away in his pants pocket. 'You could maybe be partially disabled. You think I could say that?'

Roehmer glanced through the lobby door. The entrance to the Massey house was as visible and clear as in a perfectly focused photograph. A passing car might obstruct his sightline, but only for a second.

'Yes, I think you could say that,' Roehmer said.

At ten minutes past midnight Laurence Adams closed his book and put on his sheepskin jacket, the linchpin of his go-between costume.

Julian, sitting erect in his chair next to the telephone, said, 'What do you think you're doing?'

'I'm putting on my jacket.'

'Are you cold?'

'No. I just felt like putting it on for no good reason.'

It wasn't the truth. He had found himself staring at the pages of the book, reading and rereading the same sentence, and he hoped that the slight physical exertion of putting on the jacket might break the spell.

'You must be cold. You're shivering. Are you scared?'

'I'm not shivering, not in the slightest.' Last night the old fool had complained because he *hadn't* had his jacket on.

'What time is it?' Julian said.

Laurence looked at his watch. 'Twelve minutes past twelve. It's getting on.'

'You put your jacket on as a hint that you would like to go home.'

'That's ridiculous.'

'You were expressing a subconscious wish – don't try to deny it.'

Laurence stared at him angrily but didn't say anything. He returned to his chair and picked up his book. *Dick Diver . . . Dick Diver said . . . Dick Diver . . .*

'Don't you dare let me down,' Julian said.

She strained beneath him, forgetful of her injured hand, trying to compensate for the indifference of his performance by the intensity of her own. He moved up and down on her with his customary narcissistic grace, but he was as detached as a man doing push-ups. Writhing, manipulating her body and his, mouthing obscenities that aroused her more than they affected Wally, she eventually brought them both to climax.

Wally wanted them to get up at once. She prevailed on him to linger until she had finished her postcoital cigarette. But he kept glancing at his watch, so she stubbed out her cigarette half-smoked and released him.

It was twelve-fifteen.

She had seduced him – overcoming his indifference only by the crudest advances imaginable – with the purpose of diverting him and calming his nerves, but also as a sentimental gesture, a valedictory. It was all coming to an end, an incredible two weeks in another world. It seemed an immeasurable distance in time since she had shattered the glass in Julian's picture, pushed him to the floor, run from the apartment and gone on her rampage of hostility with the doorman and the bus driver, allowed herself to be picked up in the Pleasant Times . . .

Wally came back naked from the shower. He turned on the light and began to dress. She lay back and admired his beauty for what was probably the last time. He drew a pink T-shirt on over his head, and emerged scowling.

'You going to hang out in bed forever?'

So much for sex as therapy.

At twelve-forty-five, for the second time since he had taken up his post in the lobby, Roehmer went out and warmed up the engine of his car.

'You want it ready to go if you have to take off real quick?' the doorman said.

Roehmer nodded. That was the idea. That, plus the fact that even five minutes of sitting relieved the strain on his legs. He had been standing in the lobby, never taking his eyes from the entrance to Massey's building, for more than two hours now. His eyes were watery, his stomach rumbled. His mouth was dry and spitless.

Well, that was detective work, wasn't it?

The telephone rang.

Laurence Adams closed his book with a snap. It was sixteen minutes past one. Julian snatched up the telephone.

'Yes?' His voice was hoarse.

'Is this Adams there? Just answer yes or no.'

'Yes. He's sitting – '

'Shut up!'

Julian clamped his lips shut.

'You got the money?'

'Yes.'

'Write this down. Take a taxi to the phone booth at the south-west corner of Broadway and Ninety-fifth. When the phone rings, identify yourself . . . Laurence Adams identify himself. Got it?'

'Yes. Take a taxi to – '

'If the cops or the FBI is involved, I'll chop her fucking head off just like her finger.'

'No, no, trust me – '

'If I get the money, you'll get her back in about eight hours. If anything goes wrong, I'll mail you her head.'

'Eight hours? Why do I have to wait – '

The phone was dead. Julian gestured furiously at Laurence Adams as he ran out of the room. Laurence,

351

bewildered by Julian's exit, walked over and read the note he had made on the pad: *booth sw corner 9 th-Bway*. There was a sudden, loud, strangulated cry from inside the apartment. Laurence dashed out of the sitting-room. Agnes came from the TV room and followed him down the hallway. They found Julian in the den, standing in front of the safe, rocking his head back and forth in his hands.

'The money,' Julian said. 'I can't remember the combination.'

The phone rang at twenty minutes past one. Wally said, 'Hi, Richard,' and they listened. Standing beside him, Nella could hear the drone of Richard's voice, but not what he was saying. 'About ten minutes from now. Right. Take care, Richard.' He hung up.

'Everything all right?'

'Adams should be at Broadway and Ninety-fifth in about ten minutes. Jesus, it's getting real close, baby.'

'Do you want to do the door now?'

'I have to call in ten minutes. Maybe I should wait until after.'

'It won't take anything like ten minutes.'

'Running down and then up again, I might be out of breath, and I won't sound good on the phone.'

'Maybe I would be breathing hard, but not you, Wally, not somebody in your condition.'

His lip quirked in a smile. 'Okay.'

She timed him. He was back in a little over three minutes, a little excited, a little flushed, but breathing quite normally.

When Laurence Adams appeared, carrying a valise and following the doorman out of the building, Roehmer had the feeling that he wasn't real but some fantasy projection of what he had been hoping for for the past three hours. So he had to rouse himself to get started. But once he was outside, the cold air revived him. He ducked into his car, started the engine, and, after a few cars went by, pulled out into the left lane. There was a red light at the corner.

He saw a taxi draw up to the canopy of Massey's building. But Laurence Adams drew back from the open cab door, shaking his head. The doorman was bending over to say something to the cabdriver. After a moment the cab pulled away. The doorman moved out into the street and blew his whistle. Roehmer made a U-turn when the light changed to green, and pulled up. A taxi went by him and turned into the kerb at Massey's house. This time Adams got in. The doorman shut the door and the cab moved off.

Roehmer kept a full block behind the cab. It turned west at Ninety-sixth and he followed, cheating on the light. When it turned right at Madison, he anticipated that it would make a left at Ninety-seventh and take the transverse crosstown to the West Side. It did. He slowed down and allowed two cars to slip in between him and Adams's cab.

As the taxicab entered the Ninety-sixth Street transverse, Laurence Adams asked the driver if he couldn't go a little faster.

The driver turned his head and said mildly, 'Got no wings. You think I can jump over them other cars?'

He was a bare half length behind the car in front. 'Sorry,' Laurence said. 'But once we get through the transverse . . . I'm in a hurry.'

The driver said, 'So what else is new?'

The note of resigned complaint made Laurence want to justify himself, to protest that his was no knee-jerk impatience but – literally – a matter of life and death, and that the failing memory of an old man had created a predicament that might truly be fatal. But it wasn't fair to harp on Julian's lapse. He had already suffered enough. Oh dear, since Ford had pardoned Nixon that reasonably humanitarian sentiment had become bitterly comical.

It had been awful, seeing him standing beside that bulbous old-fashioned safe, pounding his fists against his temples, as if to beat remembrance into them by sheer force. He was making a low keening sound, eerie and primitive. Agnes said there was a copy of the combination somewhere in the bedroom dresser, and she ran out, her rump twitching under her green silk dressing-gown. He and Julian followed after her. The master bedroom, which he had never seen before, was a huge chamber cluttered with what struck him as being the detritus of some rarely used Hollywood storage room. Agnes was tossing clothing out of drawers on to the floor, ransacking a collection of odd boxes containing junk jewellery, cuff links, tiepins, old coins. Julian kept screaming at her to hurry up. At last she located a tiny slip of paper at the bottom of a red manilla envelope. Julian grabbed it from her and ran back to the den. He fumbled with the combination, failing twice before the tumblers clicked in place and the massive door opened. Julian wrenched the valise out of the safe and pushed it into Laurence's hands, then took his arm and half-pulled him through the house to the anteroom.

'Don't you let me down,' Julian shouted as the elevator door shut.

Although at least five minutes had been spent in finding the combination to the safe, and he was jittery himself now, Laurence had dismissed the first taxi that drew up outside (remembering how promptly the nutcracker had arrived last night) and taken a second only after a careful scrutiny of the driver.

The taxi crossed Central Park West, made the light at Columbus, was briefly halted at Amsterdam, and sped on to Broadway. The phone at Ninety-fifth Street was one of the enclosed kind. Laurence handed the driver a ten-dollar bill, and told him to keep the change. The driver looked surprised and kept the bill in sight, as if offering him the option of changing his mind. As Laurence climbed out of the cab, he heard the phone ringing. He hurled himself into the booth and lunged at the instrument, but the ringing had already stopped.

'No answer.'

There was a note of anxiety in Wally's voice. She took the instrument from his hand and cradled it. 'Try again in about a minute.'

354

'He oughta be there by now,' Wally said. 'I don't like it.'

'He'll be there,' Nella said.

'Richard timed it, and you know Richard, he never makes a mistake. He should be there.'

'He might have had trouble getting a cab, or there might have been a traffic tie-up.'

'That's pure bullshit.' The colour of his eyes had paled. 'He's not coming, I feel it in my bones.'

'Try it again, Wally.'

She read off the number to him as he dialled.

Laurence grabbed at the phone with the first trill of the bell. 'Yes?'

'Who are you?'

He recognised the voice as the one of the night before. 'This is Laurence Adams. I'm sorry to be late – '

'Here's what you have to do. Cross the street to the east side of Broadway. You got that?'

'Yes.'

'Take the first cab that comes along.'

'First cab, yes.'

'Have him take you to the phone booth on the west side of Seventh Avenue and Christopher, just past the newsstand. Make it fast. I'll phone you there.'

'Will there be many more? I'm concerned about carrying all this money – '

'Christopher and Seventh in the Village. Do like you're told, or you'll never see Nella again. I mean, you want her head in the mail?'

The phone clicked. Laurence felt a wave of weakness. He thought, I don't know how much more I can take. I'm not cut out for this . . . He relieved his tension by drawing a deep breath, picked up the valise, and left the booth.

Richard had lit up his OFF DUTY sign and double-parked near the south-west corner of Broadway and Ninety-sixth Street, five minutes before the earliest moment that Laurence Adams might have arrived. The doors of the cab were locked. A few times people tried the doors. He shook his head at them and they went away, except for one big guy, who gave the side of the cab a kick. Ordinarily he would have risen to the insult (God knows why cabbies felt protective about the shitty rattletraps they drove), but now he ignored it. Without having to look at his watch, he knew that Adams was late.

He spotted a cab crossing Broadway, with its left-turn signal blinking. It pulled up at Ninety-fifth and Laurence Adams stepped out, carrying a valise. Adams went into the phone booth. From the tail of his eye Richard saw a black sedan make the left turn from Ninety-sixth. It was a Ford Fairlane, '75 or '76. It seemed to him to be slowing down before it came to the phone booth, but then he realised that it had paused to let Adams's taxi pull away. It went on again.

He turned his attention back to the phone booth. Adams was wedging his back against the glass door. Good move, considering all the weirdos in the neighbourhood. Somebody was rapping on the window beside him. It was a woman, asking if he was free. He pointed upwards in the direction of the OFF DUTY sign. She made a face at him and went away.

In the booth, Laurence Adams had the receiver to his ear. Richard started the cab. When Adams came out of the phone booth, he seemed to be a little shaky, but he was following instructions. He waited for the traffic light to turn green, then crossed to the east side of Broadway and immediately started looking for a cab. In his rearview mirror Richard saw a cab a block back, waiting for the light to change. He waited until Adams hailed the cab and got in. After Adams's cab went by, he edged over to the outside lane so he could make the left turn at Ninety-sixth. He turned at West End and headed south, to a quiet street in the Forties, where he pulled over and smeared some mud, which he took from a can, on his rear licence plate. Then he headed downtown again.

When Roehmer saw Laurence Adams cross Broadway and signal for a taxi, he drove to the corner of Ninety-fourth, turned into the area between the wings of the median strip, and waited there. He saw Adams get into a Checker cab, which pleased him. Its size and distinctive shape made it easily identifiable; he could lie back at a distance with less chance of confusing his prey with other cabs. As soon as Adams got in, Roehmer turned on to Broadway. The Checker signalled a right turn. Good, Roehmer thought, a taxi driver who used his directional signals – a rare find. It meant he could follow his turns without crowding him.

The Checker turned right on Columbus and headed downtown. Now all Roehmer had to do was lie back a block or two and keep his eye on the progressive traffic lights. The Checker swept across the complicated inter-section at Lincoln Center and continued downtown.

As they approached the Port Authority Bus Terminal on Forty-first, Roehmer wondered if the exchange was going to take place in the terminal. There was a police installation just inside the Ninth Avenue entrance, but he would have to be awfully sure of himself before he risked asking for help. The question became academic when the Checker swept on past the terminal, past the entrance to the Lincoln Tunnel, and across Thirty-fourth Street. There was just enough traffic on the avenue to allow him easy pursuit without being conspicuous.

The cab signalled a left turn at Eighteenth Street. Roehmer slowed down, and by the time he made the turn himself the Checker was three-quarters down the block. He dawdled, crossed Eighth, and dawdled again when the Checker stopped for a red light at Seventh and signalled a right turn. On Seventh he allowed the Checker to take a lead of two blocks. A professional might know, or at least suspect, that he was being followed, but Laurence Adams had no reason to check the rear window. The Checker crossed Fourteenth Street and continued along Seventh past St Vincent's Hospital. Fine, stay straight on, Roehmer thought, and I won't have any trouble.

He was two blocks back when he saw the Checker stopped at the corner of Christopher and Seventh. He saw Laurence Adams get out and enter a phone booth.

*

Even more than Eighty-sixth Street last night, the streets were teeming with people. Laurence, in what had become ritual, wedged the valise into the space between the phone and the side of the booth, placed his shoulder against it, and pretended to be speaking into the phone.

Curiously enough, he didn't feel nervous now – or, to put it another way, his nervousness was overlaid by a sort of headiness. Somewhere on the taxi ride downtown he had realised, for the first time, that there was a kind of spice to the adventure. True, he hadn't particularly distinguished himself thus far, but on the other hand he had brought it off, such as it was, without mishap.

He became aware that he had stopped simulating a conversation and, as if to make amends for his oversight, spoke aloud. 'Well, here we are on the second leg of the great kidnap plot. Nella? Be of good cheer, darling, Professor Adams, AB, MA, PhD, is coming to the rescue, the man on taxi-back, the gallant, the noted academic picaresque . . .'

His smile took him by surprise.

As soon as Wally finished dialling, Nella raised up on her toes and pressed her cheek against his, tilting the phone so that she could listen in.

The phone rang once, and then Laurence was saying hello.

'Indentify yourself,' Wally said.

Indentify? Oh, Wally, he's going to write 'spelling' in some margin of his mind.

'This is Laurence Adams.'

'Okay. See the taxicab parked right outside of the booth?'

'Yes. I see it.'

'Soon as I finish, I want you to get into that taxicab. The driver will say your name. If he don't say your name, get right out again and back to the phone. But if he does, do exactly like he tells you. You got that?'

'Yes.'

'You gonna do exactly like he says? Yes or no?'

'Yes.'

'Do it.' Wally hung up.

'Perfect, Wally,' Nella said. 'You were Mr Perfection.'

The taxi took off so abruptly that Laurence knew even before the driver spoke that he had not taken the wrong cab; or, more exactly, that the wrong cab had not taken its place beside the phone booth.

'Laurence Adams – right?'

The driver was wearing a wool cap, pulled down low over the back of his neck, meeting the collar of his sweater. His voice was flat, almost without inflection.

'Yes, I'm Laurence Adams. Where are we going?'

The driver didn't answer. He drove swiftly down Seventh Avenue, lifting his head from time to time to glance at his rearview mirror.

'Would you tell me where we're going, please?'

The cab swerved suddenly, on a reckless diagonal to the left, and made a rocking turn into a dark street lined with lofts. It shot forward and, by Laurence's estimate, must have been doing fifty by the time it was halfway down the street. At the corner the driver braked hard, and the cab skidded into a right turn. Laurence lost his balance and was thrown against the side of the cab. He straightened up and braced himself against the back of the seat.

The cab made a left turn, a right, and then swung into a broad street with a centre divider that Laurence thought he recognised as Houston Street. It ran through a red light, and at the next corner turned right, once again going through a red light. Two blocks further on it turned again.

Laurence gave up trying to figure out where they were, and concentrated on anticipating the jarring turns so that he wouldn't lose his balance again. The afflatus he had felt in the phone booth had vanished. But his feeling of utter helplessness roused a sense of indignation in him.

Sliding forward on the seat, he said, 'Look, you, I insist on knowing where you're taking me.'

The driver whipped his head around and shouted, 'Shut your fucking mouth. You don't sit there quiet, I'll kill you.'

The fury of the voice made Laurence recoil. He sat well

back in the seat. His face was burning from fear and with shame at how easily he had let himself be intimidated. The noted academic picaresque? The world-renowned coward! The cab turned, turned again, and he thought he recognised the old buildings and lofts of Lafayette Street; if so, they were now heading back uptown.

He became aware that the cab had slowed considerably. It occurred to him for the first time that all the wild manoeuvring had been designed to throw off pursuit. And if that was so, the driver must be satisfied that he had succeeded. A block further the cab turned on to a dreary deserted street of lofts, one- and two-storey buildings, aged storefronts with thick, broken gilt lettering that looked as if they dated back to the Civil War. In the middle of the block the driver pulled over to the kerb beside an empty loading platform and stopped.

Half-turning, he slid his partition back and said, 'Give me the valise.'

Laurence picked up the valise and placed it in the opening. He had a fleeting vision of himself ramming the valise into the back of the driver's neck, but the impulse died and left him trembling. The driver turned and hauled the valise into the front seat. It was done quickly, and Laurence could see nothing except a glimpse of a pale face almost entirely obscured by the wool cap.

'Get out,' the driver said.

'What?'

'Get out of the fucking cab, you asshole!'

It was too sudden: he felt somehow cheated, short-changed. He sat without moving.

'You sonofabitch, get out of the fucking cab!'

The driver struck him as being suddenly insensate with rage. His head and shoulders had become rigid. Laurence pressed down on the door handle, but didn't quite open it. In a voice that he hoped would be resolute, but which shamed him by emerging as a croak, he said, 'I'm entitled to know when you're going to release Nella.'

'Get out!'

'We've kept our part of the bargain,' Laurence said. 'I'm entitled to know – '

'If you don't get right the hell out of this cab, I swear I'm going to kill her. You gonna get out?'

The driver spoke softly, but the suppressed rage, the menace, were unmistakable, frightening. Laurence opened the door and got out. He was barely clear of the cab before it roared away from the kerb with squealing tyres. By the time it occurred to Laurence to look at its licence plate, it had almost reached the end of the street. Its brake lights gleamed red, and it disappeared around the corner.

He started to trudge back towards Lafayette Street, feeling spent and unutterably depressed, wondering what the chances were of finding a taxicab before he was mugged.

Chapter 25

Except for the dull glow behind the windows at the rear of the Pleasant Times, there were no lights to be seen in any of the surrounding buildings. Of course there was always the possibility of an insomniac at an unlit window staring hopelessly out into the darkness, but that was a chance they had to take.

Nella was peering through the edge of a blind. Wally was just behind her, his breathing measured but somewhat heavier than usual. It was ten minutes past two. They had gone to the window as soon as Wally had finished his second call to Laurence, although they reckoned that they had about fifteen minutes to wait.

She looked at the shadowy yard, a tiny patch of beaten earth with a bit of garbage here, a beer can there – a smidgen of city dirt in which even weeds disdained to grow. But now its ordinariness was transformed – it had the slightly unreal, weighted appearance of an arena, a stage dressed for the entrance of an actor. Richard. His appearance would be prefigured by his shadow against the window. Then the window would slide up, and he would step over the low sill. He would cross the eight or ten paces of yard and disappear through the unlatched rear door of the building. The arena would be deserted again, and the action would take place offstage.

Richard would circle the bottom of the staircase cautiously, make sure that no one was walking up or down, then start up. Wally would be waiting for him at the apartment door. He would take the shopping bag containing the money and hand him the identical bag with the athletic gear. Richard would go downstairs again, out into the yard, and back through the window. He would have been seen entering the Pleasant Times with a shopping bag, and he would have one when he came out of the john. He would ask McGarry to hold it for Wally. If

McGarry looked inside the bag he would find jock-straps, socks, and sweat shirts. Richard would get into his cab, switch off his OFF DUTY sign, and start cruising for passengers. If he was lucky, he might have another profitable night.

It wasn't perfect, or entirely without risk, but it was a feasible alternative to having Richard seen by the guard in the lobby. The guard, in Richard's characterisation, was a nosey bastard, and he would be curious not only about the bag, but about Richard's presence there during his working hours. It established a witness to his carrying a bag, *making a delivery*, shortly after the exchange of the ransom money. Although there was no reason for him to connect the two, if anything went wrong later, his testimony would be damaging.

The way Richard put it was that his turning up at the house was 'out of line' with his normal routine. On the other hand, his appearance at the Pleasant Times wouldn't case any comment. It was well known that taxi drivers had trouble finding a place to relieve themselves, and it would be natural for Richard to use the facilities at the Pleasant Times, where he was known. He had done it before.

When the idea first came up, Nella was disposed to reject it; perhaps out of pique at having overlooked the presence of the guard in the lobby – she, who prided herself on thinking of the smallest and seemingly most insignificant detail, often to Richard's and Wally's annoyance – but surely because the bag presented a serious problem; Richard would be seen going into the john with a shopping bag and coming out without one. But the balance had tipped when she hit on the idea of identical shopping bags. She was tickled by her own ingenuity: establishing the innocence of the shopping bag (McGarry surely couldn't resist examining its contents) turned a liability of sorts into an asset.

Wally, reverting to an old fantasy, had suggested lowering a bucket into the yard, but that had seemed too melodramatic even for her own theatrical taste. The rear door, located behind the main staircase, and down a few steps to ground level, was much more practical. It was a half-dozen paces from the windows of the Pleasant Times. Richard could slip in in a matter of seconds after he climbed through the window of the john.

She had also vetoed Wally's desire to go downstairs and exchange bags with Richard at the back door. Since there was no strict timetable for Richard's arrival at the Pleasant Times, it meant having to hang around waiting for an indefinite period of time, and that had seemed chancy. In any event, she felt that the more Richard did – and the less Wally – the better.

She realised that Wally was pressed against her, and that he had an erection. She turned to look at him.

'Oh, God,' he whispered, 'you realise that in a little while we're gonna have a million dollars?'

Hence the hard-on, Nella: money is an aphrodisiac.

Roehmer knew he had lost him through slowness – not in the speed of his car but his mind. When Laurence Adams had popped out of the phone booth and into the taxi, it hadn't occurred to him to be suspicious of the loitering cab, although suspicion – of anything and everything – should have been his prevailing state of mind. Even the cab's racing, wheel-spinning start hadn't alerted him; taxi drivers would do that. The cab's diagonal cut across Seventh Avenue to make a left turn put him in the picture, but by then it was already too late. He still had him in sight, though just barely, after making his own cowboy turn off Seventh; the red glow of the tail-lights gave him away. And he still had him, more or less by guesswork, when the cab turned left.

But after that it was hopeless, though he kept trying, wrenching his car into desperate turns, speeding to corners and turning again. On Allen Street – he couldn't have said how he had gotten there – he spotted a cab speeding a block ahead of him. He pursued it recklessly, caught it at Delancey Street, cut it off, and jumped out with his gun in hand. The occupants of the cab were a young couple in outlandish costumes who were probably returning from a disco.

At that point – or earlier, if he was going to be truthful – there was nothing left for him to do but to go home. Instead he quartered the streets aimlessly, turning uptown, downtown, to east or to west without any design, hoping blindly for a miracle. Miracles occurred now and then – he had been the beneficiary of a couple of them in his career – but none quite as miraculous as the one he was praying for now.

Finally a measure of reason returned. He stopped in the middle of an anonymous dark street and told himself to stop being an asshole. The balloon had gone up and he hadn't seen it because he had been nodding. He went on to the end of the block and looked for street signs to guide him home.

Richard had used up maybe seven or eight minutes shaking the black Fairlane, but the schedule now wasn't all that tight, except that Wally and Nella might start getting anxious. He drove a few blocks at random from where he had kicked Laurence Adams out, and pulled up midway along another dark, deserted street. He turned off all his lights but kept his motor running, opened the valise, and dumped the neatly arranged stacks of bills on the seat beside him. He opened the door, got out, and flung the empty valise across the street on to the sidewalk. It gave a bounce or two and came to rest against the wall of an old building.

Without bothering to put his lights on, he drove a zigzag pattern for another few blocks and pulled up again. He began to transfer the money from the seat to the shopping bag, placing the stacks neatly along the bottom and then piling them up layer by layer. When he was finished, he spread one of Wally's new sweat shirts over the top of the bag, tucking in its edges precisely, so that nothing was visible beneath it.

He drove to the end of the street, turned on his headlights and OFF DUTY sign, and headed uptown.

The newspaper delivery truck moved very slowly along the street, feeling its way. When it stopped, two of the three men in the truck got out. After a moment or two of searching, they found the valise.

The man who had remained in the truck called out softly, 'Got it?'

One of the other two, holding the suitcase dangling open, said bitterly, 'Sure. The bug worked beautifully. It's another triumph for science.'

Richard pulled up in front of the Pleasant Times. At this time of night most cops would overlook a double-parked taxi, and anyway, he figured to be back out in a few minutes. If the Gents was occupied, he would go into the Ladies; it was done all the time.

He made sure the sweat shirt was tucked in firmly around the top of the shopping bag before getting out of the cab. The bag was quite a weight. The one with the gym stuff in it would be a lot lighter. It figured: money should weigh more than jockstraps.

He opened the door into the darkness of the Pleasant Times. Down at the centre of the bar it was busier than he expected. It didn't matter. He felt his way through the narrow aisle between the bar and the wall. Past the jukebox, four or five people were standing against the wall. He saw McGarry behind the bar, and started to wave to him.

Somebody was at the cash register.

Richard stopped abruptly, but by then a short, squat PR, wearing a roll-collar sweater and a small red cap, was pointing a gun at him.

'Come on in, man,' the PR said, moving towards him. 'Come on in and against the wall, man.'

He spotted three more of them – two behind the bar, and one patting down the regulars facing the wall. They all had guns.

'I tol' you don' stand there, man,' the PR said, raising his voice. 'Up against the fucking wall.'

'Okay, okay,' Richard said.

When he had seen all those people against the wall, Richard thought, he should have guessed what was happening, and there might still have been time to run back out the door. Now it was too late. Behind the bar McGarry's face was as white as his shirt.

'You gonna move?' The PR was yelling, shifting the grip on his gun. 'Or I gotta cool you off?'

Richard caught him in the chest with his lowered shoulder, slamming him sidewards into the bar. He started running, past the bar and into the booth area at the rear. He heard shouts behind him as he pounded towards the door of the Gents, and a shot went by him into the wall. Then there were a lot of shots, and just as he pulled the door open, he felt something smack into the back of his thigh. The force of it pushed him forward into the john and he stumbled and almost fell. He pulled the door shut and latched it. Shots were coming through the door, sending wood splinters flying as he stepped to the window and pulled it up. He was straddling the sill when the door crashed open behind him. A shot smashed the top pane of the window above his head. He left a smear of blood on the sill as he fell through the window into the yard.

He got to his feet, holding the shopping bag against his body, and hobbled across the yard towards the rear door of the ·partment building. Blood was gushing from his thigh.

Wally was complaining, as he had been for the past ten minutes, when they heard the first shot.

'I know Richard wouldn't be late unless something – '

The shot froze him to silence, and his hand, holding the blind away from the wall so that they could look past its edge into the yard, began to shake. There were more shots, echoing through the stillness of the night, and Nella saw Richard straddling the window of the Gents. The glass in the window above him exploded. Behind her, Wally had begun to whimper.

Richard fell, but got right up and started to limp across the yard. A figure appeared in the window behind him, a man wearing a cap, pointing a gun. Wally shouted a warning in a hoarse, agonised scream. The man in the window started firing. Richard pitched forward abruptly. He fell across the shopping bag and lay absolutely still, and Nella knew that he was dead. She started to back away from the window, but she saw Richard's body make a series of small movements, and she thought that she was mistaken, that he was still alive, until she realised that he was being tugged by bullets striking him, each one marking its entry point with a dark splotch. The melodrama had turned into Grand Guignol.

The man in the cap gave a shout of triumph and withdrew. In the surrounding buildings windows were lighting up. Behind her, Wally was leaning against the wall and speaking brokenly. She thought at first that he was mouthing nonsense, but it was a foreign language – Russian, or a Ukrainian dialect. He was bent, slumped, his powerful body dragged down as if it were melting.

She sidled by him and as she walked out of the room she heard a spasm of sobbing. She passed through the foyer, unlocked the front door, and went out. As she started down the steps, the thought struck her, without seeming irrelevant or inconsequential in the least, that she would be cold, dressed only in the late Richard's trousers and sweater.

The first shot was muffled, and might have been a backfire, but the volley that followed was unmistakable. Automatically, Roehmer's foot stamped down on the accelerator. It was stupid, letting his ass hang out, but gunfire in the night was a cop's business, and he had reacted to it by reflex.

By rights he should have been home in bed, which was where he had been heading after losing the cab with Laurence Adams in it. Or so he had thought. But by the time he hit the thirties he had long ago decided to cruise through the girl's old neighbourhood – where she had been seen, where McGarry saw her, where she might be holed up. At the same time, he knew it was futile, an appropriate goodbye to a case that had involved him more deeply than any other he had ever handled, and with less solid motivation, or, anyway, a motivation without validity in the context of police work. It was a homage to a twenty-five-year-old love affair, which made him a prime horse's ass. To look at it another way, he was punishing himself for all his sins – past, present, and imagined – sucking on the bitter fruit of failure instead of simply spitting it out.

He slipped across Lexington against a red light and sped along towards Third, where the shots had seemed to come from.

She was more than halfway down the stairs when she heard clattering footsteps behind her, mingled with shouts. Amplified by the narrow staircase, the sounds echoed with a kind of hollow, ghostly menace. She quickened her pace, hugging her wounded hand close to her body to keep it from jolting.

She knew he was gaining on her – the sound above her was closer, and his voice was full of rage, sounding more full-bodied than she had ever heard it before, stripped of its carefully nurtured gentility, acquired to fit the Yale man, the model, the seeker after celebrity and success. He was no more than a flight behind her when she reached bottom. A man was half-rising from behind the desk in the lobby. She ran past him on shaking legs, pulled the door open, and started down the three steps that led to the outer door. As she wrenched it open, she heard Wally come through the lobby door. He leaped down the steps, but she was already outside, in the sudden coldness of the street. A man slipped between two parked cars on to the sidewalk. He was carrying a gun.

She tried to swerve, to veer away from the man with the gun and at the same time flee from Wally, who was charging at her from behind. But momentum carried her forward, and it was just a split second before she stumbled into his arms that she recognised the man with the gun as Detective Roehmer.

The next day, holding forth in the squad room, Roehmer would say that he felt no surprise whatsoever to see Nella Massey come running out of the building. Actually, what he had felt was similar to catnapping at his desk and dreaming about the lieutenant, then waking up and *seeing* the lieutenant. It wasn't unexpected, but logical, if a little bit unsettling.

He had been driving past the building when he heard shouting, and turning, saw the girl through the glass doors of the lobby. He hit his brake and came out of the car running, his gun in his hand. He opened his arms to take the impact of her body, and closed his arms around her with a wild feeling of relief and pleasure, as if he had just won a sweet victory after a long and uncertain courtship.

The man who was chasing her was a stud, a beachboy, a muscular powerhouse. He was yelling, and there was a look on his face of rage and – it was only much later that Roehmer could name it – of grief. Roehmer pointed the gun, bracing himself, not knowing if the man would, or even could, stop his rush.

'Freeze,' he yelled. 'Police officer. Don't move.'

The man came to a skidding stop. He was wearing a pink T-shirt, tight around smooth, bulging biceps. He raised his hand and pointed it at the girl.

'Move back,' Roehmer said. 'Back up against the building.'

The man didn't move. He started to spout in some foreign language.

'I told you to move back.' Roehmer motioned with the gun. 'Do what I say, you.'

The girl lifted her head from his chest, and turned her head slowly. She looked at the man in the pink T-shirt and screamed, 'Don't let him come near me. I'm Nella Massey. He's the kidnapper, the man who kidnapped me. Help me.'

She turned back to him and buried her face. The man in the pink T-shirt rocked back a pace, and then took a step forward, his handsome face stricken, outraged.

'She's lying! The dirty bitch! She's a dirty liar!'

Roehmer heard a window go up, then a second. A man in the lobby of the building was staring out in disbelief. In about two minutes, Roehmer thought, we'll have a nice little audience.

'Oh, my God!' Nella held up her hand, heavily

bandaged, with a grotesque space between the third and fifth fingers. 'He did this to me!'

'Liar!' the man in the T-shirt screamed. 'Tell the truth, it was your idea, you planned the whole thing . . .'

He began to move forward. Nella screamed. Roehmer waved his gun.

'Don't let him come near me! He'll hurt me again! Stop him, oh, stop him, don't let him hurt me! Stop him!'

Roehmer didn't know, and would never know, if he could have gotten up in a courtroom and sworn that by 'stop' the girl meant 'shoot'. But her whole body was pressed against him now, an entreaty and a promise. He knew that she was offering herself to him. A slight pressure on the trigger and that handsome sonofabitch would go flying backwards, his powerful chest bursting with blood. He had shot a man once before (and received a commendation for it) and he knew what a slug could do to a body. He felt the urgency and warmth of the girl's body, and he understood without question that he was being given a second chance, after twenty-five years.

The man in the T-shirt, sensing some new energy in the way he held the gun now, began to back away, his hand held up in front of him, half in pleading, half to ward off a bullet. Suddenly his face collapsed, as if, Roehmer thought, he could gauge the primitive force of the girl's straining body (the bastard knows all about it, he was her lover), and, having nothing like it to offer himself, or anything to counteract it, was as good as dead.

His arm tightened around the girl, returned her embrace fiercely. Her face turned upwards to his and she said, 'You believe me, don't you?'

She had more in mind than the kidnapping. She was also asking him to believe the promise of her body, the fierce warranty of the heat at its centre that was searching out the hot rising centre of his own. Beyond her uplifted face the man in the pink T-shirt was crying into his hands. Roehmer heard sirens somewhere on Third Avenue. The sound reached a crescendo, then ran down into silence.

'It's the truth!' she was screaming. 'The truth!'

'Look, your uncle will hire the very best defence lawyers – '

'It's the truth!' she screamed again. 'Believe me – I'm telling the truth!'

'The truth.' He was still holding her tightly. 'The truth, Nella. It'll come to court, but with your lawyers against his lawyers, your truth will prevail.'

Right, Roehmer, that's what it was all about. The Peggys and the Nellas would always prevail, and, one way or another, the people like the stud in the pink T-shirt would not. The Roehmers were somewhere in between – they survived. Some truths were more powerful than others.

He pushed her away and, holding her at arm's length as much to restrain himself as her, said, 'You have the right to remain silent and refuse to answer questions. Do you understand?'

She was barely aware of Wally, weeping in the background. As Roehmer intoned the pat phrases of *Miranda*, his lumpy face devoid of expression, she thought of the future. Yes, as Roehmer had said, Julian would hire the best lawyers to defend her. Julian didn't have to believe in her innocence. He wouldn't let her go to jail, wouldn't tolerate her appearing guilty in the public eye, because she was of his blood, the blood of dukes and druids. What he possessed was the best; he could not abide that it be sullied. The blood of druids, Nella, it's very thick blood, and the money of the descendants of druids is very powerful medicine. Sorry, Wally, you don't stand a chance.

And neither do you, Nella. You'll never be free of Julian now. Not for the rest of his long life, not for the rest of your own.

'I'm going to have to put cuffs on the both of you,' Roehmer said. His voice was flat, colourless. 'I'll try to be careful of your finger, miss.'

DEEP BENEATH THE SEA
A DEADLY TRAP AWAITS . . .

SEA LEOPARD

Craig Thomas

The British nuclear submarine *HMS Proteus* carries
the most sophisticated anti-detection equipment in the
world. Codenamed 'LEOPARD', the top-secret anti-sonar
systems render *Proteus* undetectable to the Russians. Sea
trials completed, *Proteus*' first mission is to chart the new
Soviet underwater defence system which poses the most
deadly threat to NATO's northern flank.

But *Proteus* picks up a distress signal. From a Soviet
submarine lying crippled on the sea floor. And as she sets
out on her rescue mission the Russians prepare to spring a
devastating deathtrap twenty fathoms beneath the ocean . . .

ADVENTURE/THRILLER   0 7221 8453 0   £1.95

TRAVERSE OF THE GODS

by Bob Langley

The Eiger, 1944 – In a desperate attempt to turn defeat into victory, German and American mountaineers are locked in an appalling struggle on the notorious North Wall of Europe's deadliest mountain – a struggle with vital implications for the development of the atomic bomb.

'Brilliant . . . in a class by itself'
Jack Higgins

'Written in the best adventure tradition'
Publishers Weekly

ADVENTURE/THRILLER   0 7221 5410 0   £1.50

And don't miss Bob Langley's other exciting thrillers:
DEATH STALK
WAR OF THE RUNNING FOX
WARLORDS
– also available in Sphere Books

I, SAID THE SPY

by Derek Lambert

Fact: Each year a nucleus of the wealthiest and most influential members of the Western world meet to discuss the future of the world's superpowers at a secret conference called Bilderberg.

A glamorous millionairess just sighting loneliness from the foothills of middle-age . . . a French industrialist whose wealth matches his masochism and meanness . . . a whizz-kid of the seventies conducting a life-long love affair with diamonds, these are just three of the Bilderbergers who have grown to confuse position with invulnerability. A mistake which could prove lethal when a crazed assassin is on the loose . . . a journalist dedicated to exposing the conference infiltrates their midst . . . and intelligence agents from Moscow, Washington and London penetrate Bilderberg's defences to reveal a conspiracy of mind-boggling proportions . . .

I, SAID THE SPY is a novel on a grand scale which sweeps the reader along on a wave of all-out excitement and suspense until the final stunning climax.

ADVENTURE/THRILLER   0 7221 5346 5   £1.75

A selection of bestsellers from SPHERE

FICTION

PALOMINO	Danielle Steel	£1.75 ☐
CALIFORNIA DREAMERS	Norman Bogner	£1.75 ☐
NELLA	John Godey	£1.75 ☐
RAILROAD	Graham Masterton	£2.75 ☐
HAND-ME-DOWNS	Rhea Kohan	£1.75 ☐

FILM & TV TIE-INS

WHOSE LIFE IS IT ANYWAY?	David Benedictus	£1.25 ☐
FORT APACHE, THE BRONX	Heywood Gould	£1.75 ☐
ON THE LINE	Anthony Minghella	£1.25 ☐
SHARKY'S MACHINE	William Diehl	£1.75 ☐
FIREFOX	Craig Thomas	£1.75 ☐

NON-FICTION

YOUR CHILD AND THE ZODIAC	Teri King	£1.50 ☐
THE PAPAL VISIT	Timothy O'Sullivan	£2.50 ☐
THE SURVIVOR	Jack Eisner	£1.75 ☐
THE COUNTRY DIARY OF AN EDWARDIAN LADY	Edith Holden	£4.50 ☐
OPENING UP	Geoff Boycott	£1.75 ☐

All Sphere books are available at your local bookshop or newsagent, or can be ordered direct from the publisher. Just tick the titles you want and fill in the form below.

Name ─────────────────────────────

Address ───────────────────────────

───────────────────────────────────